The Best AMERICAN SHORT STORIES 2010

GUEST EDITORS OF
THE BEST AMERICAN SHORT STORIES

The Best
AMERICAN
SHORT
STORIES®
2010

Selected from
U.S. and Canadian Magazines
by RICHARD RUSSO
with HEIDI PITLOR

With an Introduction by Richard Russo

HOUGHTON MIFFLIN HARCOURT
BOSTON • NEW YORK 2010

ISSN 0067-6233
ISBN 978-0-547-05528-2
ISBN 978-0-547-05532-9 (pbk.)

Printed in the United States of America

DOH 10 9 8 7 6 5

"Donkey Greedy, Donkey Gets Punched" by Steve Almond. First published in *Tin House*, vol. 10, no. 4. From the forthcoming *God Bless America* by Steve Almond, to be published in 2011, copyright © by Steve Almond. Used by permission of Lookout Books.

"Into Silence" by Marlin Barton. First published in *Sewanee Review*, July-September 2009. Copyright © 2009 by Marlin Barton. Reprinted by permission of Marlin Barton.

"The Cousins" by Charles Baxter. First published in *Tin House*, Issue 40. From the forthcoming *Gryphon* by Charles Baxter, to be published 2011, copyright © 2011 by Charles Baxter. Used by permission of Pantheon Books, a division of Random House, Inc.

"Safari" by Jennifer Egan. First published in *The New Yorker*, January 11, 2010. From *A Visit from the Goon Squad* by Jennifer Egan, copyright © 2010 by Jennifer Egan. Used by permission of Alfred A. Knopf, a division of Random House, Inc.

"Someone Ought to Tell Her There's Nowhere to Go" by Danielle Evans. First published in *A Public Space*, no. 9. From *Before You Suffocate Your Own Fool Self* by Danielle Evans. Copyright © 2009 by Danielle Evans. Used by permission of Riverhead Books, an imprint of Penguin Group (USA) Inc.

"The Valetudinarian" by Joshua Ferris. First published in *The New Yorker*, August 3, 2009. Copyright © 2009 by Joshua Ferris. Reprinted by permission of *The New Yorker*.

Contents

Foreword

OVER THE PAST DECADE, several magazines known for their stellar short fiction have ceased publication: *Story, DoubleTake,* and *Ontario Review.* Others have seen their budgets slashed. According to *Virginia Quarterly Review* editor Ted Genoways's galvanizing essay in *Mother Jones,* Louisiana State University cut more than 20 percent of *Southern Review*'s budget, and Middlebury College has given an ultimatum to *New England Review:* break even within two years or go under. Still others, typically high-circulation, general-interest magazines, publish far less short fiction than they used to: *Esquire* has cut back, as has *The Atlantic,* which annexed its fiction in one summer issue, though it recently began publishing one story a month on Amazon's Kindle. To my knowledge, *GQ, Elle, Redbook, Ms., Seventeen,* and more have stopped publishing stories altogether.

News like this makes me queasy. Five of the twenty stories that appear in this year's book were published in magazines mentioned above. I read about fifty fewer magazines this year than Katrina Kenison read in 2000, although I suspect that if more online magazines submitted their stories to me, the numbers would be comparable. Still, it is indisputable that American literary journals are in danger.

The world of book publishing is weathering a similar sea change. Nearly all publishers have downsized or merged or at the very least "reorganized." The recession has left too many talented fiction editors without jobs. Nonfiction is seen as easier to market and sell, just as novels are thought to be easier to publish than books of short fiction. A young writer with a completed story collection is likely, perhaps more than ever before, to hear from agents and potential editors, "I'd rather see a novel." Short stories—as well as novels and books of nonfiction—must now compete not only with TV and movies but also with blogs, tweets, Facebook, texts, iPhone apps, and countless other forms of digital entertainment. A new electronic reader seems to be introduced to the consuming public each month. More than one editor has called the rapidly changing situation in electronic publishing—the strained relationship between Amazon.com and book publishers, the fight to determine the pricing of e-books, the battle for readers overall—"the Wild West."

Short fiction lost some of its masters during the past decade: Saul Bellow, John Updike, and J. D. Salinger, for starters. It would be easy to say that this was not a good decade for the short story.

But the past ten years have ushered in just as many reasons for readers of short fiction to celebrate. Newer magazines like *Tin House* and *McSweeney's* have picked up where *Story* and some others left off. I'm always glad to read smaller journals and annuals like *New England Review, American Short Fiction, Agni, Crazyhorse, Ecotone, The Cincinnati Review, Epoch, Georgia Review, A Public Space, Santa Monica Review,* and this year they did not disappoint. Far from it. Editors of mid- and smaller-circulation journals can take risks, dig into that slush pile, and publish that first-time author. One of the most rewarding aspects of my job is the thrill of discovery that comes with first reading a talented young author. This year Richard Russo and I were overjoyed to come across Wayne Harrison, Brendan Mathews, Téa Obreht, Lori Ostlund, and Maggie Shipstead. Of course, the short story is a form that lends itself to newer writers: it is not as daunting as the novel, perhaps not as revelatory as poetry.

The mere length of short stories is better suited to emerging technology than most other literary forms. Many magazines, like *TriQuarterly* and *Ascent,* have migrated online. I suspect far more will end up there in order to cut production costs. The announcement that *The Atlantic* would sell stories through Kindle prompted the *New York Times* to proclaim, "Let the iTunes-ization of short fiction begin." Does this mean that Alice Munro now must compete directly with Lady Gaga? That readers will create "playlists" of their favorite short stories? Will writers other than Rick Moody tweet short stories? Check back with me in a decade. Frankly, all this change does make me a little uncomfortable. Still, I know many diehard readers who swear by their Kindle. People like me, who cling to the concept of a book as a book or a magazine as an, ahem, magazine might need a kick in the pants. Narrativemagazine.com publishes some of the best fiction out there. A story is, after all, a story. A. O. Scott wrote in the *New York Times:* "The death of the novel is yesterday's news. The death of print may be tomorrow's headline. But the great American short story is still being written, and awaits its readers."

There is more good news for the American short story. In 2004 Larry Dark started The Story Prize to honor collections of short stories publicly and financially. Exciting new story writers like Kevin Moffett, Wells Tower (whose first collection was reviewed on the front page of the *New York Times Book Review*), Karen Russell, and Lauren Groff are gaining attention. And our masters continue to dazzle: this year, wonderful stories by Charles Baxter, James Lasdun, Jill McCorkle, and Jim Shepard appear in this book.

And what about the overall quality of short fiction these days? Though defining this feels a bit like assigning a grade to all babies born in a given time period, I found it healthy. This year was a slow burner, and at the start Richard Russo and I wondered whether we would find enough stories to fill this book. But by the end of summer and into early fall, we were swimming in exceptional stories. By the end of the year, Mr. Russo had a difficult time choosing just twenty stories for the book and one hundred for the list at the back, so this year we opted to include a handful of extras in the list of distinguished stories that we felt deserved the citation. Mr. Russo took his job seriously and read along with me throughout the year. I enjoyed diagnosing various stories with him and hearing his astute thoughts about so many writers. I will miss our armchair psychologizing and his warm sense of humor.

As we head into a new decade and approach the one hundredth anniversary of this series in 2015, there is cause for concern as well as cause to rejoice. It's easy to think of the economy as the enormous, amorphous, untouchable mass that it is, but there are small things readers can do to ensure that in the coming decade we continue to reap the benefits of a healthy American literature. Subscribe to one literary journal, either on paper or online. Buy a short story collection by a young author. We must support our smaller magazines if we are to support our talented new writers. We must support our young writers if we expect quality literature—and a healthy culture—in ten or twenty or thirty years. I'm not entirely worried about our stories arriving in the form of paper or print. I am more concerned that the literature itself is nurtured, that young and established writers continue to be supported by magazine and book publishers, as well as the reading public.

I thank Nicole Angeloro for all her support, as well as Kate Flaherty, Summer Smith, Lori Glazer, and Carla Gray.

The stories chosen for this anthology were originally published between January 2009 and January 2010. The qualifications for selection are (1) original publication in nationally distributed American or Canadian periodicals; (2) publication in English by writers who are American or Canadian, or who have made the United States their home; (3) original publication as short stories (excerpts from novels are not knowingly considered). A list of magazines consulted for this volume appears at the back of the book. Editors who wish their short fiction to be considered for next year's edition should send their publication or hard copies of online publications to Heidi Pitlor, c/o *The Best American Short Stories*, Houghton Mifflin Harcourt, 222 Berkeley Street, Boston, Massachusetts, 02116.

HEIDI PITLOR

Introduction

IN THE LATE 1980s, when I was a young assistant professor at Southern Illinois University, Isaac Bashevis Singer visited campus. The English department had a small budget for visiting writers, but only the Honors College had funds sufficient to entice someone of Singer's stature to a place like Carbondale, Illinois, which meant that we had to share him with the entire university. Mr. Singer was elderly and quite frail, his vision and hearing not what they once were, though his physical diminishments belied a still razor-sharp intelligence and wit. He traveled with his wife, and they were attentively cared for by the university, but for a man in his nineties he was worked pretty hard. In the afternoon, both undergraduate and grad students, as well as faculty from a variety of university disciplines, convened in a large room with an oblong table, at the head of which Mr. Singer had been ensconced. The students were awarded seats at the table, whereas their professors, chafing visibly at the arrangement, were consigned to an outer ring of folding chairs and reminded that the purpose of the session was to allow students to enter a dialogue with the great man, that *their* questions got priority. Seated at the very farthest remove from her husband was Mrs. Singer.

The first student question was obviously a plant. "Mr. Singer?" said one of the undergraduates. The old man had trouble locating the voice, lost as it was in the ambient noise of the room—people settling into their chairs, whispering in nervous anticipation—but finally saw the raised hand. "Mr. Singer? Could you tell us, please, What is the purpose of literature?"

Mr. Singer smiled broadly at the question, as if this were the first time he had ever heard it and was delighted to know the answer. "The purpose of literature," he said clearly, meeting the student's eye, "is to entertain and to instruct."

He let his voice fall. Next question.

The undergraduate students looked at the graduate students, who looked at the outer ring of faculty. Clearly, everyone expected more. The question, after all, was the sort likely to generate whole classes of heated, unresolved debate, but here was a Nobel Prize winner who seemed to think that ten words sufficed to put the matter to rest.

"But Mr. Singer," the student persisted. "Shouldn't literature also—"

Singer held up his hand. "To entertain . . . ," he repeated, pausing to allow his wisdom on the subject to sink in, ". . . and to instruct."

Though he couldn't have been clearer or more adamant, the question proved resilient. Over the next hour several other attempts were made by faculty and students to get their distinguished visitor to elaborate on the other possible uses (political? cultural?) of literature, but each time he demurred. Near the end of the session, an aggrieved voice rang out, "But in your own stories, don't you always . . ." At the sound of this new voice, Mr. Singer's head, which had begun to droop, snapped up, his eyes darting around the room, anxious to locate the source of this new objection. "You?" he said, squinting at his wife who sat in the farthest reaches of his milky vision. "You! I don't have enough problems?"

To entertain and to instruct. Interestingly, he never reversed the order. Literature, he seemed to suggest, couldn't possibly instruct without first entertaining; nor did he fail to pause dramatically between "entertain" and "instruct," as if he feared his listeners were more likely to forget the first purpose than the second. Who could blame him? I might have been a young, wet-behind-the-ears junior professor, but counting grad school, I'd been in the lit biz for a good decade and had witnessed firsthand the propensity of my lit colleagues to mine both poetry and prose fiction for its sparkling nuggets of meaning (instruction) while allowing its many delights to run off like so much slurry. The very word "entertain" connotes to such folk a lack of seriousness, as if the ability to engage and delight readers amounted to a mere parlor trick. The desire to please, some would maintain, is akin to pandering. The writer's real job is not to court the affection of readers but to force them to confront hard truths. Back in grad school I'd flirted with such ideas myself, but lately I'd come to suspect that the desire to show people a good time is a generous impulse rooted in humility. The artist acknowledges both the existence and importance of others. He comes to us bearing a gift he hopes will please us. He starts out making the thing for himself, perhaps, but at some point he realizes he wants to share it, which is why he spends long hours reshaping the thing, lovingly honing its details in the hopes it will please us, that it will be a gift worth the giving and receiving.

But of course it's unfair to blame English teachers. Too often writers themselves, like composers terrified of being dismissed as "melody makers," give the impression that "instruction" is the big game worth stalking. Graham Greene, for instance, drew a distinction between his "serious novels" and "entertainments" like *The Third Man,* leaving readers to wonder if he was blind to what a fine piece of writing the latter is. Though I'm sure Mr. Singer would have allowed that not everyone who uses the word "entertaining" means the same thing by it, he appeared to want no part of such snobbery. His point seemed to be that while we might not all agree on what we find "entertaining," we're unlikely to confuse it with what's commonly meant by "instructive." One is a horse and the other's a cart, and in his opinion one belonged in front, the other behind. I left that afternoon session grinning from ear to ear, convinced I'd found an ally, even if he was just visiting.

That night Singer read to a packed auditorium. Given the paces he'd already been put through, I expected him to be exhausted, but instead he seemed invigorated. Either he'd had a nap or been fed a good meal (I can't imagine where, in Carbondale), or he was just pleased that with the afternoon's rough interrogation behind him, his only remaining task was to disappear into one of his magical tales. Most nonwriters don't understand how wonderful it is for an author to lose himself (to lose, literally, his self) in a story he's written, or how similar the experience of doing so is to that of a nonwriter who loses himself in a stranger's story: for a time, you, your life, your troubles . . . none of it matters. Granted, writers do feed off receptive audiences, and there's always an element of performance, but it's the disappearance, especially after a long day of smiling and hand-shaking and answering questions, that the writer craves. Dickens is said to have read himself to death in huge auditoriums, losing himself night after night to Bill Sykes's murder of Nancy in *Oliver Twist*. The best art has always had the power to seduce its creator.

Whoever worked the sound system the night of Mr. Singer's reading was given a delicate task. The faculty member whose job it was to introduce Mr. Singer was young and robust of voice, whereas the writer himself needed a significant boost from the microphone. His hellos were barely audible, but as he thanked the audience for coming to hear him read, the unseen sound engineer in the rear of the auditorium gradually brought up the volume until the small man before the microphone could be heard throughout the cavernous space. Here, like a new plot point introduced into a narrative already under way, the law of unintended consequences kicked in. Because the whole podium was now alive, the mic amplifying not just the speaker's voice but every other sound. When the toe of his shoe encountered the base of the lectern, a deep explosion resulted, the reverberations of which he had to patiently wait out before continuing, though he seemed innocent of his own causal relationship to the disturbance. My wife and I were seated near the front of the auditorium, and when Singer set down the thick sheaf of pages on the podium with another resounding boom, we regarded each other with chagrin. Did he mean to read them all? Was it his intention in this manner to exact literary revenge for the afternoon's What-is-the-purpose-of-literature discussion?

He began to read, and after about twenty seconds—far too soon, it seemed—he finished and turned the first page, and I realized that, yes, of course, he meant to read them all, but there were only three or four sentences on each; the font had been magnified to accommodate the reader's failing vision. Before he could move on to page two, though, page one had to be dispensed with. Apparently the manuscript had been fastened with a large staple, not paper-clipped, and the sheaf was too thick for each page to be easily folded underneath the ones still to be read, so Mr. Singer decided, reasonably enough, simply to detach the finished page, which came free, reluctantly, with a loud *pop*. But now the poor man had another problem. The lectern was narrow, and there was nowhere to put the detached page. He thought about this for a second and arrived at a workable solution, simply letting go of it. No doubt he expected the page to drop straight down and come to rest at his feet on the elevated stage. Instead it caught an air current and swooped out into the audience, where those seated in the front rows rose in a wave to field it. There was a ripple of nervous laughter which, blessedly, Mr. Singer appeared not to hear. He was finished with the second page now, and after a brief struggle and with a sound not unlike a cork being extracted from a champagne bottle, it too came free of its staple and wafted out into the audience. I leaned over to Barbara, my wife, and whispered, "Dear God." There had to be at least fifty pages in the sheaf. This was going to happen fifty more times? I wasn't sure I could bear it. Mr. Singer himself, though, had the determined look of a man who'd endured worse, and so I resumed my prayer, silently now. "Dear God, let this grand old man make it through his story. Give him his well-earned triumph. Do not make a mockery of him."

Does God listen to the prayers of agnostic young novelists offered on behalf of elderly Nobel laureates? You tell me. After about twenty grueling pages, half of which ended up in the audience, Mr. Singer, finishing another page, gave his now customary page tug, but this time, despite his efforts, there was no *pop*. The page remained stubbornly affixed. He tugged again . . . still nothing (*Dear God dear God dear God*). On the third try—a mighty yank this time—there was a detonation, and out into the audience fluttered not one page but two, each describing its own terrible arc. The page he needed to continue his story had broken containment, sailed out into the audience without his permission. All, I concluded, my heart sinking, was lost.

But I was wrong. Only momentarily flustered, the old man reached into his suit jacket and took out another manuscript. "This sometimes happens," he admitted ruefully. And not just to him, he seemed to imply, but rather to all who soldier on in the face of life's myriad difficulties, expected (the frailty that comes with age) and unexpected (*You! I don't have enough problems?*). Undaunted, he began to read a whole new story, a backup, the thing he'd learned long ago that it's better to have and not need than to need and not have. He'd come to entertain us, to give us the best he had to offer, and he meant to do just that. Did he need the money at this point?

I believe and devoutly hope not. The impression he gave was of a man deeply grateful at such an advanced age to have so many devoted readers in a place he'd never been to before, people whose lives he'd touched by putting pen to paper. He'd never met them and wouldn't meet them tonight. There were too many of them and there was just one of him, and when he was finished reading this new story, he'd be whisked away, empty of energy and even his magical words. But right now he enjoyed being among us strangers, giving us the gift of his voice. He read the second story in its entirety, calmly and without a glitch, as if his ninety-some years had taught him that he was unlikely to be thwarted twice in the same evening. He'd done all a man could reasonably do to anticipate and stave off disaster. It would have to be enough. Bathed in sweat and admiration, I felt—what's the word?—instructed. Note to self: *this is how it's done.*

To entertain and to instruct.

I'll leave the defining of these two crucial terms to others and say only that I was wonderfully entertained and instructed by the twenty riveting stories in this year's *Best American*. It's a showcase of twenty writers' often breathtaking talents, but there's no showing off, and the stories themselves—rich and varied—are blessedly free of the narcissism of the age. I'm pleased to report that there are no triumphs of style over substance, and the language, while often beautiful and sometimes absolutely electric, is always in the service of narrative. The writers may have begun by writing for themselves, as the late J. D. Salinger famously claimed to do, but in the end they turned outward, offering us the gift of what they'd crafted with such care, hoping we'd be pleased. And you will be. Narrowing the roughly two hundred and fifty stories I read to the final twenty felt like some sort of literary waterboarding. At the back of this book is a list of another hundred or so stories culled by Heidi Pitlor from the thousands she read this year in magazines large and small, and I strongly encourage you to search these out and read them, even though I know you'll prefer some of them to the ones I chose and, along with their authors, hold my taste against me, but there you are and here am I. In one of my own most favorite stories in the anthology, one character, a father who's taken up story writing late in life, remarks that stories are like dreams. His son, also a writer, disagrees. Stories, he claims, are like jars full of bees. You unscrew the lid and out come the bees. Maybe in the end that's all guest editors do: we choose the stories that contain the most bees, the tales that sting us good, leaving us surprised and sore at first, then free to worry at our leisure the tender, inflamed spot, our attention focused, ourselves wide awake and alive.

RICHARD RUSSO

The Best
AMERICAN
SHORT
STORIES
2010

STEVE ALMOND

Donkey Greedy, Donkey Gets Punched

FROM *Tin House*

DR. RAYMOND OSS HAD BECOME, in the restless leisure of his late middle age, a poker player. He had a weakness for the game and the ruthless depressives it attracted, one of which he probably was, fair enough, though it wasn't something he wanted known. Oss was a psychoanalyst in private practice and the head of two committees at the San Francisco Institute. He was a short man with a meticulous Trotsky beard and a flair for hats that did not suit him. He cured souls, very expensively, from an office near his home in Redwood City.

On Saturday mornings, Oss put on a sweat suit and orthotic tennis shoes and told Sharon he was off to his tai chi class. Then he shot up 101 straight to Artichoke Joe's in San Bruno, where he played Texas Hold'em at the $3/6 table for five hours straight. He mucked eighty percent of his hands, bluffed only on the button, and lost a little more than he won.

He didn't mind losing, either, if the cards were to blame. It was only when he screwed up — when he failed to see a flush developing or got slow-played by some grinning Chinese maniac — that he felt the pinch of genuine rage. And even these hands offered a certain masochistic pleasure, a mortification that was swift and public.

It was an inconvenient arrangement, tawdry from certain angles, but Oss couldn't help himself. The moment he spotted the dismal pink stucco of the casino's façade, the sea of bent cigarettes rising from the giant ashtray under the awning, he felt a squirt of brainless adrenaline. He had become addicted to the garlic and ginger prawns, too, a dish so richly infiltrated with MSG that it made his tongue go numb. Sometimes, toward the end of a session, having made his third and final promise to cash in after the next hand, Oss would sit back and let the sensations wash over him: the clack of Pai Gow tiles being stirred, the nimble flicking of the cards, the confusion of colognes and nicotine, the monstrous lonely twitch of the place. He loved Artichoke Joe's, especially while hating it.

One day, Oss arrived home to find Sharon waiting in his den. She pulled out a green eyeshade and a deck of cards and began dealing them onto his oriental rug. She'd done theater in college.

"How long have you known?"

Sharon frowned.

Jacob (age eleven) had tipped her off, the little shit. "He hacked into your computer," Sharon said.

"I didn't hack into anything," Jacob yelled from the hallway. "I just clicked the History tab for, like, one second."

Sharon began speaking in her calm social-worker tone. Oss glanced at the scattered cards — a cluster of four hearts, queen high — and thought of his henpecked father. "You could have told me," Sharon said. "I would have understood."

He didn't want his wife's understanding. He had enough of that already. He wanted her indignation, her censure, the stain of his moral insufficiencies tossed between them like a bet. But she saw his Duplicity and raised her Forgiveness.

So he bid Artichoke Joe's farewell — farewell green felt! Farewell ginger prawns! — and began playing in a weekly game with fellow analysts. The twenty-dollar buy-in, the nonalcoholic beer, the arthritic dithering over a seventy-five-cent raise; it was his penance.

Overall, he felt himself vaguely improved. He began to hike the Stanford Hills and reread Dostoevsky and brought Sharon to the Swiss Alps for a month. His older son, Ike, insisted on calling him Cisco, it being his impression that the Cisco Kid had been a famous gambler. Jacob continued to sneak into his office in the hopes of catching him playing online. "Check it before you wreck it, daddy-o," he warned. Oss wanted very much to strike the boy, just once, near the eye.

*

Gary Sharpe appeared in his office that fall. Oss would recall this coincidence later with an odd blend of pride and shame. Sharpe was tall and pale, handsome in a sneering way. He sat miserably and squinted. "So how's this work? Do I hand you my checkbook now, or wait till the end of the session?"

"This is a consultation," Oss said. "We're merely trying—"

"Or maybe I should just dump the cash at your feet?"

Oss sighed without appearing to. It was one of his tricks. "Small, unmarked bills work best. Now why don't you tell me why you're here."

Sharpe shook his head. "My wife."

"She suggested you come?"

"Suggested. You could say that. She's a shrink, too. Her supervisor is some pal of yours. Dr. Penn. I'm not sure how it works with you people. She feels I'm depressed owing to unresolved issues with my father, who, by the way, died when I was seventeen. So technically I have issues with my dead father."

"And you feel?"

Sharpe inspected his fingernails. "I'm in a volatile business. I've explained this to her a few thousand times."

"So you're not depressed?"

"Depressed. Christ. Whatever happened to 'sad'? I guess there's no dough in sadness. As for your next question, yeah, I've done the drugs. Paxil, Wellbutrin, some new one they've got called Kweez-lemonkey. That one goes up your ass as a minty fresh gel."

Oss laughed. "Sounds refreshing."

"Right. I get the funny shrink. Perfect." Sharpe fake-yawned. He looked like he hadn't slept in a few weeks.

"Are you aware of what an analysis entails?"

"My wife filled me in. I lie on my back and complain about what an asshole everyone is. Then, when you've made enough to pay for your new deck, the angels blow a trumpet and I'm cured. What a fucking racket. You people should carry guns."

"I do," Oss said.

Sharpe would be back, the bluster said as much. He'd blame it on his wife for a few weeks, then they could begin the work. "What is it exactly you do, Mr. Sharpe?"

"I play cards," he said. "I take money from people who don't want it anymore."

*

So this was his new patient: Gary "Card" Sharpe, winner of the 2003 World Series of Poker, enfant terrible of the World Poker Tour, notorious for his table talk, his braying laugh, his signature line of poker-themed clothing and paraphernalia (Look Sharpe™).

On Friday, Oss spotted Penn in the parking garage.

"Thanks for the referral."

Penn smiled. "One greedy prick deserves another." He zapped his trunk open and began removing stuffed animals. Penn was always doing things like this, things that made no sense. "His wife's a real sweetheart. She'll leave him if he doesn't shape up."

"No pressure, though."

"Take it as a compliment. You'll know what he's talking about, anyway. All the lingo. Down and dirty. Double down."

Oss took off his derby and inspected the rim. "I wasn't aware you considered me such an expert at poker."

"I wasn't aware you considered me such an idiot." Penn tapped his brow with a yellow monkey. "Come on, Ray. Tai chi? How long have I known you?"

"He's going to hassle me about the fee nonstop."

"Of course he is," Penn replied. "He's a gambler. That's how he keeps score. Speaking of which, you in Friday?"

Penn played in the weekly game. He held his cards as if the ink were still wet and studied them like runes. Then he lost cheerfully. Everyone loved Penn, in the same way they sort of hated Oss.

For the most part, Sharpe talked poker. His disquisitions inevitably began, *You know what I fucking hate?* He fucking hated the Internet. He fucking hated the TV coverage. He fucking hated the travel.

"You ever been in the Reno airport before dawn, Oss?"

"Can't say I've had the pleasure."

"I fucking hate that place. It's like hell with slot machines. Even the air smells sad. Care to guess why I was there so early? So I could get back from a tournament in time for this shit-ass session."

"How'd you do?"

Sharpe shrugged. "Twelve K, plus sponsor money. We wound up chopping the pot at the final table. You know what that means? It means we got rid of all the donkeys, the shit players, then split the prize money."

"Sounds like easy money," Oss said.

Sharpe bristled. "Easy?" he said.

"I just meant—"

"I know what you meant," Sharpe said. "I'm sure a guy in your position—you don't think playing poker takes much brainpower, do you? It's just a bunch of cigar smoke and dumb luck. What's your game anyway, doc? Bridge? You probably sit around on Saturday night playing penny-a-point, creaming your fucking chinos because somebody made small slam in hearts." Sharpe's upper lip curled. "You know who you fucking remind me of? My fucking dad."

Now we're getting somewhere, Oss thought. He waited a moment before asking, "How so?"

"Oh, you'd like that, wouldn't you?"

Oss sighed his silent sigh. "This isn't a poker game, Gary. You don't win by hiding your cards."

"I don't win at all," Sharpe said. "I just give all the chips to you."

"I can only help if you're forthcoming with me."

Sharpe exhaled through his nose. "So now you're Dr. Phil? Dr. Phil: the midget version with the stupid hats." He sneered. "What the fuck is up with these hats anyways? You're bald, doc. Deal with it."

Oss was secretly thrilled to be treating Sharpe. The depth of his rage was refreshing. It returned Oss to his adolescence, to the loathing he so lavishly apportioned to his own father, who sold hardware, who developed pathetic infatuations with his prominent customers. (My good friend Dr. Lindell. My good friend Magistrate Johns.) The old man, with his Brooklyn brogue and small-time dreams. *A man who gambles,* he liked to say, *is a man who doesn't want his shoit.*

Sharpe could be tender, too. He was terrified of losing his wife. "Back in college, she figured I'd go to some hedge fund. I told her as much. Look: she's not thrilled with the choices I've made. But she's got a better heart than me, doc. That's more or less the basis of our marriage."

Oss was stunned to discover that Sharpe had a child as well, a boy named Doyle. "Sharp little bastard," Sharpe said. "He slaughters me at everything. Concentration. Go Fish."

"A born card counter, eh?"

"No no no," Sharpe said. "He's not going to wind up rotting in some casino. He's got a real imagination."

"Poker doesn't require imagination?"

"Donkey greedy. Donkey gets punched. The rest is just math. He gets the creative stuff from Kate, these crazy little comic books he draws, he does all the plots himself. Seven years old! Every dad says this shit, I guess. But you know, sometimes he looks at me and I'll realize for a second how fragile he is. It makes me want to cry." Sharpe swallowed hard; his ear flushed for a moment. "I have no idea why. It's like I want to protect him from some terrible thing and I don't even know what."

Oss urged Sharpe to think about what that thing might be, but by the next session, he'd retreated to the old troughs of grievance. "You know what I fucking hate," he said. "All these guys from Google, with their mirror shades and their goatees. Chin pussies, I call them. You can't swing a dead cat in Artichoke Joe's without hitting Google trash."

Oss froze for a moment.

"What?" Sharpe said. "Why'd you stop taking notes?"

Oss sat back and scratched out Did-not-Did-not-Did-not. "You were saying?" he said.

"Wait a second." Sharpe smiled. "I just said something that threw you off. Don't bullshit a bullshitter, doc."

Oss's tongue tingled. He could taste the ginger prawns. "I suppose I was surprised you'd play at a local casino. Wouldn't people recognize you?"

"Of course they fucking recognize me."

"But wouldn't that make it tough? Why would anyone play against you?"

Sharpe did his full-throated bray. "You're kidding, right, doc? Everyone in that place wants to play me. For fuck's sake. I'm like Barry Bonds to these donks. Only they can play against me. They can even beat me. Shit. It's mostly up to the cards."

"I see," Oss said. For a moment he imagined what it might be like to sit across the table from Sharpe, the sort of irrational hatred a guy like him could generate.

"That's what I hate about these Google guys. They've got all this dumb money, more than they know how to squander. So they throw it at me for a few hours and brag about that one gut-shot they hit for the next ten years. That's not gambling, it's Disneyland. Gambling is about people ruining their fucking lives."

"So that's your goal? To ruin your life?"

Sharpe's brow crimped and Oss, studying his face from behind, noticed for the first time that the sneer on his lip was in fact the result of a small scar.

"You have to realize what you are," Sharpe said. "If you're a gambler, you're a gambler. That's how your nerves fire. I wake up every morning thinking about that next great bet. You can get all high and mighty and call that an addiction. Or you can call it what it is: fucking desire. I'll tell you this, there's nothing sadder than a gambler in denial. I should know. My dad was one."

Oss waited for Sharpe to elaborate. It was a lot of what he did.

The silence dragged on.

"What?" Sharpe said finally. "What the fuck do you want from me?"

In August, Sharpe returned from the World Series of Poker in a black mood. He'd been knocked out of the tournament on the third day, a humiliation Oss had witnessed (with some relish) on ESPN2.

"I've got a tell," Sharpe said to Oss now. "I fucking know it. There's no other way to explain it. You know what a tell is, right? That's like something that gives away how you feel. Like that swallowed sigh thing you do when you're frustrated. That's a tell."

Oss sat back in his chair.

"Don't act so surprised," Sharpe said. "This is what I do for a living, okay, doc? I read people. We're in the same business that way, only I look them in the eye before I take their money. Now I need some fucking help from you, for once, because obviously I'm doing something I'm not aware of."

"What happened?"

Sharpe threw up his hands as if he were tossing a salad, a salad at which he was furious. "Bad cards. Bad beats. That I can handle. I'll scrape by with shit luck. But this was different. I let it get personal, which is, rule one: it's never fucking personal. Because how else does a puke like Bill Tandy sniff out three bluffs in a row?"

"Who's Bill Tandy?"

"My exact fucking point, doc." Sharpe closed his eyes. "This guy,

Mr. Retired Real Estate Puke from Tucson, he sits there eyeballing me for ten seconds and suddenly he pops his tongue under his lip, which is what he does when he knows he's got a guy beat—it's his tell."

From where he was sitting, Oss could see the cuff of Sharpe's right ear redden again. "Couldn't he have just been guessing?" Oss said.

"He had jack-high crap," Sharpe muttered. "You don't guess against me with jack-high crap. Even an old donkey knows that. No, he saw something. This fucker saw something. And I want you to tell me what."

"Me?"

"I've been paying you a grand a week. You're supposed to be so observant, so wise to my subconscious. It's about time you offered some return on my fucking investment."

"I didn't realize it was my job to make you a better poker player," Oss said.

Sharpe glared at the ceiling. "It's your job to make me a happier person, you little shit."

"Winning doesn't seem to make you a happier person, Gary."

"Meaning what?"

Oss remained silent.

"You are a complete french-fried asshole, Oss. I pity your fucking wife and the disfigured dwarf children that sprang from her loins. Honestly. You're worse than my old man."

"I take it he didn't approve of your career."

Sharpe grinned. "No, he didn't. And he spanked me on my little bum in front of all my friends and I cried and cried. Wah-wah-wah. Then I tried to kill him, but I went blind instead and stumbled into a giant cave that smelled like my mother's snatch. God you're obvious."

As a younger analyst, Oss would have laughed and let Sharpe jump the hook. But he had come to recognize disgust as the first form of disclosure. "You said earlier that your father was a gambler in denial. What did you mean?"

Sharpe let out an exasperated sigh. "He worked in the financial sector. He played the market. That's all I meant. All those guys are gamblers. The whole fucking thing's a big bet."

"What happened to him?"

"He made a bad bet."

"And?"

"And he hung himself."

Was this another bluff? It was hard to tell with Sharpe.

When he finally spoke again his voice had lost its belligerence. It wasn't soft so much as deflated. "My dad made his nut off something called 'portfolio insurance.' The idea was that you paid a premium to limit your losses. Then came the crash of eighty-seven and the whole thing blew up." Sharpe shook his head. "And the reason it blew up is simple: he was selling the fantasy of risk-free gambling—which doesn't exist. So he lost everything and took some rope out to the garage and my mom and me were left to scrounge through his estate for rent money." Sharpe smiled his sneering smile. "This is the guy who lectured me about responsibility, about doing the right thing."

Oss didn't say anything for a time. He thought, oddly, of his own father, the way he fingered each coin from his palm onto the counter when making a purchase. Pop was a child of the Depression. He had tasted poverty. And still, Oss found his elaborate caution around money shameful.

"I can see why you might be angry at him," Oss said.

Sharpe closed his eyes. "I'm not angry," he said. The cuff of his ear flushed. "He had a shitty hand and he lost. The end."

It wasn't as if the discoloration was obvious. You'd really have to be looking to spot it. But then, that was what pros did. They looked for signs.

Oss's first impulse was to drop a hint, maybe suggest a longer hairstyle. But the more he pondered the matter, the more misguided this seemed. His role was to help the patient come to terms with the unbearable facts and feelings of his history. In fact, it was the loss at poker that had induced Sharpe (finally) to discuss his father. Was it also true that Oss derived a certain pleasure from withholding? That it served as a form of revenge against an equally withholding and, at times, emotionally abusive patient? It was possible.

One thing was clear: the closer Sharpe drew to the sources of his depression, the more recalcitrant he grew. One sweltering June afternoon, he showed up in an obvious state of inebriation. "I've had a few," was how he put it.

"Any particular reason?" Oss said.

"A few works better than one." Sharpe belched. "Anyways, I've decided you want me to lose. The sadder and more fucked up I become, the more dough you make."

"You're my bread and butter?"

"You said it, Ossipoo." Sharpe shuffled an invisible stack of chips. "You also get off on looking down on me. You think I'm some cretin. Like I should read more books or something."

Oss thought of Dostoevsky's gambler, Alexei. He had always imagined the character in a green velvet waistcoat, watching the roulette wheel spin. Freud argued that Dostoevsky—like most gamblers—subconsciously wanted to lose. He sought to punish himself for the death of his parents. His father had been a vicious drunk, murdered by his serfs, supposedly. The novelist had done that one better, letting the Karamazov boys do the deed themselves. Was there no love so disastrous as that between a son and father? Oss himself was still a wreck when it came to his pop, whose gentle hand he had held even as death took him under.

"Are you fucking listening to me?" Sharpe said.

"Of course," Oss said.

"What was I just talking about?"

Oss stared down at his notes. Absurdly, his eyes were stinging. "You were asking me, for perhaps the hundredth time, why you should keep coming here."

"And?"

"We are trying to understand your discontent. This is not easy work," Oss said.

"Oh for fuck's sake."

Sharpe began traveling overseas on what he called "the sheik circuit." Dubai, the Emirates. "Hey," he said, when Oss complained about missed sessions, "the price is right. You want I should ask any of them if they need a nice Jewy analyst?" He continued to appear for sessions drunk. He flew into paranoid rages. He celebrated his year anniversary as a patient by presenting Oss with a bill for forty-eight thousand dollars, requesting a full refund "for failure to deliver the contracted services."

Oss prescribed medications intended to ameliorate the bipolar symptoms. He urged Sharpe to cut back on alcohol and poker. Sharpe responded by flouting his bills.

A week before Thanksgiving, he shambled into the office and

nodded at Oss's hat rack. "Tell me you didn't wear the fucking be-
ret outside this office. Christ. You're like a one-man stupid-looking
contest." He plopped down on his back. His unlaced sneakers
thwacked the couch.

"We've discussed payment at length. That discussion is now over.
You either pay your outstanding fees or we terminate."

"Would you accept chips?" Sharpe reached into his pocket. "No?
Ooooh, the silent treatment. I must be in trouble."

"You're not a child, Gary."

"I love it when you get all stern, doc. I really do. It makes me
think of me dear old da!" Sharpe rubbed at his eyes dramatically.
"He was a lot like you, Ossipoo, a little donkey who thought he was
a big shark. And look how that turned out. You know what he was
wearing when I found him swinging from the rafters?"

"Hold on a moment," Oss said.

"A silk ascot. Right under the rope. I shit you not, doc. He's got
the fat blue face, his tongue's hanging out, his eyes are about to
pop from their sockets, there's shit dripping from his pants, and
the stupid fuck—"

"Is this true?" Oss said. "If this is true—"

But Sharpe had said too much. They both knew it. "You think I
need this shit? You think I ever needed this shit?" he brayed, but
his voice cracked around the sound. "Fuck you, doc. No, seriously.
We're done here."

It was a sad moment for Oss, because he loved his patients, even
the difficult ones, for the weaknesses they laid before him, for their
courage, and because it had been Sharpe, after all, who looked like
an animal, a beast of burden, charging blindly from his office, off
into a world that could bring him no peace.

"You did what you had to do," said Penn, to whom Oss inevitably
and resentfully confided. "Some patients can't be saved."

Sharon was less sympathetic. "He sounds like a royal asshole,"
she said that evening.

"Mom said a-hole!" Jacob shrieked.

"Shut up," Oss roared. "Shut your mouth until further notice."

Jacob held his cheek as if he'd been slapped. Sharon stared at
him in horror.

"The kid has to learn not to be a tattletale," Oss said. "All right,
look. I apologize. It's been a long day."

Oss tried to put Gary Sharpe out of mind. But he kept turning up: on the poker shows, loud and unhappy, with bloodshot eyes. Oss missed him. While his other patients murmured their soft complaints, his mind drifted to desirable poker hands. Ace/jack suited. Pocket queens. He found himself volunteering to do weekend Costco runs, knowing these would lead him past Artichoke Joe's. He limited himself to one game per month, then two.

It was nearly a year later, on a sleepy Tuesday afternoon, that Oss looked up from his seat and saw his former patient striding across the casino floor. He wore a tracksuit the same color as his stubble. Oss knew he should muck his hand and slip out quietly. But he hesitated just long enough to allow Sharpe to spot him.

There was a buzz in place by now, several folks at his elbow. Sharpe made straight for Oss. "Don't I know you?" he said.

Oss looked up and smiled.

"How the hell are you?" Sharpe seemed genuinely glad to see him. "I didn't realize you played here."

"I don't, really," Oss said. "Occasionally."

The other players at the table stared at him in astonishment. You, their eyes said. Really?

The manager of the poker section hurried over and began genuflecting. Sharpe stepped away from the table so they could finish up the hand. He did some backslapping, signed one of his hats for a trembling Indian kid, posed for photos. Then he smiled and nodded at an empty seat across from Oss. "Mind if I join you gents?"

"We're happy to start a no-limit table," the manager said.

"No no," Sharpe said. "Just want to play a few hands. No big deal."

"You can have my seat," Oss said. "I was just about to cash out."

"Come on now," Sharpe said. "You're going to hurt my feelings, doc." He dropped into the empty seat. "I was hoping you might teach me a few things."

The dealer glanced at Oss. Staying at the table was clearly the wrong thing to do on about six levels. But the air around him was crackling with a strange electricity. He shrugged and nodded.

It was immediately obvious the speed with which Sharpe processed information: table position, pot odds. His eyes flicked from face to face on the flop. It was something like watching a shark — the grace and efficiency of his aggression. His outbursts, so petulant on TV, came off as charming in person, a way of relieving the essential tedium of the game. When Oss took a pot with two small pairs, Sharpe applauded. "Thattaboy," he said.

For his part, Oss avoided looking at Sharpe, and in particular at his ears.

"How you two know each other?" the dealer said.

"Doc was an adviser of mine for a time." Sharpe grinned. "He has, despite that idiotic Greek fisherman's cap, a keen financial sense."

Everyone laughed.

"What kind of advice you give?" the dealer said.

"The expensive kind," Sharpe roared.

Oss waited for the laughter to subside. "How are things going?" he asked.

"My wife's going to take fifty percent of everything." Sharpe downed the rest of his beer and gestured for another. "Aside from that it's jim-fucking-dandy."

"I'm so sorry," Oss said.

Sharpe sneered. "It's not like I'm going to kill myself."

Oss wanted to pull him aside, to talk to him privately. But they were at the poker table, a place where the only intimacy permitted was between a man and his own fortune. It was time for Oss to go.

The problem—and it really was a problem—was that he'd been dealt two cards by now. Good cards.

These were, in fact, the best cards he'd gotten all day. The bet came to him and he raised. Everyone folded except Sharpe, who was the big blind. "Alone at last," he said.

Oss laughed uncomfortably.

The flop came:

This gave Oss two pair, aces and kings, an exceptional hand. He thought briefly about checking. Perhaps it was best to get through the hand and get out. Instead, he bet the limit.

Sharpe glanced at Oss. "Mighty proud of that pair, are you? I'd be, too. But you shouldn't tell the whole table, doc." He inhaled loudly through his nose. Oss realized, with a start, that Sharpe was imitating him.

"That's just cruel," someone murmured.

"No, that's poker," Sharpe snapped. "I just did the good doctor a big favor. Saved him a good deal of money down the line. More than he ever did for me." He finished his beer. "I raise."

Oss could feel the room start to thrum. He looked at the flop again and did some quick math. The chances that Sharpe had three of a kind were one in 2,500. He might be playing for the club flush, but that was a dumb bet. "Re-raise," Oss said.

Sharpe smiled. "Oh for fuck's sake, doc. You already cost me fifty grand. What's a little more?"

The turn card was the two of clubs.

If Sharpe was looking for a flush, he'd just made it. He might also have a three/four, which would give him a straight, though that would mean he'd drawn to an inside straight, something he would never do. No, if anything, Sharpe had the flush. But the odds on that were one in five. Two pair still made Oss a heavy favorite. "I'll bet," he said. "I don't think you have the flush."

"You're right," Sharpe said unhappily. "But I'll raise anyway."

Oss looked up. A small crowd had begun to form. Or maybe it had been there all along, to watch the great Gary Sharpe clobber some poor donkey. That's what he was to these folks: a donkey. A dilettante with a nasty little midweek habit. They were just waiting for him to fold.

"Re-raise."

Sharpe sat back. Another beer had disappeared down his throat. "Well now, doc, I hope those oats feel good. But do me a favor, since you're so confident: let's at least stop playing kiddie poker." He turned to the manager. "Can we make this a no-limit game?"

The crowd let out a murmur.

The manager said, "It's a limit table, Gary. I really can't do that."

"A little side wager then? How about that?"

The manager regarded Sharpe in bureaucratic despair. "The casino cannot be party to any such arrangement. That'd be between you gentlemen."

"Excellent," Sharpe said. "I'd say we've got enough witnesses. So what if we say I see your six, and raise you ten thousand dollars on the side."

Oss cleared his throat. "You're kidding, I assume."

"No sir."

"I think it's best if we just stick to the table limits."

Sharpe began nodding. "Oh I see, little man. You just want to play the safe game, nothing that could get you hurt. Does your wife even know you're here? How fucking sad."

Oss glanced at Sharpe's ears, just for a second. He knew it was some kind of violation—of analytic trust, of basic decency—but he couldn't restrain himself. They were as pale as the rest of him.

"What's the matter, doc? You don't look so hot," Sharpe brayed. "All right. Listen. I'm gonna do you another favor, for old time's sake. In front of all these nice folks and God himself, I'm gonna tell you to fold. Just throw your cards in the middle of the table and be done with it, little man. Go home and tell your wife a good lie."

It was an astonishing display. A few people in the crowd whistled. Someone said, "Classic Sharpe."

Oss reached for his cards. He certainly meant to fold, to put an end to this foolishness. But he paused for a moment first.

Sharpe gulped at his beer. "Okay, we're all done here, folks. The good doctor is all done pretending. That's okay, doc. Just walk away. There's no shame when you're beat." The cuff of his right ear flushed. "You want to see the hand you lost to? Would that help?" Sharpe made as if to reach for his cards. His ear had gone crimson now.

Oss felt his chest start to fizz. His hands, which had been hovering over his cards, trembled. He clasped them together and nearly burst into laughter. "I appreciate all your kind advice," he said. "But I guess I'll have to call anyway."

"Okay," Sharpe said loudly. "I tried. I honestly tried. I'm no longer responsible for what happens next. That's on you, doc."

Oss realized, with a twinge of pity, that Sharpe was trapped. He'd gotten himself in too deep, allowed it to become personal.

The dealer turned over the river card. It was the ace of spades.

The board now looked like this:

Oss couldn't quite believe his eyes. He had hit a full house on the river, aces over kings. Even if Sharpe wasn't bluffing, even if he'd made his flush, Oss had him beat. It seemed almost cruel.

Sharpe glanced at the fifth card, as if it was of no great concern to him. "One more round of betting," he said. "You feeling lucky?"

"Check," Oss said.

"Ten thousand," Sharpe said. He was plainly out of his mind.

Oss cleared his throat again. "Listen," he said, "I think this has gone far enough."

Sharpe turned to the crowd and brayed. "I'm not sure if you're entirely familiar with your options here, doc. You've got three: call, raise, or fold."

"Okay," Oss said. "I get it."

But Sharpe wasn't done. He was never done. "More than a year of my life you wasted with your overpriced psychobabble bullshit," he murmured. "And here's the funny part: you actually think that shit matters, that you're saving people with your little spells and incantations. Are you starting to get it, doc? This is what matters, right here." He gestured to the cards that lay between them, then to the crowd. "So don't disappoint all these nice folks, doc. They came here to see what happens next."

Oss closed his eyes and considered how he had arrived at this point. He knew some of it was his fault. But was it his fault that he'd been dealt a monster hand? Was it his fault that his opponent was a psychotic asshole? Hell, if anything, he'd tried to help the psychotic asshole.

Sharpe was now leering at him (psychotically) and blowing beer fumes across the table. "Be a good boy," he bellowed. "Save your shirt. Remember: guys like me always beat guys like you."

"Double it," Oss said.

He couldn't quite believe the words had come out of his mouth. He honestly hadn't meant to say them. But the moment he did, his body surged with joy. He felt as if he might be floating. "Double it," he said again.

The crowd let out a whoop.

The manager drew a cell phone from his pocket and began dialing frantically.

"Let's make it an even forty," Sharpe shot back. He was slurring now. "That's right. Forty thousand, you greedy bastard. You want to hang yourself in public, here's your chance. I can't save you."

A great calm descended on Oss. He had seen patients for more than half his life. Whatever tumult they created in the present, it all traced back to the past. Whatever wrath they aimed at him, he was merely a hired stand-in. And so here was the famous Gary Sharpe, face to face at last with his father. He wanted to destroy the old man, but deep down he wanted to destroy himself more.

He'd been unable to convince Sharpe on the analytic couch. But perhaps here, at the poker table, which had become his refuge, his final hiding place, the lesson might stick. "Let's make it an even fifty thousand dollars," Oss said.

"Okay now," said the manager, "now that, that's the final raise, okay? Okay guys? I don't care what the private arrangement is."

The crowd hissed, but Sharpe held up his hands for silence. He looked remarkably serene, resigned to his fate. "Fair enough," he said. "I call. Now do what you came here to do, doc. No hard feelings." He leered again and Oss saw not the garish smile but the faint scar on his lip. It made him want to weep, to see how far human beings would go to hide from the truth of themselves.

There was nothing else for him to do, though, so Oss turned over his cards. He could hear the crowd roar. "I'm sorry," he said. "I truly am. I didn't want it to come to this."

"Sure you did," Sharpe said. He smiled gently. Then he turned over his cards:

There was a moment of confused silence, then the crowd let out a collective gasp. "Take a good look," Sharpe said.

Oss inspected the community cards again. The green felt took on a queasy shimmer. He saw Sharpe's hand now:

A straight flush.

The shock hit Oss in waves. He felt the nerves in his neck constrict. He was having trouble breathing. All around him was noise and jostling. Two or three people reached to comfort him. Sharpe rose from his seat and walked around the table. He squatted down and gestured for the others to step back.

Oss stared at his ears, which seemed now to be blazing.

"Yeah, my wife was kind enough to tip me off, just before she gave me the boot. And you know the crazy thing? Alcohol has the exact same physiological effect on me. Imagine that! What are the odds, doc?"

Oss found that his hands were still clasped, but there was no feeling in either of them. It was as if he were dead now, as if he were holding the hand of his own dead father.

"Now don't go worrying about the dough. We can set up a payment plan, something weekly." Sharpe tried for a grin, but it wouldn't hold.

"What in God's name have I done?" Oss whispered. He suspected he was weeping. His cheeks certainly felt wet.

"Settle down now, doc." Oss felt a hand laid upon his shoulder with unbearable tenderness. The room was a bright blur, at the center of which hovered Sharpe's face; the sneer was gone, replaced by a familiar sorrow. Already his triumph was slipping away, into the unbending shadows of vengeance. "The man who can't lose always does," he said softly. "Did you learn nothing from our work?"

MARLIN BARTON

Into Silence

FROM *The Sewanee Review*

FROM WHERE SHE SAT at the end of the porch she noticed a tall man walking toward her house. The sight of a stranger in River-field always raised curiosity, and strangers did come through with some regularity these days, looking for work they knew they wouldn't find or for food they hoped they'd be offered. They were lost men, lost from family and friends, and the closest they could come to home was someone else's doorstep.

This man, though, wasn't walking alone, and to see her mother walking beside him struck her as a little odd. She'd never been one to offer help to those passing through. The faces that held hunger and want didn't seem to move her beyond a concern for herself and her daughter, two women alone.

As they neared the house, she saw how small her mother looked beside him. And yet it wasn't just his height that rendered her mother so small. There was some other dimension to him. Maybe it was his carriage or something in his demeanor that she'd see or feel more clearly when they were closer.

Soon they stood at the steps, and she saw the angular lines of his face and his sharp eyes examining, shifting from one point to another, taking in the house, and her. Then her mother was talking, out loud, not with her hands. "Janey, this is Mr. Clark. I met him up at Anderson's store. He's going to take a look at the room under the stairs."

Her mother spoke too slowly and carefully, so that Janey could be sure to read each word as it was said. She had told her mother many times that she didn't have to do this, but her mother almost always did. When they were in front of people Janey didn't have to hear how it must have sounded to be embarrassed.

Mr. Clark looked at her and nodded but didn't speak. She saw one thing clearly about him now. He wasn't one of those lost men that traveled through. His clothes were clean and fit him well, and his hat, which he removed to reveal a mixture of dark and graying hair cut close, looked almost new. The shirt he wore was neatly pressed, the sleeves rolled up just high enough to show muscular forearms. He'd come here for some purpose. She saw that. She wondered if her mother knew what.

He kept looking at Janey, intently, but not staring. His eyes were a dark brown, like creek water that ran through rich soil. She grew uncomfortable after a moment. Maybe, because of the way her mother had spoken, he suspected she was deaf. It would be like her mother not to have mentioned it. Perhaps he was waiting to see if she'd speak so that he could confirm his suspicion. She simply left her silence open to interpretation.

"Will you show him the room?" her mother said.

She nodded again, stood, and then turned so that he would follow her. The front door opened into a small entrance hall. To the left, narrow stairs wound their way up to the second story, which they didn't use, and to the right was the door that opened into the living room and the rest of the house. Directly ahead and beneath a portion of the stairs was a single bedroom that didn't connect to any other room. Her mother had rented it off and on the last few years when money had become too tight. She hadn't wanted to do it. Janey knew she'd felt embarrassed at such a public announcement that money was short.

She opened the door and a close musty smell came to her. He walked past and went to the one window and raised it. She felt a sudden cross-breeze that cleansed the air and ruffled her clothing. Then she smelled the sharp, masculine scent of gasoline or motor oil and knew it must have come from his hands. He turned and looked at her, and she grew uncomfortable again under his gaze, though she didn't feel as if he were looking at her as a woman, the way a woman might want if it was the right man. She felt she'd gone past the age for that and into a settled middle age. It was a passing she'd mourned, then gotten over.

He lifted his hand slowly and held it in front of his chest. His palm was stained with what looked like motor oil. She couldn't have been more surprised at the sight of his fingers moving. "I like the room," he spelled out. "I'll take it."

That was all. No conversation, no explanation about when or why he'd learned to speak, or how he'd known for certain that she was deaf. But his large fingers had moved quickly and easily.

He walked past her again, and this time she followed him. He spoke briefly to her mother, then went down the porch steps and away, his movements purposeful, businesslike.

"He's going to get his car from where he left it at the store," her mother said.

She started to tell her mother how he had spoken, then decided not to, at least for now. It would be some small thing she could keep to herself, or maybe for herself.

Only two other people in Riverfield had ever known how to speak to her, an Episcopal minister who'd finally moved to a larger church in Selma, and Louise Anderson, whose son owned the store where the man was now headed. Louise had learned as an offer of friendship, and when she visited, the two of them sitting out on the porch, their hands flying with words and sometimes a little gossip, her mother would stand in the dark of the doorway, watching, and would finally emerge and tell Janey that she needed her for some chore, usually one that had either already been done or didn't need doing. She'd always been this way, continually calling Janey to her, but after Janey's father had died, it had grown worse.

Janey signed a question for her mother now.

"He works for the WPA," she said, again speaking too slowly. "Travels around the state taking pictures."

"Of what?"

"Buildings. Old houses and slave quarters, plantation homes. Says there are people like him doing this all over the South."

"Our house?" Janey said.

Her mother nodded and looked down. She knew why. The house wasn't what it had been. The roof needed replacing. The steps were warped. Her grandfather, Jason Teclaw, had built the house with slave labor, and made a large comfortable home, the one oddity in its design the columns across the front and side of the house. The branch stubs at the tops of the tree trunks they'd used had never been completely cut away, so each column looked as though

it grew up out of the ground. There were knotholes, too, visible in
the sides of each column, and now that the paint on the house was
completely gone, the columns looked even more like trees that
had reached a certain height and had their growth stunted or
stopped. Bricks around the cellar walls had come loose, leaving
holes into the darkness that had once been, for a brief period, the
saloon that had gotten her grandfather kicked out of the Methodist congregation. He'd then bought the Episcopal church that
stood in the next county, had it dismantled and shipped across the
Tennahpush River, and finally erected where it stood now, just
down the road from where Janey had heard her last sound.

   Music was her entry into silence. She'd been only ten years old,
sitting on the end of the porch above the steps, listening to the
Episcopal choir rehearse "Our God to Whom We Turn" not fifty
yards away. Their voices had carried easily through the open
church doors and on the light breeze, and that breeze had felt like
music itself against her skin. Then her head began to reel and spin,
and she fell backwards into sound and air and finally nothing as all
her senses went dark.

   She woke into darkness nights later, there in her room, in her
bed. She'd called out from her confusion as any child would, and
her mother was there instantly, always her mother. But something
sounded wrong, or had not sounded, except inside her where illness and confusion grew. She hadn't heard herself, hadn't heard
the call she'd made—*Mama.* And though her mother was already
gripping her tightly, she'd called out again, but only into silence,
which is where she lived now, had been living for so many years
that she didn't feel uncomfortable inside its invisibility. Sometimes
she thought it saved her, gave her a separate place to retreat into as
far as she might need at any given moment—and there were moments.

After he had unloaded his car and carried in his suitcase and camera and other equipment, Mr. Clark asked her about meals. "He
wants room and board," she told her mother, who was pleased at
the chance to bring in a little more money.

   He ate a supper of soup and cornbread with them that night, at
the table in the middle of the kitchen. They'd had plenty of soup
left from the day before, and Janey had made the cornbread her-

self, though it was never as good as her mother's, which her mother always found ways to point out.

"Nice to have good cooking," Mr. Clark said, but he wouldn't respond to the protests pointed at him by her mother about how poor the soup tasted. He appeared indifferent to the hints for another compliment. He mostly remained silent, nodding when he had to, and watching first her mother, then her, studying them, it seemed, from some far-removed place, where quiet held value.

But the quiet soon became more than her mother could bear. "Are you married, Mr. Clark?" she said. She spoke quickly, abruptly. Janey wondered if her mother hadn't wanted her to read the question, but she'd seen the shape of the words. She'd also noticed earlier that he didn't wear a wedding ring, just as her mother must have noticed.

He nodded *yes*, but offered nothing else, not even his wife's name.

Then her mother must have asked another question, but her face had been turned away.

"She's staying with her folks now, in Calera, while I travel," he said.

"Children?" she spoke quickly again, but Janey had seen.

"No," he said and looked down, as though children had been something denied him.

Her mother's expression turned suddenly sad. "I don't know what I'd do without my daughter beside me," she said, and Janey looked then at Mr. Clark, and his eyes shifted back and forth between them. Finally he looked away, as though he'd taken some partial measure of them, or perhaps she'd only imagined it.

In the morning he loaded his camera and tripod into his car. He'd told her mother at breakfast, when she asked, that he'd begin with some of the buildings clustered around the post office and the store. It was a short walk, but he couldn't have carried everything he needed, so loading the car was a necessity.

He had hardly acknowledged Janey at breakfast, but now, after closing the car door, he walked toward where she sat. She tensed at his approach, perhaps because of his own tense expression. He looked tired, irritated. Maybe her mother had said something to him, or asked one too many questions.

"You might be able to help me," he signed.

She'd half expected him to say he'd be leaving by the end of the day, and felt more relief at his asking her for help than she would have anticipated. Afraid of him or not, she liked what his presence made her feel. "If I can," she spelled with her fingers.

"I'll need to know something about the buildings, the ones I take pictures of, for my notes. Maybe tonight you can tell me some history about them, who built them."

"I'd be glad to try. I can certainly tell you about this house."

She watched him back out of the drive, and felt glad to be needed, useful in some small way. When she stood to go inside, she caught her mother watching from the door.

"You didn't tell me," her mother said.

"What?"

"You know."

"That he knows how to speak to me?"

"Yes, that."

"No, I didn't tell you," she said, suddenly bold, thrusting her hand as she formed the letters and made her irritation clear.

Her mother turned and walked into the house. Janey felt her footsteps in the boards of the porch. The floor had always carried her mother's anger. She'd learned this first as a little girl when her mother and father argued. Their words might not have existed as sound for her, but anger always caused its own vibration.

She hadn't been exactly sure why they argued all those years ago, but sensed, the way a child will, that it was usually about her. And when she grew older she decided that it must have been about what she could and couldn't do, about what would be allowed and what wouldn't, and finally about what would be done with her, or for her, though she couldn't have put all of this into words as a child, words thought or spoken — in any form.

After their arguments her mother would come to her, take her into the kitchen while she worked, keeping her close, the stove's heat encircling her, pressing against her, taking her breath almost with its expansion through the room. Then her father might come in later, pick her up or take her by the hand, and quickly they would go out of the house and up to the store or maybe to the depot to watch the afternoon train arrive and depart northward. He would sit with her, hold her hand, smoke his cigar, the smell and smoke surrounding them in a masculine world of men loading and unloading, of coal and iron rails and more smoke and dreams of departure, the two of them headed away.

And then they did head away, but not before more silences and anger that she felt kept her parents from listening to each other, each made deaf in his or her own way. But the day arrived when, her suitcases packed, she and her father boarded the train for Talladega. After three days, he left her there, settled, as best she could be at the age of twelve, in her dorm room and in a school for the deaf and blind.

She'd loved it there, had learned the alphabet on her fingers and how to sign, and how to read lips. She'd continued, finally, with her regular schooling too, and taken art, and began to paint with oils. The other children there were like her, lived in her world of silence that was no longer quiet but filled with the voices of fingers and hands flying—thin fingers, long fingers, the beautiful hands of boys. It was wonderful to be able to give shape to words. She knew that her speaking voice was something she'd had less and less control over, and so seldom used it. Now words came through her fingers, the muscles there growing stronger and more sure, giving her a voice again, a voice that wanted to shout, or even sing.

Her mother wouldn't visit, but wrote desperate letters about home, about missing her and wanting her there, those cursive words on the page like pieces of string tying and knotting her emotions. During her trips home she taught her father to speak to her, but for the longest time her mother could not, or would not, learn. "You can read lips," she would say. "That's enough for me."

"What about me?" she'd sign, and, of course, no answer came, and wouldn't have even if she'd forced herself to ask it aloud, from out of her throat and off her tongue.

Her mother wouldn't want her to go places with her father, would become silent and withdrawn when they returned. She didn't want Janey going to the store by herself, even for a quick errand. One day her mother found her playing in the woods behind their house, and when she wouldn't follow her mother home, her mother grabbed her by the arm and yanked her through the trees. She finally yanked back and shouted at her, not in words but in her old voice that expressed all she felt in one great vibration. Her mother spoke with a hand then. She slapped her hard across her face.

When she left for school a week later, her mother wouldn't go with them to the depot but held her at the door. She felt her mother shaking and knew her mother loved her, but love was sometimes like silence, beautiful but hard to bear. At the train station her father told her, "She can't help herself. I don't know why. I never have."

Late that morning, from her place on the porch, she watched Mr. Clark work around the buildings in town. He moved his camera from one position to another, then disappeared beneath the black cloth before moving again. At intervals he'd go inside the store or speak to people passing. She'd thought he would come home for lunch, but he must have eaten at the store, perhaps asking questions for his notes. Maybe he wouldn't need her after all.

That afternoon she saw him load his car and expected him to soon pull into their drive, but watched with surprise, and disappointment, as he drove directly past, picking up speed and raising dust behind him. She spotted Uncle Silas, the old black man who'd worked for her father's side of the family, in the back seat and knew then where they were headed, several miles away to the old home of her father's people, her cousins, some of them several times removed. The house stood three stories with a cupola and had white columns and a grand porch, with slave quarters behind. He'd want pictures of all that, of course. Her mother wouldn't have wanted her to go up there with them. There was a distance between her mother and her father's people. It had always been there.

Her mother was bathing when he finally drove in. She'd been put out that he hadn't come at the time she'd told him supper would be ready. "Tardiness is rude," she had said.

Janey waited, gave him time to put his things away, then went and tapped on his door, and as her knuckles hit against the wood, she felt that the door was closed on some secret, something private and obscure that she shouldn't approach.

The door opened suddenly, and he stood there with a small towel in one hand. She'd filled the washbasin on his dresser with fresh water earlier. He looked tired, but not angry or irritated.

"Supper's ready for you," she signed.

He nodded and followed her.

Once they reached the kitchen she fixed his plate and set it before him. He looked at her and motioned to the chair across the table. She hadn't known if she should sit with him or not and felt relief at his invitation.

He only ate at first and didn't try to speak, his hands being occupied. She sat and waited, watched him bent over his plate. Each movement he made was so deliberate and sure. His masculine demeanor seemed to make the whole house feel different, as if the house had a slightly altered design. He stopped eating finally and put his knife and fork down.

"People at the store told me what I needed for my notes. Others too. Everyone was curious and wanted to talk. It's like that everywhere."

She was certain that he saw her disappointment, no matter how hard she tried to hide it. He apologized then for being late, and it was as though he felt a need to say something considerate to assuage her feelings. He went on and told her, too, after taking a few bites, about driving out to the antebellum home of her father's side of the family, being polite enough not to mention the disrepair it was in. "Someone in town told me about the house," he was saying, and she saw that he'd begun to speak aloud as he signed —his lips were forming words—and she felt confused, couldn't understand why he would do this. She couldn't read his lips and watch him sign at the same time. He must have known that. He paused and studied her, watched her expression more closely. "I could have asked you to ride out there with me, couldn't I? You might have wanted to go. You might have enjoyed that. Some time away from here." He motioned around the room.

She looked toward the kitchen door, not aware at first why she turned that way. Perhaps she'd simply turned away from him out of embarrassment, or perhaps she understood, on some unconscious level, what she hadn't a moment before. Her mother was standing there. She'd been listening to him. He had wanted her to hear.

When she turned back to him she read his lips. "Why don't you go with me tomorrow?"

She felt the quick vibration of her mother's approach but wouldn't turn to face her. "Yes, ma'am," he was saying, looking past Janey. "I know, but she could help me. Be a guide. I could even pay her a little. Why don't we ask her?"

Janey saw his hard gaze still focused on her mother, maybe even

gathered strength from it, and she stood then, turned to her
mother, and saw her mother's anger and fear, the way she'd always
seen them after her father had explained her mother as best he
could. She drew in her breath and forced the two breath-filled
words out in a hoarse whisper that might have sounded, for all she
knew, like a sick child or someone dying. "I'll go," she said.

Her mother stared at her in surprise, and Janey wasn't sure if her
mother was more shocked that she had used what was left of her
voice, or at what she'd said. Mr. Clark showed no reaction at all but
took another bite of food and drank from his glass.

"You can't. You just can't," her mother said. "I need you to help
me with some things around the house tomorrow."

"No," she signed, then shook her head. "You don't."

"You know good and well I do. There's cleaning to be done."

"It will wait," she said and walked out before her mother could.

She went to her room and imagined the two of them at the table
still, imagined what they might be saying, and her father came to
mind suddenly. It was as if Mr. Clark had become, for the moment,
the man her father had been, the two of them in there now acting
out the old ritual of her parents, except this time she had spoken,
and they both had heard her wishes.

She could still hear her father's voice, the memory of it clear in a
way that her mother's wasn't. It had been deep, but not extraordinarily so, and gentle, though when he scolded her there was a
sharpness to it that crushed her and made her want forgiveness,
which always came quickly, and he would hold her and wipe her
tears and smile.

It was the telegram that took him away from her, the one her
mother sent and that she received at school. "Come home," it said.
"Your father has died of fever." She was fifteen, and even then, after the first shock, she realized that the demand to *come home* had
come first, as if coming home were more important than the death
of her father. So she went, and saw her father buried, suffered the
quiet of the funeral that she could not hear but only feel. A few
days later she walked to the grave alone and left her handprints in
the mound of dirt over his casket and body.

She stayed then, not quite strong enough without him to get
back on the train, though she planned to and spoke of it as if she
would, her mother ignoring her.

Two months later the school shipped her belongings home. The first she knew of it was when they were delivered from the depot in the back of a wagon. She saw the boxes and felt somehow that her life had been returned to her mother. Each box bore her mother's name.

Janey didn't see her the next morning, and she didn't look in her room to check on her, which is what she knew her mother wanted. Instead she bathed and dressed early, then fixed breakfast and packed a lunch for herself and Mr. Clark, putting everything away afterward, leaving no plate of food covered with a cloth.

She planned to take him up the road to Oakhill, show him the old house at the top of the hill, and introduce him to the people there. If she'd given him directions he could have found it on his own, but that didn't matter. He'd asked her to go with him, and he'd known what he'd really been asking. She'd entered into the conspiracy with him and needed to see it through. Not to would have been a kind of failure.

After he loaded the car she climbed into the passenger seat. When he stopped and filled up with gas at the store she saw people looking at her in the car and enjoyed their curiosity. He drove too fast, and she felt an exhilaration at their increasing speed and at the plume of dust they raised that blocked her view of everything behind them. Neither tried to speak, and she had the feeling that even if his hands hadn't been busy, he would have remained quiet. The look on his face in profile was hard set, concentrated on something beyond driving it seemed.

The road rose toward Oakhill and at the top before they turned into the long drive that led to the house she saw the open pastures and fields spread out before her like a patchwork quilt and suddenly felt like a child wanting to run across them, as if they lay there waiting for her. A silly notion, but it made her smile.

The house stood beyond the oak grove and came into full view after they rounded a final curve. It was two-story with small white columns. No mansion, but clearly built by a landowning family.

They got out of the car and walked up the steps to the porch. Janey knocked on the screen door and waited for Mrs. Spence to come, but instead an older black woman Janey knew as Aunt Minnie appeared in the hall and opened the door. She nodded at Janey and said, "How you, Miss Janey?" Then looked at the strange man beside her. "I bet you that picture man. I done heard about you."

Mr. Clark spoke, but Janey didn't catch any of his words.

"The mister and missus, they done gone into town, up to Valhia. Is you come to take pictures?"

Janey watched him speak this time. He asked if he could at least take pictures of the outside of the house since the owners weren't home.

She nodded. "They won't mind that, I don't reckon. What about my house, out back? You gon' take a picture of it? You can go inside. It's mine. Least I calls it mine." She smiled. "I'd like a picture took of it."

"I was going to ask you if I could," he said. "Inside too."

Janey wondered if he was speaking the truth or humoring her.

"Come on around," the woman said. "You can do the big house later."

They followed. Mr. Clark carried only a small camera around his neck. The large camera with the tripod and black cloth he left in the car for now.

Several outbuildings stood directly behind the house. One of them, Janey imagined, had been a kitchen back when they were built separately so heat wouldn't overtake the house in summer and, in case of fire, wouldn't burn down the entire home. Farther on stood a small, unpainted shack, one window to the right of the door. It had already occurred to her that she had never been in a black person's house, or in the house of someone so poor. She knew her mother hadn't either, just as her mother had never let those lost men traveling through come to the back door and eat a meal. Janey realized that if her mother had been with them, she would never set foot inside where they were headed, would be appalled at the idea, and wouldn't let Janey inside, not without protest and argument.

"My grandmother was born a slave in this house," the woman said now. "We always worked for the Spences. Far back as I know of."

Mr. Clark stopped and took several pictures of the front of the house. "You don't mind if we go on in?" he said when he finished.

"I keeps my house clean always. Not ashamed of anything I got either."

They walked onto the small porch and boards gave under their feet. Aunt Minnie went in first, then Mr. Clark. Janey held back a moment, imagined again what her mother would say if she knew, then stepped through the doorway into the cramped slave house and felt, in some place within herself, as if she'd walked into one of those open fields she had seen from the car, was straying like some child running just ahead of her mother.

The house was clean, neat, the bed made with a colorful quilt across it. Newspaper pages that had not yet yellowed covered the walls, cut and pasted as carefully as any new store-bought wallpaper. A calendar from Anderson's store with May twenty-third circled hung by the door. There was a back window, and she noticed how clean the panes were, how the light broke through them and opened the room, made it somehow larger, as if it brought the whole of outdoors inside. The small black stove was wiped down, and the few pots and pans hung in order on the wall behind it. Aunt Minnie had been right. There was nothing here to be ashamed of, nothing to look down upon. Janey wished this were a place she could stay and felt a sense of envy. Then she decided no — she felt a kind of admiration for Minnie.

Mr. Clark took pictures, including one of Minnie in a chair beside the bed. She wasn't smiling but seemed at ease with herself and everything around her.

Once they were back outside, Mr. Clark got his large camera and set it up for pictures of the main house. He moved every few minutes, capturing the house at different angles. When he finished he told Minnie that he'd come again and see about taking some pictures inside, if the people didn't mind.

"Come on. They be glad to see you," she said. Then she asked if she might have a copy of the picture he'd taken of her.

"I'll see to it," he said. "It'll be a while, but I'll send it."

In the car Janey asked if he'd ever taken pictures inside a house like Minnie's.

"No," he said, and didn't elaborate. "I need those people home when I go back," he added after a moment.

His whole demeanor had changed, and Janey felt that she'd been chastised, that it was somehow her fault that the Spences hadn't been home.

A question came to her, one that she had to ask, though she

feared the answer. "Do people often ask for copies of the photographs you take?"

"All the time," he signed, then put the car into gear.

"Do you send them?"

He looked away, kept his eyes on the narrow drive, and both hands on the wheel.

They drove to several churches spread around the countryside, their conversation minimal. He took pictures both inside and out, working quickly and methodically, clearly knowing exactly what he wanted as soon as he saw each structure. They ate a late lunch that she'd packed at a table on the grounds of a small A.M.E. church, and she didn't try to speak. He seemed even further removed, already traveling on his own. She wondered where he was in his mind, wondered if she had done something to make him more distant.

Late that afternoon he told her he wanted to head back, but had one more stop in mind, the Episcopal church near her house. When they parked in front of it she began to tell him how the church had been brought across the river and why. "Later," he signed. "Tell me later." Then he got out of the car.

She stood well away from him while he worked, wandered into the graveyard behind the church, and finally to her father's grave. The grass grew thick and neat over it, but she recalled the mound of bare dirt, the way it had felt against her hands when she placed them there, the way their prints looked so perfectly made, but so empty.

He appeared then, setting up his camera, and waited for her to move, without asking, so he could take a picture of the back of the church with the gravestones in the foreground.

She obliged him, went around the building and sat on the steps at the double side doors. In a little while he walked around from the front and approached her, without his camera. He was clearly ready to go. She didn't move but looked up at him, then began to speak. He didn't turn away now but watched, though impatiently, it seemed. She didn't care.

"The last sound I ever heard came from here, through these open doors. Choir voices, all joined together. They were beautiful. A final gift to me."

She placed her hands in her lap and remained still, not really looking to see if he reacted or not to what she'd said. He turned slowly and walked away, but she didn't follow. She could easily walk home by herself, decided she'd like to do just that, but not quite yet. She wanted to be alone.

He came back though, carrying the small camera around his neck. She looked up at him but kept still. He raised the camera slowly, peered through it, then lowered it after a moment and stepped toward her. He reached out with his right hand and touched her just under her chin. The warmth of his fingers made a dampness on her skin. He gently turned her face at a more downward angle, then backed away and adjusted the camera. She watched the shutter close and open and imagined the sound it made, imagined what part of her the camera might capture.

Her mother had been up while they were gone. Janey saw a book left open on the sofa, and there was a single dish left in the kitchen sink. She wondered if her mother had heard them pull into the drive and gone quickly to her room, not expecting them back quite so early. She was probably in bed, pretending to be asleep. Of course it was possible that she was sick. She did tire more easily these last few years. Still Janey wouldn't go to her, and if she didn't, she knew that her mother would finally show herself.

She did, before good dark came. Janey was sitting in a chair on the porch, by herself, considering what she might do about supper. Her mother walked out of her bedroom door, the one that opened directly onto the porch and that she seldom used. She sat down in the chair next to Janey.

"Have you not been feeling well today?" Janey knew what the answer would be.

Her mother shook her head, then looked away for a moment.

"Do you feel like you can eat something?"

"Whatever you can fix," she said, then turned away again. It was something she did often, the turning away, a way of ignoring Janey, of not listening, because it took sight for her to be listened to. Sometimes it amused Janey, her mother's turning, but not now. She had been ignored enough today. She thought about telling her mother where they'd gone, about going inside Aunt Minnie's house and taking pictures—just to see her reaction, for spite, she guessed. But she stayed quiet. Upsetting her mother would have been too easy, and maybe pointless.

She watched the evening come on, remembered the glissando of locusts at this time of year from when she was a little girl, and wondered if they were out there now, appearing from their years-long silence and making their one sound.

Her mother looked toward the front door and Janey saw Mr. Clark had walked out of his room. He'd changed into a fresh shirt and was rolling the sleeves up. He greeted her mother, then stood before them as if he had something important to say. This time Janey turned, perhaps afraid of what he might announce. He wouldn't be staying with them for months, or even weeks. How many more days would it be?

When she looked back at them she saw the words *colored churches* form on Mr. Clark's lips. Her mother's eyes widened. "You went inside them?"

"A few," he said, studying her, measuring her reaction. He looked at Janey then, as though he were waiting on her to speak, and when she didn't he continued, his eyes lingering on her, perhaps taking some measure of her this time. "We went in one of the shacks up at Oakhill. Aunt Minnie's house. An old slave quarters."

Her mother looked down at her feet, closed her eyes, and slowly shook her head, as if she'd received news that someone was ill. "You shouldn't be going into colored people's houses, Janey," she said. "At least the Spences weren't home to see you."

Mr. Clark seemed to be waiting on Janey again, and something inside her didn't want to disappoint him.

"Why not?" she said. "Why not go into a colored person's house?"

"You know why. Because it doesn't look good." She stood, seemed to have regained her strength, and walked back into her bedroom, clearly unwilling to respond to any more such absurd-sounding questions.

Mr. Clark nodded at Janey, which she understood as a kind of approval, but something about it bothered her, made her feel presided over, and the way he stood there, above her, made her uncomfortable, as she had felt with him early on. Before she realized what he was doing, he walked to the end of the porch, down the steps, and kept going, past his parked car—headed to the store, she imagined. She realized she would be eating alone that night.

*

Her mother remained secluded in the morning, which Janey had expected. What she hadn't been sure of was whether or not Mr. Clark wanted her to go along with him again, but at breakfast he made clear that he did. She told him about some of the larger houses down toward the Tennahpush River that he might want to look at. He seemed more open to listening to her today, his mood changed from the day before.

She made a lunch for them while he loaded his car. When she walked out the front door and pulled it to behind her, she suddenly expected to see her mother's door open, and it did. Her mother stood there in her bedclothes and without a robe, motioning to Janey, the door angled between herself and Mr. Clark at his car.

"What, Mother?" she signed.

"I don't feel well."

"I know that."

"I mean I'm worse today."

Janey took a few steps toward her and then looked past the oddly made columns surrounding the porch. Mr. Clark stood against the front of his car, his arms folded, watching her, waiting.

"My chest hurts," her mother said, "and my breath doesn't come easy. You know I don't have a normal heartbeat."

Janey knew about the irregular heart, and had heard all these complaints before, too many times to take them seriously.

"Come here," her mother said, and held out a piece of paper. "Please, I've got to get back in bed."

Janey walked to her and took the paper. It was a note to Dr. Hannah asking him to come see her.

"There's nothing wrong with you," she said. "We both know that."

"You can't go with that man today. I need you here," she said aloud. "I need you to bring the doctor here." For once she wasn't speaking slowly.

Janey looked and saw Mr. Clark at the bottom of the steps now, waiting, impatient, wanting what he wanted from her. Her mother pulled the door closer to her, but didn't retreat back into the room, though she seemed to sense Mr. Clark's nearness.

She wanted to retreat, to surrender into the most silent of places within herself, where her own thoughts couldn't find voice.

"All right," she said finally. "I'll stay and get him just to prove to you there's nothing wrong, and that's the only reason. I'll go with him tomorrow."

Her mother nodded, clearly relieved, and slowly shut the door.

Janey walked down to Mr. Clark. He hadn't moved. His expression said nothing.

"I can't go today," she signed. "I've got to get the doctor. Tomorrow I'll go."

"There's nothing wrong with her." He signed the words.

"I know."

"Then get in the car. Now."

"I can't."

He focused his eyes on her the way he might when he looked through a camera, capturing her, exposing her weakness for her to see. His face showed neither pity nor disgust. Whatever was there she couldn't read the way she could spoken words, and he didn't give her any further opportunity. He turned, climbed inside his car, and drove away, leaving her standing alone in the middle of the drive. She pulled her mother's note from her pocket, held it in her hand, and felt for a moment as if it were meant for her, like one of her mother's letters that came for her when she'd been at school.

Dr. Hannah walked out of her mother's room, his black bag in his hand. He looked tired already, even at midmorning. He began to speak carefully, and quietly, she knew, so that her mother couldn't overhear. "There's nothing wrong, other than maybe nerves."

"Her heart?" Janey wrote on a small notepad.

"She's had an arrhythmia since I first came here and saw her as a patient, but there's been no deterioration. I'm certain of that. My only mistake was telling her about it."

"So she's fine?"

He nodded. "I gave her a shot, a mild sedative, to calm her nerves. That's all."

"Thank you," she wrote.

He smiled slightly and touched her shoulder for a moment, the way her father might have. She imagined that going into people's homes and seeing to the ill had taught him a lot about what people needed, both the sick and the well.

She checked on her mother after lunch and found her sitting up in bed.

"I'm feeling better now. I knew seeing Dr. Hannah would help."

Janey didn't respond, didn't move past the door's threshold.

"I'm going to bathe and dress," her mother said. "Could you fix me something to eat? I'll take it in my room so I won't tire myself out."

She slowly signed yes, glad for the moment that she no longer used speech, because she knew how angry her tone would have sounded. But what would that have mattered? Except for the fact that she was most angry at herself. For staying. She should have been in the car with Mr. Clark. He wouldn't be here much longer, and after he was gone nothing would be changed. Perhaps that was what made her most angry. His presence had shown her something that she'd kept her eyes closed to—a willful blindness on her part, another killing of the senses.

She finally carried a tray to her mother and saw that she'd dressed and put on makeup.

"This is so nice. Thank you," her mother said slowly.

Janey only nodded.

She wasn't aware that Mr. Clark had returned until she looked out a front window and happened to see his camera set up in the yard. She didn't see him, though, and then there he was, back at the camera, about to pull the dark cloth over his head. She tried to picture what he saw—the rusted roof, the unpainted boards, the strange columns with branches cut short, all of it upside down, and she felt as though everything inside herself had fallen out of place, all of it turned by his hand.

He moved the camera from one place to another, and she watched from various windows, careful to stand far enough away so that her image wasn't captured behind a pane.

When she saw him photographing the back of the house she walked onto the porch and waited for him to come back around front. She wondered if he would take pictures inside too. Sometimes he did, sometimes not.

It surprised her when she saw him at his car in the drive, bent over beside it, but there he was, loading his equipment again. He was going back out. She could go with him now that she had seen to her mother. Perhaps that was why he'd come, not just to take the pictures but to give her another opportunity. She stood when he finished loading, ready to leave without a word to her mother, and he turned and saw her. She expected him to motion to her, or to speak with his hands, but after the briefest glance her way, he opened the driver's side door and climbed in, his face shadowed by the brim of his hat, and then all of him disappeared behind the glare of the sun on the windshield.

His coming in the middle of the afternoon must have been only one more stop for him, one more house to photograph and move away from. But he had to have come when he did for a reason. It would have made so much more sense for him to take pictures of her house as his last stop of the day. Maybe he had been taunting her, or speaking his anger at her as loudly as he knew how—treating her as no more important than a stranger at yet another stop.

He backed all the way to the road, and though there were no cars coming from either direction, he sat idling. Moments passed. She was puzzled, and couldn't see if he was looking her way or not. She remained still, waiting, for what she didn't know. Maybe he was waiting too, giving her one more chance to come down the steps on her own. Then he was gone.

It was well past dark, late, in fact, after eleven o'clock, when he returned. She felt his steps through the house, felt his door closing. She looked out her front window to see if he would make the trips to unload his car, which was something he never failed to do, but he didn't come back out. Maybe he'd driven all the way to town, to Demarville, for a meal at the hotel, and then found a drink somewhere. Or maybe he'd found a drink here and had never gone into town at all or bothered with supper.

She didn't sleep. At eleven thirty she sat up in bed and pulled on her robe. She stood then, telling herself she was going into the kitchen, but when she found it empty, as she knew she would, she walked slowly and softly to the front door, opened it, and stepped into the house's entryway. The distance he had shown her the last two days drew her to his door, and emboldened now in the way she should have been earlier in the day, she knocked twice.

He opened the door after a moment. A lamp was burning, and she saw he was still dressed in shirt and pants. She also smelled liquor, strongly, but he appeared in control of himself, though he looked disheveled, his shirttail out, his sleeves rolled up loosely, not into his usual neat cuffs, though revealing again his strong forearms. He motioned for her to sit in the one chair, and he sat on a chest at the foot of the bed. He didn't seem surprised to see her, which she found unsettling.

She started to tell him that she'd wanted to leave with him after he'd taken pictures of her house, but she decided he already knew that. There was no need to say it.

"If you'd just waited another minute," she signed, knowing he'd understand.

Except for a barely perceptible nod, if only to let her know that he was reading her, he didn't respond.

His silence was as frustrating as before. She needed him to talk. He already knew what she had to say. Did he have anything at all to say to her?

He looked at her through squinted, shadowed eyes. "I knew about you before I came," he signed.

"How?" she said. "What did you know?"

"That a deaf woman and her mother lived here, that they sometimes rented a room. In one town, I ask about the next, or what might be the next. So I heard that, and came."

"Why?" she asked, uncertain if he would say more.

He remained still at first, his hands at rest. Then he looked at her, studied her. "I was told there were places here I ought to take pictures of. This place too, the columns with the limbs on them. I wanted to see that, to make a record of it."

She waited again, for what he hadn't said yet. She saw that she would have to push him. "The deaf woman you heard about—I'm part of why you came."

He nodded, but that was all.

"Why?"

"My mother," he said, as though she could follow.

The lamp grew dimmer and the shift in light seemed to carry him further away from her.

"My mother lost her hearing when I was very young. She was still young too, but I didn't know how young, not then. I learned to sign as she learned." He paused, then his hands seemed to find the words in the air. "My father didn't."

"What?"

"Didn't learn. Didn't treat her well. He never had."

She became bold again, understanding through some instinct she didn't know she had, then spelling it out. "He hit her."

He nodded again, slowly, even further away from her now, carried away by memory, and perhaps more alcohol than she'd realized.

"She suffered. It was terrible. There were awful beatings, and more and more of them."

She saw the anger in him still, in his face and clenched fists. It had been there all along, when he'd first walked to the porch with her mother, but it had taken this long to recognize it, and words from him to understand it.

"What happened?" She asked the question with a building fear, not of him but of what the answer might be.

"She took me. We left in the night."

She sighed with relief, but another question came to her. "She's dead now?" She felt she knew the answer.

"Yes." His hands stopped a moment, hung in the air. "It didn't take him long. He found her."

She took the words from his hands, felt the weight of them within her. "And you?" she managed to ask.

He shrugged his shoulders. He was through—or almost.

"Your wife?" she said then, trying to imagine the life he might have made for himself, already fearing the answer.

"There's no wife. There never has been."

She simply nodded.

"My mother tried. She did what she could, for me and for herself. I owe her a debt for that, and have to find someone to pay."

Even in the dim room she saw the brightness in his eyes, their focus directly on her, and she became afraid, of him this time, and of what she caught glimpses of behind the reflection of light in his eyes. She felt she saw ghosts within him, his mother's and his own ghost, small and lost.

She awoke knowing that he was gone. When she rose and checked his room, she found the door open, the bed made, and none of his belongings. He'd left the window open too for some reason. She felt the cross-breeze.

Within an hour she'd dressed and tried to occupy herself with cleaning, but her work was careless, and she knew it. She finally put the dusting cloth away and gave in to a sense of mourning for something lost.

Her mother hadn't gotten up by noon. Perhaps this was her way of making Janey check on her. It wouldn't work, not this time. But after an hour passed, she entered the room and saw her mother was awake but still in bed and wouldn't rise from her pillow. Janey walked closer and started to sign, but she saw the stare then and knew, saw the lack of any movement, not even the gentle lifting and falling of the sheet across her body.

She felt a greater loss to mourn now, and it fell upon her heavily, in a way she might not have expected. She sat at the foot of the bed, looked again at her mother's stare, and wondered if she had known death was coming. Had it come from inside her, out of the irregular beat of her heart, or had she seen it walk into the room and bend over her, its hands reaching for the pillow on which she now lay? She felt she knew the answer, but knew she would not speak it, would say only that her mother had been up after Mr. Clark left, if anyone wanted to ask. If no one did, her silence would speak for her, as it always had.

CHARLES BAXTER

The Cousins

FROM *Tin House*

MY COUSIN BRANTFORD was named for our grandfather, who
had made a fortune from a device used in aircraft navigation. I
suppose it saved lives. A bad-tempered man with a scar above his
cheekbone, my grandfather believed that the rich were rewarded
for their merits and the poor deserved what they got. He did not
care for his own grandchildren and referred to my cousin as "the
little prince." In all fairness, he didn't like me either.

Brantford had roared through his college fund so rapidly that by
the age of twenty-three he was down to pocket change. One bright
spring day when I was visiting New York City and had called him
up, he insisted on taking me to lunch at a midtown restaurant
where the cost of the entrees was so high that a respectful noonday
hush hung over its skeletal postmodern interior. Muttering oli-
garchs with monogrammed shirt cuffs gazed at entering patrons
with a languid alertness. The maître d' wore one of those dark blue
restaurant suits, and the wine list had been printed on velvety pages
set in a stainless-steel three-ring binder.

By the time my cousin arrived, I had read the menu four times.
He was late. You had to know Brantford to get used to him. A friend
of mine said that my cousin looked like the mayor of a ruined city.
Appearances mattered a great deal to Brantford, but his own were
on a gradual slide. His face had a permanent alcoholic flush. His
brownish-blond hair was parted on the right side and was too long
by a few millimeters, trailing over his collar. Although he dressed
well in flannel trousers and cordovan shoes, you could see the telltale food stains on his shirt, and the expression underneath his

blond mustache had something subtly wrong with it—he smiled with a strangely discouraged and stale affability.

"Bunny," he said to me, sitting down with an audible expunging of air. He still used my childhood name. No one else did. He didn't give me a hug because we don't do that. "I see you've gotten started. You're having a martini?"

I nodded. "Morning tune-up," I said.

"Brave choice," Brantford grinned, simultaneously waving down the server. "Waitress," he said, pointing at my drink, "I'll have one of those. Very dry, please, no olive." The server nodded before giving Brantford a thin professional smile and gliding over to the bar.

We had a kind of solidarity, Brantford and I. I had two decades on him, but we were oddly similar, more like brothers than cousins. I had always seen in him some better qualities than those I actually possessed. For example, he was one of those people who always make you happier the moment you see them.

Before his drink arrived, we caught ourselves up. Brantford's mother, Aunt Margaret, had by that time been married to several different husbands, including a three-star army general, and she currently resided in a small apartment cluttered with knickknacks near the corner of Ninety-second and Broadway.

Having spent herself in a wild youth and at all times been given to manias, Brantford's mother had started taking a new medication called ElysiumMax, which seemed to be keeping her on a steady course where life was concerned. Brantford instructed me to please phone her while I was in town, and I said I would. As for Brantford's two half-sisters, they were doing fine.

With this information out of the way, I asked Brantford how he was.

"I don't know. It's strange. Sometimes at night I have the feeling that I've murdered somebody." He stopped and glanced down at the tableware. "Someone's dead. Only I don't know who or what, or when I did it. I must've killed somebody. I'm sure of it. Thank you," he said with his first real smile of the day, as the server placed a martini in front of him.

"Well, that's just crazy," I said. "You haven't killed anyone."

"Doesn't matter if I have or haven't," he said, "if it feels that way. Maybe I should take a vacation."

"Brantford," I said. "You can't take a vacation. You don't work." I waited for a moment. "Do you?"

"Well," he said, "I'd like to. Besides, I work, in my way," he claimed, taking a sip of the martini. "And don't forget that I can be anything I want to be." This sentence was enunciated carefully and with precise despair, as if it had served as one of those lifelong mottoes that he no longer believed in.

What year was this? 1994? When someone begins to carry on as my cousin did, I'm never sure what to say. Tact is required. As a teenager, Brantford had told me that he aspired to be a concert pianist, and I was the one who had to remind him that he wasn't a musician and didn't play the piano. But Brantford had seen a fiery angel somewhere in the sky and thought it might descend on him. I hate those angels. I haven't always behaved well when people open their hearts to me.

"Well, what about the animals?" I asked. Brantford was always caring for damaged animals and had done so from the time he was a boy. He found them in streets and alleys and nursed them back to health and then let them go. But they tended to fall in with him and to get crushes on him. In whatever apartment or house he lived in, you would find recovering cats, mutts, and sparrows barking and chirping and mewling in response to him.

"No, not that," he said. "I would never make a living off those critters," he said. "That's a sideline. I love them too much."

"Veterinary school?" I asked.

"No, I couldn't. Absolutely not. I don't want to practice that kind of medicine with them," he said, as if he were speaking of family members. "If I made money off those little guys, I'd lose the gift. Besides, I don't have the discipline to get through another school. Willpower is not my strong suit. The world runs on willpower," he said, as if perplexed. He put his head back into his hands. "Willpower! Anyhow, would you please explain to me why it feels as if I've committed a murder?"

When I had first come to New York in the 1970s as an aspiring actor, I rode the subways everywhere, particularly the number 6, which in those days was still the Lexington IRT line. Sitting on that train one afternoon, squeezed between my fellow passengers as I helped one of them, a schoolboy, with a nosebleed, I felt pleased with myself. I had assimilated. Having come to New York from the Midwest, I was anticipating my big break and meanwhile waited tables at a little bistro near Astor Place. Mine was a familiar story, one of those drabby little tales of ideals and artistic high-mindedness that wouldn't bear repeating if it weren't for the woman with whom I was then involved.

She had a quietly insubstantial quality. When you looked away from her, you couldn't be sure that she'd still be there when you looked back again. She knew how to vanish quickly from scenes she didn't like. Her ability to dematerialize was purposeful and was complicated by her appearance: day and night, she wore dark glasses. She had a sensitivity to light, a photophobia, which she had acquired as a result of a corneal infection. In those days, her casual friends thought that the dark glasses constituted a praiseworthy affectation. "She looks very cool," they would say.

Even her name—Giulietta, spelled in the Italian manner— seemed like an affectation. But Giulietta it was, the name with which, as a Catholic, she had been baptized. We'd met at the bistro where I carried menus and trays laden with food back and forth. Dining alone, cornered under a light fixture, she was reading a book by Bruno Bettelheim, and I deliberately served her a risotto entree that she hadn't ordered. I wanted to provoke her to conversation, even if it was hostile. I couldn't see her eyes behind those dark glasses, but I wanted to. Self-possession in any form attracts me, especially at night, in cities. Anyway, my studied incompetence as a waiter amused her. Eventually she gave me her phone number.

She worked in Brooklyn at a special school for mildly autistic and emotionally impaired little kids. The first time we slept together we had to move the teddy bears and the copies of *The New Yorker* off her bed. Sophistication and a certain childlike guilelessness lived side by side in her behavior. On Sunday morning she watched cartoons and *Meet the Press,* and in the afternoon she listened to the Bartók quartets while smoking marijuana, which she claimed was good for her eyesight. In her bathtub was a rubber duck, and in the living room a copy of *Anna Karenina,* which she had read three times.

We were inventive and energetic in our lovemaking, Giulietta and I, but her eyes stayed hidden no matter how dark it was. From her, I knew nothing of the look of recognition a woman can give to a man. All the same, I was beginning to love her. She comforted me and sustained me by attaching me to ordinary things: reading the Sunday paper in bed, making bad jokes—the rewards of plain everyday life.

One night I took her uptown for a party, near Columbia, at the apartment of another actor—Freddy Avery, who also happened to be a poet. Like many actors, Freddy enjoyed performing and was good at mimicry, and his parties tended to be raucous. You could easily commit an error in tone at those parties. You'd expose yourself as a hayseed if you were too sincere about anything. There was an Iron Law of Irony at Freddy's parties, so I was worried that if Giulietta and I arrived too early, we'd be mocked. No one was ever prompt at Freddy's parties (they always began at their midpoint, if I could put it that way), so we ducked into a bar to waste a bit of time before going up.

Under a leaded-glass, greenish lamp hanging down over our booth, Giulietta took my hand. "We don't have to go to this . . . thing," she said. "We could just escape to a movie and then head home."

"No," I said. "We have to do this. Anyway, all the movies have started."

"What's the big deal with this party, Benjamin?" she asked me. I couldn't see her eyes behind her dark glasses, but I knew they were trained on me. She wore a dark blue blouse, and her hair had been pinned back with a rainbow-colored barrette. The fingers of her hands, now on the table, had a long, aristocratic delicacy, but she bit her nails; the tips of her fingers had a raggedy appearance.

"Oh, interesting people will be there," I said. "Other actors. And literary types, you know, and dancers. They'll make you laugh."

"No," she said. "They'll make *you* laugh." She took a sip of her beer. She lit up a cigarette and blew the smoke toward the ceiling. "Dancers can't converse anyway. They're all autoerotic. If we go to this, I'm only doing it because of you. I want you to know that."

"Thank you," I said. "Listen, could you do me a favor?"

"Anything," she nodded.

"Well, it's one of those parties where the guests . . ."

"What?"

"It's like this. Those people are clever. You know, it's one of those uptown crowds. So what I'm asking is . . . do you think you could be clever tonight, please? As a favor to me? I know you can be like that. You can be funny; I know you, Giulietta. I've seen you sparkle. So could you be amusing? That's really all I ask."

This was years ago. Men were still asking women—or telling them—how to behave in public. I flinch, now, thinking about that request, but it didn't seem like much of anything to me back then. Giulietta leaned back and took her hand away from mine. Then she cleared her throat.

"You are so funny." She wasn't smiling. She seemed to be evaluating me. "Yes," she said. "Yes, all right." She dug her right index fingernail into the wood of the table, as if making a calculation. "I can be clever if you want me to be."

After buzzing us up, Freddy Avery met us at the door of his apartment with an expression of jovial melancholy. "Hey hey hey," he said, ushering us in. "Ah. And this is Giulietta," he continued, staring at her dark glasses and her rainbow barrette. "Howdy do. You look like that character in the movie where the flowers started singing. Wasn't that sort of freaky and great?" He didn't wait for our answer. "It was a special effect. Flowers don't actually know how to sing. So it was sentimental. Well," he said, "now that you're both here, you brave kids should get something to drink. Help yourselves. Welcome, like I said." Even Freddy's bad grammar was between quotation marks.

Giulietta drifted away from me, and I found myself near the refrigerator listening to a tall, strikingly attractive brunette. She didn't introduce herself. With a vaguely French accent, she launched into a little speech. "I have something you must explain," she said. "I can't make good sense of who I am now. And so, what am I? First I am a candidate for one me, and then I am another. I am blown about. Just a little leaf—that is my self. What do you think I will be?" She didn't wait for me to answer. "I ask, 'Who am I, Renée?' I cannot sleep, wondering. Is life like this, in America? Full of such puzzles? Do you believe it is like this?"

I nodded. I said, "That's a very good accent you have there." She began to forage around in her purse as if she hadn't heard me. I hurried toward the living room and found myself in a corner next to another guest, the famous Pulitzer Prize–winning poet Burroughs Hammond, who was sitting in the only available chair. Freddy had befriended him, I had heard, at a literary gathering, and had taught the poet how to modulate his voice during readings. At the present moment, Burroughs Hammond was gripping a bottle of ginger ale and smoking an unfiltered mentholated cigarette. No one seemed to be engaging him in conversation. Apparently, he had intimidated the other guests, all of whom had wandered away from his corner.

I knew who he was. Everyone did. He was built like a linebacker —he had played high school football in Ohio—but he had a perpetually oversensitive expression on his wide face. "The hothouse flower inside the Mack Truck" was one phrase I had heard to describe him. He had survived bouts of alcoholism and two broken marriages, had lost custody of his children, and had finally moved to New York, where he had sobered up. His poems, some of which I knew by heart, typically dealt with the sudden explosion of the inner life in the midst of an almost fatal loneliness. I particularly liked the concluding lines of "Poem with Several Birds," about a moment of resigned spiritual radiance:

> Some god or other must be tracing, now,
> its way, this way, and the blossoms
> like the god are suspended in midair,
> and seeing shivers in the face of all this brilliance.

I had repeated those lines to myself as I waited tables and took orders for salads. The fierce delicacy of Burroughs Hammond's poetry! On those nights when I had despaired and had waited for a god, any one of them, to arrive, his poetry had kept me sane. So when I spotted him at Freddy Avery's, I introduced myself and told him that I knew his poems and loved them. Gazing up at me through his thick horn-rim glasses, he asked politely what I did for a living. I said I waited tables, was an unemployed actor, and was working on a screenplay. He asked me what my screenplay was about and what it was called. I told him that it was a horror film and was entitled *Planet of Bugs*.

My screenplay had little chance of intriguing the poet, and at that moment I remembered something that Lorca had once said to Neruda. I thought it might get Burroughs Hammond's attention. "'The greatest poet of the age,'" I said, "to quote Lorca, 'is

Mickey Mouse.' So my ambition is to get great poetry up on the
screen, just as Walt Disney did. Comic poetry. And horror poetry,
too. Horror has a kind of poetry up on the screen. But I think most
poets just don't get it. But you do. I mean, Yeats didn't understand.
He couldn't even write a single play with actual human speech in
it. His Irish peasants—! And T. S. Eliot's plays! All those Christian
zombies. Zombie poetry written for other zombies. They were both
such rotten playwrights—they thought they knew the vernacular,
but they didn't. That's a real failing. Their time is past. You're a
better poet, and when critics in the future start to evaluate—"

"—You," he said. He lifted his right arm and pointed at me. Suddenly I felt that I was in the presence of an Old Testament prophet
who wasn't kidding and had never been kidding about anything.
"You are the scum of the Earth," he said calmly. I backed away from
him. He continued to point at me. "You are the scum of the Earth,"
he repeated.

Everyone was looking at him, and when that job had been completed, everyone was looking at me. Some Charles Mingus riffs
thudded out of the record player. Then the other guests started
laughing at my embarrassment. I glanced around to see where Giulietta had gone to, because I needed to make a rapid escape from
that party and I needed her to help me demonstrate a certain
mindfulness. But she wasn't anywhere now that I needed her, not
in the living room, not in the kitchen, or the hallway, or the bathroom. After searching for her, I descended the stairs from the
apartment as quickly as I could and found myself back out on the
street.

Now, years later, I no longer remember which one of the nearest
subway stops I found that night. I can remember the consoling
smell of New York City air, the feeling that perhaps anonymity
might provide me with some relief. I shouted at a light pole. I
walked a few blocks, brushed against several pedestrians, descended another set of stairs, reached into my pocket, and pulled
out a subway token. In my right hand, I discovered that I was still
holding on to a plastic cup with beer in it.

Only one other man stood on the subway platform that night.
The express came speeding through on the middle tracks. The
trains were all spray-painted with graffiti in those days, and they'd

rattle into the stations looking like giant multicolored mechanical caterpillars—amusement park rides scrawled over with beautifully creepy hieroglyphs, preceded by a tornado-like racket and a blast of salty fetid air.

The other man standing on the platform looked like the winos that Burroughs Hammond had written about in his fragmentary hymns to life following those nights he had spent in the drunk tank. *No other life could be as precious to me / as this one,* he had written. If only I could experience some kindly feeling for a stranger, I thought, possibly I might find myself redeemed by the Fates who were quietly ordering my humiliations, one after the other.

Therefore, I did what you never do on a subway platform. I exchanged a glance with the other man.

He approached me. On his face there appeared for a moment an expression of the deepest lucidity. He raised his eyelids as if flabbergasted by my very existence. I noticed that he was wearing over his torn shirt a leather vest stained with dark red blotches—blood or wine, I suppose now. He wore no socks. For the second time that evening, someone pointed at me. "That's a beer you have," he said, his voice burbling up as if through clogged plumbing. "Is there extra?"

I handed over the plastic cup to him. He took a swig. Then, his eyes deep in mad concentration, he yanked down his trousers zipper and urinated into the beer. He handed the cup back to me.

I took the cup out of this poor madman's grasp and put it down on the subway platform, and then I hauled back and slugged him in the face. He fell immediately. My knuckles stung. He began to crawl toward the subway tracks, and I heard distantly the local train rumbling toward the station, approaching us. With the studied calm of an accomplished actor who has had one or two early successes, I left that subway station and ascended the stairs two at a time to the street. Then, conscience-crippled and heartsick, I went back. I couldn't see the man I had hit. Finally I returned to the street and flagged down a taxi and returned to my apartment.

For the next few days, I checked the newspapers for reports of an accidental death in the subway of a drunk who had crawled into the path of a train, and when I didn't find any such story, I began to feel as if I had dreamed up the entire evening from start to finish, or, rather, that someone else had dreamed it up for me and put me as the lead actor into it—this cautionary tale whose moral was that I had no gift for the life I'd been leading. I took to bed the way you do when you have to think something out. My identity having overtaken me, I called in sick to the restaurant and didn't manage to get to an audition I had scheduled. A lethargy thrummed through me, and I dreamed that someone pointed at my body stretched out on the floor and said, "It's dead." What frightened me was not my death, but that pronoun: "I" had become an "it."

There's no profit in dwelling on the foolishness of one's youth. Everyone's past is a mess. And I wouldn't have thought of my days as an actor if it weren't for my cousin Brantford's having told me twenty years later over lunch in an expensive restaurant that he felt as if he had killed someone, and if my cousin and I hadn't had a kind of solidarity. By that time, Giulietta and I had children of our own, two boys, Elijah and Jacob, and the guttering seediness of New York in the 1970s was distant history, and I only came to the city to visit my cousin and my aunt. By then, I was a visitor from Minnesota, where we had moved and where I was a partner in the firm of Wilwersheid and Lampe. I was no longer an inhabitant of New York. I had become a family man and a tourist.

Do I need to prove that I love my wife and children, or that my existence has become terribly precious to me? They hold me to this earth. Once, back then in my twenties, all I wanted to do was to throw my life away. But then, somehow, usually by accident, you experience joy. And the problem with joy is that it binds you to life; it makes you greedy for more happiness. You experience avarice. You hope your life will go on forever.

A day or so after having lunch with Brantford, I went up to visit Aunt Margaret. She had started to bend over from the osteoporosis that would cripple her, or maybe it was the calcium-reducing effects of her antidepressant and the diet of Kung Pao chicken, vodka, and cigarettes she lived on. She was terrifyingly lucid, as always. The vodka merely seemed to have sharpened her wits. She was so unblurred, I hoped she wasn't about to go into one of her tailspins. Copies of *Foreign Affairs* lay around her apartment near the porcelain figurines. NPR drifted in from a radio on the windowsill. She had been reading Tacitus, she told me. "*The Annals of Imperial Rome.* Have you ever read it, Benjamin?"

"No," I said. I sank back on the sofa, irritating one of the cats, who leaped up away from me before taking up a position on the windowsill.

"You should. I can't read the Latin anymore, but I can read it in English. Frighteningly relevant. During the reign of Tiberius, Sejanus's daughter is arrested and led away. 'What did I do? Where are you taking me? I won't do it again,' this girl says. My God. Think of all the thousands who have said those very words in this century. I've said them myself. I used to say them to my father."

"Your father?"

"Of course. He could be cruel. He would lead me away, and he punished me. He probably had his reasons. He knew me. Well, I was a terrible girl," she said dreamily. "I was willful. Always getting into situations. I was . . . forward. *There's* an antiquated adjective. Well. These days, if I were young again, I could come into my own, no one would even be paying the slightest attention to me. I'd go from boy to boy like a bee sampling flowers, but in those days, they called us 'wild' and they hid us away. Thank god for progress. Have you seen Brantford, by the way?"

I told her I'd had lunch with him and that he'd said he felt as if he had killed somebody.

"Really. I wonder what he's thinking. He must be all worn out. Is he still drinking? Did he tell you about his girlfriend? That child of his?"

"What child? No, he didn't tell me. Who's this?"

"Funny that he didn't tell you." She stood up and went over to a miniature grandfather clock, only eight inches high, on the mantel. "Heavens," she said, "where are my manners? I should offer you some tea. Or maybe a sandwich." This customary politeness sounded odd coming from her.

"No, thank you." I shook my head. "Aunt Margaret, what child are you talking about?"

"It's not a baby, not yet. Don't misunderstand me. They haven't had a baby, those two. But Brantford's found a girlfriend, and she might as well be a baby, she's so young. Eighteen years old, for heaven's sake. He discovered her in a department store, selling clothes behind the counter. Shirts and things. She's another one of his strays. And of course he doesn't have a dime to his name anymore, and he takes her everywhere on his credit cards when he's not living off of her, and he still doesn't have a clue what to do with himself. Animals all over the place, but no job. He spends all day teaching dogs how to walk and birds how to fly. I suppose it's my fault. They'll blame me. They blame me for everything."

"What's her name? This girl?" I asked. "He didn't mention her to me."

"Camille," Aunt Margaret told me. "And of course she's beautiful—they all are, at that age—but so what? A nineteenth-century name and a beautiful face and figure and no personality at all and no money. They think love is everything, and they get sentimental, but love really isn't much. Just a little girl, this Camille. She likes the animals, of course, but she doesn't know what she's getting into with him." She looked at me slyly. "Do you still envy him? You mustn't envy or pity him, you know. And how is Giulietta?" Aunt Margaret had never approved of Giulietta and thought my marriage to her had been ill-advised. "And your darling children? Those boys? How are they, Benjamin?"

Aunt Margaret turned out to be wrong about Camille, who was not a sentimentalist after all. I met her for the first time at the memorial service five years after she and my cousin Brantford had become a couple. By then, she and Brantford had had a son, Robert, and my cousin had ended his life by stepping out into an intersection into the path of an oncoming taxi at the corner of Park Avenue and Eighty-second Street. If he couldn't live in that neighborhood, he could at least die there. He suffered a ruptured spleen, and his heart stopped before they admitted him to the ER. He had entered that intersection against a red light—it was unclear whether he had been careless or suicidal, but it was midday, and my cousin was accustomed to city traffic. Well. You always want to reserve judgment, but the blood analysis showed that he had been sober. I wish he had been drunk. We could have blamed it on that, and it would have been a kind of consolation, and we would have thought better of him.

One witness reported that Brantford had rushed onto Park Avenue to rescue a dog that had been running south. Maybe that was it.

In the months before his death, he had found a job working in the produce department at a grocery. When he couldn't manage the tasks that he considered beneath him—stacking the pears and lining up the tomatoes—he took a position as a clerk behind the counter at a pet food store on Avenue B. A nametag dangled from his shirt. He told me by telephone he hated that anyone coming into the store could find out his first name and then use it. It offended him. But he loved the store and could have worked there forever if it hadn't gone out of business. After that, he worked briefly at a collection agency making phone calls to deadbeats. He edited one issue of a humorous Web literary magazine entitled the *Potboiler.* What Brantford had expected from life and what it had actually given him must have been so distinct and so dissonant that he probably felt his dignity dropping away little by little until he simply wasn't himself anymore. He didn't seem to be anybody and he had no resources of humility to help turn that nothingness into a refuge. He and Camille lived in a cluttered little walkup in Brooklyn. I think he must have felt quietly panic-stricken, him and his animals. Time was going to run out on all of them. There would be no more fixes.

I wanted to help him—he was almost a model for me, but not quite—but I didn't know how to exercise compassion with him, or how to express the pity that Aunt Margaret said I shouldn't feel. I think my example sometimes goaded him into despair, as did his furred and feathered patients, who couldn't stand life without him.

At the memorial service, Camille carried the baby in a front pack, and she walked through the doors of the church in a blast of sunlight that seemed to cascade around her and then to advance before her as she proceeded up the aisle. Sunlight from the stained-glass windows caught her in momentary droplets and parallelograms of blues and reds. When she reached the first pew, she projected the tender, brave dignity of a woman on whom too many burdens have been placed too quickly.

Afterwards, following the eulogies and the hymns, Camille and I stood out on the lawn. Aunt Margaret, with whom I had been sitting, had gone back to Manhattan in a hired car. Camille had seemed surprised by me and had given me an astonished look when I approached her, my hand out.

"Ah, it's you," she said. "The cousin. I wondered if you'd come."

I gave her a hug.

"Sorry," she said, tearfully grinning. "You startled me. You're family, and your face is a little like Branty's. You have the same cheerful scowl, you two." She lifted baby Robert, who had been crying, out of the front pack, opened her blouse, drew back her bra and set the baby there to nurse. "Why didn't you ever come to see us?" she asked me, fixing me with a steady expression of wonderment as she nursed the baby. "He loved you. He said so. He called you 'Bunny.' Just like one of his animals."

"Yes. I didn't think . . . I don't think that Brantford wanted me to see him," I said. "And it was always like a zoo, wherever he was."

"That's unkind. We had to give the animals away, back to the official rescuers. It was *not* like a zoo. Zoos are noisy. The inmates don't want to be there. Brantford's creatures loved him and kept still if he wanted them to be. Why'd you say that? I'm sure he invited you over whenever you were in town."

She looked at me with an expression of honesty, solemn and accusing. I said, "Isn't it a beautiful day?"

"Yes. It's always a beautiful day. That's not the subject."

I had the feeling that I would never have a normal conversation with this woman. "You were so *good* for him," I blurted out, and her expression did not change. "But you should have seen through him. He must have wanted to keep you for himself and his birds and cats and dogs. You were his last precious possession. And, no, he really *didn't* invite me to meet you. Something happened to him," I said, a bit manically. "He turned into something he hadn't been. Maybe that was it. Being poor."

"Oh," she said, after turning back toward me and sizing me up, "*poor.* Well. We liked being poor. It was sort of Buddhist. It was harder for him than for me. We lived as a family, I'll say that. And I loved him. He was a sweetie, and very devoted to me and Robert and his animals." She hoisted the baby and burped him. "He had a very old soul. He wasn't a suicide, if that's what you're thinking. Are you all right?"

"Why?"

"You look like you're going to faint."

"Oh, I'm managing," I said. In truth, my head felt as if the late-afternoon sunlight were going right through the skull bones with ease, soaking the gray matter with photons. "Listen," I asked her, "do you want to go for a drink?"

"I can't drink," she said. "I'm nursing. And you're married, and you have children." How old-fashioned she was! I decided to press forward anyway.

"All right, then," I said. "Let's have coffee."

There is a peculiar lull that takes over New York in early afternoon, around two thirty. In the neighborhood coffee shops, the city's initial morning energy drains out and a pleasant tedium, a trance, holds sway for a few minutes. In any other civilized urban setting, the people would be taking siestas. Here, voices grow subdued and gestures remain incomplete. You lean back in your chair to watch the vapor trails aimed toward LaGuardia or Newark, and for once no one calls you, there is nothing to do. Radios are tuned to baseball, and conversations stop as you drift off to imagine the runner on second, edging toward third. Camille and I went into a little greasy spoon called Here to Eat and sat down at a table near the front window. The cook stared out at the blurring sidewalk, his eyelids heavy. He seemed massively indifferent to our presence and our general needs. The server barely noticed that we were there. She sat at one of the counter stools working on a crossword. No one even looked up.

Eventually the server brought us two cups of stale, burned coffee.

"At last," I said. "I thought it'd never come."

The baby was asleep in the crook of Camille's right arm. After a few minutes of pleasantries, Camille asked me, "So. Why are you here?"

"Why am I here? I'm here because of Brantford. For his memory. We were always close."

"You were?" she said.

"I thought so," I replied.

Her face, I now noticed, had the roundedness that women's faces acquire after childbirth. Errant bangs fell over her forehead, and she blew a stream of air upward toward them. She gave me a straight look. "He talked about you as his long-lost brother, the one who never came to see him."

"Please. I——"

She wasn't finished "You look alike," she said, "but that doesn't mean that you were alike. You could have been his identical twin and you wouldn't have been any closer to him than you are now. Anyway, what was I asking? Oh, yes. Why are you here? With me? Now."

"For coffee. To talk. To get to know you." I straightened my neck-tie. "After all, he was my cousin." I thought for a moment. "I loved him. He was better than me. I need to talk about him, and you didn't plan a reception. Isn't that unusual?"

"No, it isn't. You wanted to get to know me?" She leaned back and licked her chapped lips.

"Yes."

"Kind of belated, isn't it?" She sipped the hot coffee and then set it down.

"Belated?"

"Given the circumstances?" She gazed out the window, then lifted the baby to her shoulder again. "For the personal intimacies? For the details?" Her sudden modulation in tone was very pure. So was her irony. She had a kind of emotional puritanism that de-spised the parade of shadows on the wall, of which I was the cur-rent one.

"Okay. Why do you think I'm here?" I asked her, taken aback by her behavior. The inside of my mouth had turned to cotton; rude-ness does that to me.

"You're here to exercise your compassion," she said quickly. "And to serve up some awful belated charity. And, finally, to pa-tronize me." She smiled at me. "*La belle pauvre.* How's that? Think that sounds about right?"

"You're a tough one," I said. "I wasn't going to patronize you at all." She squirmed in the booth as if her physical discomfort could be shed from her skin and dropped on the floor. "Well, you proba-bly weren't planning on it, I'll give you credit for that." She poured more cream into her coffee. My heart was thumping away in my chest. "Look at you," she said. "Goddamn it, you have a crush on me. I can tell. I can always tell about things like that."

She started humming "In a Sentimental Mood." After a moment, she said, "You men. You're really something, you guys." She bit at a fingernail. "At least Branty had his animals. They'll escort him into heaven."

"I don't know why you're talking this way to me," I said. "You're being unnecessarily cruel."

"It's my generation," she said. "We get to the point. But I went a bit too far. It's been a hard day. I was crying all morning. I can't think straight. My apologies."

"Actually," I said. "I don't get you at all." This wasn't quite true.

"Good. At last."

We sat there for a while.

"You're a lawyer, aren't you?"

"Yes," I said. She stirred her coffee. Her spoon clicked against the cup.

"Big firm?"

"Yeah." Outside the diner, traffic passed on Lexington. The moon was visible in the sky. I could see it.

"Well, do me a favor, all right? Don't ask me about Brantford's debts." She settled back in the booth, while the server came and poured more burned coffee into her cup. "I don't need any professional advice just now."

I stared at her.

"Actually," she said, "I could use some money. To tide me over, et cetera. Your Aunt Margaret said that you would generously donate something for the cause." She gave me a vague look. "'Benjamin will come to your aid,' she said. And, yes, I can see that you will." She smiled. "Think of me as a wounded bird."

"How much do you need?" I asked.

"You really love this, don't you?" She gave me another careless smile. "You're in your element."

"No," I said. "I'm not sure I've ever had a conversation like this before."

"Well, you've had it now. Okay," she said. "I'll tell you what. You have my address. Send me a check. You'll enjoy sending the check, and then more checks after that. So that's your assignment. You're one of those guys who loves to exercise his pity, his empathy. You're one of those rare, sensitive men with a big bank account. Just send that check."

"And in return?"

"In return," she said, "I'll like you. I'll have a nice meal with you whenever you're in town. I'll give you a grateful little kiss on the cheek." She began to cry and then, abruptly, stopped. She pulled out a handkerchief from her purse and blew her nose.

"No, you won't. Why on earth do you say that?"

"You're absolutely right, I won't. I wanted to see how you'd react. I thought I'd rattle your cage. I'm grief-stricken. And I'm giddy." She laughed merrily, and the baby startled and lifted his little hands. "Poor guy, you'll never figure out any of this."

"Exactly right," I said. "You think I'm oblivious to things, don't you?"

"I have no idea, but if I do think so," she said thoughtfully, "I'll let you know. I didn't fifteen minutes ago."

"It seems," I said, "that you want to keep me in a posture of perpetual contrition." I was suddenly proud of that phrase. It summed everything up.

"Ha. 'Perpetual contrition.' Well, that'd be a start. You really don't know what Brantford thought of you, do you? Look: call your wife. Tell her about me. It'd be good for you, good for you both. Because you're . . ."

I reached out and took her hand before she could pronounce the condemning adjective or the noun she had picked out. It was a preemptive move. It was either that or slapping her. "That's quite enough," I said. I held on to her hand for dear life. The skin was warm and damp, and she didn't pull it away. For five minutes we sat there holding hands in silence. Then I dropped some money on the table for the coffee. Her baby began to cry. I identified with that sound. As I stood up, she said, "You shouldn't have been afraid."

She was capable of therapeutic misrepresentation. I knew I would indeed start sending her those checks before very long—thousands of dollars, every year. It would go on and on. I would be paying this particular bill forever. I owed them that.

"I'm a storm at sea," she said. "A basket case. Who knows? We might become friends after all." She laughed again, inappropriately (I thought), and I saw on her arm a tattoo of a chickadee, and on the other arm, a tattoo of a smiling dog.

Back in the hotel, I called Giulietta, and I told her everything that Camille had ordered me to say.

That night, I walked down a few blocks to a small neighborhood market, where I stole a Gala apple—I put it into my jacket pocket—and a bunch of flowers, which I carried out onto the street, holding them ostentatiously in front of me. If you have the right expression on your face, you can shoplift anything. I had learned that from my acting classes. More than enough money resided in my wallet for purchases, but shoplifting apparently was called for. It was an emotional necessity. I packed the apple in my suitcase and took the flowers into the hotel bathroom and put them into the sink before filling the sink with water. But I realized belatedly that there was no way I would be able to get them back home before they wilted.

So after I had arrived in the Minneapolis airport the next day, I bought another spray of flowers from one of those airport florists. Out on the street, I found a cab.

The driver smiled at the flowers I was carrying. "Very nice. You are surely a gentleman," he said, with a clear, clipped accent. I asked him where he was from, and he said he was Ethiopian. I told him that at first I had thought perhaps he was a Somali, since so many cabdrivers in Minneapolis were from there.

He made an odd guttural noise. "Oh, no, not Somali," he said. "Extremely not. I am Ethiopian . . . very different," he said. "We do not look the same, either," he said crossly.

I complimented him on his excellent English. "Yes, yes," he said impatiently, wanting to get back to the subject of Ethiopians and Somalis. "We Ethiopians went into their country, you know. Americans do not always realize this. The Somalis should have been grateful to us, but they were not. They never are. We made an effort to stop their civil war. But they like war, the Somalis. And they do not respect the law, so it is all war, to them. A Somali does not respect the law. He does not have it in him."

I said I didn't know that.

"For who are those flowers?" he asked. "Your wife?"

"Yes," I told him.

"They are pretty except for the lilies." He drove onto the entry ramp of the freeway. The turn signal in the cab sounded like a heart monitor. "Myself, I do not care for lilies. Do you know what we say about Somalis, what we Ethiopians say? We say, 'The Somali has nine hearts.' This means: a Somali will not reveal his heart to you. He will reveal a false heart, not his true one. But you get past that, in time, and you get to the second heart. This heart is also and once again false. In repetition you will be shown and told the thing which is not. You will never get to the ninth heart, which is the true one, the door to the soul. The Somali keeps that heart to himself."

"The thing which is not?" I asked him. Outside, the sun had set.

"You do not understand this?" He looked at me in the rearview mirror. "This very important matter?"

"Well, maybe I do," I said. "You know, my wife works with Somali children."

The cabdriver did not say anything, but he tugged at his ear.

"Somali children in Minneapolis have a very high rate of autism," I said. "It's strange. No one seems to knows why. Some say it's the diet, some say that they don't get enough sunlight. Anyway, my wife works with Somali children."

"Trying to make them normal?" the cabdriver asked. "Oh, well. You are a good man, to give her flowers." He gazed out at the night. "Look at this dark air," he said. "It will snow soon."

With my suitcase, my apple, and my flowers, I stood waiting on the front porch of our house. Instead of unlocking the door as I normally would have, I thought I would ring the bell just as a stranger might, a someone who hopes to be welcomed. I always enjoyed surprising Giulietta and the boys whenever I returned from trips, and with that male pride in homecoming from a battle, large or small, I was eager to tell them tales about where I had been and what I had done and whom I had defeated and the trophies with which I had returned. Standing on the welcome mat, I looked inside through the windows into the entryway and beyond into the living room, and I saw my son Jacob lying on the floor reading from his history textbook. His class had been studying the American Revolution. He ran his hand through his hair. He needed a haircut. He had a sweet, studious look on his face, and I felt proud of him beyond measure. I rang the bell. They would all rush to greet me.

The bell apparently wasn't working, and Jacob didn't move from his settled position. I would have to fix that bell. I released my grip on the suitcase and headed toward the side door, where we had another doorbell. Again I rang and again no one answered. If it had made a noise, I couldn't hear it. So I went around to the back, brushing past the hateful peonies, stepping over a broken sidewalk stone, and I took up a spot in the grassy yard, still carrying my spray of flowers. Behind me, I could smell a skunk, and I heard a car alarm in the distance. If I had been Brantford, all the yard animals would have approached me. But if I had been Brantford, I wouldn't be living in this house. I wouldn't be here.

Giulietta sat in the back den. I could see her through the windows. She was home-tutoring a little Somali girl, guiding her along a balance beam a few inches off the floor, and when that task was finished, they began to toss a beanbag back and forth to each other, practicing midline exercises. Her parents sat on two chairs by the wall, watching her, the mother dressed in a flowing robe.

I felt the presence of my cousin next to me out there in the yard, and in that contagious silence I was reminded of my beautiful wife and children who were stubbornly not coming to the door in response to my little joke with the doorbell. So I rapped on the window expecting to startle Giulietta, but when she looked up, I could not see through her dark glasses to where she was looking, nor could I tell whether she really intended to let me into the house ever again.

I have loved this life so much. I was prepared to wait out there forever.

JENNIFER EGAN

Safari

FROM *The New Yorker*

"REMEMBER, CHARLIE? In Hawaii? When we went to the beach at night and it started to rain?" Rolph is talking to his older sister, Charlene, who despises her real name. But because they're crouched around a bonfire with the other people on the safari, and because Rolph doesn't speak up all that often, and because their father, Lou, sitting behind them on a camp chair, is a record producer whose personal life is of general interest, those near enough to hear are listening closely. "Remember? How Mom and Dad stayed at the table for one more drink—"

"Impossible," their father interjects, with a wink at the elderly bird-watching ladies to his left. Both women wear their binoculars even in the dark, as if hoping to spot birds in the firelit tree overhead.

"Remember, Charlie? How the beach was still warm, and that crazy wind was blowing?"

But Charlie is focused on her father's legs, which have intertwined behind her with those of his girlfriend, Mindy. Soon Lou and Mindy will bid the group good night and retreat to their tent, where they'll make love on one of its narrow rickety cots, or possibly on the ground. From the adjacent tent, which she and Rolph share, Charlie, who is fourteen, can hear them—not sounds, exactly, but movement. Rolph, at eleven, is too young to notice.

Charlie throws back her head, startling her father. Lou is in his late thirties, his square-jawed surfer's face gone a little draggy under the eyes. "You were married to Mom on that trip," she informs him, her voice distorted by the arching of her neck, which is encircled by a puka shell choker.

"Yes, Charlie," Lou says. "I'm aware of that."

The bird-watching ladies trade a sad smile. Lou is one of those men whose restless charm has generated a contrail of personal upheaval that is practically visible behind him: two failed marriages and two more kids back home in L.A., who were too young to bring on this three-week safari. The safari is a new business venture of Lou's old army buddy Ramsey, with whom he drank and misbehaved, having barely avoided Korea almost twenty years ago.

Rolph pulls at his sister's shoulder. He wants her to remember, to feel it all again: the wind, the endless black ocean, the two of them peering into the dark as if awaiting a signal from their distant, grownup lives. "Remember, Charlie?"

"Yeah," Charlie says, narrowing her eyes. "I do remember that."

The Samburu warriors have arrived—four of them, two holding drums, and a child in the shadows minding a yellow long-horned cow. They came yesterday, too, after the morning game run, when Lou and Mindy were "napping." That was when Charlie exchanged shy glances with the most beautiful warrior, who has scar-tissue designs coiled like railroad tracks over the rigorous architecture of his chest and shoulders and back.

Charlie stands up and moves closer to the warriors: a slender girl in shorts and a raw-cotton shirt with small round buttons made of wood. Her teeth are slightly crooked. When the drummers pat their drums, Charlie's warrior and the other one begin to sing: guttural noises pried from their abdomens. She sways in front of them. During her ten days in Africa, she has begun to act differently— like one of the girls who intimidate her back home. In a cinderblock town that the group visited a few days ago, she drank a muddy-looking concoction in a bar and wound up trading away her silver butterfly earrings (a birthday gift from her father) in a hut belonging to a very young woman whose breasts were leaking milk. She was late returning to the jeeps; Albert, who works for Ramsey, had to go and find her. "Prepare yourself," he warned. "Your dad is having kittens." Charlie didn't care then, and doesn't now; there's a charge for her in simply commanding the fickle beam of her father's attention, feeling his disquiet as she dances, alone, by the fire.

Lou lets go of Mindy's hand and sits up straight. He has an urge to grab his daughter's skinny arm and yank her away from the warriors, but does no such thing, of course. That would be letting her win.

The warrior smiles at Charlie. He's nineteen, and has lived away from his village since he was ten. But he has sung for enough American tourists to recognize that, in her world, Charlie is a child.

"Son," Lou says, into Rolph's ear, "let's take a walk."

The boy rises from the dust and walks with his father away from the fire. Twelve tents, each sleeping two safari guests, form a circle around it, along with three outhouses and a shower stall, where water warmed on the fire is released from a sack with a rope pull. Out of view are some smaller tents for the staff, and then the black, muttering expanse of the bush, where they've been cautioned never to go.

"Your sister's acting nuts," Lou says, striding into the dark.

"Why?" Rolph asks. He hasn't noticed anything nutty in Charlie's behavior. But his father hears the question differently.

"Women are crazy," he says. "You could spend a goddam lifetime trying to figure out why."

"Mom's not."

"True," Lou reflects, calmer now. "In fact, your mother's not crazy enough."

The singing and drumbeats fall suddenly away, leaving Lou and Rolph alone under a sharp moon.

"What about Mindy?" Rolph asks. "Is she crazy?"

"Good question," Lou says. "What do you think?"

"She likes to read. She brought a lot of books."

"Did she?"

"I like her," Rolph says. "But I don't know if she's crazy. Or what the right amount is."

Lou puts his arm around Rolph. If he were an introspective man, he would have understood years ago that his son is the one person in the world who has the power to soothe him. And that, although he expects Rolph to resemble him, what he most enjoys in his son is the many ways in which he is different: quiet, reflective, attuned to the natural world and the pain of others.

"Who cares," Lou says. "Right?"

"Right," Rolph says, and the women fall away like the drumbeats, leaving him and his father together, an invincible unit amid the burbling, whispering bush. The sky is crammed with stars. Rolph closes his eyes and opens them again. He is in Africa with his father. He thinks, I'll remember this night for the rest of my life. And he's right.

When they finally return to camp, the warriors have gone. Only a few diehards from the Phoenix faction (as Lou calls the safari members who hail from there) are still sitting by the fire, comparing the day's animal sightings. Rolph creeps into his tent, pulls off his pants, and climbs onto his cot in a T-shirt and underwear. He assumes that Charlie is asleep. When she speaks, he can hear in her voice that she's been crying.

"Where did you go?" she says.

"What on earth have you got in that backpack?"

It's Cora, Lou's travel agent. She hates Mindy, but Mindy doesn't take it personally—it's structural hatred, a term she coined herself and is finding highly useful on this trip. A single woman in her forties who wears high-collared shirts to conceal the thready sinews of her neck will structurally despise the twenty-three-year-old girlfriend of a powerful male who not only employs said middle-aged female but is paying her way on this trip.

"Anthropology books," Mindy tells Cora. "I'm in the Ph.D. program at Berkeley."

"Why don't you read them?"

"Carsick," Mindy says, which is plausible, God knows, in the shuddering jeeps, though untrue. She isn't sure why she hasn't cracked her Boas or Malinowski or Julian Jaynes, but assumes that she must be acquiring knowledge in other ways that will prove equally fruitful. In bold moments, fueled by the boiled black coffee that is served each morning in the meal tent, Mindy has even wondered whether her insights on the links between social structure and emotional response amount to more than a rehash of Lévi-Strauss—a refinement, a contemporary application. She's only in her second year of coursework.

Their jeep is the last in a line of five, nosing along a dirt road through grassland whose apparent brown masks a wide internal spectrum of color: purples, greens, reds. Albert, the surly Englishman who is Ramsey's second-in-command, is driving. Mindy has managed to avoid Albert's jeep for several days, but he has developed a reputation for discovering the best animals, so although there's no game run today—they're relocating to the hills, where they'll spend the night in a hotel for the first time this trip—the children begged to ride with him. And keeping Lou's children happy, or as close to happy as is structurally possible, is part of Mindy's job.

Structural resentment: The adolescent daughter of a twice-divorced male will be unable to tolerate the presence of his new girlfriend, and will do everything in her limited power to distract him from said girlfriend's presence, her own nascent sexuality being her chief weapon.

Structural affection: A twice-divorced male's preadolescent son (and favorite child) will embrace and accept his father's new girl-friend because he hasn't yet learned to separate his father's loves and desires from his own. In a sense, he, too, will love and desire her, and she will feel maternal toward him, though she isn't old enough to be his mother.

Structural incompatibility: A powerful twice-divorced male will be unable to acknowledge, much less sanction, the ambitions of a much younger female mate. By definition, their relationship will be temporary.

Structural desire: The much younger temporary female mate of a powerful male will be inexorably drawn to the single male within range who disdains her mate's power.

Albert drives with one elbow out the window. He has been a largely silent presence on this safari, eating quickly in the meal tent, providing terse answers to people's questions ("Where do you live?" "Mombasa." "How long have you been in Africa?" "Eight years." "What brought you here?" "This and that"). He rarely joins the group around the fire after dinner. On a trip to the outhouse one night, Mindy glimpsed him at the other fire, near the staff tents, drinking a beer and laughing with the Kikuyu drivers. With the tour group, he rarely smiles. Whenever his eyes happen to graze Mindy's, she senses that he feels shame on her behalf: because of her prettiness; because she sleeps with Lou; because she keeps telling herself that this trip constitutes anthropological research into group dynamics and ethnographic enclaves, when really what she's after is luxury, adventure, and a break from her four insomniac roommates.

Next to Albert, in the shotgun seat, Chronos is ranting about animals. He's the bassist for the Mat Hatters, one of the groups that Lou produces, and has come on the trip as Lou's guest, along with the Hatters' guitarist and a girlfriend each. These four are locked in a visceral animal-sighting competition. (*Structural fixation:* a collective, contextually induced obsession that becomes a temporary locus of greed, competition, and envy.) They challenge one another nightly over who saw more and at what range, invoking witnesses from their respective jeeps and promising definitive proof when they develop their film, back home.

Behind Albert sits Cora, the travel agent, and beside her, gazing out his window, is Dean, a blond actor whose genius for stating the obvious—"It's hot," or "The sun is setting," or "There aren't many trees"—is a staple source of amusement for Mindy. Dean is starring in a movie whose soundtrack Lou is helping to create; the presumption seems to be that its release will bring Dean immediate and stratospheric fame. In the seat behind him, Rolph and Charlie are showing their *Mad* magazine to Mildred, one of the bird-watching ladies. She or her companion, Fiona, can usually be found near Lou, who flirts with them tirelessly and needles them to take him bird-watching. His indulgence of these women in their seventies (strangers to him before this trip) intrigues Mindy; she can find no structural reason for it.

In the last row, beside Mindy, Lou opens the large aluminum case where his new camera is partitioned in its foam padding, like a dismantled rifle, and thrusts his torso from the open roof, ignoring the rule to stay seated while the jeep is moving. Albert swerves suddenly, and Lou is knocked back down, camera smacking his forehead. He swears at Albert, but the words are lost in the jeep's wobbly jostle through tall grass. After a minute or two of chaotic driving, they emerge a few feet from a pride of lions. Everyone gawks in startled silence—it's the closest they've been to any animal on this trip. The motor is still running, Albert's hand tentatively on the wheel, but the lions appear so relaxed, so indifferent, that he kills the engine. In the ticking motor silence they can hear the lions breathe: two females, one male, three cubs. The cubs and one of the females are gorging on a bloody zebra carcass. The others are dozing.

"They're eating," Dean says.

Chronos's hands shake as he spools film into his camera. "Fuck," he keeps muttering. "Fuck."

Albert lights a cigarette—forbidden in the brush—and waits, as indifferent to the scene as if he had paused outside a restroom.

"Can we stand?" the children ask. "Is it safe?"

"I'm sure as hell going to," Lou says.

Lou, Charlie, Rolph, Chronos, and Dean all climb onto their seats and jam their upper halves through the open roof. Mindy is now effectively alone inside the jeep with Albert, Cora, and Mildred, who peers at the lions through her bird-watching binoculars.

"How did you know?" Mindy asks, after a silence.

Albert swivels around to look at her down the length of the jeep. He has unruly hair and a soft brown mustache. There is a suggestion of humor in his face. "Just a guess."

"From half a mile away?"

"He probably has a sixth sense," Cora says, "after so many years here."

Albert turns back around and blows smoke through his open window.

"Did you see something?" Mindy says, persisting.

She doesn't expect Albert to turn again, but he does, leaning over the back of his seat, his eyes meeting hers between the children's bare legs. Mindy feels a jolt of attraction roughly akin to having someone seize her intestines and twist. She understands now that it's mutual; she sees this in Albert's face.

"Broken bushes," he says. "Like something got chased. It could have been nothing."

Cora, sensing her exclusion, sighs wearily. "Can someone come down so I can look, too?" she calls to those above the roof.

"Coming," Lou says, but Chronos is faster, ducking back into the front seat and then leaning out his window. Cora rises in her big print skirt. Mindy's face pounds with blood. Her own window, like Albert's, is on the jeep's left side, facing away from the lions. Mindy watches him wet his fingers and snuff out his cigarette. They sit in silence, hands dangling separately from their windows, a warm breeze stirring the hair on their arms, ignoring the most spectacular animal sighting of the safari.

"You're driving me crazy," Albert says, very softly. The sound seems to travel out his window and back in through Mindy's, like one of those whispering tubes. "You must know that."

"I didn't," she murmurs back.

"Well, you are."

"My hands are tied."

"Forever?"

She smiles. "Please. An interlude."

"Then?"

"Grad school. Berkeley."

Albert chuckles. Mindy isn't sure what the chuckle means—is it funny that she's in graduate school, or that Berkeley and Mombasa, where he lives, are irreconcilable locations?

"Chronos, you crazy fuck, get back in here."

It's Lou's voice, from overhead. But Mindy feels sluggish, almost drugged, and reacts only when she hears the change in Albert's voice. "No," he hisses. "No! Back in the jeep."

Chronos is skulking among the lions, holding his camera close to the faces of the sleeping male and female, taking pictures.

"Walk backward," Albert says, with hushed urgency. "Backward, Chronos, gently."

Movement comes from a direction that no one is expecting: the lioness gnawing at the zebra. She vaults at Chronos in an agile, gravity-defying spring that anyone with a house cat would recognize. She lands on his head, flattening him instantly. There are screams, a gunshot, and those overhead tumble back into their seats so violently that at first Mindy thinks they've been shot. But it's the lioness; Albert has killed her with a rifle he'd secreted somewhere, maybe under his seat. The other lions have scattered; all that's left is the zebra carcass and the body of the lioness, Chronos's legs splayed beneath her.

Albert, Lou, Dean, and Cora bolt from the jeep. Mindy starts to follow, but Lou pushes her back, and she realizes that he wants her to stay with his children. She leans over the back of their seat and puts an arm around each of them. As they stare through the open windows, a wave of nausea rolls through Mindy; she feels in danger of passing out. Mildred is still in her spot beside the children, and it occurs to Mindy, vaguely, that the elderly bird-watcher was inside the jeep the whole time that she and Albert were talking.

"Is Chronos dead?" Rolph asks flatly.

"I'm sure he's not," Mindy says.

"Why isn't he moving?"

"The lion is on top of him. See, they're pulling her off. He's probably fine under there."

"There's blood on the lion's mouth," Charlie says.

"That's from the zebra. Remember, she was eating the zebra?"

It takes enormous effort to keep her teeth from chattering, but Mindy knows that she must hide her terror from the children — her belief that whatever turns out to have happened is her fault.

They wait in pulsing isolation, surrounded by the hot, blank day. Mildred rests a knobby hand on Mindy's shoulder, and Mindy feels her eyes fill with tears. "He'll be fine," the old woman says gently. "You watch."

By the time the group assembles in the bar of the mountain hotel after dinner, everyone seems to have gained something. Chronos has won a blistering victory over his bandmate and both girlfriends, at the cost of thirty-two stitches on his left cheek that you could argue are also a gain (he's a rock star, after all) and several huge antibiotic pills administered by an English surgeon with hooded eyes and beery breath — an old friend of Albert's, whom he unearthed in a cinder-block town about an hour away from the lions.

Albert has gained the status of a hero, though you wouldn't know it to look at him. He gulps a bourbon and mutters his responses to the giddy queries of the Phoenix faction. No one has yet confronted him on the damning basics: Why were you in the bush? How did you get so close to the lions? Why didn't you stop Chronos from getting out of the jeep? But Albert knows that Ramsey, his boss, will ask these questions, and that they will likely lead to his being fired: the latest in a series of failures brought on by what his mother, back in Minehead, calls his "self-destructive tendencies."

The passengers in Albert's jeep have gained a story that they'll tell for the rest of their lives. They are witnesses, to be questioned endlessly about what they saw and heard and felt. A gang of children, including Rolph, Charlie, a set of eight-year-old twin boys from Phoenix, and Louise, a chubby twelve-year-old, leave the bar and stampede along a slatted path to a blind beside a watering hole: a wooden hut full of long benches with a slot they can peek through, invisible to the animals. It's dark inside. They rush to the slot, but no animals are drinking at the moment.

"Did you actually see the lion?" Louise asks, with wonder.

"Lion*ess*," Rolph says. "There were two, plus a lion. And three cubs."

"She means the one that got shot," Charlie says, impatiently. "Obviously we saw it. We were inches away!"

"Feet," Rolph says, correcting her.

"Feet are *made* out of inches," Charlie says. "We saw everything."

Rolph has already started to hate these conversations — the pant-ing excitement behind them, the way Charlie seems to revel in it. A thought has been troubling him. "I wonder what will happen to the cubs," he says. "The lioness who got shot must have been their mom — she was eating with them."

"Not necessarily," Charlie says.

"But if she was."

"Maybe the dad will take care of them," Charlie says, doubtfully. The other children are quiet, considering the question.

"Lions tend to raise their cubs communally" — a voice comes from the far end of the blind. Mildred and Fiona were already there or have just arrived; being old and female, they're easily missed. "The pride will likely take care of them," Fiona says, "even if the one killed was their mother."

"Which it might not have been," Charlie adds.

"Which it might not have been," Mildred agrees.

It doesn't occur to the children to ask Mildred, who was also in the jeep, what she saw.

"I'm going back," Rolph tells his sister.

He follows the path up to the hotel. His father and Mindy are still in the smoky bar; the strange, celebratory feeling unnerves Rolph. His mind bends again and again to the jeep, but his memo-ries are a muddle: the lioness springing; a jerk of impact from the gun; Chronos moaning during the drive to the doctor, blood col-lecting in an actual puddle under his head on the floor of the jeep, like in a comic book. All of it is suffused with the feel of Mindy holding him from behind, her cheek against his head, her smell: not bready, like his mom's, but salty, bitter almost — a smell that seems akin to that of the lions themselves.

He stands by his father, who pauses in the middle of an army story he's telling with Ramsey. "You tired, son?"

"Want me to walk you upstairs?" Mindy asks, and Rolph nods: he does want that.

The blue, mosquito-y night pushes in from the hotel windows. Outside the bar, Rolph is suddenly less tired. Mindy collects his key from the front desk, then says, "Let's go out on the porch."

They step outside. Dark as it is, the silhouettes of mountains against the sky are even darker. Rolph can dimly hear the voices of the other children, down in the blind. He's relieved to have escaped them. He stands with Mindy at the edge of the porch and looks at the mountains. Rolph senses her waiting for something and he waits, too, his heart stamping.

There is a cough farther down the porch. Rolph sees the orange tip of a cigarette move in the dark, and Albert comes toward them with a creak of boots. "Hello there," he says to Rolph. He doesn't speak to Mindy, and Rolph decides that the one hello must be for both of them.

"Hello," he greets Albert.

"What are you up to?" Albert asks.

Rolph turns to Mindy. "What are we up to?"

"Enjoying the night," she says, still facing the mountains, but her voice is tense. "We should go up," she tells Rolph, and walks abruptly back inside. Rolph is troubled by her rudeness. "Are you coming?" he asks Albert.

"Why not?"

As the three of them ascend the stairs, Rolph feels an odd pressure to make conversation. "Is your room up here, too?" he asks.

"Down the hall," Albert says. "Room 3."

Mindy unlocks the door to Rolph's room and steps in, leaving Albert in the hall. Rolph is suddenly angry with her.

"Want to see my room?" he asks Albert. "Mine and Charlie's?"

Mindy emits a single syllable of laughter — the way his mother laughs when things have annoyed her to the point of absurdity. Albert steps into his room. It's plain, with wooden furniture and dusty flowered curtains, but after ten nights in tents it feels lavish.

"Very nice," Albert says. Mindy crosses her arms and stares out the window. There is a feeling in the room that Rolph can't identify. He's angry with Mindy and thinks that Albert must be, too. *Women are crazy.* Mindy's body is slender and elastic; she could slip through a keyhole, or under a door. Her thin purple sweater rises and falls quickly as she breathes. Rolph is surprised by how angry he is.

Albert taps a cigarette from his pack, but doesn't light it. It is unfiltered, tobacco emerging from both ends. "Well," he says. "Good night, you two."

Rolph had imagined Mindy tucking him into bed, her arm around him as it was in the jeep. Now this seems out of the question. He can't change into his pajamas with Mindy there; he doesn't even want her to see his pajamas, which have small blue elves all over them. "I'm fine," he tells her, hearing the coldness in his voice. "You can go back."

"Okay," she says. She turns down his bed, plumps the pillow, adjusts the open window. Rolph senses her finding reasons not to leave the room.

"Your dad and I will be just next door," Mindy says. "You know that, right?"

"Duh," he mutters. Then, chastened, he says, "I know."

Five days later, they take a long, very old train overnight to Mombasa. Every few minutes, it slows down just enough for people to leap from the doors, bundles clutched to their chests, and for others to scramble on. Lou's group and the Phoenix faction install themselves in the cramped bar car, which they share with African men in suits and bowler hats. Charlie is allowed to drink one beer, but she sneaks two more with the help of handsome Dean, who stands beside her narrow barstool. "You're sunburned," he says, pressing a finger to Charlie's cheek. "The African sun is strong."

"True," Charlie says, grinning as she swigs her beer. Now that Mindy has pointed out Dean's platitudes, Charlie finds him hilarious.

"You have to wear sunscreen," he says.

"I know—I did."

"Once isn't enough. You have to reapply."

Charlie catches Mindy's eye and succumbs to giggles. Her father moves close. "What's so funny?"

"Life," Charlie says, leaning against him.

"Life!" Lou snorts. "How old are you?"

He hugs her to him. When Charlie was little, he did this all the time, but as she grows older it happens less. Her father is warm, almost hot, his heartbeat like someone banging on a heavy door.

"Ow," Lou says. "Your quill is stabbing me." It's a black-and-white porcupine quill—she found it in the hills and uses it to pin up her long hair. Her father slides it out, and the tangled golden mass of Charlie's hair collapses onto her shoulders like a shattered window. She's aware of Dean watching.

"I like this," Lou says, squinting at the quill's translucent point. "It's a dangerous weapon."

"Weapons are necessary," Dean says.

*

By the next afternoon, the safari-goers have settled into a hotel a half-hour up the coast from Mombasa. On a white beach traversed by knobby-chested men selling beads and gourds, Mildred and Fiona gamely appear in floral-print swimsuits, binoculars still at their necks. The livid Medusa tattoo on Chronos's chest is less startling than his small potbelly—a disillusioning trait he shares with a number of the men, though not Lou, who is lean, a little ropy, tanned from occasional surfing. He walks toward the cream-colored sea with his arm around Mindy, who looks even better than expected (and expectations were high) in her sparkling blue bikini.

After a swim, Lou goes in search of spears and snorkeling gear, resisting the temptation to follow Mindy back to their room, though clearly she'd like him to. She's gone bananas in the sack since they left the tents—hungry for it now, pawing Lou's clothes off at odd moments, ready to start again when he's barely finished. He feels tenderly toward Mindy, now that the trip is winding down. She's studying at Berkeley, and Lou has never traveled for a woman. It's doubtful that he'll lay eyes on her again.

Rolph and Charlie are reading in the sand under a palm tree when Lou gets back with the snorkeling equipment, but Rolph puts aside *The Hobbit* without protest and stands. Charlie ignores them, and Lou wonders momentarily if he should have included her. He and Rolph walk to the edge of the sea and pull on their masks and flippers, hanging their spears from belts at their sides. Rolph looks thin; he needs more exercise. He's timid in the water. His mother is a reader and a gardener, and Lou is constantly having to fight her influence. He wishes that Rolph could live with him, but his lawyer just shakes his head whenever he mentions it. The fish are beautiful, easy targets, nibbling at coral. Lou has speared seven by the time he realizes that Rolph hasn't killed a single one.

"What's the problem, son?" he asks, when they surface.

"I just like watching them," Rolph says.

They've drifted toward a spit of rocks extending into the sea. Carefully they climb from the water. The tide pools throng with starfish and urchins and sea cucumbers; Rolph crouches, poring over them. Lou's fish hang from a netted bag at his waist. From the beach, Mindy is watching them through Fiona's binoculars. She waves, and Lou and Rolph wave back.

"Dad," Rolph asks, lifting a tiny green crab from a tide pool, "what do you think about Mindy?"

"Mindy's great. Why?"

The crab splays its little claws; Lou notes with approval that his son knows how to hold it safely. Rolph squints up at him. "You know. Is she the right amount of crazy?"

Lou gives a hoot of laughter. He'd forgotten the earlier conversation, but Rolph forgets nothing—a quality that delights his father. "She's crazy enough. But crazy isn't everything."

"I think she's rude," Rolph says.

"Rude to *you?*"

"No. To Albert."

Lou turns to his son, cocking his head. "Albert?"

Rolph releases the crab and begins to tell the story. He remembers each thing—the porch, the stairs, "Room 3"—realizing as he speaks how much he has wanted to tell his father this, as punishment to Mindy. Lou listens keenly, without interrupting. But as Rolph goes on he senses the story landing heavily, in a way he doesn't understand. When he finishes talking, his father takes a long breath and lets it out. He looks back at the beach. It's nearly sunset, and people are shaking the fine white sand from their towels and packing up for the day. The hotel has a disco, and the group plans to go dancing there after dinner.

"When exactly did this happen?" Lou asks.

"The same day as the lions—that night." Rolph waits a moment, then asks, "Why do you think she was rude like that?"

"Women are cunts," his father says. "That's why."

Rolph gapes at him. His father is angry, a muscle jumping in his jaw, and without warning Rolph is angry, too: assailed by a deep, sickening rage that stirs in him very occasionally—most often when he and Charlie come back from a riotous weekend around their father's pool, rock stars jamming on the roof, guacamole and big pots of chili, to find their mother alone in her bungalow, drinking peppermint tea. Rage at this man who casts everyone aside.

"They are not—" He can't make himself repeat the word.

"They are," Lou says tightly. "Pretty soon you'll know it for sure."

Rolph turns away from his father. There is nowhere to go, so he jumps into the sea and begins slowly paddling his way back toward the shore. The sun is low, the water choppy and full of shadows. Rolph imagines sharks just under his feet, but he doesn't turn or look back. He keeps swimming toward that white sand, knowing instinctively that his struggle to stay afloat is the most exquisite torture he can concoct for his father—knowing also that, if he sinks, Lou will jump in instantly and save him.

That night, Rolph and Charlie are allowed to have wine at dinner. Rolph dislikes the sour taste, but enjoys the swimmy blur it makes of his surroundings: the giant beaklike flowers all over the dining room; his father's speared fish cooked by the chef with olives and tomatoes; Mindy in a shimmery green dress. His father's arm is around her. He isn't angry anymore, so neither is Rolph.

Lou has spent the past hour in bed, fucking Mindy senseless. Now he keeps one hand on her slim thigh, reaching under her hem, waiting for that cloudy look she gets. Lou is a man who cannot tolerate defeat—can't *perceive* it as anything but a spur to his own inevitable victory. He doesn't give a shit about Albert—Albert is invisible, Albert is nothing. (In fact, Albert has left the group and returned to his Mombasa apartment.) What matters now is that *Mindy* understand this.

He refills Mildred's and Fiona's wineglasses until their cheeks are patchy and flushed. "You still haven't taken me bird-watching," he chides them. "I keep asking, but it never happens."

"We could go tomorrow," Mildred says. "There are some coastal birds we're hoping to see."

"Is that a promise?"

"A solemn promise."

"Come on," Charlie whispers to Rolph. "Let's go outside."

They slip from the crowded dining room and skitter onto the silvery beach. The palm trees make a slapping, rainy sound, but the air is dry.

"It's like Hawaii," Rolph says, wanting it to be true. The ingredients are there: the dark, the beach, his sister. But it doesn't feel the same.

"Without the rain," Charlie says.

"Without Mom," Rolph says.

"I think Dad's going to marry Mindy," Charlie says.

"No way! He doesn't love her."

"So? He can still marry her."

They sink onto the sand, still faintly warm, radiating a lunar glow. The ghost sea tumbles against it.

"She's not so bad," Charlie says.

"I don't like her. And why are you the world's expert?"

Charlie shrugs. "I know Dad."

Charlie doesn't yet know herself. Four years from now, at eighteen, she'll join a cult across the Mexican border whose charismatic leader promotes a diet of raw eggs; she'll nearly die from salmonella poisoning before Lou rescues her. A cocaine habit will require partial reconstruction of her nose, changing her appearance, and a series of feckless, domineering men will leave her solitary in her late twenties, trying to broker peace between Rolph and Lou, who will have stopped speaking.

But Charlie *does* know her father. He'll marry Mindy because that's what winning means, and because Mindy's eagerness to finish this odd episode and return to her studies will last until precisely the moment when she unlocks the door to her Berkeley apartment and walks into the smell of simmering lentils: one of the cheap stews that she and her roommates survive on. She'll collapse onto the swaybacked couch they found on the sidewalk and unpack her many books, realizing that in the weeks of lugging them through Africa she has read virtually nothing. And when the phone rings her heart will flip.

Structural dissatisfaction: Returning to circumstances that once pleased you, after having experienced a more thrilling or opulent way of life, and finding that you can no longer tolerate them.

Suddenly, Rolph and Charlie are galloping up the beach, drawn by the pulse of light and music from the open-air disco. They run barefoot into the crowd, trailing powdery sand onto a translucent dance floor overlaid on lozenges of flashing color. The shuddering bass line seems to interfere with Rolph's heartbeat.

"C'mon," Charlie says. "Let's dance."

She begins to undulate in front of him—the way the new Charlie is planning to dance when she gets home. But Rolph is embarrassed; he can't dance that way. The rest of the group surrounds them. Louise, the twelve-year-old, is dancing with Dean, the actor. Ramsey flings his arms around one of the Phoenix-faction moms. Lou and Mindy dance close together, their whole bodies touching,

but Mindy is thinking of Albert, as she will, periodically, after marrying Lou and having two daughters, Lou's fifth and sixth children, in quick succession, as if sprinting against the inevitable drift
of his attention. On paper he'll be penniless, and Mindy will end
up working as a travel agent to support her little girls. For a time,
her life will be joyless; the girls will seem to cry too much, and she'll
think longingly of this trip to Africa as the last perfect moment of
her life, when she still had a choice, when she was free and unen-
cumbered. She'll dream senselessly, futilely, of Albert, wondering
what he is doing at particular moments, and how her life would
have turned out if she'd run away with him as he suggested, half
joking, when she visited him in Room 3. Later, of course, she'll recognize "Albert" as nothing more than a focus of regret for her own
immaturity and disastrous choices. When both her children are in
high school, she'll finally resume her studies, complete her Ph.D.
at UCLA, and begin an academic career at forty-five, spending long
periods doing social-structures fieldwork in the Brazilian rain forest. Her youngest daughter will go to work for Lou, become his
protégée, and inherit his business.

"Look," Charlie tells Rolph, over the music. "The bird-watchers
are watching us."

Mildred and Fiona are sitting on chairs beside the dance floor,
waving in their long print dresses. It's the first time the children
have seen them without binoculars.

"Maybe we remind them of birds," Charlie says.

"Or maybe when there are no birds they watch people," Rolph
says.

"Come on, Rolphus," Charlie says. "Dance with me."

She takes hold of his hands. As they move together, Rolph feels
his self-consciousness miraculously fade, as if he were growing up
right there on the dance floor, becoming a boy who dances with
girls like his sister. Charlie feels it, too. In fact, this particular memory is one she'll return to again and again, for the rest of her life,
long after Rolph has shot himself in the head in their father's
house at twenty-eight: her brother as a boy, hair slicked flat, eyes
sparkling, shyly learning to dance. But the woman who remembers
won't be Charlie; after Rolph dies, she'll revert to her real name—
Charlene—unlatching herself forever from the girl who danced
with her brother in Africa. Charlene will cut her hair short and go

to law school. When she gives birth to a son, she'll want to name him Rolph, but her parents will still be too shattered for her to do this. So she'll call him that privately, just in her mind, and years later she'll stand with her mother among a crowd of cheering parents beside a field, watching him play, a dreamy look on his face as he glances at the sky.

"Charlie!" Rolph says. "Guess what I just figured out."

Charlie leans toward her brother, who is grinning with his news. He cups both hands into her hair to be heard above the thudding beat. His warm, sweet breath fills her ear.

"I don't think those ladies were ever watching birds," Rolph says.

DANIELLE EVANS

Someone Ought to Tell Her There's Nowhere to Go

FROM *A Public Space*

GEORGIE KNEW BEFORE HE LEFT that Lanae would be fucking Kenny by the time he got back to Virginia. At least she'd been up-front about it, not like all those other husbands and wives and girl-friends and boyfriends, shined up and cheesing for the five o'clock news on the day their lovers shipped out, and then jumping into bed with each other before the plane landed. When he'd told La-nae about his orders, she'd just lifted an eyebrow, shook her head, and said, "I told you not to join the goddamn army." Before he left for basic training, she'd stopped seeing him, stopped taking his calls even, said, "I'm not waiting for you to come home dead, and I'm damn sure not having Esther upset when you get killed."

That was how he knew she loved him at least a little bit; she'd brought the kids into it. Lanae wasn't like some single mothers, al-ways throwing their kid up in people's faces. She was fiercely pro-tective of Esther, kept her apart from everything, even him, and they'd been in each other's lives so long that he didn't believe for a second that she was really through with him this time. Still, he missed her when everyone else was getting loved visibly and he was standing there with no one to say good-bye to. Even her love was strategic, goddamn her, and he felt more violently toward the men he imagined touching her in his absence than toward the imagi-nary enemy they'd been war-gaming against. On the plane he had stared out of the window at more water than he'd ever seen at once, and thought of the look on her face when he said good-bye.

She had come to his going-away party like it was nothing, showed

up in skintight jeans and that cheap but sweet-smelling baby powder perfume and spent a good twenty minutes exchanging pleasantries with his mother before she even said hello to him. She'd
brought a cake that she'd picked up from the bakery at the second
restaurant she worked at, told one of the church ladies she was
thinking of starting her own cake business. *Really?* he thought, before she winked at him and put a silver fingernail to her lips. Lanae
could cook a little, but the only time Georgie remembered her trying to bake she'd burnt a cake she'd made from boxed mix and
then tried to cover it up with pink frosting. Esther wouldn't touch
the thing, and he'd run out and gotten a Minnie Mouse ice cream
cake from the grocery store. He'd found himself silently listing
these non-secrets, the things about Lanae he was certain of: she
couldn't bake, there was a thin but awful scar running down the
back of her right calf, her eyes were amber in the right light.

They'd grown up down the street from each other. He could not
remember a time before they were friends, but she'd had enough
time to get married and divorced and produce a little girl before
he thought to kiss her for the first time, only a few months before
he'd gotten his orders. In fairness, she was not exactly beautiful; it
had taken some time for him to see past that. Her face was pleasant
but plain, her features so simple that if she were a cartoon she'd
seem deliberately underdrawn. She was not big, exactly, but pil-
lowy, like if you pressed your hand into her it would keep sinking
and sinking because there was nothing solid to her. It bothered
him to think of Kenny putting his hand on her that way, Kenny
who'd once assigned numbers to all the waitresses at Ruby Tuesday
based on the quality of their asses, Kenny who'd probably never be
gentle enough to notice what her body did while it was his.

It wasn't Lanae who met him at the airport when he landed back
where he'd started. It was his mother, looking small in the crowd of
people waiting for arrivals. Some of them were bored, leaning up
against the wall like they were in line for a restaurant table, others
peered around the gate like paparazzi waiting for the right shot to
happen. His mother was up in front, squinting at him like she
wasn't sure he was real. She was in her nurse's uniform, and it
made her look a little ominous. When he came through security
she ran up to hug him so he couldn't breathe. "Baby," she said,
then asked how the connecting flight had been, and then talked

about everything but what mattered. Perhaps after all of his letters home she was used to unanswered questions, because she didn't ask any, not about the war, not about his health, not about the conditions of his honorable discharge or what he intended to do upon his return to civilian society.

She was all weather and light gossip through the parking lot. "The cherry blossoms are beautiful this year," she was saying as they rode down the Dulles Toll Road, and if it had been Lanae saying something like that he would have said *Cherry blossoms? Are you fucking kidding me?* but because it was his mother things kept up like that all the way around 395 and back to Alexandria. It was still too early in the morning for real rush-hour traffic, and they made it in twenty minutes. The house was as he'd remembered it, old, the bright robin's egg blue of the paint cheerful in a painfully false way, like a woman wearing red lipstick and layers of foundation caked over wrinkles. Inside, the surfaces were all coated with a thin layer of dust, and it made him feel guilty his mother had to do all of this housework herself, even though when he was home he almost never cleaned anything.

He'd barely put his bags down when she was off to work, still not able to take the whole day off. She left with promises of dinner later. In her absence it struck him that it had been a long time since he'd heard silence. In the desert there was always noise. When it was not the radio, or people talking, or shouting, or shouting at him, it was the dull purr of machinery providing a constant background soundtrack, or the rhythmic pulse of sniper fire. Now it was a weekday in the suburbs and the lack of human presence made him anxious. He turned the TV on and off four times, flipping through talk shows and soap operas and thinking this was something like what had happened to him: someone had changed the channel on his life.

The abruptness of the transition overrode the need for social protocol, so without calling first he got into the old Buick and drove to Lanae's, the feel of the leather steering wheel strange beneath his hands. The brakes screeched every time he stepped on them, and he realized he should have asked his mother how the car was running before taking it anywhere, but the problem seemed appropriate—he had started this motion, and the best thing to do was not to stop it.

Kenny's car outside of Lanae's duplex did not surprise him, nor did it deter him. He parked in one of the visitor spaces and walked up to ring the bell.

"Son of a bitch! What's good?" Kenny asked when he answered the door, as if Georgie had been gone for a year on a beer run.

"I'm back," he said, unnecessarily. "How you been, man?"

Kenny looked like he'd been Kenny. He'd always been a big guy, but he was getting soft around the middle. His hair was freshly cut in a fade, and he was already in uniform, wearing a shiny gold nametag that said KENNETH, and beneath that, MANAGER, which had not been true when Georgie left. Georgie could smell the apartment through the door, Lanae's perfume and floral air freshener not masking that something had been cooked with grease that morning.

"Not bad," he said. "I've been holding it down over here while you been holding it down over there. Glad you came back in one piece."

Kenny gave him a one-armed hug, and for a minute Georgie felt like an asshole for wanting to say *Holding it down? You've been serving people KFC.*

"Look man, I was on my way to work, but we'll catch up later, all right?" Kenny said, moving out of the doorway to reveal Lanae standing there, still in the T-shirt she'd slept in. Her hair was pulled back in a headscarf, and it made her eyes look huge. Kenny was out the door with a nod and a shoulder clasp, not so much as a backward glance at Lanae standing there. The casual way he left them alone together bothered Georgie. He wasn't sure if Kenny didn't consider him a threat or simply didn't care what Lanae did; either way he was annoyed.

"Hey," said Lanae, her voice soft, and he realized he hadn't thought this visit through any further than that.

"Hi," he said, and looked at the clock on the wall, which was an hour behind schedule. He thought to mention this, then thought against it.

"Georgie!" Esther yelled through the silence, running out of the kitchen, her face sticky with pancake syrup. He was relieved she remembered his name. Her hair was done in pigtails with little pink barrettes on them; they matched her socks and skirt. Lanae could win a prize for coordinating things.

"Look at you, little ma," he said, scooping her up and kissing her cheek. "Look how big you got."

"Look how bad she got, you mean," Lanae said. "Tell Georgie how you got kicked out of day care."

"I got kicked out of day care," Esther said matter-of-factly. Georgie tried not to laugh. Lanae rolled her eyes.

"She hides too much," she said. "Every time they take the kids somewhere, this one hides, and they gotta hold everyone up looking for her. Last time they found her, she scratched the teacher who tried to get her back on the bus. She can't pull this kind of stuff when she starts kindergarten."

Lanae sighed, and reached up to put her fingers in her hair, but all it did was push the scarf back. Take it off, he wanted to say. Take it off, and put clothes on. He wanted it to feel like real life again, like their life again, and with him dressed and wearing cologne for the first time in months, and her standing there in a scarf and T-shirt, all shiny Vaselined thighs and gold toenails, they looked mismatched.

"Look, have some breakfast if you want it," she said. "I'll be out in a second. I need to take a shower, and then I gotta work on finding this one a babysitter before my shift starts."

"When does it start?"

"Two."

"I can watch her. I'm free."

Lanae gave him an appraising look. "What *are* you doing these days?"

"Today, nothing."

"Tomorrow?"

"Don't know yet."

"I talked to your mom a little while ago," Lanae said, which was her way of telling him she knew. Of course she knew. How could Lanae not know, gossipy mother or no gossipy mother?

"I'm fine," he said. "I'll take good care of her."

"If Dee doesn't get back to me, you might have to," said Lanae. She walked off and Georgie made himself at home in her kitchen, grabbing a plate from the dish rack and taking the last of the eggs and bacon from the pans on the stove. Esther sat beside him and colored as he poured syrup over his breakfast.

"So what do you keep hiding from?" he asked.

"Nothing." Esther shrugged. "I just like the trip places better. Day care smells funny and the kids are dumb."

"What did I tell you about stupid people?" Georgie asked.

"I forget." Esther squinted. "You were gone a long time."

"Well, I'm back now, and you're not going to let stupid people bother you anymore," Georgie said, even though neither of these promises was his to make.

Honestly, watching Esther was good for him. His mother was perplexed, Kenny was amused, Lanae was skeptical. But Esther could not go back to her old day care, and Dee, the woman down the street who ran an unlicensed day care in her living room, plopped the kids in front of the downstairs television all afternoon and could only be torn away from her soaps upstairs if one of them hit someone or broke something. It wasn't hard for Georgie to be the best alternative. He became adequate as a caretaker. He took Esther on trips. They read and reread her favorite books. He learned to cut the crusts off of peanut butter and jelly sandwiches. Over and above her protests that the old sitter had let the kids stay up to watch *Comic View,* he made sure she was washed and in bed and wearing matching pajamas by the time Lanae and Kenny got home from their evening shifts.

"Are you sure it doesn't remind you . . . ," his mother started once, after gently suggesting he look for a real job, but she let the thought trail off unfinished.

"I wasn't *babysitting* over there, ma."

"I know," she said, but she didn't.

The truth was Esther was the opposite of a reminder. In his old life, his job had been to knock on strangers' doors in the middle of the night, hold them at gunpoint, and convince them to trust him. That was the easiest part of it. They went at night because during daytime the snipers had a clear shot at them, and anyone who opened the door, but even in the dark, a bullet or an IED could take you out like that. Sometimes when they got to a house there were already bodies. Other times there was nothing—a thin film of dust over whatever was left—things too heavy for the family to carry and too worthless for anyone to steal.

The sisters were sitting in the dark, huddled on the floor with their parents, when Georgie's unit pushed through the door. Pretty girls, big black eyes and sleepy baby-doll faces. The little one had cried when they first came through the door, and the older one, maybe nine, had clamped her hand tightly over the younger girl's mouth, like they'd been ordered not to make any noise. The father had been soft-spoken—angry, but reasonable. Usually, Georgie stood back and kept an eye out for trouble, let the lieutenant do the talking, but this time he went over to the girls himself, reached out his hand and shook their tiny ones, moist with heat and fear. He handed them each a piece of the candy they were supposed to give to children in cooperative families, and stepped back awkwardly. The older one smiled back at him, her missing two front teeth somehow reminding him of home.

They were not, in the grand scheme of things, anyone special. There were kids dying all over the place. Still, when they went back the next day, to see if the father would answer some more questions about his neighbors, and the girls were lying there, throats slit, bullets to the head, blood everywhere but parents nowhere to be found, he stepped outside the house to vomit.

When Georgie was twelve, a station wagon had skidded on the ice and swerved into his father's Tercel, crushing the car and half of his father, who had bled into an irreversible coma before Georgie and his mother got to the hospital to see him. Because his mother had to be sedated at the news, he'd stood at his father's bedside alone, staring at the body, the way the part beneath the sheet was unnaturally crumpled, the way his face began to look like melted wax, the way his lips remained slightly parted.

Georgie hadn't known, at first, that the sisters would stick with him like that.

"What's fucked up," Georgie said to Jones two days after, "is that I wished for a minute it was our guys who did it, some psycho who lost it. The way that kid looked at me. Like she really thought I came to save her. I don't want to think about them coming for her family because we made them talk. I don't want to be the reason they did her like that."

"What's the difference between you and some other asshole?" Jones said. "Either nobody's responsible for nothing, or every last motherfucker on this planet is going to hell someday."

After that, he'd turn around in the shower, the girls would be there. He'd be sleeping, and he'd open his eyes to see the little one hiding in the corner of his room. He was jumpy and too spooked to sleep. He told Ramirez about it, and Ramirez said you didn't get to pick your ghosts, your ghosts picked you.

"Still," he said. "Lieutenant sends you to talk to someone, don't say that shit. White people don't believe in ghosts."

But he told the doctors everything, and then some. He didn't care anymore what his file said, as long as it got him the fuck out of that place. And the truth is, right before the army let him go, sent him packing with a prescription and a once-a-month check-in with the shrink at the VA hospital, it had gotten really bad. One night he was sure the older girl had come to him in a dream and told him Peterson had come back and killed her, skinny Peterson who didn't even like to kill the beetles that slipped into their blankets every night, but nonetheless he'd held Peterson at gunpoint until Ramirez came in and snapped him out of it. Another time, he got convinced Jones really was going to kill him one day, and ran up to him outside of mess hall, grabbing for his pistol; three or four guys had to pull him off. Once, in the daytime, he thought he saw one of the dead girls, bold as brass, standing outside on the street they were patrolling. He went to shake her by the shoulders, ask her what she'd been playing at, pretending to be dead all this time, but he'd only just grabbed her when Ramirez pulled him off of her, shaking his head, and when he looked back at the girl's tear-streaked face before she ran for it like there was no tomorrow, he realized she was someone else entirely. Ramirez put an arm around him and started to say something, then seemed to think better of it. He looked down the road at the place that girl had just been, and shook his head.

"The fuck you think she's running to so fast anyway? Someone ought to tell her there's nowhere to go."

Sometimes Esther called him Daddy. When it started out, it seemed harmless enough. They were always going places that encouraged fantasy. Chuck E. Cheese's, where the giant rat sang and served pizza. The movies, where princesses lived happily ever after. The zoo, where animals who could have killed you in their natural state looked bored and docile behind high fences. Glitter Girl, Esther's favorite store in the mall, where girls three and up could get manicures, and any girl of any age could buy a crown or a pink T-shirt that said *Rock Star*. What was a pretend family relationship, compared to all that? Besides, it made people less nervous. When

she'd introduced him to strangers as her babysitter, all six feet
and two hundred and five pounds of him, they'd raised their eyebrows and looked at him as though he might be some kind of pred-
ator. Now people thought it was sweet when they went places together.

"This is my daddy," Esther told the manicurist at Glitter Girl,
where Georgie had just let Esther get her nails painted fuchsia. She
smiled at him conspiratorially. He had reminded her, gently, that
Mommy might not understand about their make-believe family,
and they should keep it to themselves for now.

"Day off, huh?" said the manicurist. She looked like a college
kid, a cute redhead with dangly pom-pom earrings. Judging by the
pocketbook she'd draped over the chair beside her, she was working there for kicks—if the logo on the bag was real, it was worth
three of Georgie's old army paychecks.

"I'm on leave," he said. "Army. I was in Iraq for a year. Just trying
to spend as much time with her as I can before I head back." He sat
up straighter, afraid somehow she'd see through the lie and refuse
to believe he'd been a soldier at all. When they'd walked in, she'd
looked at him with polite skepticism, as if in one glance she could
tell that Esther's coordinated clothes came from Target, that he
was out of real work and his gold watch was a knockoff that sometimes turned his wrist green, like perhaps the pity in her smile
would show them they were in the wrong store, without the humiliation of price tags.

"Wow," she murmured now, almost deferentially. She looked up
and swept an arc of red hair away from her face so she could look
at him directly. "A year in Iraq. I can't imagine. Of course you'll
spend all the time you can with her. They grow up so fast." She
shook her head with a sincerity he found oddly charming in a
woman who worked in a store that sold halter tops for girls with no
breasts.

"Tell you what, sweetheart," she said to Esther. "Since your daddy's
such a brave man, and you're such a good girl for letting him go
off and protect us, I'm going to do a little something extra for you.
Do you want some nail gems?"

Esther nodded, and Georgie turned his head away so the manicurist wouldn't see him smirk. Nail gems. Cherry blossoms. The
things people offered him by way of consolation.

*

When Esther's nails were drying, tiny heart-shaped rhinestones in the center of each one, and the salesgirl had gone to wait on the next customer, a miniature blonde with a functional RAZR phone but no parent in sight, Esther turned to him accusingly.

"You're going away," she said.

"I'm not," he said.

"You told the lady you were."

"It was pretend," he said, closing his eyes. "This is a make-believe place, it's okay to pretend here. Just like I'm your pretend daddy."

He realized he had bought her silence on one lie by offering her another, but he couldn't see any way out of it. So they wouldn't tell Lanae. So the salesgirl would flirt with him a little and do a little something extra for Esther next time. He *had* made sacrifices. Esther deserved nice things. Her mother worked two jobs and her real father was somewhere in Texas with his second wife. So what if it was the wrong things they were being rewarded for?

At the counter, he pulled out his wallet and paid for Esther's manicure with the only card that wasn't maxed out. Esther ignored the transaction entirely, wandering to the other end of the counter and reappearing with a purple flier. It had a holographic background, and under the fluorescent mall light seemed, appropriately, to glitter.

Come see Mindy with Glitter Girl! exclaimed the flier. Mindy was a tiny brunette, nine, maybe, who popped a gum bubble and held one hand on her hip, and the other extended to show off her nails, purple with gold stars in the middle.

"Everybody wants to see Mindy," said the manicurist. She winked at them, then ducked down to file his receipt.

"Maybe we could go," he said, reaching for the flier Esther was holding, but the smile that started from her dimples faded just as quickly.

"I don't really wanna," she said "It's prolly dumb anyway."

He followed her eyes to the ticket price, and understood that she'd taken in the number of zeros. He was stung, for a minute, that even a barely-five-year-old was that acutely aware of his limitations, then charmed by her willingness to protect him from them. It shouldn't be like that, he thought, a kid shouldn't understand that there's anything her parents can't do. Then again, he was not her father. He was a babysitter. He had less than a quarter the price of a ticket in his personal bank account—what was left of his disability check after he helped his mother out with the rent and utilities. He spent most of what Lanae paid him to watch Esther on Esther herself, because it made Lanae feel good to pay him, and him feel good not to take her money. He folded the Mindy flier into his pocket, and gently pulled off the twenty-dollar glittering tiara Esther had perched on her head to leave it on the counter. "Mommy will come back and get it later," he lied, over and above her objections. Even the way he disappointed her came as a relief.

Of course, the thought had crossed his mind. He never thought Kenny and Lanae were the real thing, didn't even think they did, really. Things had changed between her and Kenny in the year Georgie had been gone, softened and become more comfortable than whatever casual on-again, off-again thing they had before she and Georgie had dated, but he wasn't inclined to believe it was real. He pictured himself and Lanae as statues on a wedding cake —they were a pair. Kenny was a pastime. How could Georgie not hope that when she saw the way he was with Esther, she'd see he belonged with both of them?

But it wasn't like that was the *reason* he liked watching her. Not the only reason. Esther was a good kid. He thought it meant something, the way she didn't act up with him, didn't fuss and hide the way she used to at day care. But yeah, he got to talk to Lanae some. At night, when Lanae came home, and Esther was in bed, and Kenny was still at work for an hour, because being manager meant he was the last to leave the KFC, they talked a little. Usually he turned on a TV show right before she came in, so he could pretend he was watching it, but mostly he didn't need the excuse to stay. It was Lanae who had sat with him that week after his father had died, Lanae who, when she found out she was pregnant with Esther, had called him, not her husband or her best girlfriend. There was an easy kind of comfort between them, and when she came home and sat beside him on the couch and kicked off her flats and began to rub her own tired feet with mint-scented lotion, it was only his fear of upsetting something that kept him from reaching out to do it for her.

*

When Lanae came home the day he'd taken Esther to the mall, he wanted to tell her about the girl, the way she'd smiled at him, and scan her face for a flicker of jealousy. Then he remembered he'd earned the smile by lying. So instead he unfolded the Mindy flier from his pocket and passed it to her.

"Can you believe this shit?" he asked. "Five hundred a pop for a kids' show? When we were kids we were happy if we got five dollars for the movies and a dollar for some candy to sneak in."

"Hey." Lanae grinned. "I wanted two dollars, for candy *and* a soda. You were cheap." She held the flier at arm's length, then turned it sideways, like Mindy would make more sense that way. "Esther wants to go to this?"

"The lady at Glitter Girl said all the girls do. She said in most cities the tickets already sold out."

"That whole store is creepy anyway. And even if it was free, Esther don't need to be at a show where some nine-year-old in a belly shirt is singing at people to *come pop her bubble*. Fucking perverts," Lanae said.

"Who's a pervert?" asked Kenny. Georgie hadn't heard him come in, but Lanae didn't look surprised to see him standing in the doorway. He was carrying a steaming, grease-spotted bag that was meant to be dinner, which was usually Georgie's cue to leave. As Kenny walked toward them, Georgie slid away from Lanae on the couch, not because they'd been especially close to begin with, but because he wanted to maintain the illusion that they might have been. But Lanae stood up anyway, to kiss Kenny on the cheek as she handed him the flier.

"These people," said Lanae, "are perverts."

Kenny shook his head at the flier. Georgie silently reminded himself of the sophomore Kenny had dated their senior year of high school, a girl not much bigger than Mindy, and how Kenny had used to joke about how easy it was to pick her up and throw her around the room during sex.

"Esther ain't going to this shit," Kenny said. "This is nonsense."

"She can't," said Georgie. "You can't afford it."

Kenny stepped toward him, then back again just as quickly.

"Fuck you man," said Kenny. "Fuck you and the two dollars an hour we pay you."

He pounded a fist at the wall beside him, and then walked toward the hallway. A second later Georgie heard the bedroom door slam.

"Georgie," said Lanae, already walking after Kenny. "You don't have to be an asshole. He's not the way you remember him. He's trying. You need to try harder. And this Mindy shit? Esther will forget about it. Kids don't know. Next week she'll be just as worked up about wanting fifty cents for bubblegum."

But Esther couldn't forget about it. Mindy was on the side of the bus they took to the zoo. Mindy was on the nightly news, and every other commercial between kids' TV shows. Mindy was on the radio, lisping, *Pop my bub-ble, pop pop my bub-ble.* What he felt for Mindy was barely short of violence. He restrained himself from shouting back at the posters, and the radio, and the television: *Mindy, what is your position on civilians in combat zones? Mindy, what's your position on waterboarding? Mindy, do you think Iraq was a mistake?* He got letters, occasionally, from people who were still there—one from Jones, one from Ramirez, three from guys he didn't know that well and figured must have been lonely enough that they'd write to anyone. He hadn't read them.

He went back to the mall alone on the Saturday after he'd pissed Kenny off. He told himself he was there to talk to the manicure girl, pick up a little present for Esther and meanwhile maybe get something going on in his life besides wet dreams about Lanae, who'd been curt with him ever since the thing he said to Kenny. But when he got to the store, the redhead was leaning across the counter, giving a closed-mouth kiss on the lips to a kid in a UVA sweatshirt. He looked like an advertisement for fraternities. Georgie started to walk out, convinced he'd been wrong about the whole plan, but when the boyfriend turned around and walked away from the counter, the redhead saw him and waved.

"Hey!" she called. "Where's your little girl?"

"I came to pick up something to surprise her," he said. "She's been asking for a princess dress to go with the crown her mom got her."

He was pleased with the lie, until the redhead, whose nametag read ANNIE, led him over to the dress section and he realized he'd worn suits to weddings that cost less.

"Come to think of it," he said, "I'm not sure of her size. Maybe I oughta come back with her mother. Meantime, maybe she would like a wand."

"That's a good idea," said Annie. "All the kids are into magic these days."

Annie grabbed the wand that matched the crown and led him back to the register. The Mindy fliers had been replaced by a counter-length overhead banner. Mindy's head sat suspended on a background of pink bubbles.

"What's this Mindy kid do, anyway?" he asked.

"She sings."

"She sing well?"

"It's just cute, mostly. She has her own TV show, and her older sister sings too, but sexier. You get tickets for your daughter?"

"Nah," he said. "Bit pricey, for a five-year-old. Maybe next year."

"They ought to pay you people more. It's a shame. It's important, what you do."

She said this like someone who had read it somewhere. It would have seemed stupid to disagree and pathetic to nod, so he stood there, waiting for his change.

"Hey," said Annie. "We're having this contest to win tickets to the show. Limo ride, dinner, backstage passes, the whole shebang. All you have to do is make a video of your daughter saying why she wants to go. I bet if your daughter talks about how good she was while you were gone, she'd have a shot. It's right here, the contest info," she said, picking up a flier and circling the website. "Doesn't have to be anything fancy—you could do it on a camera phone."

"Thanks," he said, reaching to take the bag from her.

"Really," she said. "I mean it. Who's got a better story than you? Deadline's Tuesday. It'd be nice, if they gave it to someone who deserved it."

He liked to think that Annie's encouragement was tacit consent. He liked to think that if he'd had longer to think about it, he would have realized it was a bad idea. But as it was, by Sunday he'd convinced himself that it was a good idea, and by Monday he'd convinced Esther, who, after hearing the word *limousine,* needed only the slightest convincing that this was not the *bad* kind of lie. And when she started the first time, it wasn't even a lie, really. "Hi Glitter Girl," she began, all on her own, "for a whole year while he was in Iraq, I missed my daddy." Okay so he wasn't her father, but he liked to think she *had* missed him that much. When she said how much she wanted for him to take her to the show now that he was back, he thought it was honest: she wanted not just to see the show but to see it with him. He had downloaded the video from his phone and played it back for her, and was ready to send it like that, when Esther decided it wasn't good enough.

"Let's tell how you saved people," she said. "We have more time left."

He hesitated, but before he could say no, she asked him to tell her who he'd saved, and looking at her, the hopeful glimmer in her eyes, her pigtails tied with elastics with red beads on the end, matching her jumpsuit and the ruffles on her socks, he realized her intentions had been more sincere than his. How could they not be? Esther didn't doubt for a second that he had a heroic story to tell. He closed his eyes.

"Two girls," he said, finally. "A girl about Mindy's age. She was missing her two front teeth. And her little sister, who she loved a lot. Some bad men wanted to hurt them, and I scared off the bad men and helped them get away."

"Where'd they go then?"

"Back to their families," he said. He opened his mouth to say something, but nothing came out.

"Start the movie over," Esther said. "I'm going to say that too."

Somehow, he was not expecting the cameras. It was such a small thing, he'd thought. But there was Esther's video, labeled, *Contest Winner!: Esther, age 5, Alexandria, VA,* right on the Glitter Girl website. It was only a small relief that this was the last place Lanae would ever go herself, but who knew who else might stumble upon it? He'd named himself as her parent, given his name and phone and authorized the use of the images, and now he had messages, not just from Glitter Girl, who'd called to get their particulars, but from the *Washington Post,* and Channels 4 and 7 News. Even after the first few, he thought he could get this back in the bottle, that Lanae would never need to know. In his bathroom mirror, in the morning, he practiced what to say to the journalists to make them go away. He tried to think of ways to answer questions without making them think to ask more.

Listen, he told the Channel 4 reporter, I'd love to do a story, but Esther's mother has this crazy ex-boyfriend who's been threatening her for years, and if Esther's last name or picture were in the paper, we could be in a lot of trouble. Look, he told the Channel 7 reporter, the kid's been through hell this year, with me gone and her mom barely holding it together. It was hard enough for her to say it once. Please contact Glitter Girl for official publicity.

It was the *Post* reporter that did them in, the *Post* reporter and the free makeover Esther was supposed to get on her official prize pickup day. He figured it was back-page news, and anyway, Esther was so excited about it. They would paint her nails and take some pictures and give them the tickets, and that would be the end of it. When they walked into the store a week later, there was a giant pink welcome banner that proclaimed *Congratulations Esther!* and clouds of pale pink and white balloons. All of the employees and invited local media clapped their hands. Annie was there, beaming at them when they walked in, like she'd just won a prize for her science fair project. The CEO of Glitter Girl, a severe-looking woman with incongruous big blond hair, hugged Esther and shook his hand. Mindy's music played on repeat over the loudspeakers.

There was cake, and sparkling cider. The CEO gave a heartfelt toast. Annie gave him a hug, and slipped her phone number into his pocket. One of the other employees led Esther off. She came back in a sequined pink dress, a long brown wig, fluttery fake eyelashes, pink lipstick, and shiny purple nails. People took pictures. He was alarmed at first but she turned to him and smiled like he'd never seen a kid smile before, and he thought it couldn't be so bad, to give someone exactly what she wanted. Finally, the CEO of Glitter Girl handed them the tickets. She said Esther had already received some fan mail, and handed him a pile of letters. He looked at the return addresses: California, Florida, New York, Canada.

"Is there anything you'd like to say to all your fans, Esther?" shouted one of the reporters.

"I want to say," said Esther, "I am so happy to win this, but mostly I am so happy to have my daddy."

She turned and winked at him. She smiled a movie star grin. There was lipstick on her teeth. For the first time, he realized how badly he'd messed up.

It was two days later the first story ran. Esther had told the *Post* reporter her mommy worked at the Ruby Tuesday on Route 7, but when the reporter called her there to get a quote, Lanae had no idea what she was talking about, said she did have a daughter named Esther, but her daughter's father was in Texas and had never been in the army, and her daughter wasn't allowed in Glitter Girl or at any Mindy concert.

She called him on her break to ask him about it, but he said it must have been a mix-up, he didn't know anything about it.

"You'd damn well better not be lying to me, Georgie," she said, which meant she already knew he was.

That night he called the number Annie had given to him, wondered if she could meet him somewhere, pictured her long legs wrapped around his.

"Look," she said softly, "I'm sorry. I was being impulsive the other day. You're married, and I'm engaged, and I'm really proud of you, but it's just better if everything stays aboveboard. Let's not hurt anyone we don't have to."

Georgie hung up. He went downstairs and watched television with his mother, until she turned it off and looked at him.

"You know I watch the news during my break at the hospital," she said.

"Uh-huh," said Georgie. "They're not still shortchanging you your break time, are they?"

"Don't change the subject. Other day I coulda swore I saw Esther on TV. Channel 9. All dressed up like some hoochie princess, and talking about her *daddy,* who was in the *army.*"

"Small world," said Georgie. "A lot of coincidences."

But it was a lie, about the world being small. It was big enough. By the time he drove to Lanae's house the next morning, there was a small crowd of reporters outside. They didn't even notice him pull up. Kenny kept opening the door, telling them they had the wrong house. Finally, he had to go to work, walked out in his uniform. Flashbulbs snapped.

"Are you the one who encouraged the child to lie, or does the mother have another boyfriend?" yelled one reporter.

Georgie couldn't hear what Kenny said back, but for the first time in his life, Georgie thought Kenny looked brave.

"Did you do this for the money?" yelled another. "Was this the child's idea?"

All day, it was like that. Long after Kenny had left, the reporters hung out on the front steps, broadcasting to each other. Lanae had already given back the tickets; beyond that, she had given no comment. He could imagine the face she made when she refused to comment, the steely eyes, the way everything about her could freeze.

"How," the reporters wanted to know, "did this happen?"

Their smugness made him angry. There were so many things they could never understand about how, so many explanations they'd never bother to demand. How could it not have happened?

At night, when no one had opened the door for hours, the reporters trickled off, one by one, their questions still unanswered. Lanae must have taken the day off from work; her car was still in its parking space, the lights in the house still on. Finally, he made his way to the house and rang the doorbell. She was at the peephole in an instant. She left the chain on and opened the door as wide as it could go without releasing it.

"Georgie," she said. She shook her head, then leaned her forehead against the edge of the door so that just her eyeball was looking at his. "Georgie, go away."

"Lanae," he said. "You know I didn't mean it to go like this."

"Georgie, my five-year-old's been crying all day. My phone number, here and at my job, is on the Internet. People from Iowa to goddamn Denmark have been calling my house all day, calling my baby a liar and a little bitch. She's confused. You're confused. I think you need to go for a while."

"Where?" he asked.

He waited there on the front step until she'd turned her head from his, stepped back into the house, and squeezed the door shut. He kept standing there, long after the porch light went off, not so much making an argument as waiting for an answer.

JOSHUA FERRIS

The Valetudinarian

FROM The New Yorker

THE DAY AFTER Arty Groys and his wife retired to Florida, she
was killed in a head-on collision with a man fleeing the state to escape the discovery of frauds perpetrated under the guise of good
citizenship. Arty found himself bereft in a strange land. He knew
none of the street names or city centers. His condominium was un-
derfurnished and undecorated. The cemetery where Meredith was
buried was too bright and too hot on the day of the interment and
on every visit thereafter. Whenever Arty had imagined one of them
at the other's funeral, he had pictured rain, black-clad figures under black umbrellas, the cumbersome dispersal of the gathered
through mud in the lowest spirits. He saw Meredith leaning down
to grasp at one last memory as their daughter, Gina, bent to encourage her to stand, both women weeping — for it was always Arty
who died in Arty's daydreams. But on the day that Meredith was
laid to rest golf and tennis beckoned to retirees in radiant waves of
sun, and the fishermen of Tarpon Cove sported cheerfully with the
devilish snook.

To the surprise of his children, Arty didn't return to Ohio. Over
time they got the sense that he had stalled, then that his wheels
had shifted into reverse, and then that he was heading backward at
full speed, toward some oncoming atrocity — a slow and entirely
psychological reenactment of their mother's death. He was without responsibilities after a long professional career, and for three
years now he had been without the one person, helpmeet and bick-
ering companion, who could shake him out of his recliner and
force him into the world.

His worst instincts claimed him. He started a feud with Mrs. Zegerman, his neighbor in Bequia Tower, one of three tall condominium buildings overlooking Naples Bay just west of the Tamiami Trail. Arty suggested in a note slipped under Mrs. Zegerman's door that her Shih Tzu, Cookie, whose incessant yapping came right through the walls, deserved to be shot by Nazis. Mrs. Zegerman accused him of being an anti-Semite. Arty countered that he was not an anti-Semite but an anti–Shih Tzu and that all Shih Tzus should be rounded up. A few days later, Mrs. Zegerman found an unopened box of rat poison near the potted phlox beside her welcome mat, and the tension escalated from there.

In other respects, Arty withdrew. His brooding caused him to lose golf partners and alienated him somewhat from his one true friend, fit and generous Jimmy Denton. Jimmy had come down to Florida after making a killing in the Danville (Illinois, not Connecticut) real estate market. Jimmy had taken Arty golfing and talked baseball with him, but now it was growing late on Arty's birthday, and he had not yet received a call from Jimmy or from any of his children. He was starting to feel as unloved as he had the day of his ninth birthday, when only two of the eleven invited guests showed up to his party, a pair of twins who took off their shirts and came together at the arm to show where they had been separated.

He was instantly relieved to hear the first ring of the phone, an old rotary that vibrated with the vigor of the Mechanical Age. He let it rumble and stop, rumble and stop three full times so that the caller would not suspect how lonely he was. After the third ring, he snatched it up. He let the pause grow and then said a very casual hello. It was his daughter, Gina, who lived by herself in a horse stable in Belmont.

"Happy birthday, Daddy!" she cried into his ear. "Happy birthday, happy birthday!"

"Oh, Gina, God bless you for calling," Arty said. "Happy birthday to me. Happy birthday to your old man."

"I'm sorry I didn't call earlier, but we had to put a horse down today. His name was The Jolly Bones, and he was absolutely everyone's favorite. He was almost sort of human. This one time —"

"My gallbladder's ruined," Arty declared.

"Your gallbladder, Daddy? How did that happen?"

"Yes, my gallbladder. Dr. Klutchmaw says it has to be removed. First a low-glucose plasma concentration, then the heart, now the gallbladder. I have never given a thought to my gallbladder my entire life, but evidently it wears down like an old tire. I didn't mean to make such terrible decisions."

"What decisions are those, Dad?"

"Klutchmaw tells me I could have prevented this if I had stayed away from fatty foods forty years ago, but no one gives you a manual, Gina. No one hands you a manual."

"I wish you wouldn't be so gloomy," Gina said. "Not today. Not on your birthday."

"I want you to do yourself a favor and stay away from fatty foods, my girl, because a worn-out gallbladder is no walk in the park. Klutchmaw has a man who plans to remove it and that means going under the anesthetic, and I may be diabetic. I'm waiting on the test results."

"Well, that sounds good," Gina said. "But what about today, Daddy, what do you plan to do on your birthday?"

"If I had known about all of this forty years ago, I wouldn't be so gloomy today, but no one gives you a manual. The cigarettes ruined my bowels and I smoked them only ten years before I noticed the warnings. When I go, I have a feeling it will be because of the lungs or the bowels and not the heart after all."

"Do you have a golf game lined up today, Daddy?"

"I'm too fat to play golf anymore," Arty said. "It's a good thing you called when you did, sweetheart. I was just about to go into the kitchen and attack the Oreos."

Gina stayed on the line until she was called away. They were having a little ceremony for The Jolly Bones. She encouraged Arty to get out of the house for what remained of his birthday and to have a good time, maybe by riding his bicycle.

The sun was never so part of the earth's essence and beauty as when its golden meniscus quivered at the edge of Arty's balcony, at the top of his sliding glass doors, and his condo, furnished at last with that marriage of wicker and cushions, filled with the light of a dying day, which colored the clouds and restored to the sky all the pastoral visions of the earliest era.

After finishing the Oreos and three glasses of milk, Arty struggled not to dial a number long committed to memory. Doing so went against Klutchmaw's express demands, and it might tie up the phone right as someone was calling to pass along kind birthday wishes. But in the end he reasoned there was no point aging another year if you couldn't spoil yourself. A familiar voice answered after only half a ring. It was Brad. Brad put in the order for a large meat-lover's pizza and a two-liter Sprite. Anxious about tying up the line, Arty nevertheless announced that it was his birthday.

"Happy birthday, Arty," Brad said. "How old are you?"

"Yes, happy birthday to me. Thank you, Brad. I'm a composite sixty-six, but that doesn't tell the whole story. I've lost much of my aerobic potential, so I put the lungs at about a hundred. I put the legs at eighty-five. How old are you, Brad? They don't give you a manual, you know. I don't want you to be shocked when they tell you they're coming to pull all your teeth."

"Arty, man, the other lines are screaming. Can we talk tomorrow?"

"I'll talk to you tomorrow, Brad, you bet. God bless for calling. Happy birthday to me."

"Happy birthday, Arty."

By one of those good fortunes of timing that lonely people long for, the phone began to ring just seconds after Arty set down the receiver. This racket of activity gave an impression of momentary pandemonium that brought joy to Arty's one day. Again, he let the phone ring three interminable times before answering, and then, as the mouthpiece traveled through the air toward his lips, said casually, ". . . think they're going to have a wonderful year this year."

"Dad?"

It was his son, Paul, calling from San Francisco. Paul worked in a hospice where he sat among the terminally ill and watched them die. Arty was proud of him—Paul had given his life to a good cause—though not as proud as he would have been if Paul were the owner of a chain of hospices scattered across the country.

"Oh, Pauly, God bless you for calling," Arty said. "Happy birthday to me."

"Is there someone there with you, Dad? Should I call back?"

"No, it's just my friend Jimmy Denton. You know Jimmy. We're sitting here talking baseball. You know I love talking baseball with an old friend."

"Well, I'm just calling to wish you a happy birthday."

"I talked to Dr. Klutchmaw's office today," Arty said. "It doesn't look good."

"Remind me again," Paul said. "Which one is Klutchmaw?"

"Dr. Klutchmaw is my internist. He tells me the manufacturer is recalling the stent. There's a flaw in the thing. It's not fair, Pauly."

"They don't hand out manuals, do they, Pop."

"No, they don't. You think your heart stent is going to last you forever, and then the manufacturer recalls the damn thing."

"Well, everything's okay here. The children are fine, Dana's fine. Matter of fact, she's sitting next to me and wants to wish you a happy birthday. Here she is."

"Hold on, Paul, hold it just a second before you give the phone to Dana. I want to tell you something, son. Now listen to me, Paul. Odds are, you're going to get fat. You're going to get goddam fat and you're going to get the gout. You're going to have hypertension and high cholesterol and you're going to be put on drugs with the worst side effects. They'll make you sweat in odd places. You won't be able to focus or count. Your children will grow distant. Dana will be dead. And you'll be lonely, Paul. I should have told you this years ago, to prepare you, but I didn't know it myself. I just want you to be prepared."

There was a long pause before Dana's voice said, "Hello? Arty?"

"Oh, hello, Dana."

"Happy birthday, Arty."

"God bless you. Happy birthday to me."

Arty spoke to his daughter-in-law for a while about heart stents, gallstones, impacted bowels, insulin shots, and stomach ulcers before he announced that he was being referred to an oncologist for twinges that might indicate a tumor.

"Oof!" Dana cried. "Meredith, you can't do that, honey, you're too big! Arty, Meredith just ran into the room and jumped on my lap. I'm on the phone with Grandpa, honey. Do you want to say hi to Grandpa? It's his birthday today. Say happy birthday to Grandpa."

A great battle of wills commenced behind a fortress of muffled static that collapsed totally in brief intervals during which Arty heard Dana scream, "Meredith Ann! Talk to your—" and Meredith howl as if in terrible pain, before a silence prevailed and a teary Meredith said, "Hello?"

"Hello, Meredith. It's your grandpa."

"Hello," Meredith said.

"Happy birthday to me."

"Happy birfday."

Like many older people who find themselves on the phone with
children of unstable attention spans, Arty began to talk nonstop,
flinging at his granddaughter every expression of pride and love,
interspersed with questions intended not to sate a genuine curiosity but to confirm Meredith's continued presence on the other end
of the line. Arty was convinced that she had no interest in him, that
as far as little Meredith was concerned he was as good as dead. This
provoked the panic that fueled the blithering that he hoped might
overcome Meredith's annihilating silence. He asked if she knew
what an internist was.

"An internist is just a doctor," he explained. "My internist's name
is Klutchmaw. I'm not crazy about him, but he takes my insurance.
One day you'll understand what an important measure of a good
doctor that is. Do you like going to the doctor? I don't like it because it always means there might be something terribly wrong
with me. You should be very happy that there's nothing wrong with
you yet, Meredith. You have your teeth, you can go outside and run
around, your bowels have yet to liquefy."

Arty paused a moment. Where was he going with this conversation, and would her parents approve? Yet seconds later he continued, for when if not now to relay to her the stealth of years, the
inexorable betrayals of the body, the perfidiousness of the eventu-
alities?

"They don't give you a manual, Meredith, and who's going to
prepare you if not your grandpa? I'm not going to go pussyfoot-
ing around your bowel movements on account of your innocence,
because one day you're going to wake up and wonder why the
world perpetrated treacherous lies against such a perfect creature
as yourself, and I want you to look back on your old grandpa and
remember him as somebody who told you the truth about what's
in store for you, and not as one of these propagandists for perpetual youth just because right now your constitutionals happen to be
nice and firm. Do you know what a constitutional is, Meredith? I
will tell you."

Meredith dropped the phone and ran out of the room. Arty
spoke tinnily into the carpet. After a while the phone went dead
and then, a few hours later, began to ring, which sent Paul into a
frenzy. He finally came upon it on the floor of the bedroom and
wondered why he had left it there of all places.

*

Arty had hoped Jimmy Denton would call, but after his conversation with Meredith, despite his importuning eyes, the stolid black machine remained mute. He imagined a conversation with Jimmy, who, knowing that it was his birthday, would indulge him, on this one day only, as he expressed yet again his mystification that Bob Sherwood and Chaz Yalinsky no longer invited him to play golf. They'd made a great foursome, Jimmy and Arty against Bob and Chaz. But now he had no one to play golf with, no friend but Jimmy, no companion in life—not even one person who might call him on his birthday.

The doorbell rang. Mrs. Zegerman's Shih Tzu pierced the air with high-pitched barks, which ordinarily felt to Arty like an axe whooshing around his head, but as he moved from rug to Spanish tile he tried not to let it get to him, because someone, oh someone was at his door. He dismissed a late delivery of flowers from one of his children in favor of his old friend Jimmy Denton, there to take him for a beer after shaking free of Jojo, his lusty and calisthenic Oriental wife, who had never liked Arty and made no attempt to hide it. But just as he was about to open the door he realized with a sinking heart that it was probably not flowers and probably not Jimmy Denton but Dusty, Brad's counterpart, there to deliver the meat-lover's and two-liter.

It was not Dusty.

Standing opposite him, partially lit by the bulb shining from its gaslight cage, was a young woman dressed in a miniskirt of stretch fabric and a bosomy blouse of silver lamé. Beneath her makeup lay a pallor that had been set in place by long, hard winters. Her hair, straining to be blond, had washed out into a color resembling sugarless gum of a lesser flavor. It fell to her shoulders in two coarse and wavy cascades. She carried nothing in her hands, no purse, no personal possessions of any kind, but when Arty opened the door she raised her hand and dimmed her eye, taking one last drag from a cigarette before extinguishing it under her bright silver heel.

"You are Arty Growsie?"

"Groys," Arty said.

"Your friend is Jimmy?"

"Jimmy Denton?"

"Is not necessary to know last name."

Arty was pretty sure the woman was a prostitute. He was at his core a fearful, law-abiding, overly cautious man, yet he let her walk

past him into his apartment without a word. She was spritzed for a
cheap night at a loud club. Before shutting the door, he sensed, by
way of Cookie's silence, Mrs. Zegerman at her peephole, holding
the trembling dog to her crêpe-paper chest.

The girl took a seat on the wicker sofa. Arty situated himself next
to her, not so close as to fall within the weather of her communica-
ble diseases but not so far as to appear rude. He was touched that
Jimmy Denton would do this for him. The last time he'd seen
Jimmy, at the dog track, Jimmy had said that Arty's yapping was as
annoying as his faggot cousin's at family gatherings. Arty had been
going on about Bob and Chaz just as one of Jimmy's dogs had come
in dead last. Arty excused himself, and bought a hot dog and a
jumbo pretzel, which he ate in the car as he drove home. They
hadn't spoken since.

"Well, God bless you for coming," he said to the girl, reaching out to touch her hand but pulling back in time. "God bless you
and God bless Jimmy Denton. It's my birthday, and I was feeling
lonely."

"Ridiculous for handsome and strong man ever to feel lonely,"
the girl said.

"I am no longer handsome and I am no longer strong," Arty said.
"I'm fat and I have a bad heart and my internist has warned me
that I'm on the edge of diabetes."

The girl said, "Two requirements to continue." She reached into
her bra and pulled out a condom and a blue pill. "Condom is necessary to use during making love. Erection pill is added expense
but is paid for already by your friend."

"Well, happy birthday to me," Arty said. "Happy birthday to old
Arty Groys. But I'm afraid I can't take that pill. It is expressly forbidden to me by my internist, Dr. Klutchmaw. It interferes with the
nitrates I take for my bad heart."

"Do you need pill to make penis work?"

Arty nodded his head.

"We gave it good try then," the girl said as she stood.

Arty surprised himself by reaching out and grabbing her hand.
"Wait," he said. "Don't leave. Have you eaten? I have a pizza coming. We could have dinner."

"You eat greasy pizza and you have bad heart?"

"Please, sit down."

The girl sat.

"Pizza is one of my compensations," Arty said. "I don't have to take a pill to eat a pizza. Well, to lower my cholesterol and blood pressure, but that's different. I eat the pizza and take those pills, but I don't die. I take that pill, I could die. I could have a heart attack."

"Friend of mine from my country swallowed twenty-four pills with liquid pipe cleaner and then took razor blade and cut open her veins from wrist to elbow," the girl said. "Now she lives in North Carolina and works at Holiday Inn."

A stunned abatement of his own concerns stole over Arty and forced him to look at the girl more closely. She stared back at him with the neutral innocence of a child waiting obediently for the start of a piano lesson.

"She survived?"

"Now she is married to American undertaker who steals all her money, but he doesn't beat her, so is okay for time being. He fought for America in Vietnam War. Did you fight for America in Vietnam War?"

Her questions ended not in an inquisitorial lilt but with a descending, matter-of-fact thud.

"I was in the service from 1963 to 1966."

"Were you shot?"

"Shot? I was never shot. I fixed chairs and typewriters and other things. I never left Texas."

"I have been shot twice. Here," she said, "and here." She showed him two scars, each a quarter-size debit of loose yellow skin, one in the stomach and one in the leg.

"What was *that?*" he asked.

She lifted her blouse again. "This? From exploded appendix. Ambulance driver took his sweet time. Nurse and doctor take their sweet time. Everyone is taking their sweet time while I am drowning in poison. I am in hospital twenty-six days."

"How old are you?"

"Eighteen."

"Eighteen?"

"I am not telling real age to anyone."

Arty looked at her again. Though he guessed that she was no older than thirty, her pale demeanor and sodden dye job had consigned her to an eternal middle age. He imagined her on her days off lighting cigarettes from noon till dawn, imagined them burning down in a room defined by drawn shades and muttering talk shows. He saw the crow's-feet that worked against her beauty, but he also saw the beauty. She must have a robust constitution, he thought, immune to colds and despair, unsentimentally surviving. He knew that if he had been born into the same conditions that she had been born into, he wouldn't have made it to nine, ten at most. He had said it a hundred times, a thousand, a hundred thousand, to whoever would listen, but now he merely thought it, with that shock of having stumbled upon a perfect demonstration of the rule: "They don't give you a manual."

"I have question," she said. "Life is so tough, you are afraid of one little pill? It is one little nothing. You take it and we have good time. Maybe I come back next week. Every week we have good time together, and you no longer sit on this nice sofa and think, Oh, poor me, I'm so lonely, I'm such lonely old man."

She was close now. He was starting to like her overbearing perfume. She placed the pill on his knee. He stared at it. He had never had to consider this option before. He rarely met new people; he was too scared of rejection. Yet here was a girl willing to take him in her arms and kindly ignore the humbling sight of him blundering his way toward ecstasy. Those stern warnings to heart patients not to take such pills—they were probably just the exaggerations of executives afraid of lawsuits.

The girl straightened herself on the sofa and reached around her back and untied something essential. She lifted her blouse to reveal the kind of breasts that Arty believed were seen up close only by men who dealt cocaine or played professional football. There was disbelief, and then there was what passed beyond the realm of the comprehensible into the sensuous world of warrior kings. Dusty arrived with the pizza. Arty ignored the doorbell.

Mrs. Zegerman resembled a mosquito. She had long, thin limbs and a small, very concentrated face whose severe features were drawn dramatically forward, culminating in a sharply pointed nose.

She had passed the day waiting for an apology from Ilsa Brooks, with whom she had had a falling-out after arguing over a movie they had seen together on a recent Sunday afternoon. Ilsa had thought the film was a return to the screwball romantic comedies of the nineteen-thirties, but Mrs. Zegerman wanted to know in what nineteen-thirties comedy was everything "F this" and "F that." Ilsa told her to get with the times. Mrs. Zegerman responded by saying that matters of common decency were timeless, and now the two women weren't speaking.

She was preparing for bed when she thought she heard the doorbell ring again, and again her first thought was that it had to be Ilsa, come to apologize. It would be such a relief to have her matinee partner back again, but as her bare feet left the Persian rug for the red Spanish tile she remembered that Ilsa had returned north to Chillicothe on Wednesday, and she quickly reverted to the opinion that her former friend's ideas of both movies and morals were wanting.

Through the peephole, she watched the pizza boy pointlessly ringing Arty's doorbell until she could take it no more. She stepped out into the open-air vestibule to explain the situation: Arty Groys was inside that condo with a woman who had appeared half naked on his doorstep. Mrs. Zegerman was convinced that the two of them were in there interrelating. It was shameful and disgusting. It was also holding up commerce.

"Arty's in there with a woman?" the boy said. "Our Arty?"

She had no idea what he meant by "our."

"You sure he didn't just kick off?"

"He's not dead," she replied.

"Well, God damn," the boy said, removing the pizza from its spacesuit pouch and placing it with the Sprite to one side of Arty's door before nodding good-bye and galloping down the stairs. "Tell him it's on the house!" he cried. This was not the first time she had watched him go. He was a well-tanned boy. Perhaps he surfed. For a brief second, she imagined her body warmed by the sun and her head pillowed by the sand, while out in the distance he waved to her between surging whitecaps.

She stepped back inside her apartment and picked up Cookie. She decided to wait there for Arty to emerge with his floozy so that she could give him a piece of her mind. A moment later, Arty's door slammed like a shot. Mrs. Zegerman turned in time to catch a glimpse of the departing girl, who fled down the same stairs as the delivery boy while quickly buttoning her blouse, carrying her silver heels in one hand. Mrs. Zegerman naturally assumed that she had been repulsed by the sight of Arty's horrible penis. Then a long time passed at the peephole, and Arty didn't come out for his pizza.

Mrs. Zegerman found Arty on the floor of his living room. She was thrown into a panic that emptied her mind entirely of common sense. She simply did not know what to do, and the sensation of helplessness resounded with only one thing she remembered in all her years: the terror of the day that Mr. Zegerman had stumbled while walking along the wharf and hit his head on that utterly purposeless green metal thingy. She remembered the seep of his warm blood through her summer dress as she cried out for help. Now it was her neighbor whom she might have loved for years and years, so swiftly and completely had she been struck dumb at the sight of him. He had collapsed between wicker sofa and African coffee table, his legs hairless and white as wax, his stomach a great pale mound, and his face as pinched and pink as crab shell.

"Oh, thank God," Arty said, when he caught sight of his neighbor. "Call the paramedics, Mrs. Zeger—"

He was cut off by a terrible grip, a twisting vine-strangle of the heart—but his words kicked Mrs. Zegerman into high gear. She rushed over to him throbbing with adrenaline and clamped one of his arms around her slender neck like a nutcracker. She restored him to respectability by returning to its rightful place the underwear that dangled around one ankle. Supporting his bulk all the way to the elevator, she planned to get him downstairs and drive him to the hospital in her Mazda. If she had learned one thing from the death of Mr. Zegerman, it was never to put your faith in the timeliness of men who drive ambulances. But they had to wait too long, much too long, for the infernal elevator, which liked to clamor below with buckling metal and other echoes of motion the minute the call button was pressed, but tended to dally there before zooming right past, up and up, to some grander view of Bequia Tower. At last she told Arty that they would have to take the stairs, and she carried him over to their brink and started the descent with her weighty dying charge. On the final flight, however, they got tangled up and he flew off her, bouncing down brutally step after step, while it was everything she could do to catch the banister and not follow him. She took one look at the twitching body that lay in a yellow patch of security light and, scared that she had killed him, raced upstairs again to call an ambulance.

She outsmarted the hospital by telling the nurses that she was Arty's wife. They didn't question her, and she had license to come and go as she wished. The first two days, he was incommunicado, lost beneath a breathing apparatus when he was not in surgery. To move out of the ICU into a regular unit took another five days, by which time she had found his insurance card and called his children.

"What does this mean?" Paul asked her when she broke the news. "Will he live?"

"How will he get around?" Gina asked. "Who will take care of him?"

Mrs. Zegerman assured them that she would not abandon Arty until one of them could make it down to Florida, and even after they had left again. It occurred to her that perhaps he had said something to his children about her, as she didn't have to explain her involvement beyond mentioning the fact that she was a neighbor.

Arty's knee was in bad shape from the fall. Once his heart had fully recovered, he would need an operation to determine the extent of the ligament damage, followed by a long period of physical therapy. His weight would be a significant impediment to recovery. The orthopedic surgeon predicted that it might be as long as a year before her husband walked again.

Mrs. Zegerman took the elevator up to his hospital room. The coarse, almost particulate sun was showering in through the window, filling the small antiseptic space with a false radiance. There was no need for sun, as his children's flowers had wilted and died days earlier, and the competition between the outside heat and the central air only made the room feel claustrophobic and unpleasant. These things might have gone unnoticed had her first observation not covered her in a thin sweat of panic: the bed was empty. Arty was not in his room. Had he had another heart attack? Had he died overnight? Overnight! Gone. She wished she had never got involved. Oh, damn it. The dog was enough.

Suddenly the toilet roared and the bathroom door was thrown open. Arty Groys came staggering out, favoring his good leg while fiddling with the fly of the pressed trousers she had brought for

him the day before. Mrs. Zegerman was beside herself, for he was
walking in defiance of the doctor's predictions. She rushed over to
him with exclamations of dismay.

"What are you doing up and about, Mr. Groys? Your knee is in
no condition for you to be walking around, to say nothing of your
heart."

"God bless you, Mrs. Zegerman, God bless you," he said. "But
the heart has never been better, and the knee is only knocked off
center a little. If I had remembered to take that cane with me, I
would hardly have noticed a thing."

Mrs. Zegerman saw an ivory-handled cane in the far corner of
the room. She turned to Arty with surprise, as though she had just
found something unsavory in his sock drawer. She had been with
him practically every waking minute since he had entered the hospital. "Where did that come from?" she asked.

"We must get out of here, Mrs. Zegerman," Arty said. "We must
get over to Jimmy Denton's house."

"Who's Jimmy Denton?"

"Jimmy Denton is the man responsible for all this, God bless
him. He never visited or sent flowers, but no doubt his Asiatic wife
is to blame for that. She must have closely guarded the fact that I
was dying only ten miles away. She has always been jealous of our
friendship. Now, we must do this on the sly. Are you ready?"

"But you haven't even been released yet, Mr. Groys."

"Mrs. Zegerman, I must see Jimmy Denton. He knows how to
put me in contact with the girl who saved my life."

Mrs. Zegerman was under the impression that she had been the
one who had saved his life. Nevertheless, she found herself sneaking Arty Groys out of the hospital. They simply walked down the
corridor, into the elevator, and out the main exit. He did remarkably well with the assistance of his cane.

"They did a fine job in there," he said, "but I'm happy to be leaving. Too many people die in hospitals. You're safer on a Chinese
beach with those scavengers and their rusted circuit boards. And
would you look at that," he added, when they had walked through
the automatic doors and entered the day. "The sun is shining so
gloriously. Two weeks ago, I would have called that glare."

Jimmy and Jojo Denton lived in a gated community whose thriving
heart was a golf course dotted with sun-dappled ponds—a per-

fectly manicured oasis of hurricane-proof Spanish Colonials, manatee mailboxes, and geriatric promiscuity. Mrs. Zegerman, staying put at Arty's insistence, watched her neighbor get out of the car in front of a gaudy palazzo and limp across the dense lawn. He returned not five minutes later, hastily shutting the door.

"Jojo dropped a dime, Mrs. Zegerman. We have to get to East Naples, and pronto. Apparently, they all crowd into a single apartment unit. The thought of it just tears the heart out of my chest."

"Who are you talking about, Mr. Groys?"

"The young lady who saved my life. Now, please, Mrs. Zegerman, put the car in motion and head east."

Mrs. Zegerman thought that it was imperative to get Arty Groys home, to set him up, with his bad leg and weak heart, in bed or on his sofa, with pillows and remotes and restorative liquids, and to discuss his dietary preferences, so that she would know what to buy at the grocery store. She had believed that he was in for a long convalescence, and that the obvious indifference with which the widower's children treated their father guaranteed that she would preside with crowned authority over many months of incremental improvement.

But Arty's sudden mobility had made her heart sink. The long months of slow, sequestered progress vanished instantly, casting doubts on her plans, and his oblique agenda in East Naples reduced her to feeling like a mere chauffeur. They were heading down a swath of highway raised out of the wetlands, past a schizophrenic landscape of saw grass prairies and strip malls, where the road signs warned of panthers and the billboards advertised alligator zoos and other South Florida attractions. Mrs. Zegerman came to understand, through Arty's roundabout explanation, that his friend Jimmy had spent two hundred dollars on a birthday present for him. There had been no way for Jimmy to tell his wife that he'd lost that much at the dog track, so that morning he'd had to come clean. His wife immediately put in a call to the Collier County Task Force Initiative, with whom she had worked in the past to enforce speed limits in her subdivision and to establish random sobriety tests at crucial intersections. At some point, after putting two and two together, Mrs. Zegerman stopped listening.

Arty guided them into an apartment complex and through a maze of speed bumps. To the right and left stood building after gray generic building. They went past a Dumpster center and a large barricade of metal mailboxes while Arty searched squint-eyed for the right apartment. They had to circle three times before he found it.

She braked quickly at his command. He turned away from the apartment complex to look at her. "Thank you for the ride, Mrs. Zegerman," he said. "There's no sense in mixing you up any further in all this. I'll take a taxi home."

As he climbed out of the car, she was speechless. She was hurt, she was confused, and most of all she was angry at herself for feeling an absurd but overwhelming sensation of abandonment.

"Mr. Groys," she said, "don't you need your cane?"

"No, thank you, Mrs. Zegerman. That cane just slows me down."

"But you shouldn't even be walking!" she cried.

"Isn't it something?"

He slammed the door. She immediately leaned over the passenger seat and manually rolled down the window. "Arty!" she cried.

He turned with surprising grace and peered back at her from a distance of a dozen feet. "Yes?"

She stared at him through the open window. She was propping herself up on the passenger seat with the splayed fingers of one hand. He stared back at her in the full dazzle of the sun. "Arty," she repeated. "In all the years we've been neighbors, why have you never asked me my first name?"

Arty stood awhile in silence before limping back to Mrs. Zegerman. He bent down to the window. "I don't know why," he said. "What is it?"

"It's Ruth," she said. "Although my friends call me Ruthie."

"May I call you Ruthie?"

She had straightened up and taken hold of the steering wheel again. She turned to stare out the windshield while he peered in at her. She replied without looking over. "I suppose that would be fine," she said at last.

He did not know what to expect and imagined he might encounter some specimen of pimp—the dagger-dark madam or tracksuited thug—but it was a petite black girl who answered his knock and asked him who his appointment was with. After Arty had described her (he didn't even know her name!), the black girl led him to a dental office loveseat in a gloomy room whose only decoration was a mounted poster of a Budweiser logo, and disappeared down the hall of what was otherwise the kind of apartment that recent grads pile into as one pursues acting, the other a law degree, a third some kind of entrepreneurial scheme, and a fourth the dollar tips handed out at gentlemen's clubs. The barren despondency of the place depressed him and challenged his resolution, arrived at during his recovery, to see the girl again. He had been living as a dead man for years, and without her sudden presence in his suffocating cloister, coaxing and tempting him, he would certainly have died a dead man. He planned to offer to retire any debts she might have accrued and to furnish her with education funds. Was this preposterous? Would she laugh in his face?

Something prompted him to rise and walk over to the window. He widened a gap in the Venetian blinds and squinted out into the sun. He had a view of the entire parking lot and he saw, once his eyes had fully adjusted, a car he believed to be Mrs. Zegerman's, parked beside a gleaming black motorcycle. It was Mrs. Zegerman's, all right, for she herself was in the front seat. But what was she still doing there? He narrowed his squint and focused all his attention. Her forehead rested against the top arc of the steering wheel, then her chin, then her forehead again. As she shifted, heaving, between these two positions, he caught glimpses of her face, contorted, wet, until finally she sat silent a moment, chin on steering wheel, watery eyes blinking in the happy sun. Then she righted herself, retrieved a tissue from the glove box, and blew her nose. It was as if he were seeing her for the first time.

His attention was called away from Mrs. Zegerman by first one and then a second squad car pulling up outside the building, their sun-muted siren lights twirling unnoticed by anyone but him. His still delicate heart came to a stop, as if suddenly cast in stone, only to shatter into pieces when it came charging back. Jojo Denton had remarkable pull. Four Collier County police officers stepped out and began to confer, then approach, by which time he had let the blinds snap back and was rushing toward the rear rooms.

He found her brushing her hair in front of a bathroom mirror. She turned and saw him standing in the doorway. She backed up at the mere sight of him — his eyes were still bruised from his fall, his forehead was pinkly scarred, and his pale sweaty demeanor was ghastly. She issued something quick and terrified in a language he could not identify. "I don't believe it!" she finally cried in English. "I leave you one-hundred-percent dead man."

"You remember!" he said, happily but a little breathlessly. "I have survived and I have come to thank you, but first we have to get out of here. Jojo Denton dropped a dime and the cops are right outside."

"Cops?"

"Is there a back exit?" he asked.

He didn't wait for an answer. He reached in and grabbed her hand and pulled her with him. He limped briskly to a sliding glass door in one of the bedrooms, where he struggled to undo the stubborn metal lock. While this was going on, he turned to her and said, "Do you remember the pill?"

"The pill?"

"The one I refused to take," he said. "You persuaded me to take it, do you remember? How did you know what to say to me?" he asked. "How did you know what I needed to hear?"

"You stupid!" she cried, having taken over. "Glass door is open whole time!"

They left just as a thundering knock landed on the front door and reverberated through the apartment. He raced down to be in front of her, his knee be damned, and turned back to speak as they descended the stairs. "How did you know?"

"Know what?"

"How did you know what to say to get me to take that pill?"

"Are you so stupid? I am prostitute!"

"No, no, it was something more," he said. When they reached the bottom of the stairs, he brought her to a halt and said, "I want to take care of you. I want to pay your debts. Let me pay your debts and fund a college education for you."

"This is very tired routine," she said, "and not good timing."

Upstairs, invisible, they heard the commotion of the ensuing bust. They hurried across an expanse of treeless yard to the front of the apartment complex. Cars washed by on the street. He refused to allow his knee to bother him as he ran beside the girl. He was simply happy that he had survived to declare his intentions. He had no ulterior motive. What she did with his offer was up to her.

Soon they were several blocks away. There was no cop or squad car in sight, and he could have stopped. But he didn't stop, not

even when he turned and saw Mrs. Zegerman. She was driving
slowly, turning her face from him to the road and back to him
again. She pulled ahead and angled in to the curb. She rolled
down the window and shouted something he couldn't hear on account of his heavy breathing. He smiled at her. He let go of the
girl's hand to wave. He wanted to tell her many things, like how
sorry he was to have been cruel to her dog, and how surprised even
he was at how well his leg was holding up. Or maybe his strength
was only an illusion, just as it had been one summer when he was a
boy playing ball, that day he attempted to steal second and was
forced to slide as the ball neared the infielder's glove. The infielder
missed, and the ball went long, and when he saw that he was free
for a run to third he jumped up and took off, despite the hairline
fracture that would make itself known—through a pain that came
with a dawning awareness of what lay in store—only later, long after he had passed the third-base coach gesturing like mad and
made it home, graceful as a dancer, bodiless, ageless, immortal, a
boy on a summer day with a heart as big as the sun, with all his
troubles, his sorrows, his losses, all his whole long life still ahead of
him, still unknown, unable on that still golden field to cast its tall,
unvanquishable, ever-dimming shadow.

LAUREN GROFF

Delicate Edible Birds

FROM *Glimmer Train*

BECAUSE IT HAD RAINED and the rain had caught the black soot of the factories as they burned, Paris in the dark seemed covered by a dusky skin, almost as though it were living. The arches in the façades were the curve of a throat, the street corners elbows, and in the silence Bern could almost hear the warm thumpings of some heart deep beneath the residue of civilizations. Perhaps it was always there, but only audible now, in the dinless, abandoned city. As the last of the evacuees spun through the streets on their bicycles, they cast the puddles up into great wings of dark water behind them. Paris seemed so gentle as it awaited the Germans.

There was a fillip of sulfur and light as Parnell lit two cigarettes and placed one between Bern's lips. In the flare, she saw Viktor's eyes watching her in the rearview mirror and the pink rolls of the back of Frank's neck. Then the match went out again, and in the darkness she was no longer flesh, only the bright, hot smoke in her lungs.

It was all over: they had awoken in the middle of the night to unnatural silence, and rose to an abandoned hotel, the door of each empty room solemnly thrust open, the beds identically smooth. In the breakfast room, the geranium's soil was damp and their coffee was hot on the sideboard, but there was no one there but them. They were journalists; they had seen Czechoslovakia, Poland, Norway, Belgium; they knew what this meant. They hurried, then, and Viktor somehow procured the jeep, and Lucci bicycled off for the photo. Just an hour, murmured the little Italian, and he sailed off bravely toward the invasion while Frank spluttered and fussed, and

Viktor grew stony, and Parnell rolled cigarette after cigarette, each as perfect as a machine's. They waited in the jeep and they waited.

Now the street gleamed with brighter light, but still no Lucci. She sensed the tarry massing at the edge of Paris where the Germans were undoubtedly pushing in and felt a wildness rise up in her. But there was Parnell's hand on her thigh, squeezing, and she was grateful, though comfort like this was not what she was hungry for. She had to do something; she wanted to shout; and so she said, voice low and furious, Fucking Reynaud. Fucking Reynaud, handing the city over to the Germans. A real man would stand and fight.

In the rearview mirror she saw Viktor wince. Bern was the first woman he'd ever heard curse so, he once told her, and it was as if a beautiful lily suddenly belched forth a terrible stench. From the looks of him, it seemed impossible that he'd never heard a woman curse; he was Russian and massive, had a head ugly as a buckshot pumpkin. One imagined that if the serfs had never been liberated, today he'd be a tough old field hand, swinging scythes and gulping down vodka like water. But, in fact, he was the son of some deposed nobleman and spoke perfect tutor English and governess French, and was known as a reporter of prose as taut and charged as electric wire. He had shadowed her since the Spanish war, and there were times she was sure that his silent presence had saved her from some shadowy danger. She knew she should resent it, but the way he looked at her, she couldn't.

Viktor, darling, she said, a serrated edge to her voice. Is there a problem?

But Viktor didn't say anything: it was Frank in his Kansas drawl who said, If Reynaud fought, my dear, poof, up in smoke goes all your precious architecture. All the civilians, smithereens. He did the sensible thing, you know. Paris remains Paris. It's what I'd have done.

It's cowardly, spat Bern.

Frank sighed and rubbed his fat hand over his head. Oh Bernie. Don't you grow tired of being the everlasting firebrand? And where the hell is that little Eyetie of ours, that's what I want to know. Let's give him ten more minutes, then scram.

Bern bristled. There weren't enough women firebrands in the world as far as she was concerned, she said; Lucci was the best

damn photographer in this damn war; and why the hell *Life* magazine paired Frank with Lucci was beyond her, when Frank could
barely write a story without a dangling preposition and bland-as-
buttermilk prose, when God knows she herself, by far the better
journalist, even if she was a girl, had to bend over like a goddamn
contortionist for *Collier's* even to let her tour the front lines, let
alone do any exciting reporting.

But Frank wasn't listening, and interrupted. Viktor, we better
get going, he said. Germans catch us, you know where you're all
headed. Me, I'm the only one who'd go free.

Parnell blinked and rubbed his handsome forehead with a
knuckle. What do you mean, Frank? he said softly.

I know it's hard, but make an effort, Parnell, said Frank. Viktor's
a Commie, Orton's a Jew, you're a Brit, and they probably wouldn't
let Lucci go, what with his wife causing all that trouble down in Italy. I'm inoffensive. He gave a snort-laugh and turned around, his
face set for Bern's attack.

There was a pause, then Bern said, softly, Good god. Parnell
gripped her thigh more tightly to hold her back, but the truth was
that she was glad for this argument, for the dirty distractions of a
fight, for just now two planes with swastikas on their wings roared
overhead into the fields south of them, then separated, curved
about, poured together like water into water, and came back over
the jeep. The journalists, despite themselves, cringed. In the silence of the planes' wake, Bern took a breath, ready to lash some
sense into Frank. But she didn't have the chance, because Parnell
gave her thigh a smack and said, voice slipping from its cultivated
heights back into its native Cockney, Bloody hell, if it isn't Lucci.

There he was now, tiny Lucci with the camera like a millstone
around his neck, throwing down the bicycle so it clattered on the
cobblestones, leaping into the jeep, saying, Gogogogogo. And Viktor threw the jeep forward even before they heard the drone behind them, and they shot out from the city into the tiny dirt road as
the motorcycles came around the bend. Two hundred feet apart
and even from that distance Bern could see the stark black of the
German officers' armbands, the light-sucking matte of their boots,
the glint in their hands from the pistols as they whined behind
them, Viktor cursing in Russian and spinning the jeep over the
dark and rutted road. Lucci was in her lap, hot with sweat and
flushed and trembling, and Bern frowned and kept her head down

and watched the lace of Lucci's eyelashes on his cheeks. And then, over the roar of the engine and wind and pebble-clatter, as the motorcyclists rapidly lost their grasp on them, falling back, Lucci opened his eyes and said, Oh, Bernice, in his Italian way, Ber-eh-nee-che; Oh, Bernice, I have it. The best photo of the war. Nazis goose-stepping through the Arc de Triomphe. You shall see. Oh, it is the sublime photo. Oh, the one to make me live forever, he said, and Bern couldn't help it; she closed her eyes; she clutched Lucci's thin shoulders and threw her head back; and, hurtling into the steel-gray dawn, she laughed and she laughed.

The day was already bright where they stopped in the hemlock copse. Bern was stretched over the hood, basking in the sun like a cat. Viktor had never seen anything so beautiful. They were waiting for Lucci to finish vomiting in the ditch; ten miles south of the city he had discovered that the Germans had shot through one of his rolled-up trouser cuffs, and he slowly unrolled the fabric and fingered the six neat holes. Turned green. Viktor had to stop the car. Now Parnell and Frank were smoking, looking back at the city behind them, and for a moment, Viktor wondered if he could just take Bern and leave the rest behind; Lucci was all right, but Parnell and Frank he despised. Parnell for obvious reasons; Frank because he was a greasy toad. But he couldn't; they were not far enough out of Paris for abandonment to be anything but cruel. The last bicyclists they had passed were now passing them and an old woman with a chicken under her arm hobbled by, the chicken's head bobbing with each step. The Germans would be along soon. In the distance there were odd mechanical sounds.

Viktor flicked his eyes over Bern and thought that though she was the most beautiful woman he knew, she was not a true beauty. He should know; he himself was a warthog, but he had grown up around swans, long-necked sisters with velvety eyes and a mother whose grace was so legendary that, among her three-dozen rejected suitors in old noble Moscow, there were still men who wept when they remembered her. Bern was too dark a blond and too light a brunette, devoid of embonpoint, her face hawkish with its great nose, and her mouth like a pink knot tied under it. Too thin, also; war whittled her down, though she was always hungry, always eating. Still, even though she was almost plain when she slept, when she was vibrant it would take a strange man to find her unattractive. In the sunshine, she radiated; her hair turned golden, her eyes green, and her skin seemed to pulse with health. In the sunshine, Viktor had to hold his hands in his pockets to keep from grabbing Bern's sole world-class attraction, her tidy rear, fleshed with a layer of smooth lard, firm and handy as a steering wheel.

The day Viktor met Bern, she was twenty-two, climbing up the stairs of a Spanish hotel just after witnessing her first battle. Her face was pink, her eyes sparked angrily. She was trembling, and shook his hand hard to introduce herself, then said, Damn! I mean, damn! and went into her room and tapped at her typewriter for an hour, until she came out to the veranda where he was waiting for her and pretending not to, and she thrust a piece of paper into his hands and demanded to know if it was good, because, you see, she was determined to be a war reporter, and she'd heard he was a good one. The man she came to Spain with, a lover, wasn't worth his weight in pig poo, and she had to learn from someone. Viktor read the article, and said it was a job well done, B. Orton, but what does B. stand for? And she said in her French horn of a voice, Ah, well, it means Bernice, but it also means that if I can fool *Collier's* into thinking I'm a man, I'm a war reporter for good, and don't you forget it. And Viktor said, To be sure. And she said he better goddamn not, because they were going to be buddies; watch out.

But they didn't become buddies yet: he went off to a different section of the front and when they met up again, it was in a hotel right after Guernica, and Viktor was having an awful time of it. He kept seeing flashes of things he tried to shunt away. Late at night he wept in the water closet, unable to stop himself, and tried to stuff his shirt in his mouth to muffle the sound, but couldn't. For fifteen minutes, there were two dark shadows in the crack under the door, Bern's feet, Bern's head on the door, listening. When she came in and took off her blouse and hitched up her skirt and smiled up at him, he couldn't think to say no.

Afterwards, he kissed the delicate slice of her chin down from her ear and asked her to marry him. And she laughed roughly, and gave him a tweak of the ear and said, Oh, well, Viktor, dear, now you've made a terrible mistake, and she vanished down the dark hallway. It was a mistake; it hadn't happened again between them, though he'd watched time and again as she disappeared down other hallways with Parnell. And he had to swallow it because she was who she was, a woman so removed from the women of his youth as to be a whole new gender. In her every small movement she was the woman of the future, a type that would swagger and curse, fall headlong, flaming into the hell of war, be as brave and tough as men, take the overflowing diarrhea of nervous frontline troops without grimacing, speak loudly and devastatingly, kick brain matter off her shoes and go unhurriedly on. When he looked at Bern, Viktor saw the future, and it was lovely and bright and as equal as things between men and women, between prole and patrician could be. And he also saw that any impulse to pin her down would only make her flitter away. Some days he hated her.

He must've sighed, because Bern shielded her eyes with one graceful hand.

Viktor, you're wearing ye olde death-head again, she said. What's the matter?

But instead of saying, for the hundredth time, Oh, Bern, why Parnell and not me; or, Oh, Bern, why won't you marry me, he gave a grimace and ground out his cigarette and said, We should be off, then, if we don't want the Krauts to catch us.

Now the others climbed up the embankment and Bern let herself slide off the hood, graceful, winking. Come on, chaps, she called out in her high honk. *Vite Vite.* We've got to make it to Tours before the Nazis bomb the bejeezus out of it.

In half an hour, the dampness had burned from the ground, and dust rose in a haze and saturated everything. The oaks that drooped over the avenue and the pocked road were so lovely in the dust cloud, they seemed to drip with honey. Strange, Parnell thought dreamily, that on a day like this there should be beauty left in the world. For a while they had been going increasingly slowly, passing thicker and thicker clumps of evacuees, whole families like packhorses, even the smallest pulling little red wagons full of bedding or small dogs or even tinier children than they. Terrible shame, he thought, terribly sad.

But later he saw a number of parties in the fields huddled over blankets spread with food, picnicking as if the occasion were a merry one, and he murmured, How lovely, wishing himself out there, with his own little ones — how the girls would enjoy it! — and Elizabeth presiding over it all with her neat sandwiches and birdly chatter about gardens and whatnot. He longed for home, longed for the house in London and his shoes shined in the morning and a proper cuppa. Looking out in the fields, he murmured again, Oh, how lovely, and hadn't thought he'd said it aloud until Bern turned her head to him and snorted, They're idiots, Parnell. Germans flew by they'd be blown to bits.

He stared at this brusque American, appalled as ever. Then she softened and cuddled against him, a good kitten, and he reminded himself that she never meant it, not really. She talked a terrible hard streak but was a dear thing inside. Reminded him of Elizabeth, in some vague way, not that Bern would ever do if he had a mind to introduce her to his wife. Elizabeth was so peculiar in that way, refusing to take tea with so-and-so for some such reason or other, and he knew that Bern in his wife's parlor would be a frightful thing; the snubbing going on over the tea and poor Bern never seeing it for a moment, honking on the way she does and getting on Elizabeth's nerves. And it was odd, wasn't it, how people changed; he was only a housepainter back in the day when he met Elizabeth, and she didn't hold it against him then, although she did make him take elocution lessons and make something of himself. He was about to follow this thought into another daydream of Elizabeth, young and naked and smelling of his house paints, when Bern interrupted, saying, So, did anyone think to bring food?

There was a long silence, until Parnell, wanting to be helpful, said, Well, rather, I brought that half a can of petrol, you know.

And I the jeep, said Viktor.

And I the stupendous photo, said Lucci.

And I the water, said Bern.

The back of Frank's neck turned red, but he said nothing. Badtempered fellow, Parnell thought, but doesn't seem to mean any real harm.

Frank? Bern prompted sweetly, but he just turned and said, Darling, you being the only female of the bunch, I thought provisions were your field.

Not now, said Lucci, throwing his hands into the air, but Bern seemed too tired to curse Frank to hell more than a few times. She bent down and rummaged in her valise and pulled out a bottle of Scotch, brandishing it like a tennis victor with a trophy.

Looks like the liquid lunch again, fellas, she grinned, and cracked the seal with her fingernail. I liberated this from the hotel bar this morning.

Now Parnell wanted to take her in his arms again. This was why he invited her into his bed every night, propping the picture of his family up on the windowsill first, a plea for them to forgive him the sin he was about to commit; *this* feminine thought for the comfort of others. He felt a bubble of elation rise in him as he took a swig of the Scotch; this is why the men were out here in the fields, fighting: for their women, for knitting and stews and flower arrangements, all the wondrous small things that keep a fellow's life pleasant. If he weren't so blasted old, Parnell would fight for it, too. And Bern had a great womanly capacity for comfort, though she kept it hidden because she thought it made her seem less like a chap than she wanted to be. Silly duck. She shouldn't hide it; it was what he liked about her, and he resolved to tell her so, maybe sometime when they were alone and not so pressed for time.

Bathed in a warm dust and a warming buzz, Parnell drifted into a pleasant waking doze as they passed the growing numbers of refugees on foot, on bicycle, on carts pulled by peasant women like pendulous-breasted oxen. They went down that insignificant road from Paris, until it emptied out, at last, into one of the major southbound arteries, to the northeast of Orléans and about sixty miles south of the city.

It was then that, pulling out onto the autoroute, Viktor cursed and stopped the jeep suddenly, jolting Parnell out of his lovely trance. Before them roiled a scene of such chaos that they, all veterans of chaos, had to take a moment to sit, absorbing, before they reacted. For instead of the neat, small clumps of refugees who had decided to take the small road they had just left, the autoroute was teeming, impossible: cars that had run out of gas were abandoned by the roadside, women in summer dresses had fainted in the heat and were fanned by wailing children, a teeming mass of man and mule and bicycle and machine was roiling down the road as far as their eyes could see, and everywhere around them were wounded people. An old woman, haute bourgeoise by her chignon and her gray silk dress, had a dried magnolia of blood blooming on her chest. Two men carrying a makeshift stretcher bore a tiny boy, waxen and still, with a tourniquet on his thigh and nothing where his knee should have been. Filling the air was a faraway keening, hushed talk, the klaxons of the few cars that were still running.

And out in the fields beyond, as if this migration were not a hundred feet from them, the backs of an old farmer and his wife as they bent to pull weeds from their crop.

Shit, said Bern, and she flew out of the jeep, into the maw of humanity, asking questions, scribbling answers. Parnell cringed, feeling a tad sheepish: this was not precisely his beat; the British people were under attack enough, they didn't need more bad news, and so his orders were to write about resistance and bravery, not innocent civilians fired upon when they fled their homes. From where he sat in the jeep he heard *bombed, machine gunned, massacred,* the airplanes strafing the émigrés about twenty miles south of Paris. Numerous dead. A two-week-old baby shot in the throat. An old man had a heart attack, just witnessing the destruction. Parnell watched as under Bern's pen the story formed, neat and relentless, threads ordered from chaos.

Frank trailed slowly behind her, gleaning, having little success at asking questions himself: his French was poor, and people did not warm to him as they always did to Bern. Viktor glowered in the jeep, keeping it a meter behind Bern as she walked beside her subjects, protecting her; dear Lucci darted hither and thither, taking photographs until he returned to the car to hide his face in his jacket, unable to see any more. For a while, Bern held a baby so its mother could shift her bundle, and she held it awkwardly. But Parnell wanted to tell her she would make a marvelous mother; as she looked down into its soft fist of a face, he knew she would. His admiration only grew when, after a while, Bern held the hand of the boy in the stretcher when he awoke and sobbed soundlessly in pain.

When she at last returned to the car, when the first bats began swooping over the fields, heralding the long dusk, she wiped and wiped at her cuff where a small coin of the boy's blood had darkened it. And when she moved closer to Parnell and looked up into his face, he saw the kind of searing look she gave him when she wanted to take him into a corner and have her furious way with him. As always, he was taken aback, though he would have complied had there been any chance; but he looked around at the roiling mass of humanity, at the others in the car—poor Viktor, he tried not to be so obvious around him—and shook his head, just slightly.

And so, disappointed, Bern turned away and said, I have four stories just dying to be published. And no fucking wire to send them.

That is why we are going to Tours, darling, said Viktor.

That's our problem, said Bern. The people out there told me. The wires are cut in Tours, too, the government's fleeing to Bordeaux. Nowhere to sleep, even the barns forty kilometers out full of people. No food. No water. General panic. La-di-dah.

A long silence, broken at last by Lucci, saying, So what is it we're to do?

Frank unfolded the map, whistling the "Marseillaise," as he was wont to do when he wanted to calm himself. There's a road, he said, three miles to the east that's smaller than this one. Takes us to Bordeaux, looks like, if in a bit of a roundabout manner.

Bordeaux, said Parnell, thinking of good wines and soft beds. He hadn't eaten in a day and his hunger had been replaced by a dull ache. How he longed for the buttery melt of pheasant in cream sauce on his tongue. How fine it would be to take a warm bath, to sleep and sleep without awakening to the sound of artillery. So Parnell said, Oh, yes, let's go on to Bordeaux, and he wondered if he spoke more strongly than usual, for Bern looked at him, a smile flickering across her face, and Lucci made a little noise of approval.

It's decided, said Viktor. On we push, and he turned into a cart path through the nearest field. When that path dead-ended in a long, lush field of barley sprouts, he drove through the young crops and they left a path of broken plants in their wake. Parnell felt sorry for those small broken plants, he did. But when he was about to mention this to Bern, he felt a little foolish for it, and said nothing after all.

They made the road by the time the sky had immolated itself in sunset. Bern would never admit it to the chaps, but she was beginning to shake with hunger; always a bad sign. As thin as she became in war, when she began to shake she needed to eat, or else suffer fits of nastiness. The jeep pressed on valiantly until the moon had risen, but it presently began to make a coughing sound and slowed to a crawl. There was an electric light glimmering ahead through the trees. Though they urged the engine along, the jeep died before they reached it. Parnell got out, uncomplaining, and Frank got out, complaining, and together they pushed until they reached the settlement.

There she saw a group of three stone buildings that, in the thin wash of moonlight, seemed to have sprung up organically from the ground, as if a natural geologic formation or a mushroom ring. In the hard-packed dirt courtyard, two skinny dogs skulked and rattled their chains. One weak bulb hung over a door, which was thrust open when Viktor honked, and an immense, bullet-shaped body blocked the light pouring from within.

Oh, he is very large, said Lucci. He will be sure to have food.

Our savior, who art in hovel, said Frank, his sharp good humor returned.

When they saw, however, that the man had the unmistakable silhouette of a rifle in his hand, and that he spoke to two other creatures who came outside behind him, also with what appeared to be rifles, the reporters did not climb out of the jeep, as they had been about to do. They waited, still and quiet, in the car, until the man came up and pointed a flashlight at their faces, one by one. When he reached Bern, he paused, and she winced so in sudden blindness that she didn't notice that he was fondling a lock of her hair until he tugged on it. When she batted at his hand he had already pulled it away, and she was left clawing air.

Excuse me, sir, said Viktor in his impeccable French, but we are hungry and tired, and would gladly pay for some food and a place to rest. And some gas, if you've got any.

The man, still invisible in the darkness, grunted, and the soft voices of the two others murmured behind him. Yes, he said in an earthy, provincial French, yes, we've got all that. Come inside and bring what you've got.

Now they all slowly slid from the jeep and walked behind him, the two other strangers dark shadows at their backs. And when they were inside the cottage all Bern saw at first was a tiny old woman paring potatoes in a dark corner, a fairy-tale grandmother who smiled, though her eyes watered, rheumy. Bern's eyes adjusted in a moment, and only then did she see the small photograph of Hitler over the mantel, one plucked daisy and a guttering candle before it, as if the führer were some syphilitic-looking saint.

Bern spun toward their host and found him grinning down at her with his dark eyes and his oily but handsome face. His arm was jutted out, his hand upraised, and on his great biceps there was an armband embroidered with a crude swastika. Heil Hitler, he boomed. Today is a great day, is it not, my friends? Please, sit. Are you hungry? Call me Nicolas.

Bern didn't know how she bore it, but in the next moment she was eating, and to her surprise it was good. A smooth white wine, hot bread, potage of carrot, even a small tin of potted meat. She scowled. It would do no one any good if she were to starve to death, but she didn't have to enjoy it. Viktor sent her warning glances from his side of the table, and Parnell kept his hand on her knee, for good measure; not as if she were really so stupid as to open her mouth and let fly; they were just making sure. By the fireplace at the far end of the room sat the two creatures who had come outside with their host to greet them, and now Bern had a hard time seeing any threat in them: they were two teenaged boys with guns in their arms, but so skinny and cringing they may as well have been girls cradling their dolls.

My sons, Nicolas had said, gesturing at them. My wife died many years ago. The boys kept their eyes averted, and on one of them Bern noticed the blue-green stamp of a fading black eye. The watery old woman kept peeling her potatoes, nodding and smiling vaguely.

For his part, their host was leaning back in his chair, watching the reporters eat and smiling his approval. When they had finished, and Frank had speared the last hunk of bread with his knife, Nicolas spoke again, softly. I am so glad my meal was to your liking, my friends. Now that you are satiated, I hope, we can come to an agreement, can we not? You mentioned that you could pay for my hospitality, did you not?

We did, said Viktor. We can. We have money. Francs, pounds, dollars. For supper tonight, of course, plus a roof over our heads, plus provisions for tomorrow. And enough fuel to get us to Bordeaux. Perhaps fifty francs would be a good deal. That is, if you please.

I do please, said Nicolas, smiling his charming smile. I do, indeed. I will give you all that you want, the food, the gas. But I do not, most unfortunately, accept currency from those places. Those countries will presently be crushed, and all that will be worthless. Just paper, a few tin coins. Now, if you had deutschemarks, that would be something, he said, and sighed a voluptuous sigh. How I am glad that I share this day with you, he said. I must admit that I have been dreaming of this day, my friends, for years.

Since the last war, said his mother from her potatoes. He has not let up about it. Germany this, Germany that. Takes a correspondence course. German. All sorts of books. Always a very smart boy.

I was a prisoner of war during the last one, Nicolas said, but, really, I was kept better there than here: they valued me more there, where I could not at first speak the language, than they do in my own country. We had schnitzel for luncheon every day. Schnitzel! A marvel of precision, the German mind. These boots here, he said, rapping his vast foot on the ground, are German-made, given to the prisoners, and they're still as good as the day I got them. I lived among those people and knew they were superior. The Germans rise, he said, dreamily. And with them a better race of man.

Oh, Christ, spat Bern, feeling herself flush with rage.

Indeed, said their host. Bern saw his eyes drop to her lap, where Parnell's hand was clutching her thigh too tightly, too high on her leg. Nicolas raised an eyebrow and gave her a private smile. Bern was not prepared for the pretty dimple in his cheek.

Viktor rushed in. Well, we have other goods. I've got a gold watch, he said, and put his father's watch on the table, looking sternly at the others. I'm sure we can rustle some more up.

Parnell gamely took the photographs of his family out of the silver frame, tucked them back into his pocket, and put the frame beside the watch. Then he added to the pile two diamond cuff links (*What,* Bern thought, amused, even now, *does he imagine he's doing with cuff links in a war?*), his engraved cigarette case, and a still wrapped bar of Pear's soap.

It's unused, he said with a significant glance at Nicolas.

I don't understand what's going on, said Frank in English, but he can have my flask if he wants it, and threw into the mix a horn-and-silver flask that he had kept hidden from all the other reporters until now. Parnell gave him an odd look; Frank only shrugged.

Bern threw in her gold bangle and it made a furious jingle on the pile.

Lucci fumbled, and found a pair of clean woolen socks in his pocket. All I have, he said cheerily in French. The watery old mother by the wood stove creaked out of her chair and hobbled up and took them, muttering how nice the wool was, how soft, what lovely socks they were, worth a lot, she was sure, and she patted Lucci on the head like a good child. The boys by the fireplace watched the pile hungrily, their eyes large in their faces.

Ah, sighed Nicolas, a pile of riches. Surely more than this family has ever seen in one place before. He played his hand around in the pile for a moment, moving this bit, then that, but shook his head, and pushed them back toward the reporters, save for the socks, which the old woman stroked in her lap like a kitten. Alas, said Nicolas, this is not what I want, either.

Well what in bloody Christ's name does he want then, said Parnell in English. But Viktor shushed him, and it was only when Bern saw the face of her good, strong Viktor pale, as if washed with bluing, that she began to feel cold. Frank gave a small whistle, as if a kettle releasing the pressure of its steam. In the wake of this sound, Nicolas looked at Bern.

Her, he said.

Into the vast, frigid silence came a snicker; Nicolas's boys, eyes like darts.

Never, Bern said. Never, never, never.

Not forever, no, Nicolas said, seeming not to understand her. I'm not a sadist, young lady. For a night. No more. Then you will be on your way tomorrow. Plenty of gas to get you to Bordeaux. Plenty of food, my mother's delicious chicken. I have been far too long without female companionship, and I am a man with strong desires. You remind me of my wife, you know. Same hair. Same, excuse me, rear end. Lovely rear end. Now tell me, my cabbage; I know you're American, but is there a chance your people were German?

A sharp blow to her ankle: Lucci kicking her; and she knew he meant to remind her that this man was both bats and had a gun. And so she said, grimly, Oh, in a way.

I knew it, he said, sitting back with his charming smile. You are the purest Aryan I have seen for some time. I knew it when I saw you.

Oh, did you, said Bern, and couldn't help herself, saw herself telling this story to a whole dinner table of guests, saw herself shrieking one day with laughter, saying, My God, he was telling a Jewess she was the most Aryan creature he'd ever seen. Even now, she gave a high little bleat of delight. Viktor, she noticed, had grown huge, was sitting up in his chair as if ready to spring; Frank was gaping, bright red, having apparently understood; even Parnell's handsome brow was knotted and black. Lucci's eyes were bowed to his lap, as if in shame.

Your answer is no, Bern said. I would rather gnaw off my own foot.

Very well, said Nicolas, making his mouth twist painfully. You may soon be doing so. I am sorry, but I'll have to keep all of you fine foreigners here until the Germans come, won't I. Prisoners. And who knows what they'll do when they find you.

You can't do that, said Viktor. We're reporters.

Oh, can't I, said Nicolas and it was not a question. Now, boys, he said to his sons. Lock them in the barn.

He stood and nodded at them all, thoughtfully, and said, Good night, and as he climbed the stairs they heard his footsteps on the boards above them, so heavy they feared that great rocks of plaster would fall down onto their heads. Then they moved, one by one, into the night, Lucci kissing the hand of the old woman in thanks for the meal.

The barn was one of the buildings of stone, dark and chill, more a cellar than a barn. Inside was a great mass of hay and a mound of potatoes and one ugly old donkey that bit at Lucci when he tried to make friends. The boys shoved the reporters inside and made a great to-do about running the chain through the handles outside and locking them in sturdily, and when the reporters were alone, with just a chink in the roof for a weak light, they settled into the hay in silence. But Parnell stood up presently and began to pace between the donkey and the door, and at last spat out, How disgusting, really. With that delivered, he sat down again.

` There was another long silence, then Bern burst out, Filthy. Filthy, filthy. I would commit hari-kari. Spectacular fucking brute. Never in my life would I sleep with a fascist.

From his corner, Frank cleared his throat. No, Bern, he said. No question. I would shoot you myself if you did it. For the principle of the thing. If there's anything we Americans know, it's principles. His voice in the darkness held a tremble, and Bern, who was never quite clear where she stood with him, felt a small easing inside of her.

No, said Parnell, nothing of the sort can happen, of course. Barbaric, really. So what, old chaps, do we do?

Bern said, Well, we sure as hell can't wait for the Germans, and they will be here, and sometime soon. And we can't escape, not at least without the gasoline.

I say, said Viktor, so quietly they could barely hear him, we murder the son of a bitch in his bed. And his two whelps. And leave the mother trussed outside for the vultures.

Wonderful, wonderful, murmured Parnell, standing then sitting

again. Your fury, Viktor, it's wonderful. In his agitation, he fumbled
for a cigarette and failed to light it three times before it glowed a
sudden orange in the dark.

Yes, but, said Lucci. But how is it we escape this place?

And you forget, said Frank, that there are three of them, and
they all have guns.

After this, a black silence enveloped them. They all sank deeply
into their thoughts. Without conferring with anyone, Lucci eventually rose and made a thick bed of hay, and they lay down together
for the warmth. Bern was in the middle, between Viktor and Lucci,
Frank and Parnell on the outside; and when Frank began to snore
and Lucci's nose let out a sleeping squeak, Viktor turned to Bern,
and put his arms around her. There, safe against his smell of body
and sweat and his own clove-like undertones, she realized how un-
surprised she was.

Even as she was now—unbathed, unkempt, exhausted—Bern
knew she had it, that same old something. She'd had her first great
love affair at sixteen, was still notorious from it. The man in question had been three times her age, the mayor of Philadelphia, but
even so they blamed her, a child. The father of a schoolmate, he
had given her a ride home from school one day in his chauffeured
car, and that was that. Over the year she was involved with him, his
wife grew skinny and sour, his daughter turned the entire school
against Bern, and her lover took her to Montreal for a week while
her parents were visiting family in Newport News. She was enrap-
tured; she felt free. She took it as her due when her lover fed her
vast meals and put her in bespoke lingerie and took her to bur-
lesque shows, and, the last night, to a dinner party given by the
kinds of friends who would be amused by a sixteen-year-old mis-
tress. In that gilt and velvet world of closed curtains and secrets
circling like electricity, there was another girl there not much older
than Bern, but uncertain and clumsy with her hands, her face
painted in roses like a porcelain doll.

Bern had still been vibrating with her strange new joy when the
butlers set the silver domes in front of them. The lights had
dimmed, and the lids were whisked away. There, on the plates,
Bern saw the tiniest bird carcasses imaginable, browned and glistening with butter. There was a collective gasp: *L'ortolan,* a woman
murmured, her voice thick with longing.

A finch, whispered her lover, bathing her ear in his wine-warmed

breath. Caught, blinded, and fattened with millet, then drowned
in Armagnac and roasted whole. A delicacy, he said, and smiled,
and she had never noticed until then that his eyeteeth were yellowed and extraordinarily long.

With the gravity of a religious ceremony, her tablemates flicked
out fresh white napkins and veiled their faces with them. The porcelain girl held hers like a mantilla for a moment before she
dropped it over her face. Bern did not: she watched, holding her
breath, as each person reached for his own small bird and made it
disappear behind the veil. For a long time, at least fifteen minutes,
there were the wet sounds of chewing, small bones cracking, a lady's voluptuous moan.

A stillness came into Bern as she observed this, a chill, as if she
were watching from a very distant place. The bird on her own plate
cooled and congealed, and she didn't even look at it when she
wrapped it in her napkin and placed it gently in her evening bag.
She watched as the others, radiant with badness or shamefaced and
shaky, came from behind their napkins, wiped their lips. A tiny
bone—a wishbone, a foot—stuck to the carmine lipstick of some
opera singer. Bern saw thin wet streaks in the porcelain girl's cheek
powder, saw she was still holding something in her mouth, and
Bern gazed hard at her until the other turned away, flushing for
real under her paint.

Later that night Bern let the tiny carcass drop from the hotel
balcony, setting it free, she thought, though it dropped like a lead
weight to the ground for some prowling beast to eat. Like that,
she who had been perhaps too amenable, too obedient—why else
could she be seduced—felt herself harden. When she returned to
Philadelphia, Bern never spoke to the man again, and the story
formed the foundation of the first piece of fiction she ever wrote,
in a hiatus between wars. After the magazine ran it, people in Paris
and New York began to call her L'ortolan behind her back. Bern
Orton; Bern Ortolan. It made a certain awful sense, Bern herself
could admit.

Now, so close to Viktor's peculiar scent, Bern felt something stirring in her again, and with her silent, cool hands undid his belt.
This is what she needed, a man coming alive in her arms, such
comfort; and though she preferred Parnell—there was no compli-
cation in him, and he was gentle and sweet to Viktor's large rough-

ness—when Viktor put his hand on her waist and slid it under the
band to hold her rear, she let him, eager. She loved this, and not
because she ever had much pleasure from it; it was a gift, the men
wanted it, and it was their gratitude that made it good; the way that
Bern was the white-hot center of another person's world for those
minutes or hours; the way for a moment it made them both forget
everything but this other skin, to forget the shattered souls drifting
over the world; how it was cracking in half.

But Viktor put his two hot hands on hers and stopped them. She
could see a tiny glint in his dark eyes as he looked at her. He lifted
her hands to his mouth and kissed them both, on the palms and
on the backs. Then he turned her about so that her back was facing him, and he held her gently around the chaste arc of her rib-
cage, his arm for her pillow, the deep beat of his heart a current,
eventually drifting her off to sleep.

Frank was up earlier than everyone else because his blasted hands
wouldn't stop shaking. Hungry, too. The others, like useless logs in
the hay, Bern all cuddled up with that crazy Russky Viktor. In the
back, the donkey stinking in his own muck. It made his skin crawl.
And when he went to the doors and peered out into the half-dark,
he saw them along the road, the refugees. Pale as death, a huddle
of them, waiting.

Frank remembered an assignment he once took to Haiti long
ago, during a time of peace when he was young, not the fat sad
sack he was now. He remembered the stories, the fear in the people's faces when they talked of the warlords who would steal souls
and turn the emptied bodies into slaves. Those people out there,
moving in the dust and dawn, seemed to have their very souls
leached from them; zombies, he thought, of war. When they sensed
someone awake in the cottage, they knocked on the door, and
when nobody answered, two of them moved on. The last, a young
man, waited for an hour, until the sun rose fully, and then half-
heartedly stole a chicken from the yard. The son with the bruised
eye stepped from the roadside and cocked his rifle under the man's
chin. The man released it and limped away.

Crazy, crazy, Frank muttered, what war makes people become.
Animals.

There was a rustle and he peered behind him, saw Bern sitting up with her lovely, sleepy eyes, hay in her hair. Frank? she said uncertainly.

What I wouldn't give, he said, for a fucking drink. His voice was shaking, too, he noticed. Bern stood, and Frank's heart lifted a bit, as she moved toward him, but then the group in the hay began to stir and his mood turned dark again. Always, always the others around. And he no match for Parnell, handsome as he was, or Viktor, who simply sweated virility. Or even Lucci, with his easy charm; and he'd seen it, there's something going on there, too, between Bern and the photographer. He might as well forget about it. Not that a cold bitch like Bern would be good for him, drive a cold dagger through his heart, more likely than not. There was something so phony about her. He'd better forget it.

But as they all rose and stretched and tried to forage for food and watched the sunbeams slowly rake across the floor of the barn, and still no Nicolas, none of the sons, not even the weepy old hag, no food but the scent of some kind of ham wafting from the cottage, he couldn't forget about it. Needled him, Bern, always. There was that one time in Oslo, anyhow, when they were drunk on aquavit, and everyone else had gone to bed. Normally Frank resorted to whores, all peroxide and bosom, but that night, when the electricity shorted out and they lit the flickering candles, there was something so dark and appealing about Bern that he put his hand on her rear and raised his eyebrow. She went still and seemed to think, and then carefully raised hers back. Bern had tasted of alcohol and copper, and afterward, rumpled and sweating, he wept and confessed that he dreamt of killing himself. Usually it's a noose, he'd said. Sometimes a gun. Sometimes I step deliberately on a land mine.

It was this that got him. That he'd said this, and to her of all people. That she'd taken it and stored it away and might use it someday. And that he couldn't shake the idea that maybe she'd only done it out of pity, slept with him. That's what he couldn't take. The pity. Frank turned away, counting his breaths through the morning to stay steady.

All day, Lucci sat staring through a crack at the clouds skimming across the delicate sky. Viktor did fifty pull-ups on a beam. Parnell smoked the last of his cigarettes and flipped the photographs of his family over and over again like playing cards. Outside, there were the sounds of a few more passersby. A strange

French owl somewhere. Someone working nearby, the clang of wood and metal.

In the midmorning, Frank couldn't take his hunger and bit into one of the raw potatoes from the sacks, but spat it out again when he saw it was black at its heart.

Before noon there was a rumble in the sky, and the way that Viktor winced, Frank understood that he had recognized the sounds as Nazi planes. If the Nazis could fly this far south without firing, he knew their troops would be only a few days away. And then the camps, which he had heard of. Bullets in the head, inmates thin as bones. He was not so sure now that he would get away scot-free.

Frank listened to the mother come out and scold her chickens; he heard Nicolas and the boys clomp back into the house for the midday meal. And he listened to each tiny noise as Nicolas unlocked the chain on the barn and thrust open the door. In the overbright sun, Nicolas was not quite so frightening. Just a peasant farmer, and not a bad-looking one at that. Young enough, younger than Frank, at least. He gabbled something inquisitive in French toward Bern, and she spat back her answer, saying, *Cochon*, which Frank knew meant pig. So: the answer still no. He felt his insides twist at this, a fury rise up in him when Nicolas laughed and gabbled something else, then slammed the door shut again, locking them in the dark.

Germans are advancing on Orléans, Viktor said for Frank's benefit.

I got it, said Frank, but he hadn't, though he couldn't let Viktor know that.

Damn Bern. She was starting to get on his nerves. Frankly, in the light of day, he didn't see what all the fuss was about. She'd slept with everyone and his brother, so why one more peasant meant anything at all, he didn't know. Phony, prissy bitch: the first time he knew he was going to report on this war (how young he seemed then, my god, not that long ago, either), the fellows back at *Life* raised their eyebrows. Say hello to Bern Orton for us, Frankie-boy, they'd said. We hear she's a hot number, and when he said, What do you mean?, sincerely admiring a woman whose moxie alone let her do what only men did, they laughed. Showed him a photograph of a young lady. Said, She looks all prim and proper, distant cousin to Eleanor Roosevelt, Main Line, all that. But don't be fooled. And they told him about the mayor she'd seduced at six-

teen; the marriages she'd broken up; the painter who'd shot himself in the heart for her. Pussy of gold, they said. Gives it away for
free.

Lucky bastard, they all said, and clapped him hard on the back.

By evening, Frank was shuddering, making the wall behind him
rattle. Felt about to die. He had nothing in America, no family, no
wife, no children, nothing but his job and baseball and a small
house near a decent brewery, but he just wanted it all to be over.
When night fell again and the moon rose in the chink in the roof
and it became painfully evident that there would be no dinner, either, Frank began to curse. The curses rattled out of his mouth like
gravel, like spittle, he couldn't stop them, he let himself go. He
cursed Nicolas, the boys, the dogs, the chickens, the old hag; he
worked himself up to curse France, the world, the United States of
America, his mother, who urged him to be a reporter, his father,
who had gotten him his first job, the *Kansas City Star, Life* magazine,
his editor, God, President Roosevelt and his ugly old wife, and—because Bern jumped in roaring to defend Eleanor, it was inevitable
—in the end he spun about and began to curse Bern.

Dammit, girl, he said, just do it. Just do it and get it over with and
we can go. I'm dying here. I feel like a fucking beehive was set loose
in me. Just do it. Please, please; we can go and we'll never talk
about it again and I can have a fucking drink.

Viktor grabbed Frank by the collar and shoved him up against
the wall. Frank struggled, but could not breathe. The barn, already
dark, went darker. And then, without saying anything, Viktor let
him go and Frank slid to the ground and wheezed there sullenly
for a long time, watching the straw before his eyes dance with his
breath, watching Bern at the far end of the room, as she combed
and combed her hair like a cat licking itself calm.

He was in the garden in Fiesole eating figs and Cinzia was there,
her hair short like a boy's and blown by the warm wind. She opened
her mouth, about to say something important—Lucci's very limbs
tingled—when Parnell sat up beside him, shouting incomprehen-
sible, strange words. Lucci sprang up in the darkness of the donkey-
smelling barn, his heart splitting in his chest. Oh, he cried. Viktor
lit a match.

In the spit and flare they saw Parnell's face, blank, seized by fear.
Then he was weeping, his handsome face in a rictus of pain. No, he

said, no, no, no, and Bern was beside him, holding his face, saying softly, Parnell, wake up, wake up, it's okay, sweetheart, it's a dream, and Frank scrambled to the wall, and Lucci sat down again, wearily, and the donkey kicked, and Viktor lit another match when the first burned out in his fingers.

Parnell rested his head on Bern's shoulder until he stopped weeping, until his breath came naturally again. He told them what he had dreamt: ranks of soldiers, black as beetles, marching in lockstep down the Strand, a child swung by its heels against a wall so its brains splattered out. London burning. Bombs falling like hailstones on the Houses of Parliament.

I want to go home, Parnell said. Please, Bern. Just let us go home.

See, said Frank from the wall, where he sat, shuddering. See, Bern. You're hurting all of us, you know. Your *morals,* he said, are hurting all of us.

Viktor moved toward Frank, but Lucci stepped between them. Frank's ill, he said quietly. He knows not what he talks. Viktor glowered down at him and Lucci steeled himself for a blow, wondered if it would kill him, but Viktor turned and sat abruptly.

When they settled again, Lucci could no longer sleep. In his mouth he still tasted figs, and he could almost smell Cinzia's hair. He thought of her as she would be now, if she were alive, in the camp at Bolzano. Probably gaunt, no longer pregnant. Still as fierce as she was as a partisan, going into the night, doing what she needed to do against the fascists. All that time Lucci had tried not to worry, stood with his chemicals pulling images from the baths in his red light, but growing more frantic as their child began to show. And one bright afternoon he watched as, far down a street too long for him to run, she was hustled into a dark car and taken.

And now, the Germans coming, perhaps even a few miles down the road. A great ugly ink stain on France, spreading. And when they overtook this barn, who's to say where they would go. Perhaps Lucci would walk into the camp and see Cinzia look up from whatever work it is they make women do; sewing, perhaps, or weeding, and she'd blanch, be furious with him for being caught. But this was wishful thinking, Lucci knew; he'd more likely be killed on the spot. Journalism was no impediment to evil. And only the willful say they do not know what's happening in Europe anymore.

And yet, he thought, there are still people like Bern, and this is good. White-hot people, people with a core of iron. Lucci had met Bern long before the war, when she was a debutante visiting Europe on the arm of some man. They met at a nightclub and she charmed him. That night, Cinzia, in the presence of a woman so beautiful, held forth to dazzle herself and danced the way that only Cinzia could dance. Bern turned to Lucci in the dim flickering light and brilliant bleat of horns and said, Giancarlo Bertolucci, your wife is spectacular. And he said, This I know, Berenice, and she threw back her head and laughed her smoke-filled laugh. Later, in his despair with Cinzia gone, when he took the job to photograph the looming war, they met up again in Czechoslovakia. When one night he knocked on her door, she opened it a crack and said, Oh, Lucci. Oh, darling, no. You see, I make it a point of honor not to see the husbands of women I adore. And he said, I understand, but it is probable I am a widow. And she said, Widower. And don't think that. Never Cinzia, she's a strong one—you can't let yourself think that, and she opened her door a little wider and gave him a long, soft kiss on his mouth. There, she said, now I know she's alive, and closed her door.

They were going to die there, in the barn. Starve. Already, they were at the end of the water in the donkey's bucket and he had seen Parnell try to eat the oats. A terrible shame to die now; it made him want to weep for the glorious world out there, that he would not be able to live and see it grow healthy again. To find Cinzia, or to avenge her. Now, in the bleak night, he hoped his heart would break and kill him before the Germans found him.

Lucci heard a scraping at the door and sat up. Probably rats; still, he crawled over to see. It was morning, but still dark, and he pressed his eye to a crack and saw the teary old woman creep back across the yard and close the cottage door with exquisite care. Lucci was heartened; there was still good in the world, perhaps. Then he smelled a smell that made him heady, crêpes, and he could isolate each of the ingredients as he never could before: butter, sugar, flour, milk, even a little rum. He felt the ground until he found the plate, and pressed his fingers into a soft stack two inches high. If he were Frank, he would eat them himself. He wasn't Frank, so he said, loudly, Excuse, and the others grumbled in the hay. Chaps, he said, and they sat up. Breakfast is served, said Lucci. Courtesy of Madame Lachrymose.

It was enough to keep them alive, not enough to make them satisfied, and by dawn they were starving again. Nicolas came early to take the donkey to the fields and recoiled at their smell, frowned. My cabbage, he called to Bern, have you come to any new conclusions? But Bern sent a scathing stream of curses in French at him and Nicolas chuckled and led the donkey into the light and locked them in again.

Frank and Parnell sat together by the wall now and conferred quietly. Lucci did not like this at all. He sat beside Bern and stroked her hair, telling her little tales that his mother had told him as a child so that she would not have to see the others in their low discussions. Viktor paced back and forth. Lucci wasn't looking at him when Viktor suddenly, around noon, turned pale, sank to his knees, and fainted.

Though Frank looked close to death, he was quick enough as Bern knelt over Viktor. He stood over her and shook her shoulder roughly. Listen, he said. You don't have to prove anything to us, you know. You're the most courageous woman we all know.

The most courageous *person*, rather, called Parnell from the wall.

I've seen you with my own two eyes, said Frank. I've seen you kick a wounded man from a door so a cottage full of women could escape. I've seen you walk through brains and guts and viscera without gagging. If you could do those things, you could sleep with Nicolas to set us free. It'd only take an hour. One hour of courage and then we can go.

It's not about courage, gentlemen, said Bern. Shut your traps.

Viktor stirred on the ground and blinked his eyes, confused, drawn and pale, and she leaned over him again, cradling his pitted face. Lucci felt ill, looking at Viktor as low as this.

Nicolas is not even that bad-looking, said Parnell, in a rush. A bit greasy, but overall quite all right. It'd be a kindness to him, actually. He hasn't had a woman in years and years, he said. Think of yourself as doing a kindness, Bernie.

And listen, said Frank. You can write about it when you're done. Imagine: a short story. Like that one you did, "L'ortolan," that won all the prizes. It's material. Be a good chap, Bern. Be a good sport.

Lucci leapt up, shouted, Enough, she will not do it. That is enough. He pushed Frank back, and though Frank was far larger than Lucci, he stumbled a little. There was a long pause, and Lucci thought he could hear everything there was to hear in the world: distant planes, the shuffle of a weary family on the road outside, the inquisitive wind rustling under the skirts of the trees, voices hushed and murmuring, moving in, moving out, like one great tide. He could hear, somewhere, singing, and thought it was his imagination. No: it was Frank, whistling the "Marseillaise" softly under his breath. Lucci looked toward Viktor, who was struggling to sit up. When he looked back, a curious glint had come into Frank's face.

Frank said, slowly, Why the hell not, Bern. Everybody knows you're a slut.

Shut up, said Viktor, voice deadly quiet, but Frank gave his sour little smile. Oh, Viktor, I'm surprised you didn't know, he said. She sleeps with just about everyone she meets. I could name hundreds of men.

I do know, Viktor said, rubbing his head wearily. She's had a few lovers. It is her right, as it is yours. As it is Parnell's, and Lucci's, and mine, Frank. At least, unlike Parnell, she's not married. Bern, at least, is not a hypocrite.

Ha! A few lovers, well, said Parnell, his voice turning Cockney, ugly. Don't you wonder, Viktor, why she won't sleep with you? I do, very much. She fucks me, you know.

I know, said Viktor, sagging. I know.

She sleeps with everyone, said Parnell. She slept with Frank, if you can believe it.

What is that supposed to mean? said Frank, but nobody heard him because now it seemed as if there were a hole ripped into the air in the barn, and Bern was alone in the middle of it. She reached out to take Viktor's face in her hands, speaking low and seriously, but Viktor shook her off.

Frank, he said, very slowly. Frank. I knew about Parnell. He's handsome, it's uncomplicated. But Frank, Bern? Him?

Bern sighed and tried to find the sauciness in her voice again, but it came out strained. I don't understand it myself. I guess I felt sorry for him, she said.

Viktor stared at her, and though it was dim in the barn, Lucci thought he saw his eyes fill. Well, Viktor said. I suppose you felt sorry for me, too.

No, said Bern, but he had already turned away, already walked to the muck and stink of the donkey's area. Viktor, she said, but he raised his hand to quiet her.

Do what needs to be done, Bern, he said. It shouldn't make a difference to you, now.

They were all looking at Bern, all of the men. She took a step back and leaned against the door to catch her breath. And Lucci saw that Viktor had changed something, had turned something with his words, and Lucci couldn't resist the change. He saw the light again in Fiesole, in his garden. He saw Cinzia; he saw a million small colors of that world, and he longed, suddenly, to be in them. He longed.

In a minute, Bern stepped closer to Lucci, searched his face. She tried to take his hand. But Lucci couldn't breathe anymore. He stepped away, he turned his back.

Bern blinked, and her voice came out raggedly. *Et tu*, Lucci, she said with a grim little smile. Then she took a deep breath and waited at the door until one of Nicolas's sons passed by, and called to him in a muted voice and told him to fetch his father. The minutes that she stood there, with her back to the men in the room, seemed like weeks, like months to Lucci. Her hair was lit golden in a sunbeam that fell in a long strip down her delicate back, down her plump behind. He wanted, terribly, to say, Stop, to say Bern's name, to stroke her soft cheek where it was bitten by the light, but in the end, he didn't do anything at all.

A sooty dusk. It had begun to drizzle, and the men waited in the jeep. Under the seats were boxes of food; terrine, bread, cheese, pickles, bottles of wine, plus a full canister of gas. They had washed themselves with water the teary old woman had heated for them; they had eaten their fill beside a fire to warm their bones. The old woman would not look at them, though she wore Lucci's woolen socks in her clogs. She held out food with a closed face, turned those perpetually watering eyes away. The two sons had paced in and out of the house with their excitement, loading the jeep with provisions. At one point, they had both disappeared upstairs, and reappeared an hour later and sat whittling by the fireplace, like dogs licking their paws, satisfied.

In the car, Viktor held his face in his hands. Frank held a bottle and his normal pink flush had already regrown across his cheeks. Parnell held an unlit cigarette and stared at his hands. Lucci held his camera, but did not take a photo.

At long last, the door of the cottage opened, and Bern came out. She had lost a great deal of weight in the last few days, and her clothing hung on her; she moved as if sore, and her lip seemed torn and bleeding, as if she had bitten through it. She climbed up beside Parnell, who glanced sideways at her, his warm eyes liquid and fearful. Viktor turned on the engine and looked at Bern in the mirror, willing her to look back; Lucci, tentatively, put his hand on her cheek. Her skin was icy and white as wax. The world seemed to slow for a moment—there was the moon like a half-closed eye —the wind had died and so everything seemed to hold its breath. But Bern would not look at Viktor, and grabbed Lucci's hand and threw it back at him.

Don't, she said, very softly. Don't touch me. Don't look at me. Go.

They didn't at first, though. They remained silent. A hawk darted suddenly down. There was the wail of a distant plane. At last, Bern again said, Go, and Viktor started up the jeep. Frank cleared his throat and turned his face toward the sky. Parnell swallowed. The engine throbbed and the jeep pulled away from the cottage, into the trees. And for hours they drove, in silence, southwest, toward a certain kind of safety.

WAYNE HARRISON

Least Resistance

FROM *The Atlantic*

NICK CAMPBELL BUILT small-block engines with more bottom end than anyone in Waterbury—some said in all New England. His shop was Out of the Hole Automotive, the name sewn in midnight blue over the pockets of our work shirts. At thirty-three, Nick was a legend, and as I pulled on my uniform each morning I felt transformed from pathetic teenager to minor superhero. So when Nick's jobs started coming back as rechecks, I was fairly devastated.

The first was a '70 Monte Carlo, whose 350 engine Nick had beefed up with a high-lift roller cam and racing pistons. Mimo, the owner, was a high-maintenance price-haggler, and I wasn't surprised when he pulled right into the bays without a ticket. "I'm not happy about this, boys," he said, lisping like he did when he was excited. Mimo was a fat man, always in a turtleneck and paperboy cap. One of his relatives was supposedly connected, but Mimo looked less like a dangerous mobster than like Dom DeLuise.

Nick, Tommy Costello, and I were all on cars at the time, and approached the Monte from different angles. Nick stopped to light a cigarette with a lack of urgency that I tried to imitate. "What's the trouble, Mimo?" he said.

"Oil's the trouble. Drips all over my garage floor." He reeked of sweet cologne. You couldn't get it off all day, if he shook your hand.

Instead of putting the Monte up on the lift, Tommy ("Tommy the Temper," as some of our regulars called him) kicked over a creeper and rolled under the car with a drop-light. At this point we could still hope that Nick's work wasn't to blame. Maybe the leak was condensation from the air conditioner, and Mimo couldn't tell oil from water. We still had options. But when Tommy rolled back out and, flat on his back, just stared at the blackened ceiling, my stomach dropped. He sat forward, one of his eyebrows raised in a look that was as close as he came to compassion. He said to Nick, "It's the drain plug."

"Don't tell me he cross-threaded it," Mimo said, lisping wildly. Tommy swung around with a mean smirk, and I could guess what was next.

"He what-ed it?" Tommy said.

"Cross-threaded."

"*Croth*-threaded?"

But Mimo hadn't seen it coming. He leaned on his car, a flush rising through his jowls as he folded his arms. "What is your problem, man?"

Tommy leaned over the dynamometer and spat in the wheel well. "My problem," he said, "is a guy pulls in here like he owns the fucking place. A guy that drops off his car every other month for more cam, more carb, more exhaust, thinking it's gonna make his dick bigger, and then don't want to pay."

"Jesus, Tommy," I said, feeling I had to say something, out of common decency.

"What's wrong with the drain plug?" Nick said.

Tommy rubbed his oil-wet fingertips. "It's loose a little bit."

"Loose?" Nick said. The word took the wind out of him. Quick as I'd ever seen him do anything, Tommy dug a five-eighths box-end out of a drawer and went back under the car. Nick, our boss, our leader, neglecting something so basic—imagine going a day unaware you forgot to put on your right shoe—was inconceivable.

Nick smoked and stared at the car dumbfounded, dazed. Mary Ann, his wife, passed by with her bookkeeping binder. The three of us, standing quiet as mourners around Mimo's car, stopped her short of the lobby door. "What's wrong?" she said.

Nick wouldn't look at her, and when she turned to me, I was torn between the loyalty I owed the two people who mattered to me most. I couldn't blow her off, and I couldn't tell on Nick. Thank God Nick spoke up then, just as Mary Ann started to walk away. "Do me a favor," he said. "Take Mimo out to the lobby and give him his money back."

"Whoa," Mimo said, a flattered, guilt-ridden knot of emotion now. "That's eighteen hundred dollars. I'd be happy with a discount."

"I don't give a damn what you're happy with," Nick said, and he threw his cigarette in the trash can, where any number of things could have gone up in flames.

What happened between Mary Ann and me started as conversations in the parts room. She'd ask me about my girlfriend, Katie, what we did on our dates, whether I said nice things to her. When Katie broke up with me a week before Christmas, I couldn't bring myself to tell Mary Ann. I was embarrassed and hurt, two things I didn't want to show, but inevitably those feelings came out, and Mary Ann and I had our first hug between thermostats and Fram oil filters. It was a big hug, which gave me a glimpse into where our friendship might lead.

Why I betrayed the one man I wanted to become wasn't clear to me then—the summer I turned nineteen—and only with the distance of time do I see the kid who thought he was exempt from the basic laws of civilized life. Sometimes, as Nick and I buttoned up a car he'd just brought back from the dead, I'd promise myself Mary Ann and I were over. But then she'd come out through the bays, not even noticing me as she started an inventory, completely focused on her job, so strong to do that when only days earlier an orgasm I'd given her had made her cry. If right then she told me to declare my love for her to Nick, I would have. I would have done almost anything.

"Chant with me," she said, late one morning in her living room. I didn't worry much about Nick coming home on our Tuesdays together. Nick was a raging workaholic, and besides, he'd never leave Tommy alone at the shop to greet customers. Sometimes Mary Ann and I left our clothes off after making love—likely as not we'd fall back into the act after a while—and as she crossed the room to the stereo, I watched her back and ass and thighs. Her body didn't disappoint me when she undressed, unlike the two girlfriends I'd been with, both of whom were thirteen years younger than Mary Ann.

The big plaster-walled living room held six framed photographs. Over the fireplace mantel Nick was standing arm in arm with

Buddy Baker after Buddy had broken 200 miles per hour at Talladega. The other pictures were of Oregon, where Nick and Mary
Ann had moved from four years ago. Rolling waves were framed
by miles of Sahara-like dunes. A lake inside a dead volcano, white
mountain peaks, lava fields that looked like the face of the moon.
Nick and Mary Ann came out East when Nick inherited the shop
from an uncle who had died of emphysema. I imagined that arriving here, in run-down Waterbury, from such a place as Oregon,
must've been like waking from a dream.

Mary Ann put in a cassette, and the sound that rose from
the speakers was unlike any I'd ever heard. Two rich voices that
could only belong to gorgeous dark-eyed Indian women sang the
first chorus. *Om namah shivaya.* Then a hundred or a thousand
voices in unison. Behind the chant were the slightest sounds, tiny
wind chimes, tiny buzzing. Then *om namah shivaya. OM NAMAH
SHIVAYA.* You could hear tears in the women's voices, anguish,
then resolve, safety. "What are they saying?"

"It's a salutation to that which we are capable of becoming."
Mary Ann took my hand and brought me to the carpet, piled my
legs in rough approximation of a lotus, and positioned herself beside me. I started to sway. It was warm, and we were naked with this
remarkable sound.

And then the phone rang. She let the machine answer, and the
sound of Nick's voice in the house shot through me like a spark-
plug jolt. "Babe, I can't find the last Carquest order . . ." When the
message was over, she turned off the chant tape, and we dressed in
the silence of Adam and Eve after the apple.

Though she herself didn't drink, Mary Ann went to the kitchen
and brought me one of Nick's Heinekens. It wasn't quite noon, but
the day already had the feel of an epic journey for us, and all com-
forts were allowed. "Do you believe in karma?" I said. She watched
me a moment, as if to see where this was going, then nodded.

"What's a good way to improve it?"

"Go to college. Do something with your life."

I lit one of her menthols, a taste I'd already come to associate
with these air-conditioned, self-indulgent mornings. "You sound
like my dad."

"Sorry," she said. She knew the story. My father had told me, one
morning before school six years earlier, that he and my mother
had outgrown each other—which was half true.

"And I like fixing cars."

"Maybe you'll find something you like better. Something friendlier to your back and knuckles."

"Nick told me you used to work on cars."

She caught her lip in her teeth, and her mind seemed to change gears. "Do you like fortune cookies? I had one the other night that said, 'Spend much money on many doors.'"

I thought about that, and shook my head. With a Chinese accent she said, "It mean go to *correge*. Open *possibirities*." I spent the next moment in love with her, a feeling that both hurt and exhilarated me. She had a young, freckled complexion, and I was already losing hair in front, my teeth stained from cigarettes and coffee. I imagined the years between us were offset. I imagined — all I could do was imagine — that if anyone saw us holding hands on the street, they would think we were the same age.

"Tommy Costello was human once," she warned. "Don't turn into him."

"I was actually thinking of Nick. All his rechecks."

She lit a cigarette for herself. "Justin, what do you think karma is?"

"Why bad things happen to good people," I said. And I thought, too late, of the baby boy they'd lost not even two years ago. If I'd offended her, she didn't show it. She brushed her permed, always damp-looking red hair behind an ear and shaped the ash of her cigarette.

"I don't think Tommy can blame karma," she said. "Out of the Hole isn't a shop, it's a circus. You guys aren't even nice to your customers."

This was often true — we modified engines for gearheads who tipped well and would've forgiven us for crapping on the floor if we juiced a dozen more ponies out of their V-8s. Tommy was worse than anyone. Mary Ann had to buy a separate coffeemaker for the bays just to keep him out of the lobby, where he got fingerprints everywhere, and swore and farted as he pleased.

"It's the path of least resistance," she said. "He has no decency, no discipline. And so his work is starting to suffer. Where's the mystery?"

The first of two mistakes I made with Mary Ann happened during sex. I was starting to worry that she'd think missionary was the only position I knew, so I asked if we could try doggy style. She looked away and freed herself from me, turned over, and waited, slumped over the sofa arm. The muscles in her back tightened, pulling down from her spine and causing her back to arc slightly. Entering her without the press of our fronts and without kissing was like breaking a spell. I apologized and turned her back, holding her fiercely, and, as if I'd just pulled her from a hole in the ice, felt her life return.

The second mistake was going into their bedroom. The door stayed closed when I was over, and one morning while she was in the bathroom I saw my chance. The room was neat, the bed made —a rustic log bed of Oregon fir, I figured. I stayed in the doorway. In a frame on the bureau was a picture of baby Joey, whose features were mostly Nick's, with Mary Ann's electric-blue eyes. Like a mini-shrine, the picture was surrounded by two plastic rings, a stuffed penguin, and a toy banana. In the mirror I saw something that drew me all the way in. On the floor, between the bed and the window, was a rumpled sleeping bag and pillow on a foam mat. I stared at it for some time and was halfway back to the door when she came in and caught me.

"Justin," she said. The pain in her voice sickened me. "I don't believe this."

"Mary Ann."

"Just leave. Get out. Go." She came around and pushed me back. She would have knocked me over had I tried to hold my ground.

This took us weeks to get over. At first she wasn't talking to me, and I felt no better than Tommy, though, unlike him, I was aware enough to feel the agony. I could see that she was suffering as well, having no one to talk to other than customers and Nick, whose mind was generally passing from valve to cylinder to exhaust, like one of those tiny cameras that swim up veins on science shows. Then one day I got a sentence: "You had no right," and then, hours later, another: "I thought I could trust you." But slowly we came back together. One afternoon she drove out to Bethlehem, the lit-tle dairy-farm town where I lived. We walked the downtown, three blocks of mostly antiques stores, and in a coffee shop she explained sudden infant death syndrome, how it was every parent's night-mare, how she woke to the sight of Nick rocking the baby, pleading with him, "Warm up. Warm up, son."

Our small table had two chairs, and to slide mine around to her side when her eyes filled up would have been loud and awkward. So I pressed her hand in both of mine and waited. In a while she managed a smile. "I didn't want to cry in here," she said.

"Why does he sleep on the floor?"

"He dreams that Joey's still in the bed. He tells me not to take it personally, but how do you not?"

Holding her hand in the coffee shop, I realized how close I'd come to blowing it with the one person in my life who needed me. Her family was back in Oregon. Her husband was distracted, about to lose his reputation and business if he couldn't pull it together. And here I was, listening. Devoted to her and listening.

The rechecks were eating Nick alive. It wasn't the number of them —maybe seven or eight all summer—but that the mistakes were careless and potentially expensive. The only pattern I noticed was what you'd expect, that the jobs happened on our busiest days, when any of us were hard-pressed just to keep our fingers out of spinning fans. For a while I toyed with the idea that Tommy was behind it somehow, but on those chaotic days all I could do was keep track of myself, never mind watching him. And what would he have to gain by ruining Nick? We weren't known for competitive pricing, and certainly not for customer service; all that kept us employed was Nick's fast-spreading reputation as a genius.

I gave Nick my full dedication. My dark secret made me the best friend I'd ever been. I'd intercept pissed-off customers and lie straight-faced that a bad batch of spark plugs was to blame for their complaints. I put myself out on a limb, and felt wonderful.

Early one afternoon Nick was helping me with a mid-'70s Formula that Firestone had sent by. They'd replaced the carburetor to the tune of five hundred dollars only to find that the idle continued to cough and skip.

Cylinders six and eight came up weak on a cylinder balance. Nick set one end of a long socket extension on the intake manifold and listened to the other end. He looked back to see the hydrocarbon count registering from the exhaust sniffer. It was up through the roof. "What do you think?"

"It needs a valve job," I said.

He brought the rpm up to 2,000 and held it, and the hydrocarbons dropped to passing levels. I was baffled. Worn valves are worn valves at any rpm.

Nick leaned back against my toolbox. He lit a cigarette off the head of one whose filter I could smell burning, he'd smoked it so far down. "You're how old?" He said.

"Nineteen on Friday. You're taking me out for Jäger shots, remember?"

He grinned more to himself than to me. "I was nineteen when I balanced and blueprinted my first 350. Every weekend out in the garage for a month. That was what you might call my defining moment."

My first reaction to this story was gloom. Here was another instance when the rest of my life seemed like not enough time to catch up with Nick. Nothing was more exhaustive and precise than blueprinting an engine, nothing. Each piston disassembled and polished, each nut and washer cleaned or replaced, accounted for. I was light-years from such a feat.

Nick squinted over his cigarette. "I don't even know if I could do it again," he said. "I think my memory's going to be toast before I'm fifty." An hour ago he'd had another recheck, a big-ticket job that started backfiring twenty minutes after the customer left. He'd pulled into the first shop off I-84 and was told that a loose head bolt was to blame.

"It happens," I said, wishing I could think of something useful to say. "I hate to think how many times I've screwed up." He chuckled, then stretched out his arms and yawned gigantically. I wanted to ask if he was getting sleep, but I couldn't trust myself not to reveal — just by the look on my face as I asked — what I knew about his home life. So I went back to work. I used propane to check for vacuum leaks. I checked timing. I wanted to prove myself better than Firestone. Things that made no sense to check, I checked. Finally I lit a cigarette and flopped over the fender mat. "Goddamn it," I said. "It's unfixable."

He picked up a ball-peen hammer, leaned on the passenger-side fender, and tapped twice on the EGR valve. Something held by suction dislodged, the engine coughed once and almost stalled, and he revved it clean. When he let go of the throttle, it idled like glass.

All I could say was "Jesus." When the fog of having witnessed a near miracle lifted, I saw the bad news as well as the good. The car was fixed, but an EGR valve wasn't even a hundred-dollar ticket, so my commission—I made that plus seven dollars an hour—would be less than five dollars.

He read over the paperwork again. Then, with the ball-peen still in hand, he stepped up to the Formula, and with one smack he cracked the back corner of the intake manifold all the way through. The idle started coughing again, and suddenly I was looking at a fifteen-hundred-dollar ticket. "Firestone's paying," he said. "Happy birthday."

Six months after she dumped me, Katie started calling the house. She said she missed me, that she felt like she'd lost her best friend. Finally I told her about my affair with Mary Ann, to try and scare her away. But Katie was persistent. "I'm worried about you, Justin," she said. "How old is she?"

"So how's UConn? You meeting any guys up there?"

"It's illegal," she said. "If she's married, that makes it adultery."

"Shut up."

"I mean, how would you feel if you were him?"

"I already know how it feels. Remember?" She'd left me for an ex-friend from Nonnewaug High. I'd driven out to her house one night and his LeMans was parked in her driveway, her Christmas tree lights blinking over his hood.

Katie sighed, and I waited another second, then hung up. I thought we were done, but two days later she called and said she'd be there for me when this was over, and I thanked her just to be civil, though I didn't see how we could ever be together again, considering how immature our love was. Life had always been easy, and was going to continue to be easy, for her. She didn't know the struggle of real people. But I was learning. In my heart I couldn't imagine ever being through with Mary Ann.

I told Mary Ann I'd never go back to Katie.

"I don't blame you," she said. "You have to learn how to trust again."

I watched to see if she was relieved at all about my resolve. We held each other's eyes, and I understood, when she leaned in and kissed me lightly, that she'd misread my sullenness. "Keep talking," she said. "Men don't learn how to talk about pain."

I could see that she needed to listen. "She liked jewelry," I said.

"She had all these little jewelry boxes in her room, so I bought her this one giant one. It's like four feet tall with two swinging doors, solid oak. And she breaks up with me a week before Christmas. By the time I realize we're not getting back together, I can't return it. So I gave it to my mom, and now, every time I walk by her room, I see that damn jewelry box."

As I spoke, I watched the vertical blinds that closed us off from the daylit world, their color that of fingers on a flashlight lens. I wondered if Mary Ann had seen how close I'd come to choking up. Yes, I still ached, but more than that, I recognized that we were connecting yet again—more undeniable evidence that she and I were made for each other.

"Wait here," she said, and in a moment she came back from her bedroom. She handed me something smooth and cool. "It's a worry stone," she said. "It helps you not be inside so much. Hold it when you're upset, and let it take the bad energy."

I rolled the stone in my palm. It was the black-green of an avocado, and I recognized it but couldn't remember from where.

"Where did you feel it?" she said. "The hurt."

I looked into her big pale eyes. "It's like you forget how to breathe."

She took my other hand and held it to her bare chest. Her heartbeat was almost something I could hold. We stayed that way, and her breathing deepened. She closed her eyes tightly, as if against an awful sound, and a trickle of coldness seeped through me.

"Sometimes," she said, sitting forward, "God, it's like it just happened. Sometimes he'd nurse so hard I was raw. I'd be in tears by the time he was done." She stared down at the old braided rug, with its frayed threads and little spills, and might have been looking into the past. "The morning after we lost him, I was so engorged, I had to pump. My body didn't understand that he was gone. I pumped six ounces and then had to pour it down the drain. That almost killed me. I would've given anything for another bloody nipple."

I pictured her at the sink watching her milk disappear, my story a pathetic whimper next to hers. I looked at the stone again, and then realized where I'd seen it before. Looking for matches one day in Nick's box, in the little top drawer where a mechanic keeps cigarettes, soda machine change, his Snap-on account book and receipts, I saw, way at the back, the twin of this little stone.

One night after hours Tommy, Nick, and I were sharing a twelve-pack while Nick finished up on an '85 IROC. The engine was crawling with vacuum lines and sensor wires, and Nick's confidence had fallen to the point of sending me to Caldor for a Polaroid camera. He'd taken shots of the engine from several angles before dismantling.

"Your folks divorced?" Nick said, glancing at me over the carburetor. I nodded, the question affirming how little he knew about me personally.

"How come your old man never taught you cars?"

"He's not like that," I said. "He buys new and sells when the warranty runs out."

"Man," Nick said, dolefully. "I don't know where I'd be without my old man taking me out to the garage. What kind of work's he do?"

"He's a, uh . . ." I glanced at Tommy, who was leaning back on a metal stool with his legs open, a Milwaukee's Best on his thigh, just kind of staring off. "He's curator at a gallery in New Haven."

"Gallery?"

"Japanese art."

"What kind of art the Japs make?" Tommy said, perking up. "Rice cakes?"

"Robes. Swords, you know. Paintings."

"*Brown Stains on the Wall,* by Who-Flung-Poo," he said and chugged his beer. His mind was sharper than you'd think, looking at his sagging, stubbled face, and I grinned, though I was becoming more and more reluctant to indulge him.

"I never really got art," Nick said.

"He a bum chum, your old man?" Tommy said.

Nick laughed. "A what?"

"A sausage jockey. A backdoor commando." His look never varied from an expression of knowing that the world and everyone in it was full of shit. "Isn't that, like, a qualification for being curator?"

"He remarried," I said. "He has two kids." It shut him up but didn't erase that damn smirk. I stared at him. "I don't know, man,"

I said. All of a sudden my stomach was quaking, but the thought of how much Mary Ann despised him made me brave. "When was the last time you had a girlfriend, Tommy? You're not a fag, are you?"

"Oh, boy," Nick said. "Let's get ready to rumble."

"I just had yours last night. Little Miss Pick-a-Hole."

"I'm serious," I said. "You need to get laid, man."

"Kid, you're going to talk your way right into a hospital room. I want your opinion, I'll have my sister beat it out of you."

"All right, guys," Nick said. "Give it a break." He checked the timing and finished up the paperwork, and I didn't look at Tommy. "You want to," Nick said in a while, "go ahead and think of me as your stand-in old man. Surrogate, or whatever."

Tommy crumpled his can and tossed it in the box with the others. "Get a room, queers," he said. Watching him head toward the lockers, I felt I'd won. I got Nick a fresh beer. "Here you go, Dad."

He took it, grinning. "All right. Not Daddy, though. Or Pop. Call me Pop, and I'll stomp a mudhole in your ass."

After that night, something changed in our relationship. Nick took on fewer cars so that he could give me jobs that were over my head and guide me through them. Not one of my cars came back, though a few of those he jumped on alone did. I saw that he cared more about my work than his own. I saw that karma, as Mary Ann had insisted, wasn't magical but just the natural course of things. He gave me what was abundant to him. He taught me how to listen to an engine as a compilation of sounds, the way dogs understand smell or winemakers experience taste. When his heart was open, and he was sharing all his secrets, I could only imagine the mechanic little Joey might have become.

Nick and Mary Ann decided the shop needed a facelift.

"Two hundred bucks if you stay all night," Nick said to me, carrying four gallons of apple-green latex from the trunk of his car. It was Saturday evening, half an hour after we'd closed. "Walls and floors," he said. "It can sit and dry tomorrow. What do you say?"

What was to say? I ran down the alley to Lou's Liquors for a case of Heineken. Lou Jr. served me without question, persuaded by my confidence even as I dropped my hill of fives and ones on the counter sign that said NO ID NO SALE. Back at the shop I swept, and Mary Ann mopped behind me—"Yo-ho-ho and a bottle of rum," she sang, swabbing the deck without plan or pattern, until she was out of breath. These days, she was more animated around the shop and more affectionate with Nick. I felt we were all probably changing for the better. Mary Ann and I talked about our pain, and we chanted, and when I laughed and cried, I laughed and cried harder.

The phone rang in the lobby, and Nick looked at his watch and said, "Benny about the Cutlass." The door hadn't even fully closed behind him when Mary Ann said, "I've got to tell you something incredible," and she took a bottle out of the case and held it out for me to open. I did, and she knocked my bottle in cheers before the first drink of alcohol I'd ever seen her take. She made a face. "I forgot how skunk-cabbagey they are."

"They're strong," I said, for once feeling more experienced about something.

"He got in bed with me last night," she said. "He slept right through to the alarm."

"Wow," I said, and I didn't see it coming, this pang, this shortness of breath. "That's really . . . I'm happy for you guys."

She had another sip and looked at me over the green bottle. "Justin," she said, "honey, we talked about this. Don't be jealous."

"I know. It's fine. We'll talk about it later," I said, ready to not think about it anymore as I dipped my roller.

"Talk about what?" she said. "What exactly do you mean?"

"Nothing," I said, her tone causing a knot to swell in my throat. "It's no big deal."

"I don't have to negotiate with you."

"That's not what I meant."

Nick came back out to the bays, but Mary Ann continued watching me, and for a panicked moment I thought she might continue the conversation. I set down my roller and cracked a beer for Nick. "All right, team," he said. "Let's make like Picasso."

Around midnight, as the first coat dried, we washed up and drove to the Peking Duck in Nick's Chevelle. We feasted on beef chow mein and Mai Tais. Mary Ann was drunk and giddy, leaning on Nick's shoulder in the booth. When the fortune cookies came, and she tore up my FINANCIAL NEWS IS IN STORE and wrote me one on a napkin, FOLLOW YOUR HEART. IT WILL LEAD YOU HOME, I knew things were all right between us again.

*

A week after the painting, the shop was bright as a new car, the beer cans gone from the back ledge, little giraffes revealed—after a scrubdown with GoJo—on the bathroom wallpaper. Nick and Mary Ann came out to the bays together one afternoon. "Justin," Nick said, "you got a minute?"

Bent over a Grand Prix, I glanced from Nick to Mary Ann for signs that everything was, all of a sudden and horrifically, out in the open. "What's going on?"

"I wanted to tell you first while Tommy's on a test drive," Nick said. "He'll be pissed, but fuck him."

"What?"

"I just sold the place to Mitch Heedy at Firestone." He grinned at me and held up his hands. "Hang on, don't go having kittens. He's going to hire you on. We already discussed it."

"You sold it?" I said.

"We're moving back to Oregon. Mary Ann's brother wants me to manage a Carquest out there. It's a glorified counter job, but it'll be less stress. Reliable income. Anyway, Mitch doesn't want Tommy, so try not to bust his ass too much."

The rest of the morning was a blur. Mary Ann stayed behind the counter helping customers, and finally I left her a note that was just a big question mark on a folded scrap.

She came out to the car I'd been trying to finish up for close to an hour. "Where's Nick?" I said.

"In his office telling Tommy." She folded her arms and glanced away. Then she sighed and looked at me again. "Be happy for me. We deserve this."

"Why didn't you tell me?"

"You, you, you," she said. "I hate to say it, but that mindset won't make you very popular with women. You'll see." She smiled, but my expression made her look away.

"I'm not joking, Mary Ann. I mean, what the fuck?"

"Don't do this," she said.

"What's in Oregon?"

She blinked at me. "Our lives."

Suddenly the lobby door crashed into the adjacent wall and stayed there, the knob half buried in the sheetrock. Tommy marched out shaking his head, Nick on his heels. "Look, Tommy," Nick said.

"Motherfucker. Get away from me." Tommy kicked over a gallon of antifreeze and disappeared into the locker room. Then the metal crash that could only be the sound of a fist launching into a locker door. Again and again.

Nick closed the door to the locker room and turned to us. "Well, that didn't go as bad as I thought."

"Can I come out to Oregon?" I said.

When he looked at me his smile broke like a boy's. "Sure, you can come. You fish?"

"I mean, what's keeping me here?" I said. "I can't stay behind without my Pop."

"What did I tell you about that?" he said, and got me around the neck. We wrestled around, and he pulled back, laughing. He wiped his eye. "All right. Keep it sad around here for Tommy's sake," he said, and went back to the lobby, where he pulled the doorknob from the wall.

When he was gone my fingers went digging in my pocket for cigarettes, sticking one in my mouth, fumbling with a match. A couple of screwdrivers rolled off my fender mat onto the floor. Mary Ann was staring at me. "I don't think that's a good idea," she said, a surge of color in her face as she bent to pick up my screwdrivers. She brought them to my toolbox and started setting them in their holders. "I'm putting my marriage back together, Justin."

"He said I could come."

"This isn't your life." She went back to the car, beside which I'd wheeled a rolling tool tray, and started gathering up my wrenches and putting them away as well. And everything became clear to me. The cigarette fell out of my lips. "Jesus," I said. "It was you."

She stared at the floor where my cigarette had fallen. "Okay. It was me what?"

"Sabotaging Nick's jobs. He wasn't fucking up."

Mary Ann sighed deeply and closed her eyes. She shook her head, smiled bitterly, and then out of nowhere she lurched forward and slapped me. I'd never been slapped before, and it burned with the ring of a low piano chord. "You took advantage of a situation. That's it. That's all that happened." These things she said with a steady, calculated voice that made her anger all the more icy.

I didn't say a word. After she went back to the lobby, I gathered sockets off the fender mat and tucked them in their plastic cases silently, as if in fear of waking someone. I didn't want to hear anything. The hammering in my chest was enough.

JAMES LASDUN

The Hollow

FROM *The Paris Review*

THE PARKERS, FATHER AND SON, came over to introduce
themselves when we moved in, five years ago. Dean, the father, was
slow to speak, awkward when he did. But Rick was talkative, his eyes
roving inquisitively over us and our boxes of possessions. A fuzz of
reddish stubble covered his neatly rounded head and pointed chin.
His voice was soft, almost velvety, with a sprung quality, each word
like a plucked banjo note. He told us he did a variety of odd jobs
in landscaping and construction. Tree work was what he enjoyed
most, the more difficult the better. He would climb up in a harness
and spiked boots to drop limbs from trees that stood too close
to people's houses to fell conventionally, or he'd drive out in his
pickup to haul storm-tangled, half-blown-over trees out of each
other's branches, then cut them up for firewood. Any jobs like that
you need doing, he told us, I'm your man.

Some time after that visit my wife and I passed two small children
climbing the steep slope of Vanderbeck Hollow. They were both in
tears, and we stopped to see if we could help. Their mother had
put them out of the car for fighting, they told us, and they were
walking home.

Home, it turned out, was Rick's house. Rick had met their
mother, Faye, a few weeks earlier, at a Harley-Davidson rally, and
she'd moved in, bringing her kids with her. Rick's father had already moved out. Faye herself we met when we dropped off the
children. She didn't seem to care about our interference in their
punishment. She was a thin, black-haired woman with pitted skin,
bright blue eyes, and a dab of hard crimson at the center of her upper lip. She didn't say much.

They had their first baby the next year, a girl. Rick used to tuck her into his hunting jacket while he worked in his front yard, fixing his trucks or sharpening his chainsaw blades. He liked being a father—from the start he'd treated Faye's two elder children as his own—but it was soon apparent that his new responsibilities were a strain for him. After a day operating the stone crusher at the Andersonville quarry or cutting rebar with one of the construction crews in town, he'd come home, eat dinner, then turn on a set of floodlights he'd rigged up to the house and start cutting and splitting firewood to make extra money. He sold it for seventy dollars a cord, which was cheap even then. I often bought a cord or two for our woodstove. Once, he asked how I made my living. "Gaming the system," I replied, intending to sound amusingly cryptic. "You must be good at it" was all he said, pointing to our new Subaru.

He bought a car for Faye, cutting wood later and later into the night to pay for it, renting a mechanical splitter from the hardware store and erecting huge log piles all around his house. A note of exasperation entered his talk; he seemed bewildered by the difficulty of making ends meet. Here he was, a young man in his prime —able to take care of his physical needs, to plow his own driveway, to fix his own roof, to hunt and butcher his own meat—and yet every day was a struggle. If it wasn't money, it was offenses to his pride, which was strung tight, like every other part of him. He was always recounting (reliving, it almost seemed) insults and slights he'd received from various bosses and other representatives of the official world, along with the defiant ripostes he'd made. When Faye got a job on the night shift at Hannaford and was kept past her clocking-out time, he called up the manager at the store: "I told that freakin' weasel to get off her back," he said to me with a satisfied grin. She was fired soon after.

To blow off steam he would barrel up and down the hill in his truck, churning up clouds of dust from the gravel surface. Or he would carry a six-pack up to the woods above the road and sit drinking among the oaks and ashes along the ridge. I would often find a can of Molson by a rock up there in the bracken where he'd dumped it—his gleaming spoor. He was building a little cabin on the other side of the ridge, he told me once. It was state land there, but he figured no one would care. What was it for? I asked him. He shrugged. "Just somewhere to go . . ."

Another time he told me he'd seen a lion up there.

"A mountain lion?"

"Yep. A catamount."

"I didn't know they lived around here." In fact I'd read that despite rumored sightings, there were no mountain lions in this area.

He gave me a glance and I saw he'd registered my disbelief, but also that he didn't hold it against me. "Yep. Came right up to the cabin. Sucker just stood there in the entranceway, big as a freakin' buffalo. I kept one of the paw prints he left in the dirt. Dug it out and let it dry. I'll show you someday."

As a boy, when the Parkers' property had marked the end of the road, he'd had the run of Vanderbeck Hollow, hunting deer and wild turkey, fishing for trout in the rock pools along the stream that wound down the deep crease between Spruce Clove and Donell Mountain. He wasn't exactly a model of ecological awareness, with his beer cans and his oil-leaking ATV that he used for dragging tree carcasses down to his truck, not to mention the roaring, fumey snowmobile he drove along the logging trails all winter, but he knew the woods up here with an intimacy that seemed its own kind of love. I walked with him up to one of the old quarries one spring morning and found myself at the receiving end of a detailed commentary on the local wildlife. To my uninformed eye, the trees and plants were more or less just an undifferentiated mass of brown and green matter, and the effect of his pointing and naming was like having a small galaxy switch itself on star by star around me. "Trout lily," he said, and a patch of yellow flowers lit up under a boulder. "Goat's rue," and a silvery-stemmed plant shone out from a clearing a few yards off. "Mountain laurel," he went on, gesturing at some dark green shrubs, "blossoms real pretty in late spring. Won't be for another month or more yet. They call 'em laurel slicks when it grows in thickets like this. Sometimes heath balds. It's poisonous—even honey made from the flowers is supposed to be poisonous. See here, the burl?" He put his finger on a hard, knot-like growth—"old-timers used to make pipes out of 'em. My dad has one."

In his lifetime he'd seen the road developed a mile and a half beyond the family property, the surrounding land sold off in twenty-acre lots, with timber frames and swimming pools and chainlink fences and NO HUNTING signs going further and fur-

ther up the hill every year, and he hated it all, though his hatred
stopped short of the actual human beings responsible for these in-
cursions. One afternoon he was standing on the road with me,
complaining about the arrival of backhoes to dig the foundation
for a new house on the property of Cora Chastine, the neighbor
below him, when Cora herself rode out of her driveway on her
chestnut mare. Seeing him, she began thanking him for a favor
he'd done her the night before, pulling a dinner guest's car out of
the ditch at one in the morning. Smiling gallantly, he assured her
it was no problem and that he hadn't minded being woken at that
hour. "Nice lady," he said in his purring voice when she rode on,
as if there were no important connection in his mind between
the person herself and her contribution to the destruction of his
haunts.

He and Faye had a second child, another girl. A hurricane—unusual in these parts—struck that year. Torrential rain had fallen
for several days before, loosening roots so that the trees came
crashing down like sixty-foot bowling pins when the wind hit, turning the woods into scenes of carnage, the trees lying in their sap
and foliage and splintered limbs like victims of a massacre, the vast
holes left by their roots gaping like bomb craters. Within the hurricane there were localized tornadoes, one of which plowed a trail
of devastation through our own woods. Rick offered to do the
cleanup for us, pointing out that there were some valuable trees we
could sell for timber. He proposed doing all the work himself over
the course of a year: to use a cousin's team of horses to drag the
timber out so as to avoid the erosion big machines caused, to load
it with a hand-winched pulley (a "come-along" was his quaint name
for this), to chop up all the crowns for firewood and haul off the
stumps to the town dump.

I hesitated, knowing he had no insurance and anticipating problems if he should injure himself. A lawyer friend told us on no account to let him do the work, and we hired a fully insured professional logging crew instead. They brought in a skidder the size of a
tugboat, a bulldozer, two tractors, and a grappler with a claw that
could grab a trunk a yard thick and hoist it thirty feet into the air.
For several weeks these machines tore through our woods, bulldoz-
ing rocks, branches, and stumps into huge unsightly piles and rip-
ping a raw red trail across streambeds and fern-filled clearings to

the landing stage by the road, where the crew loaded the limbless trunks onto a double-length trailer to sell at the lumberyard. I ran into Rick several times on the road during the operation. He never reproached us for passing him over for the job; in fact he offered good advice on how not to get cheated out of our share of the proceeds. But I felt uncomfortable seeing him walk by, as though I'd denied him work that was his by rights.

He and Faye got married the following summer. We were invited to the celebratory pig roast. It was a big party: beat-up old pickup trucks lining the road halfway down the hill and twenty or thirty motorcycles parked in the driveway. We recognized a few neighbors; otherwise it was all Faye's and Rick's biker friends in leather jackets and bandanas. At the center of the newly cleaned-up front yard a dance floor had been improvised out of bluestone slabs that Rick must have dragged from one of the old quarries up in the woods. Beside it a band was playing fast, reeling music: two fiddles, a guitar, a banjo, and a mandolin, the players belting out raucous harmonies as they flailed away at their instruments.

I liked this mountain music. I'd started listening to it a few years before and found myself susceptible to its mercurial moods and colors—more so than ever since we'd moved up here to mountains of our own, where it had come to seem conjured directly out of the bristly, unyielding landscape itself, the rapid successions of pain and sweetness, tension and release, frugality and spilling richness, arising straight out of these thickly wooded crags and gloomy gullies with their sun-shot clearings and glittering, wind-riffled creeks. I would listen to it in the car as I drove to work, an hour down the thruway. The lucrative drudgery of my job left me with a depleted sensation, as though I'd spent the days asleep or dead, but driving there and back I would play my Clinch Mountain Boys CDs at full volume, and as their frenzied, propulsive energies surged into me I would bray along at the top of my lungs, harmonizing with unabashed tunelessness, and a feeling of joy would arise in me as if a second self, full of fiery, passionate vitality were at the point of awakening inside me.

A van drove into the yard shortly after we arrived. In it was the pig for the pig roast. As a wedding joke, their friends had arranged to have the animal delivered alive instead of dead. Two of them helped the butcher lead it from the van, roping its bucking, scarlet-eyed head and shit-squirting rear end, and dragging it over to Rick. One of them handed him a gleaming knife.

"What's this?"

He stared down at the animal, writhing frantically in its ropes.

Faye had appeared, dressed in a denim skirt and red cowboy boots. She looked on, smoking a cigarette with an air of neutral but attentive interest.

"You gotta do the honors, buddy," one of the bikers said. "Duty of the groom."

There was loud laughter, a shout of "Go on, cut his goddamn throat."

"I'll cut your goddamn throat," Rick muttered. He went into the house and there was a brief, awkward hiatus. He came back out with a shotgun. Faye turned away.

"Hey, you can't do that, he has to bleed to death, don't he?" a guest said, looking at the butcher, who gave a noncommittal shrug.

Ignoring them both, Rick loaded a cartridge into the gun and fired it straight into the pig's head, splattering himself and several others with blood and brains. This set off guffaws of laughter among the bikers, and Rick himself cracked a smile. "I'll get the come-along," he said. They hoisted the pig up with the device—an archaic-looking assemblage of cords and gears and wooden pulleys —hanging it by its hind legs from a tree branch, and the butcher slit it open, spilling its innards into a bucket. Then they drove a spit through it and set it up over a halved oil drum grill, and the band, which had fallen silent during this episode, struck up again, three high voices in a blasting triad calling out, "Weeee-ill you miss me?" followed by the single morose rumble of their thick-bearded baritone: "miss me when I'm gawwwn . . ."

Rick came up to us with a bottle of applejack that he claimed to have brewed himself with fruit from his grandfather's old Prohibition orchard at the back of their lot. He insisted we take a swig from the bottle—it was pure liquid fire—then reeled away, grabbing Faye for a dance on the stone floor.

It was at this moment, watching him cavort around his bride with one hand on his hip and the other brandishing the bottle high in the air, while she stared out across the valley at the dusty emerald flank of Donell Mountain, that I registered, for the first time, the tinge of sadness in Faye's expression, underlying the more visible cold severity.

I was away much of the following year and aside from a few fleeting glimpses didn't see them again until the fall, when I ran into them at a neighbor's party. Arshin and Leanne, the hosts, were therapists, Buddhists, members of the local "healing community": Leanne shaven-headed like a Tibetan monk, Arshin gaunt and dark, a set of prayer beads forever clicking in his fingers. Their friends were mostly either acupuncturists or qigong practitioners. Rick and Faye were standing in a corner, drinking beers with a tall man in a scuffed leather jacket and a pair of muddy work boots. The three of them looked out of place among these shoeless, tea-drinking wraiths. I went over to say hello. Rick introduced their friend as his "buddy" Schuyler. I noticed a string of numbers tattooed across the back of his neck, like a serial number. He gave a nod, then faded swiftly back into what appeared to be some immensely pleasurable private reverie. Purely to make conversation I asked Rick if he was planning to sell firewood again this fall.

"Maybe."

"I'd like a cord if you are."

"Okay."

He didn't seem all that interested in talking. I moved away, wondering if I'd offended him by talking business at a social gathering. Schuyler and Faye left the party but Rick stayed on, drinking steadily. At one point he started asking women to dance, even though it wasn't that kind of party. One or two of them did, just to humor him.

The next night, at two in the morning, he started firing off his gun. The same thing happened for the next several nights. I called to ask what was going on. He answered the phone with the words "Hello, you've reached the Vanderbeck Hollow Cathouse and Abortion Clinic," then hung up. A few days later I came home from the train station to find a pile of logs dumped over the lawn. It was true that I'd asked for wood, but normally we would discuss the price and the time of delivery before Rick brought it over, and he would help me stack it. I called him that evening. Without apologizing for dumping the wood, he said he wanted a hundred and twenty dollars for it.

"That's quite a bit more than you usually charge."

"That's the price."

I stacked the wood. It seemed less than a full cord, and I said so when I took the check down to Rick the next day. He was outside, talking with Faye by the stone oven he'd built in their front yard. He barely looked at me as I spoke.

"That was a full cord," was all he said, taking the check. "I measured it."

It was only when I spoke to Arshin a few days later that I began to understand Rick's behavior, and it is only since I've spoken with a cousin of Rick's who works at the post office that I've been able to piece together the sequence of events in the month that followed.

Schuyler, their companion at Arshin's party, was not a friend of Rick's at all, let alone his "buddy," but an old acquaintance of Faye's. The exact nature of their relationship was not made apparent to any of us at this time: all we knew was that he had turned up at Rick's house, having just come out of jail, where he'd spent eighteen months for selling methamphetamine. Faye ran off with him the day after that party, leaving the four kids behind. She was gone for five nights. Those were the nights Rick fired off his gun. She came back, they had a fight, a reconciliation, then she took off again. The sequence repeated itself a third time, after which Rick told her to stay out of the house for good. She could take the children or leave them, he told her, but she had to go. At this point Faye became violently angry, throwing furniture and dishes at the walls till one of the older kids called the cops. Before they arrived Rick chamber-locked his gun and set it outside the house. "That was so the cops would see there wasn't no gun violence in the house," his cousin told me. Faye had cooled down by the time they showed up. Very calmly she told them that Rick had threatened to kill her and the children and then himself. The police, obliged to take such threats seriously, carted Rick off to the Andersonville Hospital psychiatric wing for a week's enforced observation. By the time he came out of the hospital, Faye had obtained a protection order, barring him from coming within a mile of the house.

The next few days are a mystery, obscured by conflicting reports and gaps in the record. What was known for sure was that Rick spent them at the home of a relative, a woman named Esther whom he referred to as his "second mother," his first having disappeared when he was small. He was distraught, drinking heavily, but also looking for work: intent on supporting his family even though he wasn't allowed to see them. The Saturday after Thanksgiving he took a job with a landscaper who'd been hired to do tree work on a property in town. We first heard about the accident when Arshin called on Sunday to ask if we knew whether it was true that Rick had been killed the day before: hanged, up a tree. An hour later he called back to confirm the report. A heavy branch, roped to the ground to make it fall in a particular direction, had been caught by a gust and blown the wrong way, slashing the rope across Rick's neck and chest, asphyxiating him. He was seventy feet up in the air and the fire department couldn't reach him with their cherry picker. They put out a call for a bucket ladder. A local contractor brought one and grappled him down. He was blue. The emergency helicopter on its way from Albany was sent back.

The funeral service was in town, at the Pinewood Memorial Home. It was already crowded when we arrived: young, old, suits, overalls, biker jackets, everyone in a state of raw grief. We signed the register and made our way inside. Loud, agitated whisperings rose and fell around us, anger glittering along with tears. Already there was a sense of different versions of Rick's last days forming and hardening, of details being exchanged and collected, variants disputed. The two older children sat on the front bench on one side of the chapel, fearful-looking as they had been when we first saw them, walking alone up the twilit slope of Vanderbeck Hollow. On the other side were Rick's relatives, his father sitting rigid, hands on his knees, broad back motionless.

Faye appeared from a side room with the two little girls and slid next to the older two, glancing briefly over her shoulder at the congregation, her face stricken, though whether with grief, guilt, or terror was hard to say. Even among her four children she seemed a solitary, unconnected figure.

A minister came in and told us to rise. After he read from the Bible and we sang a hymn, people went up to the front to speak. High school anecdotes were recounted, fishing stories, the time Rick was chased out of his front yard by a bear. A tall, silver-haired woman stood up. As she began speaking, I realized she was Esther, Rick's second mother. She said she'd had a long conversation with Rick a few days before his death, when he was staying with her.

"In hindsight," she continued, "*unbelievably*, I see that I have to take this conversation as the expression of Rick's last wishes."

With a firm look around the crowded chapel, she announced that he'd said he still loved Faye.

"He told me he still hoped to have another child with her, a son."

She paused a moment, then concluded:

"Therefore, Faye, I honor you as his widow, and I love you."

An unexpected brightening sensation passed through me at these words. I, like everyone else no doubt, had arrived at the funeral believing Rick had been up in that tree in a state of impaired judgment, if not outright suicidal despair, and that this was a direct result of Faye's behavior. I still did believe this to be the case, but I was caught off guard by the implicit plea for compassion in Esther's speech. I found myself thinking again of the expression I'd glimpsed on Faye's face at the wedding, gazing off into the late summer greenness of the hollow, and although I still had no more idea what it signified than I had at the time, I wondered if there was perhaps something more in the nature of a torment underlying her behavior than the purely banal selfishness and manipulation by which I had so far accounted for it.

The service ended. Whether by design or some unconscious collective assent, our departure from the chapel was conducted more formally than our arrival: a single, slow line formed, passing out by way of the casket. It was open, and there was no avoiding looking in. Ribboned envelopes were pinned to the white satin lining of the lid. *Dear Daddy*, they read, in childish handwriting. I mounted the single step, bracing myself for the encounter. There he lay: eyes closed, beard trimmed, cheeks and lips not-so-subtly made up, chalky hands together holding a turkey feather. I stared hard, trying to recognize in this assemblage of features my neighbor of five years. For a moment it seemed to me that I could make out a trace of the old mischievous grin that floated over him even when his luck was down, and it struck me—God knows why—as the look of someone who knows that despite everything having gone wrong with his life, at some other level everything was all right.

That was November. Knowing what I know now—what we all know now—I go back to that ghost of a grin on Rick's face and find I must read into it a note of resignation as well as that appearance of contentment: submission to a state of affairs as implacably out of reach of human exertion as the shift of wind that took his life. And by the same token I go back to the look on Faye's face at their wedding and find in it, beyond the general sadness, the specific expression of a person observing that nothing after all, not even the charm of one's own wedding day, is powerful enough to purge the past or stop its taint from spreading into the future. Whether this disposes of the "banal" in her subsequent actions, I am not sure, the situation being, in a sense, the precise essence of banality. Schuyler had been her foster brother from the time he was fifteen and she eleven. Arshin had the story from an acquaintance who used to work for the Andersonville Social Services. Over the course of several years, in a small house in the section of town known as the Depot Flats, he had—what?—seduced her? Taken advantage of her? Raped her? No word seems likely to fit the case, not in any useful way, which is to say in any way that might account for the disparate, volatile cluster of wants, needs, aversions, and fears the experience appears to have bequeathed her: the apparent determination to put a distance, or at any rate the obstacle of another man, between herself and Schuyler, her equally apparent undiminished susceptibility to him, her cold manner, her strange power to make a man as warm and tender as Rick fall in love with her nevertheless.

She stayed in the house all December and January, though I barely glimpsed her. Arshin claimed Schuyler was living with her, sneaking up there at night and leaving first thing in the morning, but we saw no sign of him. In February we went on vacation. When we got back there was a realtor's board up outside the house. Faye had left abruptly—for Iowa we heard later, where she had relatives —and Rick's father had decided to sell the place. It sold quickly, to a couple from New York who wanted it for a weekend home.

A few days ago I met Cora Chastine coming down the road on her mare. We stopped to talk and at some point I remarked how quiet Vanderbeck Hollow had become without Rick roaring up and down it in his truck. Cora looked blank for a moment and I wondered if she was growing forgetful in her old age. But then, in that serene, melodious voice of hers, she said:

"Do you know, I realized the other day that Rick is the first person whose life I've observed in its entirety from birth to death within my own lifetime. I was living here when he was born and I'm still living here now that he's no longer alive. Isn't that remarkable?"

I nodded politely. She gave the reins a little flick and glided on.

I'd been planning to take my usual late-afternoon walk to the top of the road and back, but something was making me restless—some faint sense of shame, no doubt, at having failed to protest that Rick's existence might be regarded as something other than merely the index of this genteel horsewoman's powers of survival—and instead of turning back I continued along the logging trail that leads from the end of the road up through the woods to the ridge.

It had been years since I'd been up there. The trail was muddy and puddled from the late thaw but the service blossoms were out, ragged yellow stars, and the budding leaves on the maples and oaks made high domes through which the last of the daylight glowed in different shades of green. Reaching the top of the ridge I followed the path down the far side, past the rusted swing gate with its STATE LAND sign and on down the uninhabited slope that faces north across Spruce Hollow.

The trees here were different: hemlocks and pines, with some kind of dark-leaved shrub growing between them, its leaf-crown held up on thin, bare, twisting gray stems like strange goblets. It took me a moment to recognize this as mountain laurel—deer must have stripped it below shoulder level, creating this eerie appearance—and I was just trying to remember the things Rick had told me about this plant the time we walked up through the woods together when my eye was caught by a straight-edged patch of darkness off in the distance. I realized, peering through the tangled undergrowth, that I was looking at a manmade structure.

Leaving the path, I made my way toward it, and I saw that it was a hut built out of logs. It stood in a small clearing. The walls were about five feet high, the peeled logs neatly notched into each other at the corners. The roof had been draped with wire-bound bundles of brush. A door made of axe-hewn planks hung in the entrance. I pushed it and it swung open onto a twilit space, and by a swift chain reaction of stimulus and remembrance, I became abruptly aware that I was standing in the cabin that Rick had built himself in order to have, as he had put it, somewhere to go.

The top few inches of the rear wall had been left open under the eaves, giving a thin view of Spruce Clove. On the dirt floor below stood a seat carved out of a pine stump, with a plank shelf fitted at

waist height into the wall beside it. An unopened can of Molson
stood on this, next to what looked like an improvised clay ashtray.

I sat on the stump, struck by the thought that this would make a
good refuge from the world if I too should ever feel the need for
somewhere to go. And then, as I was sizing up the shelf for possible
use as a desk, I saw that what I'd thought was an ashtray was not in
fact an ashtray at all. I picked it up: it was a piece of dried clay that
had been hollowed by the imprint of an enormous clawed paw.

A sudden apprehension traveled through me. Despite a strong
impulse to swing around, I stopped myself: I dislike giving way to
superstition. Even so, as I sat there gazing up at the granite out-
crops of Spruce Clove streaked in evening gold, I had an almost
overpowering sense of being looked at myself, stared at in uncom-
prehending astonishment by some wild creature standing in the
doorway.

REBECCA MAKKAI

Painted Ocean, Painted Ship

FROM *Ploughshares*

TO ALEX'S PERSONAL HORROR and professional embarrassment, the Clement College alumni magazine ran an obnoxiously
chipper blurb that September, in a special, blue-tinted box. She
read it out loud to Malcolm on the phone:

FOWL PLAY
Assistant Professor Alex Moore has taught Samuel Taylor Coleridge's
"Rime of the Ancient Mariner" quite a few times since joining the Eng-
lish Department in 2003, but she developed an unexpected intimacy
with the poem when, duck-hunting in South Australia this June, she ac-
cidentally shot and killed an actual albatross.
Moore, whose doctoral dissertation at Tufts University focused on
D. G. Rossetti and his muse Jane Burden Morris, took aim at what she
thought was a goose.
"My students are never going to let me hear the end of this," she says.
Because the birds are protected under Australian and international
laws, Moore incurred a hefty fine — hopefully the extent of that legendary bad luck! She has no plans to hang the bird around her neck. "The
wingspan was over two yards," says the 5-foot-2 Moore. "That would be
asking for it!"

Those exclamation points killed her, the way they tacked the whole
episode down as farce. And the cheery italics. None of Alex's tired
sarcasm had come through. She vowed in the future only to give
quotes via e-mail, so she could control the punctuation. ("You're
my favorite control freak," Malcolm said. "No, listen," she said. "It
affects my professional image. And '*muse*'? I never said *muse*.") Plus
there was that photo to the side, her book-jacket photo with the
half-smile, perfect for suggesting Pre-Raphaelite intrigue and scan-

dal, but here verging on the smug. A month stuck dealing with the South Australian police and Parks Department; half her grant spent on the fine; her research summer wasted; and all of it snipped down by a freelance writer named Betsy into photo, irony, pretty blue box.

And as for the bad luck, it was just starting, waiting for her back home like her postal bin of unopened mail. Not the "hefty fine" kind of luck, but the "Your career is over" kind, the "Why aren't you wearing your engagement ring?" kind.

"Didn't take you for a hunter," she heard about twenty times that first department party back.

"I'm not," she'd say, or "You don't know who you're dealing with here," or "I'm really more of a gatherer."

She ended up telling the full story, and as she talked the whole party squeezed around where she sat on the arm of the couch — even Malcolm, her fiancé, who'd seen it all happen. He was sweet to listen again, and sweeter still not to chime in with his own version. Her colleagues sat on the coffee table, the bar, the floor, and sipped their white wine. She told them how her half-brother Piet had invited her and Malcolm to his place outside Tumby Bay for June. "He's not Australian," she said. "He just thinks he is." And then once they got there, Piet, in that way of his — just masculine enough to intimidate Malcolm, just Australian enough that everything sounded like a fine, foolish adventure — convinced them to come shooting at his lake, so he wouldn't miss the last day of duck-hunting season.

"Australia is the new America," announced Leonard, her department head. Or rather, he slurred it through his beard. The new hires nodded; everyone else ignored him.

After Piet brought down three ducks and his dog had dragged them in, he wrapped Alex's hands around the gun and showed her the sightline.

"What kind of gun?" someone asked.

"I don't know. A rifle. It was wooden."

She'd seen something barely rising above the stand of trees on the small island in the lake, and shot. If she thought anything, she thought it was a white goose. It went down, crashing through the trees, and Piet sent Gonzo swimming out to it. Gonzo disappeared on the island, yapping and howling and finally reappearing, sans goose, to whimper at the water's edge.

"Christ," Piet said, and took off his clothes—all of them—to swim out. He emerged from the trees after a long minute, full frontal glory shining wet in the sun. Malcolm slapped his entire arm across his face to cover his eyes. "She's a monster!" Piet shouted. "You've slain a beast!"

Thirty minutes later, Piet, half drunk, was on the phone to his friend Reynie at the Parks Department, asking him to come out and tell them if that wasn't the biggest bloody bird he'd ever seen. They took two double kayaks out—Piet and Reynie, then Malcolm and Alex, who still hadn't seen her victim. It lay there, enormous, wings out, half on a bush, a red spot fading out to pink on the white feathers of the neck. Its whole body glared white, except the wings, tipped in glossy black. "It was beautiful," she told her colleagues. "I can't even describe it—it had to do with the light, but it was just *beautiful*."

"You shouldn't have brought me out here, Piet, Christ," Reynie had said. He put his hand on the bird's back, and Alex walked around to get a better look at the face. It had a rounded, almost cartoonish beak. "I'll have to write you up, and you'll lose your license and pay a fortune. It's a wandering bloody albatross. They're *vulnerable*."

"Vulnerable to what?" Piet had brought his camera, and he was moving the bush branches for a better shot.

"Extinction. Jesus Christ. Vulnerable's a step from endangered. Piet, I don't want to write you up, but you shouldn't have called."

Piet snapped a picture. "Didn't shoot it," he said. "*She* did. Not even *from* here, never shot a gun before. Girl's been good at everything she ever tried in her whole damn life."

"Which is how I spent the next three weeks camped in Adelaide," she told her colleagues. The ones who were out of wine took this as a cue to stretch and reload at Leonard's bar.

"Hey, great story!" Bill Tossman clapped her on the shoulder, used that loud, cheesy voice more suited to an executive schmoozing on the squash court than a professor of modern poetry. "Wish I could stay to hear the end, but my two friends and I here are late for a wedding!"

They laughed, then all started in: You must be parched! Can I get you some water? Hey, take a load off!

"You're going to do that all year," Alex said. "Aren't you."

And yes, they did, until the real bad luck became public in November and they suddenly didn't know what to say to her at all, as if she'd lost all her hair to chemo and they weren't sure whether to compliment the headscarf.

She actually taught the Coleridge that fall, and passed around a copy of the photo Piet had e-mailed her. It was an unfortunately dull section of 222, half frat boys who only took classes as a pack (one, confused by her story, later indicated in his paper that the Mariner killed the albatross because he thought it was a goose), a bunch of foreign students, mostly Korean, who never spoke, and a freshman English major named Kirstin who made every effort to turn the class into a private tutorial. They passed the photo listlessly, one of the boys raised his hand to ask how much the bird weighed, and Alex made a mighty effort to turn her answer into a discussion of the weight of sin and Coleridge's ideas about atonement.

Kirstin compared the poem to *The Scarlet Letter* and one of the boys groaned, apparently traumatized by some high school English teacher. Alex wished someone else would talk. Poor Eden Su, for instance, in the front row, was one of those Korean students. She wrote astonishing papers, better by a mile than Kirstin's, and yet she never spoke in class unless Alex asked her something directly, and even then, she whispered and pulled her hair across her mouth. Like everyone else in the department, Alex counted class participation as a chunk of the final grade, and Eden, who deserved a high A, would get a B. Before class, Alex had asked her to come to her office later, and now Eden was slowly tearing apart a cheap ballpoint pen.

By one o'clock she was in her office on the phone to Malcolm, the red leaves on the maple hitting the bottom of her window again and again. He was in Chicago, meeting with his thesis adviser. He'd be back the next night, and was asking if she wanted to grab dinner.

"I'll take you someplace nice," she said. "You'll need champagne." These meetings were probably his last before he defended, and they were going well.

"Sure," he said. "I'll leave it up to you. I just won't feel like getting dressed up."

"Right." She found herself saying it flatly and quickly, but he didn't seem to notice. So she went on. "You know, sometimes girls like getting dressed up. It makes us feel pretty."

He laughed. "Okay. Boys like to wear jeans."

"My student is here." She wasn't. "We'll talk later." She hung up.

The problem, the source of all her snippiness, her cattiness, her being such a *girl* about everything, was that since they'd gotten engaged nine months ago he had not once, not a single time except during sex, which absolutely didn't count, called her beautiful. In sharp contrast to the courtship phase, when he'd say it several times a week, one way or another. And of course she'd known the staring-into-her-eyes thing wasn't going to last forever, and it had been a crazy year, with the Australia trip and her getting stuck there, and his dissertation, but nine months and *nothing*. Not that she was counting, but she was. She'd have settled for a peck on the head and "Hey, gorgeous." A whistle when she stepped out of the shower.

She'd been so caught up in being engaged and close to tenure and publishing her articles and generally getting everything she wanted that it wasn't until those weeks in the Adelaide hotel, alone with Australian TV and her own thoughts, that she started wondering if she could live with Malcolm the rest of her life, never seeing beauty reflected back at her. And she wondered, if she felt like this now, what she'd feel like at nine months pregnant. Or fifty years old. Or twenty pounds overweight. Or terminally ill.

She felt regressive and petty and uneducated for caring about beauty, but she did. God help her, it was closely tied to her self-esteem and probably had been since about fourth grade.

Here was Eden, showing up like a prophecy, knocking with one knuckle on the open office door. Alex motioned her in. Eden's eyes had that glazed, jetlagged look common to all the foreign students. Every year Alex assumed it would wear off by October, but it never did. She'd mentioned it once to Leonard, and of course he'd had a theory. "You know why, right? They stay up all night texting their friends back home. Refuse to adjust to American time."

Eden sat on the edge of the chair, her red backpack on her lap. It almost reached her chin — a kind of canvas shield. "Eden, I just wanted to check in with you." No response. "You've been getting solid A's on your papers, but I need you to understand that twenty percent of your final grade is class participation."

"Okay." She said it through her hair, barely audible. If it hadn't been a cultural issue, Alex would have worried about depression.

"Do you feel you are participating?"

She shrugged.

"Hello? Do you?" Which was harsh. She was mad at Malcolm, not this poor girl.

Eden shrugged again. "What else could I do?" It was the most words Alex had ever heard her string together, and she was pleased to note that the English was okay. When she'd been a TA, another TA actually told her to compare foreign students' spoken English with their written English, to make sure they weren't plagiarizing. The implication being that they were more likely than native speakers to do so, something Alex had never seen borne out.

"There's nothing else you can do," she said to Eden. "You need to talk."

"Okay."

"Look, I understand that back in Korea you weren't supposed to talk in class, but you're at an American university now, and part of an American education is talking. Not just writing about literature, but *engaging*. Out loud." She always had trouble ending conversations with students, especially ones who wouldn't look her in the eye. "Is that something you think you can do?"

Eden shrugged and nodded, but she seemed upset, staring at the bookshelf behind Alex. She looked, for once, like she wanted to say something. But she didn't, just stood up and left.

Alex did take Malcolm someplace nice: Silver Plum, a twenty-minute drive from home. She overdressed, in a sheer green blouse and a silk skirt, knowing he wouldn't say anything about it at all. It was like she was daring him not to.

He was exhausted. He wore khakis and a wrinkled blue polo shirt, and he was overdue for a haircut, curls everywhere. He ordered a Scotch and gulped it down. He didn't want to talk about his dissertation, or Boston, or work. She didn't even try to bring up the plans for the wedding in May, which he'd probably have talked about, but the thought was starting to make her sick. Specifically: the fact that either, after months of preparations, he'd see her in her dress and say nothing at all, or he'd say something nice and she'd feel it was just out of duty.

"I finally met Jansen's wife," he said. Jansen was his adviser, and apparently something of a god in the world of sociolinguistics.

"Yeah? What's she like?"

"Beautiful. She's just this gorgeous, sixty-whatever woman with enormous black eyes."

"Huh."

"I mean, they're like *pools* of blackness."

"Huh."

"Not what I expected, you know? I thought she'd be some little mousy person. And she's just this amazing, exuberant, stunning woman."

Winded from the effort of that much conversation, he returned to his lasagna.

Alex caught her reflection in the window to the street, and for the love of God she looked like a circus clown, all frizz and eyes and jawbone. It was a wonder he could look at her at all. But people had found her beautiful, they really had, and one of the reasons she'd even found her specialty (vain creature that she was) was that Donna Evans, her professor in college for Nineteenth-Century British Poetry, saw her that first day of the term and said, "My God, you're a ringer for Jane Morris!" The next day, she brought in a book with Rossetti's *Proserpine* and proved it to everyone.

She wanted to grab Malcolm by the collar with one hand and say, "People would have *painted* me. If I'd lived in the right century, they would have paid me just to sit there!" But with the other hand she wanted to scratch out her face with a marker or a knife, obliterate every trace of ugliness, of gawky eighth grader, of hope.

Some feminist.

That Friday it wasn't even Leonard who called her in, but Miriam Bach, the Dean of Faculty. Alex was offered a glass of water, asked to take a seat on the soft leather couch. She wanted to compare the experience to being called to the principal's office, but that had never happened to her.

"So we received a letter from a student named Eden Su," Miriam said. She had nothing on her desk, nothing at all except her picture frames and her closed computer, and she rested her hands in her lap. "It was a request to drop your class."

"I think I know what this is about," Alex said. It had been one of about ten scenarios she'd rehearsed since receiving Miriam's e-mail, and she felt her best strategy was to turn this into a friendly debate about how hard to push foreign students, and whether the class participation component was out of order.

"I'm not sure you do. Tell me what you know about Miss Su."

"She *does* seem borderline depressed to me, although I question whether that's cultural, just a matter of reserve. She's not an English major." Miriam was staring at her, so she kept talking. "I think she's a sophomore. Very good writer."

"Yes, her writing is excellent. Tell me something: You mentioned a cultural issue. What did you mean by that?"

"Oh, I wouldn't call it an *issue.* She's just very quiet, and I'm sure that's what the letter is about, that I asked her to speak more in class. I *did* acknowledge that in her previous schooling she likely hadn't been asked to speak much. I hope that didn't upset her."

Miriam opened a desk drawer and pulled out a paper. It wasn't folded—so it was a Xerox of the letter, and who knew how many copies were out there, and why. Miriam glanced through it. "In this exchange, did you refer to her schooling in Korea?"

"Right." And then her stomach turned to a wave of acid. Miriam had asked it so casually, but no, this was the whole point. "Oh God, is she not—"

"No, she's not. She's from Minnesota, fifth-generation American. And her ethnic background is Chinese."

Alex stared stupidly forward. Could she really have mistaken a whispered Minnesotan accent for a Korean one? She started to explain that Eden never spoke, that she looked so jetlagged, but she stopped herself; it might only make things worse. She put her hand to her mouth to show that she was properly horrified, that she felt terrible on behalf of the girl. When really all she felt was horrified for herself.

Miriam looked at the letter again. "The issue, of course, is the presumption that a student who looks Asian must be foreign-born. She's quite angry, and it seems she's involved the Minority Student

Council. She says her father is very upset, but we haven't heard from him yet."

"Can I ask why Leonard isn't handling this, on a departmental level?"

"He felt uncomfortable with the situation." Of course he did. He probably didn't even understand what the issue was. She'd heard the poor man use the word "Oriental" on more than one occasion with no apparent qualms.

"May I please see the letter?" Alex held out her hand.

"Not at the moment, no, I'm afraid not." Miriam slid it back in the desk drawer. "But you'll see it soon. And I want you to know that I do understand how we make assumptions about *all* our students—background, socioeconomic status. I really do understand. If it were up to me, it would end with this conversation."

Alex didn't know what to do, and she realized some principal's office experience would have come in handy here. Did one grovel now? Burst into tears? Make a joke? It was hot, so she rolled up her sleeves. In the office of the South Australian Parks Department, she'd just told her story again and again while they plied her with tea and cookies and tried to ensure she maintained a pleasant impression of Australia despite the legal trouble. A cookie might have been nice right now.

"What's going to happen next is that the Dean of Students will recommend Miss Su take this to the Grievance Committee, and you'll just have to do a written statement. I predict that they'll discuss this briefly and dismiss it. And if there's no disciplinary action, it won't come up in your tenure review. That's my very strong prediction."

On the way to her car, she called Malcolm and canceled dinner, saying she had a monstrous headache and ten phone calls to make. She'd just have seethed silently, and she couldn't bear his asking what was wrong, trying to guess if it was something he'd said or done.

Usually, it was.

That night she drank an entire bottle of red wine, stared at *A Night at the Opera* with the sound too low to hear, and attempted to catalog any racist thoughts she'd ever entertained. When she was

five, walking in Boston, she'd grabbed her mother's hand because
there was a black man coming toward them on the sidewalk. But
she was so young, and she'd grown up in New Hampshire, for
Christ's sake.

More recently, she hated on NPR the way any reporter using
Spanish words would roll out the thickest accent possible, just to
prove to the stationmaster and the listening public that his ten
years of Spanish class had paid off and that he was down with the
people. "It's going to be a big issue with Ell-a-*diiii*-no voters," for
instance. In a way he'd never refer to "the *français* community" or
"*Deutsch* immigrants."

And there was a journalism professor, Mary Gardner, whose
creamy brown skin Alex once stared at in a faculty forum, becoming (profoundly, inexcusably) hungry for chocolate.

But that was it. Honest to God, that was it. A resentment of over-
zealous reporters, a perverse admiration of Mary Gardner's complexion, a small child's ignorance.

She hadn't even been *around* that much racism. Once, in college, a girl on her freshman hall had said, "If everyone in Asia is,
like, lactose intolerant, then how do they feed their babies? Is that
why they're all so skinny?"

It occurred to Alex, lying drunk on the couch, that if all she
could summon up was one incident of someone else's vague racism, while she could pin three on herself—no, four, let's not forget the big one—that made her the most racist person she knew.
By three hundred percent.

Malcolm called at nine to see how she was, but she was too drunk
to pick up. He called on Saturday morning, when she was too hung
over, and again on Sunday night, when she was once again too
drunk. He didn't seem terribly concerned about her absence, not
even in the Sunday message. "It's me," he said. "Just checking in.
Call me later."

She passed herself in the mirror late that night, and the gin and
the bathroom lighting made her look somehow speckled, like a
grainy photograph. She gripped the sink edge and squinted, to see
how she'd look to a stranger. Interesting, maybe. Striking. From a
certain angle, ugly, and from a certain angle, not.

Sometime after midnight, she called Malcolm's cell phone,
knowing it would be turned off. She said, slowly, trying to enunci-

ate, "It's me. *Just checking in.* I want you to know, Malcolm, that I cannot live the rest of my life being ugly. You need to know that. That is all."

She drank five glasses of water and passed out.

On Monday, Eden wasn't in class. Why this should have been a surprise, Alex had no idea. Was she expecting her to show up obediently until the registrar came through with official permission for the late drop? Did she, on some level, think this because she expected Asians to be more mindful of authority? No, no, no, she was just hung over still, from the whole long, miserable weekend, and the coffee had only made things worse. Let's be honest: she was still drunk. She thought she might be missing a couple of other Asian students, too, and the fact that she wasn't sure was a very bad sign.

"Tintern Abbey," she said, and found she had nothing else to add. "Let's read it aloud."

She ended class fifteen minutes early, threw up in the bathroom on the second floor, bought a grilled cheese from the co-op to absorb some of the alcohol, and went back up to put her head on her desk until her afternoon class.

She woke to the ring of her office phone reverberating through the desk, a hundred times louder than it should have been. It was Malcolm.

"Your cell's off," he said. Really, she had no idea where it was. "So you were pretty drunk last night." He was laughing. She remembered the phone call now, and thought she pretty much remembered what she'd said. "What were you drinking?"

"All of it."

"Everything okay?"

"You mean this morning? Yeah." She turned down openings like this all the time. Because what could she possibly say? Asking if he still found her attractive was desperate and unattractive; telling him he needed to compliment her more was worse. In either case, she'd never believe anything nice he said, ever again. She realized that what she was supposed to be upset about was Eden Su. That should have been what she was working up the nerve to tell him. But it had come down to this: after twenty-two years of schooling and five years of slogging away at her CV, she somehow cared more about her appearance than her career.

"So what's new?" he said.

And she said, "I don't think I can marry you."

Bill Tossman found her on a bench outside the library, trying not to throw up again. She was sitting very, very still, her hands clasped around a paper cup of coffee she didn't think it wise to drink. "There she sits," he said, "as idle as a painted ship upon a painted ocean." She tried to laugh or smile, but it must have come out a grimace.

"I have something for you." He sat beside her, shaking the bench just enough to make her head throb and stomach slosh. He was a big man. Small bones, and a smooth, bright face, but a soft gut that aged him. He had a crush on her. (Or at least he'd always been sweet to her. She wasn't sure she could trust her judgment any more.) Tossman was a poet, the one department member with a Pulitzer instead of a Ph.D. It made his loud voice all the more surreal.

He slipped his hand into his briefcase pocket, pulled out a rubber-banded pack of playing cards, and shuffled them on his knee. "Cut," he said, and she managed to. He took four cards off the top and laid them facedown on the bench. "Okay," he said, "flip them up."

Seven of diamonds. Seven of hearts. Seven of clubs. Seven of spades.

"See? Your luck is turning!" He grinned at her, proud of himself.

"Where'd you learn that?"

"Where'd I learn *what?*"

He was making her feel like his niece, and although it was sweet, she didn't appreciate it. On a professional level. She gathered the cards and held them out to him, but he shook his head. "No, why don't you hang onto those. And hey, I'm sorry about the whole letter thing. That shouldn't have happened. It wasn't necessary."

She stared at him, trying to comprehend. He wasn't on the Grievance Committee.

"In the paper."

"The paper?"

"Oh. Christ. You've seen it, yes? In the *Campus Telegraph*. I should
—there's a stack in the library, if you want to—okay. Hey, I'm going to run before I make more of a jackass. Look, come by if you
need to talk." He literally backed away from her—walked backwards a good ten steps, then stopped. "It's not like I don't know
about messing up, right?" He laughed at himself and walked on,
hitting his briefcase against his leg. He must have meant his marriage ending last year, and then the time he broke down sobbing in
front of his Frost seminar when they discussed images of adultery
in "The Silken Tent."

Alex held her head a few more seconds, then pushed herself
up.

The "open letter" in the *Telegraph* wasn't from Eden herself, but
the entire Minority Student Council. It named Alex, described her
conversation with Eden pretty accurately, and went on to include
"ten stereotypes about Asian-American students"—number eight
was "Asian-American students are more likely to cheat to attain
high grades"—and a quote from Leonard, stating that "the English Department works hard to include everyone."

She put a nearby *Newsweek* on the stack of *Telegraph*s, picked the
whole thing up and dropped it in the big blue recycling bin behind
the elevator. There were plenty more papers all over campus, but it
felt good to get rid of these fifty or so.

Out on the sidewalk, two girls from her Pre-Raph seminar were
waving energetically.

"Professor Moore! We waited for you for, like, twenty minutes!"

She checked her watch. She wasn't even wearing a watch. They
stood in front of her, smiling, expecting an explanation, or at least
further instructions.

She threw up on their shoes.

Her phone was ringing, but she didn't even know where it was, so
she put pillows around her ears. She'd taken two of the Vicodin
left from her knee surgery, and now everything was padded with
cotton. She had told those girls she had a stomach flu and offered
to buy them new shoes, but then they were gone and she was back
in the English Department, slumped in the door of her office, and
then Leonard was asking Tossman to call her a cab, and now she

was in bed in her clothes. Something sharp was digging into her hip, but it didn't hurt. She dug around. Seven of hearts, seven of diamonds, seven of spades, seven of clubs.

Back in her office, on the phone, Malcolm had actually laughed at first, unable to take her seriously. She held her silence until he got it. "What the hell do you mean?"

She said, "There are people who actually find me attractive."

"I don't?" His voice was an octave above normal. It bothered her now, thinking back, that she had no idea where he'd been. She didn't know whether to picture him in front of his refrigerator, lying on his bedroom floor, out on the deck, driving downtown, sitting on the toilet.

She'd said—perhaps too cryptically, in retrospect—"It's like some horrible inversion of 'The Frog Prince,' like the frog convinces the princess to kiss him, but then she finds herself transformed into a toad. And the frog goes, 'Hey, I'm about as good as you can do now, baby.'"

There was a silence that hurt her throat. He said, "I'm supposed to be a frog?"

"No. You're supposed to *get it*." She'd hung up then, but he'd probably hung up too.

She ran a hand through her hair and realized she hadn't even showered since Saturday. Her bed swayed, and the room turned to water.

Every time she taught the Pre-Raph seminar, she waited till the end of the semester to bring out the actual photographs of Jane Morris. They would see her in Rossetti's and William Morris's paintings, they'd see her needlework, they'd study the decoration of Red House. And this in addition to the lectures from an art professor about the Arts and Crafts movement, the three days spent discussing Rossetti's "The Portrait," a major focus of Alex's own thesis:

> This is her picture as she was:
> It seems a thing to wonder on,
> As though mine image in the glass
> Should tarry when myself am gone . . .

Jane Morris was as much the lynchpin of the course as she'd been the goddess of the Brotherhood—that daughter of a stableman, who posed and flirted and married and adulterated her way to the top of English society, outsmarting and outcharming the snobs. And so each year when Alex showed the photographs, the students—for some reason particularly the girls—were devastated. She wasn't half as beautiful as Rossetti and Morris had painted her. Rossetti had given gloss to her hair and depth to her eyes, added a good three inches to her neck, lengthened her fingers, straightened her nose.

It was only then that the students started to see how all Rossetti's women—Jane, Christina, Elizabeth—shared some indefinable look that wasn't their own but something Rossetti had done to them, a classical wash he'd painted over them. This was where the feminists in the class always started to have fun, and someone inevitably compared the paintbrush to the penis. At which point Alex could lean on her desk and take a breather as they screamed at each other.

She wondered now, lying in bed ignoring the phone, not about Rossetti's fetishes or the invention of the classical but about how Jane Morris felt, to look at a finished painting and see a woman more beautiful than the one she saw in the mirror. Was this the reason she started her affair with Rossetti—knowing she could only be that beautiful when she was with him—or did it feel more like a misinterpretation, an abduction?

And she thought about Rossetti himself, how she'd never considered before that he might really have *seen* Jane Morris that way, not just wished he had. The way she herself had taken an albatross for a goose, an American for a Korean. How easily is a bush supposed to be a bear.

She finally answered the phone around eleven that night, and didn't realize until she heard Leonard's voice how strongly she'd believed it to be Malcolm.

"Thank God," he said. "You're okay, then."

"How long have you been calling?"

"All day. We were starting to think—okay. What can I do to help?" She knew he wanted some kind of concrete plan to fix everything.

"Because I gotta be honest," he went on, "this doesn't look good for the whole department. As a whole."

She wasn't sure if he meant the grievance or the letter or her absence. Or the vomiting.

"Oh, come on, Leonard. It doesn't look *that* bad. Not as bad as half the stuff I've heard you say. I mean, 'oriental'? For Christ's sake, I've heard you use the word 'coed,' Leonard."

"I'm confused." He sounded tired.

"Of course you are."

And why not hang up on him, too, while she was at it?

From seventh grade (after she got over mono) through grad school, Alex had not missed a single class. Freshman year of college, her roommate had practically tackled her to keep her from leaving the dorm with a 104° fever, but Alex just kept walking, stopped to sit on the sidewalk halfway to Biochem, got up again and staggered the rest of the way. It wasn't a matter of maintaining her record, but of principle. Unlike Piet, who'd once shown up at home in the middle of the semester for "National Piet Week," which he celebrated by watching television and getting his mother, Alex's stepmother, to do all his laundry.

But the next day, she stayed home. Oddly, her phone did not ring. Maybe she'd scared Leonard off. Or maybe her students hadn't said anything, grateful for the free time. After that one missed day, she couldn't imagine going back the next, because she didn't know what to expect. She pictured walking into her 222 to find someone subbing for her. Or only three students who'd bothered showing up, the rest assuming the class had been canceled for the term. Or everyone asking if she was all right, and her not being able to lie. She wondered if her lifelong punctiliousness had just been a fear of losing her grip. She wondered if she'd known all along that one little thing going wrong in her world could unravel absolutely everything else.

She was shocked to find herself taking heart in the fact that Coleridge's Mariner had made it safely home. He'd done his penance, and continued to do his penance in telling the tale, and Alex wished for something heavy to hang around her neck, something horrendously painful. She thought of her ring, which she still hadn't removed, but hanging it on a necklace chain would only call people's attention to its absence from her finger. Instead, she took it off and put it in a Tupperware and put the Tupperware in her freezer, which she'd once heard was a good place to store jewelry.

She felt lighter, not heavier. But it was a start. She made herself go for a walk around her neighborhood, staring at people's driveways and the falling leaves and chained-up dogs and unclaimed newspapers. When she came back, there were two messages on her phone. One was from Piet. The other was from the bridal boutique, confirming her dress fitting.

Piet was in town to catch up with friends and to see a woman he'd found on the Internet.

"That's a pretty expensive date, isn't it?"

They met up the next morning, and Piet was usurping the entire red velvet couch in the back of Starbucks. "Look at it this way," he said. "I get here, which is a nice vacay for me anyhow. She feeds me, if she likes me she puts me up, and maybe in the end I come out ahead." He was getting an Australian accent, and it suited him. The sun had aged his face fifteen years in the seven he'd been there, and that suited him, too. "Listen, Al. Where the hell's your ring?"

She managed to get the story out, or at least the parts about Eden Su and going AWOL at work and calling off the engagement. Not the girl part, the part about wanting to be beautiful. "I don't know what I'm doing," she said.

He laughed. "When have you ever not known what you're doing?" He was shredding the wooden stick he'd used to stir his coffee. "What I don't get," he said, "is what's this Asian chick got to do with Malcolm."

"It's hard to explain."

"I got all day."

"It just set me off. Or maybe it was—maybe the idea that someone could look at you and just not see you at all. See something totally different that isn't even you."

"Right, but this is different. Malcolm knows you better than anyone, right?"

"Theoretically." This was the place where she might cry, if she were the kind of person who cried. "I need you to do something with me. You're not meeting this cyberwhore till tomorrow, right?"

"Sure."

"Okay, we're going to go visit my dress."

She figured, if she already owned the dress, it might as well fit her. And a lot could happen between November and May. By May, she could be marrying someone else entirely. But really, she'd gotten this stupid idea in her head that if she tried it on, something would change. She'd been hoping for something big and white and horrible to hang around her neck, hadn't she? And here it was.

It really did hang, too—it was a halter neck, crisp and shiny and gaping way too big. A little Russian woman flitted around her with pins. Maybe not Russian, she reminded herself. Maybe Lithuanian. Maybe Ukrainian. Maybe Minnesotan. Piet sat on a pink-cushioned bench and watched. "Looks great," he said. "Look even better with a ring on."

She stared in the mirror, not at the dress but at her horrible face. Her skin was dried out and her eyes were puffy, and her hair was a dark mess. She wanted a necklace with a big red stone, to match that brilliant red on the albatross's neck. What she hadn't been able to describe really to anyone about that day in Tumby Bay was the sublimity, the blinding beauty of that bird as it flew, and as it lay where it fell. She could bring back in an instant that moment of white light rising beyond the leaves, her hand shaking against the gun. The echo of the shot seeming to come first because her ears went dead, then the loud roar as they woke again. The flapping and cracking as something fell down through the trees, branch by snapping branch. She wanted black arms on her gown, to match the dead bird's wings. She wanted to take it all back, to return to that moment at the lake's edge and take back that one moment of horrible misprision. And if she'd seen that bird wrong, and seen Eden Su wrong, who was to say she hadn't seen Malcolm wrong, too? She'd been walking around blind ever since that day.

"You look miserable," Piet said. "I'm calling him right now." He pulled out his phone.

"No! Please don't."

"I already dialed." He held the phone out of her reach, like he'd done with stuffed animals when they were kids. She couldn't move away from the Russian woman's pins.

"Malcolm, listen. It's Piet. Yeah, my sister's been an idiot, she's sorry, and she's standing here in her wedding dress looking gorgeous. You'd be a fool not to take her back. What do you say?" He listened for a minute, and she could hear the rumble of Malcolm's voice, but not his words. "Sure, sure. Good man." He clicked his phone shut. "He says call him tonight and you can talk."

"I'm going to kill you."

"No, you're not."

They walked out into the street, her dress left behind in a bag like something hunted and caught and hung up. "See, your luck's turning," Piet said. "As soon as I show up."

"All that's happened is you've meddled."

There was a park up ahead, so they sat on a bench. There were geese flying overhead, real ones, with brown bodies and black faces and white chinstraps.

"So really you've got four options. You go back to Malcolm and back to work, you forget about Malcolm and focus on the job, or vice versa, or you leave it all behind and go live someplace you've always wanted to go. I mean, your problem is it's undecided. And you've never been a girl to leave things to chance, just sit there and let things happen to you. So, you take action and you select an option. One, two, three, or four."

Piet had that way of talking that you'd agree to anything he said. And if she no longer believed she could see clearly enough to find her way, at least she was starting to believe in luck. She reached into her pocket. She said, "Go ahead, pick a card."

The next morning, Eden Su was walking down the big sidewalk that cut diagonally across the campus green, hunched under a carapace of red backpack. She wore a loose, silky blue sweater over black leggings. Alex raced behind the music building so she could meet her face to face, rather than sneak up on her from behind. She had just dropped off her statement for the Grievance Committee, and it was a good one. Whatever Eden had to say, stellar writer that she was, it wouldn't hold up against Alex reasoning with the committee on an adult level.

When Alex was about ten feet away, Eden spotted her, and there was a slight trip to her step. She put her head down again, as if she planned to walk past and say nothing—which made Alex angry, rather than just desperate to end things. This girl had taken it upon herself to ruin an adult's professional reputation and tenure prospects, but now she was acting as if they were eighth-grade enemies with crushes on the same boy. And Alex wouldn't accept that. It gave her the courage to approach Eden as an adult talking to a child, rather than as a desperate woman begging a twenty-year-old for mercy.

She stopped walking right in front of her and said, "Eden." And smiled patiently.

Eden tried to look surprised. "Oh. Hi." She glanced around—not, Alex realized, out of embarrassment, but to see if any of her friends were around to witness how strange it was that a professor would accost her like this. "Professor Moore. I'm so glad you're feeling better." Instead of pulling her hair across her face, she tucked it behind her ear.

Alex had planned on asking her to explain, from her point of view, the problem. This would lead to a rational discussion in which Alex would not apologize—doing so would potentially give Eden more ammunition for her Grievance Committee statement—but they would eventually see eye to eye, and Eden would admit what a silly misunderstanding it had been. But now the girl was staring her down, and Alex didn't want to lose the little edge she had left. So she said, "Have you resolved the issue of those missed credits? You can't be picking up a new course now. Will you need to over-load in the spring?"

"Yeah, I—it's okay." Eden was starting to look uncomfortable. "Actually, what I'm doing is switching to an Independent Study with Professor Leonard. It's the same reading, but just one-on-one." Her voice was still quiet, but it was determined, and even— something Alex would never have guessed—a little supercilious. "He offered."

"Right. Well, I certainly hope you're thanking him for his time. That's an awful lot to ask of someone already teaching two courses and acting as department head."

Eden adjusted her backpack. "Okay, sure. So I'll see you later."

"Hold on." She could absolutely not let Eden be the one to end the conversation. She put a thin layer of concern in her voice. "You know, Eden, part of me wonders if the real reason you dropped this class is because you weren't getting a strong grade."

Eden just stared ahead blankly, the way she always used to.

"Maybe you haven't really been challenged like that before, and it seems I was wrong about where you're from, but speaking in class is still a part of a liberal arts education. And I can see from your recent actions that you have no problem speaking up for your-self."

Eden looked around again for those invisible, incredulous friends.

"Look at it this way, Eden. How much do you know about me? Do you know my first name? Do you know where I did my graduate work? Do you know my genetic background?"

Eden was gawking at her like she was insane and drooling. Alex found it infuriating, even with the Vicodin still in her system.

"I'm going to take your silence for a 'no.' You've probably made assumptions about me, and I'm sure most of them aren't true. For instance, I'm not American." It was a lie, from Lord knows where. "I was born in Australia. I lived there till I was eighteen. If you referred to me, say, in an article for the *Telegraph,* as an American, you'd be wrong. And one thing I could say, if I were really unreasonable, is that you were intentionally denying my Australian identity. My point is, Eden, that we can't see *anyone,* really."

The girl shifted her backpack and smiled. She didn't look uncomfortable at all anymore, just quietly, enragingly smug.

"For instance," Alex said, "I thought you were a smart person. And I appear to have been mistaken." She turned away before Eden could say anything, then looked back over her shoulder. "Hey, have a super term with Leonard! I'm sure he'll enjoy your stony silence!" She managed a ridiculous grin and walked away, pleased to note in her peripheral vision that Eden stayed planted several seconds before pulling out her phone and continuing down the sidewalk.

She showed up outside her 222 five minutes late, just to see what was going on. The door was closed, and there were voices inside. She checked the hall: just a couple of chatting students she didn't recognize, so she put her ear to the door. It was Tossman in there, talking about "The Daffodils." She went to the co-op to bide her time with greasy food.

When she walked into Tossman's office later, he actually looked frightened for a moment. Then he grinned, and in that huge voice he said, "There she is in the flesh! The sadder but wiser girl for me!"

It took her a second. "Tossman, did you just pull a Coleridge reference by way of *The Music Man?*"

"Why, yes I did." He was quite pleased with himself. He leaned back in his desk chair and bellowed out the chorus of the song, banging his ballpoint pen on a stack of student papers to keep the rhythm.

She sat on the chair reserved for nervous students. "I just flipped out at Eden Su. I was trying to patch things up, but apparently I'm not very good at it." She knocked her foot against a stack of literary magazines on the floor, sending them flying. She started to pick them up, but he stopped her. "So you're covering my 222?"

"They're good kids. Sandy took the Pre-Raph." He searched the jungle of his desk till he found his coffee mug. "And look, Alex, I hope you don't mind, I told Leonard you were having health issues, dating from your time in Australia. You can tell him I was wrong, but maybe you want to use that to explain what's been happening. I didn't say specifically what the problem was, so you could make up whatever you wanted. If you need to take time off, you know Leonard would agree. He just doesn't want a scene. And he'd recommend you anywhere, as would I. But it would be nice if you stayed." He smiled at her. He was a good man.

She let out a breath. "Tossman ex machina. You and my brother both, trying to save me from myself."

He said, "You'd do the same for me. Take a couple more days before you decide anything. Rest."

Two days later, there was an e-mail from Miriam Bach: they needed her to appear in front of the Grievance Committee after all. "This is in light of an additional encounter between you and Miss Su," she wrote. "It's only fair to advise you that Miss Su has produced a witness to the conversation." A witness? The only other students had been passing at least twenty feet away. Well, if Eden could lie, she could too. Except it was two against one, and Alex could never convince another professor or even a grade-hungry student to pretend to be her witness.

She drank a lot and called Piet and told him everything. "Yeah," he said finally, "I like your friend's idea. Say you're sick. Feminine problems, so they won't pry too much. Maybe like cysts."

She flopped down on her bed. "Sadly, I can't think of anything better."

"So why didn't you ring up Malcolm?"

"Maybe I did."

"No, I called him to see. Look, I was there when you pulled the card. Seven of hearts meant you were supposed to go all out. Job and man and your life back on track, yeah? So anyway, I set up a meeting for you guys."

"You're an ass, Piet."

"Sure." She heard him drinking something. His date had gone well, and he was staying with this woman downtown. "Look, Al, what's the moral of the whole albatross poem? Isn't it something about taking charge of your life? Like, 'I am the master of my fate and the captain of my soul,' right?"

"No. It's about loving animals. He looks at these water snakes and decides he loves them, and then he gets saved. So the moral is love all God's creatures. It's a bad poem, Piet. When you stop and think about it, it's a *really stupid poem*." She was turning into a sophomore.

"Okay, so it's about love, though. There you go. Go love your man."

They met at a little café and bakery near campus, and Alex couldn't help feeling she was in a movie. She'd watched it a thousand times, how the former lovers met for coffee — at a table by the window, so one person could watch the other leave, then sit there brokenhearted — and now here they were. Except they were back in a corner, at a table that wobbled, with someone's kids running around screaming in soccer uniforms. Malcolm maintained an expression of deep concern and leaned a little over the table, his head tilted to one side.

"I shouldn't have done that," Alex said.

"Which part?"

She managed to smile. "I'd say the entire past six months. Starting with the albatross."

"Have you been seeing someone?"

She couldn't believe he'd think that. And she was actually flattered. "No, of course not," she said. "I would never do that to you."

His cup was frozen halfway to his mouth. "No, I meant — I was asking if you were seeing, like, you know. A psychologist. A therapist."

"Oh."

"You just haven't seemed like yourself."

"Honestly, Malcolm, I've just been drunk a lot lately. I was drunk when I said I couldn't marry you."

He nodded and considered this. "How do you feel now?"

"Now? I'm sober." Intentionally avoiding the question.

He made a concerted effort to drink some coffee. He set the cup down and licked his lips. "What do you need from me?" God, the man was so sweet. And she wasn't the type to appreciate a man's kind heart while secretly wishing for the wife-beating Harley man. This really was what she wanted.

If she'd learned anything from Eden Su, it was that sitting there mutely doesn't get you anywhere. Tossman was right—she was idle, a ship frozen in a sea of trouble—and that would never do.

So she said, "I need to know how you see me."

"I think you're great, and I love you, but I think it wouldn't hurt you to get some help."

"No, I'm actually—I actually need to know what you think I *look* like."

He was confused, and for a second she thought she'd have to explain the whole thing, all her vain neediness, but then he reached into his pants pocket for a ballpoint pen, white with a blue cap. He turned over his napkin and began to draw.

"What are you doing?" She leaned to see, but he moved it behind his coffee cup. Finally he held it out, in both hands. It was a stick figure: round head, curly hair in every direction, smiling mouth, happy eyes. Under it, he'd written *Alex*.

She laughed. "That's me?" He put it down on the table and drew wavy lines emanating from her face and body. "What's that?"

"That's your amazingness."

He tilted his head and grinned at her, exactly like someone in a movie—the one the girl was supposed to end up with. And she thought, it wasn't a Rossetti, but it was good enough. And she thought, if he was dumb enough to take her back, she might be smart enough to marry him.

In future years, when she told that story, she left out the part about Malcolm. It became instead the story of why she left Clement, of how she and Malcolm ended up at State, of how sweet Tossman had been to her, that year before he killed himself. Of how even in assessing all her misprisions, she'd still missed something enormous. But where had the signs been? There had been no signs: just poor Tossman, slumped on the steps of the music building at midnight, gun in his hand. And no one seemed to know why. And really, she barely knew him. She'd only read half his books.

She'd tell the story to younger colleagues, starting with the albatross, focusing on Eden Su, ending with Tossman, whom they all knew about already. The point, the moral, was how easy it was to make assumptions, how deadly your mistakes could be. How in failing to recognize something, you could harm it or kill it or at least fail to save it. But she wondered, even as she told the story, if she wasn't still missing the point. If maybe it wasn't something, after all, about love—something she was too cold to understand.

The telling was an attempt, of course, at penance. It never did work; penance so rarely does.

BRENDAN MATHEWS

My Last Attempt to Explain to You What Happened with the Lion Tamer

FROM *The Cincinnati Review*

HE WASN'T EVEN a good lion tamer, not before you showed up. He had always looked the part, with his whip and his chair and his spangled pants, but honestly, watching him in the cage with those lions was like watching a man stagger blindfolded across a four-lane highway. One night in Glens Falls, the chair slipped from his hand, and the cats swatted it around the cage like a chew toy. In Council Bluffs, a claw snapped his patent leather bandolier like an old shoestring. And in Granite City, a lion caught the whip between its jaws and yanked him around the ring like a fish on a line. It was a minor miracle every time he stepped out of the cage—bruised and bleeding, but still intact. He didn't seem to care that the clapping was never the thunderous peal you'd expect when a man emerges from a cage full of beasts, and he didn't care that it petered out before half a minute was up. He'd just stand there with his arms raised, like some avatar of victory, and he'd beam that ivory smile and shake his blond mane. You'd think the lions had just elected him King of the Serengeti.

Looking at the scars and the shredded outfits with their missing sequins and webs of crooked stitching, I'd wonder why the guy was doing this to himself. You told me once that his father was a lion tamer, and that these things run in the family. I don't know. My old man was no clown, but maybe that skips a generation.

*

The first time I saw you, I was alone behind the big top, adjusting the mix in the confetti buckets. Most of the others were still in bed, nursing hangovers or aching limbs, asking themselves for the ten thousandth time what it was going to take to get moving today. Me, I was up early because no one else would be.

Right away I knew you were no first-of-May, no circus rookie. Five-foot-nothing, barefoot in a leotard, you strutted like you owned not just the big top but the fairgrounds it stood on, like the rest of us better get your say-so before we turned a single somersault.

"You the new girl on the flying trapeze?" I said, although I knew without asking: you smelled like chalk dust and hairspray.

"You the old clown?" you said, eyeing my tattered plaid pants and my flop-collared shirt, my white face and painted-on smile. I danced a little jig, letting my head loll from side to side, and ended with a pratfall — straight down on my keister.

"The one and only." Immediately I wished I hadn't said that.

Still, you smiled. It wasn't a toothy, whole-face-blooming-into-a-laugh sort of smile, but it was a smile. Then without another word you made tracks for the big top.

That confetti wasn't going to mix itself, but how could I take my eyes off you, with your legs like cables of braided silk? It wasn't just that you were beautiful; there are a lot of pretty ladies in the circus, tattooed and otherwise. It was that strut. I followed you into the tent, and by the time my eyes adjusted to the light filtering through the canvas you were already halfway up the ladder to the high wire. Whoa-ho, I said to myself, a double threat: the tightrope and the trapeze. The wire and the swing.

The roustabouts had started to hoist the net into place, cursing at the lines and jabbering about this broad who shows up out of nowhere and puts them to work right in the middle of a union-mandated coffee break. They were ornery that morning, still grousing about the case of Jonah's luck they'd had with the blow-off in Sandusky — the skies had opened, the canvas became cement-heavy, and the fists of soaked rope that gripped the tent pegs couldn't be pulled apart. Two days later they were still looking for someone to piss on, and a greenhorn tumbler was just the ticket.

"Hey down there," you said, your voice knifing through the morning haze. "I don't want the net!"

They kept hoisting the lines, because it's one thing to perform without a net, but no one practices without one—unless you want your first mistake to be your last. So this time you shouted, "Gentlemen!" and that stopped them in their tracks, because no one ever called them gentlemen. "I said no net!"

The net flopped to the floor, kicking up a fog of sawdust. One of them called you a crazy bitch, but I swear the words were tinged with respect, and even a little awe.

You were at the top of the ladder, and although you could have stepped lightly onto the tightrope, testing its thickness and tension, you raised your arms above your head and cartwheeled to the middle of the wire. I heard one of the razorbacks gasp. Another mumbled something that might have been a curse but could have been a prayer.

And me? My heart burst like a child's balloon. Right then and there I knew I loved you.

I made it a habit to run into you on the midway whenever I scrounged for breakfast. There was always plenty of lukewarm coffee in the pie car, but tracking down a meal that didn't come with a side of day-old funnel cakes was a challenge.

In those early days I wasn't shy about giving advice: watch out for the sword swallowers and the fire eaters, I told you, because they're only interested in one thing. And steer clear of the midget couple, Tom and Tina Thumb. They had each cheated—him with the fat lady, her with the dog-faced boy—but they were as perfectly matched as salt and pepper shakers, and neither could call it quits. But here's something I don't remember, though I've squeezed my brain like a soggy dishrag: Did you ever ask me about him? Did I ever volunteer anything that made you think, why not?

You didn't say much about yourself, and what little you told me didn't add up. Once you said you had been born into the circus, and another time that you'd run away and joined up when you were a little girl. You said your parents were your first audience, and then later that they had never seen you perform. But the one thing you didn't waver on was this: you had never worked with a net.

"It wouldn't count," you said one morning as we set up our breakfast on the counter of the ringtoss booth: bananas looted from dozing monkeys, apples left out for the Arabian stallions, honey from the trailer of the freak show's Bee Man. "It just wouldn't, if you knew you could fall and get right back up like nothing had happened."

"What if you're trying something new?" I said. "You know, in practice." You smirked. "You either know what you're doing, or you don't."

I tried to tell you I knew exactly what you were talking about— that we were like two sides of the same coin, even if it was engraved on one side with some mythic diva and on the flipside with the dull, muddy squiggle of a horse's ass. Still, I knew that when I went out there every night, the only options were mass murder or a public hanging. Either I killed, or I bombed. I don't think you got it, though—then or ever—because in your eyes you were risking the long fall from the top of the tent, and I was just another groundling hoofing it around the center ring. Come to think of it, I don't think you ever really appreciated what the rest of us did. We were just the scenery: the human cannonballs with their nightly blowups; the elephant riders preening like royalty while their pachyderms did the heavy lifting; and the clowns, sweating and grinding for every laugh, our stomachs in knots for fear that this might be the night when nobody laughs and we stand out there naked, wilting under the glare of a thousand cut-the-crap stares. Or maybe that's just me.

Looking back, I don't know what I was expecting—okay, I do, but I was smart enough to understand that it wasn't going to happen without a bop on the head, a bad case of amnesia, and a tropical island where no one could remind you who you really were.

Then came that first night: your big debut.

I should have known something was up when the lion tamer strode out of the cage in better shape than usual. No stitches required. The applause from the local gillies wasn't exactly hearty, but it seemed a little more genuine. Then, as the lights cut out on him, a single spot lasered the ringmaster, who directed the crowd's attention to the uppermost reaches of the tent, where you were frozen in place, the trapeze in your hands. "Ladies and gentlemen! I present to you the aerialist, who dances on the high wire and works magic on the trapeze. The flying girl, the acrobat of the air. Thrill to her breathtaking feats! Gape in amazement as she flirts

with death, because folks—hold on to your hats—there's nothing
between her and the ground but the force of gravity! That's right;
she does it all without a net!" I'd swear the sides of the tent snapped
like a ship's sail as the crowd, in one big gasp, sucked the oxygen
out of the big top.

You soared. Head over heels—once, twice, a third time—a hundred feet above the floor. There wasn't a sound among the yokels
who packed the bleachers, their necks craned upward, their eyes
following the klieg lights. Every time your body snapped open like
a switchblade, your sequined leotard burst into a thousand tiny
flashbulbs. When you came out of a rotation, arms extended, there
wasn't a single heart beating. You twirled and floated, riding on
the fear and wonder of the crowd, and when you finally came to
rest on the platform, they absolutely exploded.

The applause lasted for hours, or so it seemed, but eventually
the audience grew peckish for some new treat. While their eyes
were drawn to a family of Chinese acrobats, I waited near the bottom of the ladder to congratulate you—and if the opportunity
arose, to pour my heart into your hands. I counted down the dwin-
dling number of rungs (yes, the view was exquisite, and from the
tips of my size-twenty-four shoes to the top of my busted stovepipe
hat I wanted you), but before your feet touched the floor, the lion
tamer had you in his arms. He crushed you up against his chest—
I'll admit it, the guy was ripped—and you buried your hands in his
thick pile of hair. Then you kissed him.

You had never mentioned this over breakfast.

It was after that kiss that I started performing that new bit, the take-
off on the lion tamer's act, where I used Scottie terriers with tutus
around their necks for lions. I'd fill my back pockets with kibble so
the terriers would chase me in circles trying to tear the seat out of
my pants, and by the end my clothes would be shredded, my tiny
chair broken to pieces, and I'd have two or three dogs hanging
onto my padded rear. I didn't know how the lion tamer would take
it—just a joke, right, all in good fun—but after I saw him in a
clinch with you, I didn't care.

That's not true. I cared. I wanted the clamor of the crowd to
drown him: all the laughs they held back when he was in the cage
would come pouring out when they saw me. Not just because the

bit was funny but because everyone would see I was goofing on him. But it was just for laughs. Honestly. That's all I wanted.

The dog-tamer act was a big hit, but the joke was on me. I planned to go on with it right after the lion tamer finished. Bing-bang. Agony, then ecstatic laughter. The problem was, he was great that night; everything a lion tamer is supposed to be. Forceful. Authoritative. Daring. For once he lived up to the words of the ring-master's nightly, and heretofore ironic, introduction: the Man with the Indomitable Will. He cracked his whip and thrust the chair, and I couldn't tell who was more surprised, me or the lions. He shouted commands, and the beasts obeyed. Nothing too techni-cally difficult—jumping through hoops, getting the lions to sit up on their hind legs—but he pulled it off without a hitch. He even finished by prying open one animal's mouth and sticking that big blond head of his between the cat's jaws. I thought for sure the lion was going to snatch his head like a grape from a vine, but the big cat didn't even twitch. If a lion can think, I know exactly what was on its mind: Who *is* this guy? I kept asking myself the same ques-tion.

He finished to robust applause. I wouldn't say *thunderous,* but the crowd was impressed. And then it was my turn—me with criss-cross sequined bandoliers, modeled on his costume, drooping into my baggy pants. The Scotties did their part, and the audience laughed in all the right places. Laughed a lot, actually. It was a great bit, but it had none of its intended punch. It was supposed to be two parts funny, mixed with one part catharsis, spiked with a shot of derision. A satire. Or a parody—one or the other. What do I know? I'm no clown-college clown, but that's what I was aiming for. But now that he had his act together, I was the only one worth laughing at. Which is my job—I'm the one they're supposed to be laughing at—but still.

After a week of asserting his newfound mastery of all things vi-cious and feline, the lion tamer became unbearable. When he was one misstep away from being lion chow, it was easy to work up some sympathy for him—or it would have been, if I wasn't congenitally deficient in the sympathy department. But now? It was bad enough that he was in the spotlight, in the center ring, and that he had you in his life; now he seemed to think he deserved it. Maybe I was the only one who noticed, but he was acting like he, with his buffed arms and bushy mane, was the only one who belonged under the big top.

Here I go again, yakking like a sideshow barker, but I have to wonder: This high-and-mighty King of the Jungle routine didn't bother you? I've tried to convince myself that you couldn't help it, because let me tell you, some women are just drawn to lion tamers. It must be the smell of the lions—some pheromone that women can't resist. I don't know if he told you this, but even when he wasn't impressing *anyone* with his ability to Bend the Lions to His Indomitable Will, he was still getting laid like a sailor on leave. He used to talk about it all the time, and he had this way of making it sound like it was such a chore, telling me how women expect a lot from a lion tamer. In the sack, he meant. They would growl at him and curl their fingers into claws and bare their teeth. More than once a woman asked him to use his whip or to prod her with an overturned chair. And the ones who brought the lion tamer back to their apartments always wanted to see his scars. They wanted to hear the stories behind each mark and kiss the ropy flesh and say, *There now; all better.*

"You clowns have it easy," he once said. "All you have to do is make them laugh."

I swear, I almost popped him one, right in the kisser. And not with a cream pie.

Do you remember the time you told me he needed a better moniker? It was late one afternoon, as we packed for the trek to the next town. We'd had a good run through Kalamazoo, Crown Point, and the Quad Cities, but it was time to move on. You said he needed a name that looked good on a poster—an all-caps, red-letter name.

I was wrapping up bottles of seltzer, stacking pie plates, stowing the balloon-animal balloons. "How about 'The Preposterous?'" I said.

You cracked a smile—yes, you did—before you said, "I was thinking 'The Great,' or 'The Magnificent,' but those seem—"

"Incongruous?" I said.

"No," you said, the smile blooming into something larger. "Too common. Everyone thinks they're great or amazing or magnificent. It needs to be"—and here you paused—"more awesome." You cocked your head, perhaps considering a thesaurus full of possibilities. "Hey, what about that?"

"The Awful?" I said. "Sure. It's kinda catchy. It suits him."

"For someone who calls himself a clown, you're not as funny as you think," you said (trust me, I have this committed to memory). And here's the kicker: that smile hadn't faded. Can't you see what this meant to me? A smile. A chuckle. A stifled laugh. To me, these have all the come-hither power of a wink, a pout, a gaze that lasts a second too long.

And what about the time you told me he needed a new costume? "Maybe something with animal prints," you said. The image of the lion tamer in leopard-spotted jodhpurs flared into my mind: ridiculous and horrifying at once. A getup like that could put my dog-tamer bit out of business, another case of life overtaking art.

"Now that," I said, "would be awesome."

You let loose with a big laugh, and I should have been in my glory. Score one for me, and a goose egg for the lion tamer. But I was beginning to see that he had been right all along: getting a laugh was the easy part.

The funny thing was, you were burning up mental energy on how best to describe his greatness when all along you were the only thing awesome about that circus. Take it from me, who was nothing more than a tiny red-nosed planet in far-flung orbit—you were the star, and you knew it. You had to. After that first night, crowds packed the stands in town after town, waiting for your act. You did things in the upper reaches of the big top that were impossible even in a dream. Some people looked up and thought: Brave. Magical. Intoxicating. You were living a life they were too timid to even contemplate. Others saw you use the trapeze like a catapult and the tightrope like a dance floor, and then they looked at the empty space where the net was supposed to be, and they thought: Naïve. Foolish. Shameless. But they watched, just as spellbound as the others, waiting—and, I have to wonder, hoping—for you to get what you deserved. Depending who you asked, you either loved life more than the rest of us, or you craved death and spent every night auditioning a new crowd of witnesses.

Maybe that second group, the nasty naysayers, saw something that I didn't see then but do now: all that time you were up there, you weren't flying—you were falling. You dressed it up, with the flipping and the spinning and the soaring, but from the second you let go of that trapeze, you were plummeting to the unforgiving floor.

And maybe that's why none of your catchers lasted more than a week. They were close enough to see what was what. And you sure didn't make it easy on them. In every trapeze act that I've ever seen, the tumblers take turns: one night you've got your legs wrapped tight around the trapeze as you wait to catch your partner; the next you're the one counting on your partner to be there when you come out of a tuck and stick out your hands. But you were the only one who flew, and the weight of it—night after night without a net—got to be too much for them. It never seemed to bother you; if anything, it inspired you. Like I've said, you soared— or appeared to, which was good enough for everyone under the big top. But the guys waiting to reel you in—guys whose names we never bothered to learn—were worn out, used up, exhausted. And while they always caught you, they could only do it for so long. The poor, lucky saps.

Was it these small moments—packing for the next town, shooting the breeze, watching you tumble—that pushed me to say what I said? Of course it was, but it was bigger than just that. It was the whole way we lived—in trailers and tents like tinkers, like refugees, like some kind of traveling circus. The romantically inclined probably think we're one big carefree troupe, laughing and drinking and dancing the mazurka, but romance here is as rare as an honest answer. There are no harlequin tents, no barrel-roofed Gypsy wagons. Our trailers are frosted with rust. Our pitted windows spill fluorescent light onto the hard-packed fairgrounds and black-topped lots. The tents are drafty, or else stifling. From inside come shouts or sobs, or the rare soft words that only fill our hearts with envy at another's happiness or hasty climax. The only advantage of our portable habitations is our ability to cluster and recluster them, depending on the latest feuds or fondnesses, the couplings and the coming-aparts.

This is a roundabout way of saying that one night I heard noises from his trailer—thumps, bangs, the echoes of exertion—and I thought, Here we go again. Another night torturing myself with images of you and him: your teeth bared, your back arched in fe-line submission, your throat emitting a low rumble. (Please tell me, if nothing else, that you weren't one of those women.) But before I could stuff my fingers in my ears it became clear that you were grip-ing, not groaning. After weeks when I swore I could hear every whispered moment, I strained and stretched but couldn't make out a word. What filtered through the tin-can walls were the smoky remnants of anger and frustration.

I confess I went to bed happy. I think that's the name for what I was feeling; I've never been good with names. I only knew I hadn't felt it in a long time, and it made me giddy to lie there in my sheets and imagine I might have stirred something up by putting in my time and playing games with big red-letter names. I had stalked around the edges of the thing I most wanted to say, and look what happened. A rift, a breach; perhaps a doorway was opening that I could walk through. And while I was in the business of wishful thinking, I put in a request that I would have one clean shot at the bop on the head, the island, and all the rest.

Then there was that night, in that town. I don't remember where —let's just say it was somewhere in the Heartland; we spent a lot of time in the Heartland. We were walking the midway, and you were telling me how hard things were for him, with the big cats lunging and the crowd hungry for excitement. But your heart wasn't in it. You were telling me this because you always told me this.

"He's nice," you said. "He is." You stopped near the booth where the swami read palms. "He told me his father was a lion tamer, and his mother was a lion tamer's assistant. So what choice did he have?"

"I don't know," I said. "Traveling salesman? Electrical engineer? Auto-parts dealer?"

"If only it were that easy," you said. "We'd all be traveling salesmen, right?"

I felt boldness, never one of my strong suits, rising inside me, buoyed by the memory of that happiness I'd felt in the darkness of my trailer. "No, we wouldn't," I said. "You'd still be you, and I'd still be me—but he could be someone else entirely."

Your eyes had a dreamy, faraway look to them. If he were someone else entirely, would you have been more interested in him, or less? If you were someone else entirely, could that person see herself with me? If I were someone else—but that's enough of that. All of these things were spinning through my noggin, but what was I supposed to do with them? Or with you? There were no straight answers. No firm pronouncements. No signs, no portents. I was ready to burst.

That was when the words popped out of me: "Why do you do

this?" I meant everything—the trapeze, the wire, the lion tamer, the time you spent with me, the empty space where the net should be. I left it up to you to decide how much of the question you wanted to bite off.

"I guess I like it," you said, which cleared up nothing.

"You guess?"

"I must, right? Why else would I do it?" Whether you were asking a question or defending yourself, I wasn't sure. All I knew was that your eyes were on me, and the temperature out there on the midway had skyrocketed. Had it ever been so hot under the spotlights, in the tent in midsummer with the thousands sweating in their seats and the trampled straw and pissed-on sawdust rising, rising, rising through my head? Better men than me would have had an answer for you, or at least something to say. I had nothing. You were staring right at me, but your eyes were fixed on some secret spot inside you. If that door had been left open, it seemed to me that the wind was pushing it shut.

"Say something funny," you said, your eyes like jewels in the lamplight.

"I love you" tumbled out of me, the words pushing their way into the open like clowns from a car.

"That's not funny," you said, and your eyes snapped shut like I had slapped you.

And you were right. It wasn't funny—it was hilarious. Coming from me, it was absolutely ridiculous.

As time crawled from one second to the next, your head ticked from side to side in a slow-motion no, and I could feel the pressure of all the things I'd left unsaid mounting in my head. If I had been a cartoon, steam would have shot from my ears. I would have blown my stack, complete with a red whistle and smoldering dome. But I am what I am, and I did what clowns do. I started turning my arm faster and faster, as if cranking some giant flywheel, and when I couldn't go any faster I ratcheted my fist up and bopped myself smack on top of the head. It's a standard sight gag—anyone who's been to the circus has seen it a million times—that ends with a woozy roll of the eyes, a loll of the tongue, and after a second's delay, a gimpy-kneed collapse. But I left all of that out. I wasn't going for the gag. I wanted so badly to believe my arm had become a sledgehammer that could drive my body deep into the ground, deeper than the pegs that keep the big top tight, deep enough to get away from you and the truth of what I'd said, and the truth of what you felt.

This is how what happened happened: I heard you behind the cotton candy stand, and I honestly thought you were talking to me. I didn't so much hear your voice as I detected a fluttering in the atmosphere. It was a whisper, an intake of breath, nothing more. I heard it again, then again, growing louder as I drew near.

There were hay bales piled in the gap between the booth and the outer wall of the big top, and as I poked my head over the top of one, my nose rising like a poster-paint sun, I saw it all. It wasn't me you were talking to, and it wasn't the lion tamer. It wasn't me straddling you, and it wasn't the corrugated expanse of my back concealing everything but your sculpted legs and taped feet.

Ladies and gentlemen, in the center ring I give you the strong man, the human steam engine! Watch as he twists bars of solid iron like saltwater taffy! Thrill to the display of brute force as he juggles bank safes like baseballs! Nothing is beyond his power, and nothing can crush his forged steel frame!

My knees buckled, and in that moment of ecstasy (yours, of course) and agony (mine, as always), I swear I heard you laugh: a tinkling sound like a bag full of broken glass, like some candy-faced kid pounding the twinkly end of a piano.

As I staggered away, the water-squirting daisy in my lapel started gushing, and my shoes flapped against the flattened earth. That laughter followed me, echoing, louder than any tent full of yokels in any town I'd ever played. It broke over me like a tidal wave, and that's when I stumbled out onto the midway and ran right into him.

I want to make this part clear. I didn't go looking for him. I didn't have a tale to tell. I tripped; I fell; I looked up. And there he was.

He looked golden. Since his act had taken off, he had acquired a deeply bronze tan—a sheen, even—that only made him look more like the lord of some grassland kingdom. He glanced down, and before he said a word he shook that mane of his. I wouldn't have been surprised if he had roared at me. But instead he asked a simple question: Did I know where you were? I was practically deaf from the laughter ringing in my head, and there he was, looking so polished, so confident, so unshakeable. So without getting up, without dusting off my pants, without saying a word, I pointed one white-gloved hand down the path that led to the hay bales behind the cotton candy booth.

I would have explained all of this, if you had let me, but all I knew was what I heard around the midway: you were spending all of your time up on the wire, the lion tamer was holed up with his big cats, and the strong man had already been seen testing his mettle with the bearded lady. The lion tamer claimed he was putting the finishing touches on a brand-new act, something no one had ever seen before. In the meantime he was still doing the old routine, but he was slipping. And here's the part that really got me: it wasn't any fun to watch. Before, he had been oblivious, like a dopey kid trying to jam a fork into an electrical outlet. You had to admire his moxie, even if you knew he was in for a shock. Now he was just plain angry, whipping the cats through their paces. After watching this for two nights and a matinee, I put the dog-tamer bit on hiatus. He wasn't bad enough for it to be funny the way I had wanted, and he wasn't good enough for it to be funny the way the ringmaster wanted. We figured we'd muddle through with something else until his new act was ready, and then we'd bring back the Scotties. The crowd loved those Scotties.

Then, the grand finale. The night the lion tamer was going to unveil his new act, and the night I would debut a bigger and better dog-tamer bit. I wanted to hold off until I knew which way things were going to break with the lion tamer, but the ringmaster insisted. He could tell how tense things had been around the big top, and he believed that one good show could clear it all up.

From the first minutes after the come-in, as the rubes lined up and handed over their ducats, there was a buzz in the air, right up until the moment that the lights went down and the big top was bathed in black. When the spotlights came back up, the lion tamer was in the center ring, surrounded by his big cats. Only it wasn't just his big cats. It was a pride of them. He must have had a dozen lions in there. Torches guttered at every corner of the cage, and an entire row of flaming hoops was fanned out across the middle. The lions looked skittish, distracted by the spotlights, angered by all that fire, nipping at each other, and feeling decidedly unbent by the until recently Indomitable Will of the lion tamer. Who just looked awful. Like he hadn't slept in days, hadn't showered, hadn't been near a blow dryer. Even at his worst, he had always had his vanity to keep him afloat.

I don't know what he had planned. It's a safe bet that he wanted to run the entire line of cats through that fiery tunnel, just to prove it could be done — to prove that he could do it — and it might have really been something to see. When he waded in among the lions, the crowd went church-quiet. Then he started shouting, urging the lions in one direction or another, and when they didn't respond he went to the whip. He waved it over his head like a pompom, and the lions seemed happy to ignore him until he jerked it back in one quick motion and the tip of the whip bit into the haunches of the biggest cat in that cage.

The lion's yellowed eyes narrowed, and if something that big can pounce, then that's exactly what it did. No growling, no swatting, no warning. It pushed off with its meaty legs, and before the lion tamer could raise his little chair it was on top of him. Once he was on the ground, the other lions moved in.

The lights went out in the center ring — too late, I'm sure, to spare the ladies and gentlemen and children of all ages the firelit sight that would linger long after we left town. And that's when the lights came on over me and the dogs, because that's how it works in the circus. When something goes wrong, you send in the clowns. So the lights came on, and we snapped to life, the dogs with their tutu manes, and me in my spangled bandoliers and my pockets full of kibble.

The crowd was distracted for a second or two — I am the shiny penny on the sidewalk, the light bulb that flares before it dies — but when they caught on to the gist of the act, they turned on me as surely as the big cats had turned on the lion tamer. Garbage rained down on me, and I swear it wasn't until the first wadded-up bag of popcorn hit me in my big ugly mug that I realized how the dog-tamer bit must have looked. But what was I supposed to do? Pick up the Scotties and juggle them? That's the act we had ready to go. That's all I had.

I froze out there, and the second I stopped moving the Scotties dug their teeth into the seat of my pants with all their little terrier jaws could give. This indignity, not thirty feet from what was left of the lion tamer, sent the crowd into a cascade of boos—booing like I had never heard before. Thunderous. And while the crowd pelted me with paper cups and half-eaten hot dogs, I looked up into the big top and saw you on the platform, sparkling vaguely in the shadows. You had seen it all; you would understand that I was only doing my job. I tried to use my own will, which no one had ever described as indomitable, to draw your eyes off the darkened cage and over to me. I wanted you to see how I had been swept up in all of this, and to give me one sequined smile, one dewy look from those kohl-black eyes. There I was, the focus of the crowd's anger and disgust, but not for one second did I blame you for any of it: not for choosing the lion tamer, or burying your fingernails in the strong man's beefy back, or even for my own predicament—the dogs, the boos, my ass. I could have laid this at your petite, rope-burned feet, but I didn't—I couldn't—because only mess and misery connected me to you.

You could have looked at me, and all of this would have been clear. Instead, you stood on that shaky cocktail table of a platform, feeling gravity's pull. Below, the horror of the lion cage, the fury of the crowd, and one clownish heart calling out for a moment's tender notice. Which of these caused you to do what you did? Which one of us—the strong and weak, brave and cowardly, funny and foolish—steeled you for that first step? No lights lit your way, but you walked onto that wire like it could take you out of the big top and away from all of us.

JILL McCORKLE

PS

FROM *The Atlantic*

DEAR DR. LOVE,

By now you have gotten several letters from me and this will probably be the last. I don't care that you never respond. In fact, I'm glad that you don't, because if you did, a response would show a weakness in your professional ethics. In all my other letters, I have been trying to explain myself a little better because I always felt that maybe you liked Jerry more than you liked me. And what about human nature makes us all want to be the one liked the most? In those other letters I was still trying to convince you that I was the right one, but the truth is that now so much time has passed I just don't give a shit. The right/wrong stalemate is what keeps people in your office for way too long. I thought I might settle things in my mind by writing you this *final* letter. And I will tell the truth—not that I haven't told the truth in the past, I have, but let's just say I also lied.

What has been consistent and honest in all my letters is how I don't think your name works, and I still think you should change it. You might say it led you to do what you do, and you might mention other people with prophetic names like Judge Learned Hand, or someone I knew named Clay Potts, who makes mugs and stuff to sell by the highway, but I never liked the way your name feels like a bad joke to all those people who are struggling with their marriages. Maybe you should change it to Dr. Apathy, which they (the 1960s shrink set) said was the opposite of love—instead of hate—and I absolutely agree with this. In fact, I think if they ever remake *The Night of the Hunter,* which is one of my very favorite movies (or

was until Jerry got religious), they might rethink the tattoos that
the preacher has on his hands. Lord, Robert Mitchum was scary
there using his hands to show the fight between love and hate, and
him a coldblooded killer hiding behind Scripture. But imagine a
preacher (or a marriage counselor) with hands saying LOVE and
APATHY. You love all those little games; you can put your hands
behind your back and say, *Pick.*

Anyway, when you last saw me, I did not look good. In fact, I
looked like shit on a stick. Most of us coming in and out of your
home office did, you know. I know you think that you have figured
out a way so people don't see one another—five-minute intervals
and in one door and out another. It *is* a big-ass house—but truth
is, I rarely made an immediate exit. I would stop off in your little
bathroom there at the front to splash water on my face and get myself looking good enough to go pick the kids up from school.
Sometimes, you may recall, I would even have to excuse myself during a session. You might have thought I was being avoidant, but
truth is, I was bored. I suspect being bored and having your mind
wander during marriage counseling is not a good sign. I would suspect that that level of boredom should say something big. You
should tell people right up front how, if they're bored, then probably the best thing for everybody is to stop. Don't take their money,
don't make them sit there and say stupid things back and forth.

Anyway, I did like sitting there in your bathroom, the way the
white noise enveloped me and kept me from hearing all that Jerry
was probably saying about me while I wasn't there. He probably
said things like how I often rearranged the furniture or changed
the light bulbs to get a better feel to the room, or how I didn't
check the cabinets and pantry before going shopping and how he
was tired of me buying things like sugar or mayonnaise or a big can
of pepper for fear we had none back at home. He didn't like that I
bought Chef Boyardee either, even though the kids love it. Who
doesn't? I don't like being told what is *right* and what is *wrong.*

"Do you know how many bags of sugar are in that pantry?" he
would often ask, and I would say, "No! How many?" which made
him mad enough to pull out a bunch of bags and stack them there
on the floor like we might be getting ready for a flood. Then I
might say something like *Do you know how many* Sports Illustrated*s
are in the bathroom getting all wet and soggy?* or *Do you know how you*

bruised my arm when you grabbed me so hard during sex the last time we had it? But you know better, because you know Jerry. Those would be my fantasy marriage-counseling complaints, where I might also have big stinky jock sneakers in the hall and a man thinking of all the new ways he might go about satisfying me.

In reality I would say, "Do you know how many daily devotional books and Mensa quizzes are neatly stacked on the shelf in the bathroom? Do you know where the antibacterial cleanser might be, or that thing you use to scrub your tongue?" Jerry did not like for his tongue to look like a normal tongue. I don't even know who thought of a tongue brush, but I am open-minded enough that I said if he needed to, I was okay with that, that I personally didn't feel the need to scrape my own but certainly I wouldn't judge him for doing so.

You (and the whole planet Earth) were always talking about Venus and Mars, which I understand. We don't agree about the tongue brush, or the way I like toilet paper backed up to the wall and Jerry likes it spinning off the front. Different strokes and so on. But that explanation just didn't work with religion, mainly because Jerry kept trying to *save* me. "From what, Jerry?" I must have said forty times. "What are you saving me from?"

I guess coming to you was like going somewhere like Saturn or Uranus to work it out. Remember when I observed that? And then I said how sometimes a planet is *not* a planet, like Pluto for instance. All these years we thought it was a planet only to find out it wasn't. Clearly, I was too subtle for both of you, because you didn't do anything with my observation, and Jerry just shook his head and winked at you as if to say, *You see? You see how off she is?* and I said, "Up Uranus." Do you remember that? I'm hoping that you can picture us there that day: Jerry and Hannah from three suburbs over.

Anyway, I think that marriage vows should include an escape clause that says the contract is broken if one party ups and makes a big switch in religion or politics or aesthetic taste. I mean, these shifts just aren't fair, and we need an easier way out. Some people talk about marriage versus civil union. Well, I think everybody needs to be civil, and I think anybody that wants to call a relationship a marriage should have the right to do so.

I'm an open-minded person, and these days a more honest person, so I'll just go ahead and tell you that you were not our first counselor. In the beginning, we—like so many who come to you—were just hoping for an honest appraisal, like when you take your car in. Do they open the hood and just close it with disgust, like the way people often describe cancer: *They opened and then just closed her right up?* Or do they say, *Well, this vehicle might not have been the* best *choice for you, but she has miles left in her. Keep her in tires and oil and she'll probably get you where you need to go?* Or do they say, *Ah yes, she's a beauty and if you just pay attention to the subtle sounds of this complex engine then she'll be purring for life and won't you feel proud to have a hand on her wheel?*

My first choice of a therapist was Ashley Hoffman, but he is so brilliant and popular, a patient has to die for you to get an appointment. So I chose a Dr. Levine for his good Jewish name, because I had decided that the only way I could get some objectivity to counterbalance what had become Jerry's religious fervor was to find a good atheist or agnostic or Unitarian. Well, that is not information that you can find anywhere in an advertisement. So I thought I could go the more subtle route and look for a good Jewish name, which I did, only to have another bad joke played on me. Dr. Levine's mother, I discovered, was a Baptist, and that's how he had grown up down in Alabama, with Mr. Levine nowhere in sight. His accent was thicker than mine, and he used the words *bless* and *blessing* all the goddamn time. Jerry liked him, of course. Jerry likes talking to men better than he likes dealing with women, even though he won't admit it. I know you picked up on this too, but I'll come back to that. I felt that this lack of separation of church and marital state was a big conflict of interest. I wanted to tell Dr. Levine that I wanted to sue his ass for false advertisement, because the field of psychotherapy has a great and rich Hebrew heritage. But, of course, I didn't. Instead of that I told Jerry that Dr. Levine had to let all his clients go, because he was suffering a nervous breakdown of sorts, and then I opened the Yellow Pages, closed my eyes, and found you. The name *Love* sounded prophetic at the time. Ha ha.

But I did like how you always had the daily paper and *People* magazine in your bathroom, except sometimes when I started reading, I forgot that I had to go back in there and hear what a difficult person I am. Remember that time you had to come and get me and I told you I was feeling sick? What I was actually doing was reading about David Koresh and thinking how Jerry's new religion was getting on my nerves, but at least he wasn't *that* bad. Not yet anyway. Of course, I wanted to know what to be looking for in case the turn he'd already taken got worse.

Love or Apathy. The Game of Marriage. The Game of Monogamy. Some would say *Monotony*. You take turns. You go round and round. Sometimes you have to pay a penalty or lose your turn. Still, making a big change isn't easy, and that is what I was often thinking while collecting myself and watching others coming and going. The people I saw leaving who looked good and all together were already done deals, I suspect. You could tell the ones who already knew they were out of there and were just going through the motions to appease the other one enough to get a better deal during the divorce—more money, more time with the kids. I mean, so many people go to counseling for the kids, and that's a good thing when it works—kind of like a sermon when it's good and inspirational and you can use what you hear—but it can also become selfish. All that money that could go to college, and all that time that could go to taking them fun places. I mean, I spent a hell of a lot to get bored and wander around getting creeped out by your spooky violent and primitive art stuff.

I wish I could get all that money back from you. One day I added it up and it totaled at least a new car, which I really need these days. Do you remember how Jerry wanted to have me diagnosed as crazy? And then how he was hoping I had brain cancer? "Something is causing your abstract thoughts," he said. I mean no offense, well, actually I do mean a little offense, I never understood why you didn't get pissed off and tell him to let you tend to your own business. I mean, you listened to him sitting there in all his born-again glory. He would have loved a reason to have me drugged or lobotomized so I'd just drool and go along with whatever he said whenever he said it.

I am someone who does believe in the higher power of necessary medication. Amen. At times, a smidgen of this or that is just what you need. I loved the feel of Demerol when I was in labor, and I don't know what I would have done without that epidural—scream out lots of terrible things, I suspect, which I did anyway. And this drug they give you with a colonoscopy is just a dream—you're relaxed on one side, wide awake and watching television. I wanted to nominate myself for an Emmy. And I believe in spiritual highs, too. What I don't believe in is someone having the power to dictate someone else's spirituality or aesthetic code. Like if I hate corduroy, that is *my* business, not his.

But I did not *marry* a born-again person and so, yes, I did have a problem when he up and got all religious on me. That religious business was just another way to control and manipulate. "You aren't smart enough because you aren't Mensa material. You aren't neat and clean enough even when you say you're trying. You aren't saved, because you haven't cried and humiliated yourself by confessing to the congregation all the awful things you have done in life so they can heal, bless, and forgive you." That is *not* who I married. I mean, I didn't marry a luxury vehicle, I know that, but I did marry what I thought was your basic white stripped-down Corolla. I married Jerry Barnes, Toyota dealer, who in grade school was told that he scored in the genius range on some stupid aptitude test and has spent his whole life doing things like the Rubik's Cube to prove it. He was a lot of hot air but nice enough and kind of cute on a good day—a lot shorter than me but I didn't think much of it, especially since Dudley Moore and Susan Anton were an item around the time we were dating. People would say, "There's Dudley and Susan," and I liked that. I know that's stupid, but I was also only about twenty-two years old and still going to school for interior design. I liked a margarita on a Saturday afternoon and a glass of wine while cooking dinner, and so did Jerry, but now he is a teetotaler. He can't do anything halfway or in moderation. Forgive my diversion, but thinking about first meeting Jerry made me think of my neighbor's little Chihuahua, who is all the time trying to mount my Lab, Sheba, and I say, "There's Dudley and Susan." But now Dudley is dead, and very few people even remember that he was ever with Susan Anton. I loved that movie *Arthur.* Jerry did too, back when he was Jerry.

But being normal wasn't enough for Jerry, he had to always be into this or that. He always had a new hobby, and he'd go at it full tilt for a few months and then move on to another interest. He was into Sudoku and then pottery, model trains, and beer making. He wanted to take dancing lessons, and then he got interested in a kind of tag wrestling that involved grown men moving all around one another and then grabbing and holding. I referred to it as "homoerotic dance," and he accused *me* of not being open-minded, and I just said, "Whatever." I told him that I'd never in my life had any trouble finding somebody who wanted to dance with me, and he should remember that.

I am realistic enough to know that psychological or subconscious reasons often explain why people go where they go and make the choices they make. I mean, even though he tells people I'm not *saved*, I did grow up going to church, right? And where I went, a virtual feast of questionable things was happening, so I'd be a total fool *not* to question. Youth directors and choir directors and assistant this and that who took a "special interest" in the children. Some liked young girls and some liked young boys. "(I'm a) Boy Watcher." Remember that commercial? Or worse, remember those sunglasses? A slit of polarized glass so that no one could tell where you were looking—creepy. And that's why I told Jerry that if he was having some thoughts in those directions, he needed to spend some time with himself and his thoughts and his impulses and come to a personal decision. And of course, that is when he came to the personal decision that he needed to rededicate his life to the Lord and that he needed to bring me along with him. I might add that Jerry goes to a church where people want to heal homosexuals and those who are pro-choice.

You must get tired of hearing the same old thing over and over, because of course marriage fighting isn't really about the toothpaste cap left off, or the toilet seat up, or who loaded the dishwasher last. All that little nitpicky stuff usually means: *You get on my fucking nerves so bad I can't stand it.* It means: *What happened to the person I thought I was marrying?* It means: *You don't like the cat, so I don't like you.* It means: *I pretend I'm asleep when your hand brushes my back. I pretend your hand belongs to somebody else.*

Now, I'm not trying to tell you your business, but I think if I were you, I would have a series of questions that lead to a big yes-or-no answer. Should I get divorced? Ding ding ding—the answer is yes. I mean, I realize that a lot of people go into your business for a little self-help, and that's where you might very well overlap a little bit with Jerry being born-again. People with mental and emotional problems very often seek refuge in the church and the field of psychology. I'd say about eighty percent of you probably do that. And that's fine if a personal weakness leads you to a calling. I can dig it. I mean, that is what led me to interior design, after all. Everyone in my town would tell you that I grew up in a rat-hole firetrap and that my chosen profession was all about bringing color and clarity and order into a life of chaos. I mean, my mother couldn't help that she was one of those people who never cleaned house and never cared if anything matched or not. And my dad was a fireman, who should've known not to have stacks of papers everywhere with both of them chain-smoking. The cobbler's children go barefoot, like your girl I met one day on a bathroom trip, but I'll get back to that in a minute, if I remember.

By the way, if you are actually reading this letter, don't think you can charge me for the time, like that lawyer keeps doing every time I e-mail or call him back to answer a question he asked me. Just the other day he said, "How are you doing?" And I said I wasn't saying unless he stopped the clock and kept it stopped until I was done. I think he had trouble in that moment figuring out what part of himself was human and what part was not. That was the only time I had ever heard him pause in conversation, like he'd shorted out or something.

Some of my conversations with my lawyer have reminded me of those little games you had us play, which you need to know right up front do not work at all. I think you'd have to be a total idiot or someone who takes Mensa quizzes regularly to fall for such simplistic crap. I mean, anybody who ever saw *Annie Hall* knows to read the subtext.

You look so pretty today. (Like a bitch who spent too much at Nordstrom's.)

Why thank you, love. (Fuck you.)

What I know now is that, just by way of thinking those thoughts, I should not have continued shelling out two hundred bucks a pop to you. I'd have done just as well to rent a boxing ring for an hour. There's a test right there. Get in the ring and if you are — in a great moment of anger — willing to drive your fist into the face of someone you promised to cherish forever (especially if the genetics have worked such that those are now the same eyes you associate with your children), well then, Houston, we've got a problem.

So I wonder about you. Like at the end of the day, do you put your feet up and tell your wife all about us? Do you open a bottle of wine and snuggle on that big divan up in your room (I made a wrong turn once going to the bathroom) and say, "Thank God I am not living such an unhappy existence"? Does this thought make you love her more? She looks a bit older than you, and so I did wonder (when I saw the photo on your dresser) if she had had a husband before you and how you had adjusted to that or if you all have some different kind of marriage like mentor/mentee, or mother and child. Truth is, you seemed a little too interested in a lot of what Jerry had to say, and since this is my last letter to you, I'll just go ahead and say that. On some days I felt you two were picking up a frequency like a dog whistle that I just wasn't able to hear. Of course, you might just have a great gift for empathy, but then I'd have to ask where was this gift when Jerry was trying to have me committed to the attic like that woman in *Jane Eyre* who set everything on fire.

I have to admit I was curious about you and your life, especially after I met your kid and saw your room, and what I observed undermined my confidence in what you might or might not know. I mean, those enormous ornate cornices you all chose in your bedroom I can overlook. That is *my* business after all, and a lot of people make the unfortunate mistakes you did. Yellow really is a hard color to pick and work with. Any artist will tell you that. But my advice would be to go in there and start from scratch. That overhead light looks like something Liberace might've had in the bathroom.

I think your job would be easier if you had a chart of sorts that told people how they *should* feel. Here is a normal range of jealousy, and here is where you went off the deep end. Here is true compassion and concern, and here are feelings that are malicious and calculated. That's what I'd say about Jerry putting me on the prayer list at his new church. People keep leaving fruit on my steps, and I keep driving over to Jerry's house and throwing it through the window. "Stop praying for me!" I said, and he said, "I can pray for whomever I want." He said he would continue to pray for those like me — the sick and deranged. I didn't say what was on my unbrushed tongue, which shows how far I have come from the anger of it all. I am evolving each and every day. That's what I told Jerry when he sighed and stared to the heavens and mumbled something on my behalf. Instead of putting a foot in his face, as I wanted to, I just told him how at *my* church, my own personal testimony had inspired many. How I told I was born into chaos—a swirl of dust and stacked newspapers and old plastic-lined drapes that had not been opened in years—how my parents had sex that one time and then I was on my own tidying up when no one was looking and reading house magazines about decluttering and complementary colors. "I am so evolved," I told Jerry, "I never had wisdom teeth. I have an innate sense of when to get rid of what I don't need."

So, do you ever wonder what happened to us? Good old Jerry and Hannah. We went to a mediator after you, and we're still dealing with the lawyers, the kids going back and forth every week like little Ping-Pong balls. I know you see these disagreements all the time, often enough so that perhaps you can predict the ending to those like us, but aren't you ever curious, or is it just part of the job, part of the day, like you're just one of many stops on the Underground Railroad? Or maybe not, since I can't imagine a slave choosing to go back or to just sit and talk indefinitely. *Emancipation* was a word on my mind before I even knew it was there.

If I had your job, I might ask a person: *If a nuclear disaster occurred, and you had to live out those final painful days just stretched out somewhere thinking about your life—This is who I am. This is what I love. This is what I believe—who would you want hearing your whispers?* Or perhaps better: *Who do you trust to hear your whispers? Whose breath do you want mingled with your own? Whose flesh still warm beside you?*

I once heard a preacher discuss the miracles of Jesus in a way that made total sense to me. He said that science could explain the act, but that the timing was a miracle. And every now and then during that period of time we were seeing you, I would wake in the middle of the night to an old feeling, a sad feeling. Some dream had transported me back to when I could feel. And I could remember what *hope* felt like. Not happiness necessarily, but hope. A kind of natural happiness grows out of hope, a kind of longing and imagining of what might be. You know, back when I was so miserable, I read true crime all the time, the grislier the better, and I wondered, *What is wrong with me?* But I needed to reassure myself about where I was. At least I wasn't married to a serial killer. At least he didn't make me pretend to be dead or a young boy when having sex. Those aren't bodies stacked up out there in his tool shed, but little Tupperware containers filled with sorted screws and nails. The fascination with someone else's reality is a total escape (this is where I think you might come in). We look at a bad situation and say, "Whew," or we laugh/judge/ridicule. We want confessions— car wrecks, true crime, divorce battles, someone's nervous breakdown. Who is the fattest person in the family? But what kind of life is that, if you have to spend all your time filling up on all the awful stuff that is *not* your life? I had just ordered video biographies of John Wayne Gacy Jr. (sicko clown) and Jeffrey Dahmer (cannibal) when I caught a glimpse of myself in your bathroom mirror and thought, *Oh my God.* And that is when I had to slam on the brakes. I slammed on the brakes, and then the world crashed, and with the wreckage I heard silence, and with the silence I heard my own voice. I had been screaming all the while. For years I had been screaming. As in *Horton Hears a Who!*, that realization also made me see how selfish all this divorce/religion/self-analysis can be—I had not read to my children or just sat and watched their television programs with them in weeks. I had not stretched out beside them and rubbed their backs, whispered to them about all the good things that will happen in their lives, until they fell asleep. I had not done a thing to my hair in months, and I had worn the same jeans for a week straight, the same ones I had let my scarecrow wear the whole summer before. I was a mess.

Remember how I finally ended our time with you? Remember how I made a big confession that I had fucked the plumber who stopped by to make a few repairs? Well, the truth is I didn't do that at all. That's the story you hear all the time, kind of like the banker and his secretary, the professor and his student. The carpenter, electrician, plumber. The butcher and the baker and candlestick maker. That is a cliché right out of porn central. Bored wife wanders around the house all day wearing little to nothing and fucks whatever passes by. And you all believed it. Now *that* was *offensive* to me. I may be a lot of things but cliché is not one of them. And of course Jerry didn't really believe it, though he jumped on it like a dog on a bone because then he could accuse me of something specific. *Alienation of affection.* Boo hoo. And when he threatened to let it affect the decision about the kids and how we'd divide the household goods, I started singing "(I'm a) Girl Watcher," and we agreed to disagree and agree to a truce.

Though we never discussed my confession, I think deep down Jerry must know that I am too loyal a person to have screwed the plumber—loyal to the kids, loyal to my own moral code, and loyal to my own sense of aesthetics (no offense to the plumber, of course, but *not* my taste at all). No, my biggest betrayal to Jerry is that I quit trying. When I finally found my own voice, I realized I had nothing else I wanted to say to him. I stopped talking, nothing feeding nothing until nothing was huge and nothing begot nothing. Feeling nothing is not good, but it's where a lot of people stop and stay. The nothingness is so delusional and numbing. It's like stretching out in the snow and taking a little nap, and the comfort of discomfort is a scary thing. The lull into nothingness should be feared by all. I hope that as you read this letter you are actually able to identify me, to place me among the assembly line of broken parts and broken hearts that pass through your business. I hope you are able to remember how I often had to pee at the most unlikely (boring!) times and how you have always wished that you had gotten the recipe for my grandmother's pound cake, which I described so well one day when you asked me to talk about something I was proud of. I know you are proud of all those times you went to Asian and African places, but I just have to tell you, those stories are depressing. Maybe I got speared and boiled in a pot in some past life, I don't know, but those things you put on display give me the creeps. I'm afraid you'll come out there one day and find a client speared right there in the hallway with what came off your wall. But what I'm most afraid of is that people want to come there and stay, get comfortable with the little games and the burden of trying to fix something that just can't be fixed. I hope you will remember that, whatever I was, I was not apathetic. Bored? Oh dear God, yes, I was bored much of the time, but whenever I said I was bored or lonely or tired, it was my own voice saying it. I heard a voice that said, *Feel something*. And so I did, and I continue to. I wish you peace and love, Dr. Love. I wish you a happy daughter and a smooth-running vehicle and better decor. I thank you for the time you have spent reading me free of charge.

                                                    Sincerely,
                                                    Hannah from three suburbs over

PS: Enclosed is a photo of me and my kids at Disney World right after we rode Space Mountain, which is why the little one looks kind of scared. She barely made it up to the height mark that will let you ride. It was so much fun we went as many times as we could and even after screaming and carrying on and getting slung back and forth, I am proud to say that I no longer look one bit like shit on a stick.

KEVIN MOFFETT

Further Interpretations of Real-Life Events

FROM *McSweeney's*

AFTER MY FATHER RETIRED, he began writing trueish stories about fathers and sons. He had tried scuba diving, had tried being a dreams enthusiast, and now he'd come around to this. I was skeptical. I'd been writing my own trueish stories about fathers and sons for years, stories that weren't perfect, of course, but they were mine. Some were published in literary journals, and I'd even received a fan letter from Helen in Vermont, who liked the part in one of my stories where the father made the boy scratch his stepmom's back. Helen in Vermont said she found the story "enjoyable" but kind of "depressing."

The scene with the stepmom was an interpretation of an actual event. When I was ten years old my mother died. My father and I lived alone for five years, until he married Lara, a kind woman with a big laugh. He met her at a dreams conference. I liked her well enough in real life but not in the story. In the story, "End of Summer," I begrudged Lara (changed to "Laura") for marrying my father so soon after my mother died (changed to five months).

"You used to scratch your ma's back all the time," my father says in the final scene. "Why don't you ever scratch Laura's?"

Laura sits next to me, shucking peas into a bucket. The pressure builds. "If you don't scratch Laura's back," my father says, "you can forget Christmas!"

So I scratch her back. It sounds silly now, but by the end of the story, Christmas stands in for other things. It isn't just Christmas anymore.

The scene was inspired by the time my father and Lara went to Mexico City (while I was marauded by bullies and black flies at oboe camp) and brought me home a souvenir. A tin handicraft? you guess. A selection of cactus-fruit candy? No. A wooden back-scratcher with extended handle for maximum self-gratification. What's worse, *te quiero* was embossed on the handle. Which I translated at the time to mean: *I love me.* (I was off by one word.)

"Try it," my father said. His tan had a yolky tint and he wore a shirt with PROPERTY OF MEXICO on the back. It was the sort of shirt you could find anywhere.

I hiked my arm over my head and raked the backscratcher north and south along my vertebrae. "Works," I said.

"He spent all week searching for something for you," Lara said. "He even tried to haggle at the *mercado*. It was cute."

"There isn't much for a boy like you in Mexico," my father said. "The man who sold me the backscratcher, though, told me a story. All the men who left to fight during the revolution took their wives with them. They wanted to remember more . . ."

I couldn't listen. I tried to, I pretended to, nodding and going *hmm* when he said *Pancho Villa* and *wow* when he said *gunfire* and then *some story* when it was over. I excused myself, sprinted upstairs to my bedroom, slammed my door, and snapped that sorry back-scratcher over my knee like kindling.

A boy like me!

You'll never earn a living writing stories, not if you're any good at it. My mentor Harry Hodgett told me that. I must've been doing something right, because I had yet to receive a dime for my work. I day-labored at the community college teaching Prep Writing, a class for students without the necessary skills for Beginning Writing. I also taught Prep Prep Writing, for those without the skills for Prep Writing. Imagine the most abject students on earth, kids who, when you ask them to name a verb, stare like you just asked them to cluck out a polka with armpit farts.

Literary journals paid with contributors' copies and subscriptions, which was nice, because when your story was published you at least knew that everyone else in the issue would read your work. (Though, truth be told, I never did.) This was how I came to receive the autumn issue of *Vesper*—I'd been published in the spring issue. It sat on my coffee table until a few days after its arrival, when I returned home to find Carrie on my living room sofa, reading it. "Shh," she said.

I'd just come back from teaching, dispirited as usual after Shandra Jones in Prep Prep Writing told a classmate to "eat my drippins." A bomb I defused with clumsy silence, comma time!, early dismissal.

"I didn't say anything," I said.

"Shh," she said again.

An aside: I'd like to have kept Carrie out of this because I haven't figured out how to write about her. She's tall with short brown hair and brown eyes and she wears clothes and—see? I could be describing anybody. Carrie's lovely, her face is a nest for my dreams. You need distance from your subject matter. You need to approach it with the icy, lucid eye of a surgeon. I also can't write about my mother. Whenever I try, I feel like I'm attempting kidney transplants with a can opener and a handful of rubber bands.

"Amazing," she said, closing the journal. "Sad and honest and free of easy meanness. It's like the story was unfolding as I read it. That bit in the motel: wow. How come you never showed me this? It's a breakthrough."

She stood and hugged me. She smelled like bath beads. I was jealous of the person, whoever it was, who had effected this reaction in her: Carrie, whom I met in Hodgett's class, usually read my stories with barely concealed impatience.

"Breakthrough, huh?" I said casually (desperately). "Who wrote it?" She leaned in and kissed me. "You did."

I picked up the journal to make sure it wasn't the spring issue, which featured "The Longest Day of the Year," part two of my summer trilogy. It's about a boy and his father (I know, I know) driving home, arguing about the record player the father refuses to buy the boy, even though the boy totally needs it since his current one ruined two of his Yes albums, including the impossible-to-find *Time and a Word,* and—*boom*—they hit a deer. The stakes suddenly shift.

I turned to the contributors' notes. FREDERICK MOXLEY is a retired statistics professor living in Vero Beach, Florida. In his spare time he is a dreams enthusiast. This is his first published story.

"My dad!" I screamed. "He stole my name and turned me into a dreams enthusiast!"

"Your *dad* wrote this?"

"And turned me into a goddamn dreams enthusiast! Everyone'll think I've gone soft and stupid!"

"I don't think anyone really reads this journal," Carrie said. "No offense. And isn't he Frederick Moxley, too?"

"Fred! He goes by *Fred*. I go by Frederick. Ever since third grade, when there were two Freds in my class." I flipped the pages, found the story, "Mile Zero," and read the first sentence: *As a boy I always dreamed of flight.* That makes two of us, I thought. To the circus, to Tibet, to live with a nice family of Moonies. I felt tendrils of bile beanstalking up my throat. "What's he trying to do?"

"Read it," Carrie said. "I think he makes it clear what he's trying to do."

If the story was awful I could have easily endured it, I realize now. I could've called him and said if he insists on writing elderly squibs, please just use a pseudonym. Let the Moxley interested in truth and beauty, etc., publish under his real name.

But the story wasn't awful. Not by a long shot. Yes, it broke two of Hodgett's six laws of story writing (Never dramatize a dream, Never use more than one exclamation point per story), but he'd managed some genuine insight. Also he fictionalized real-life events in surprising ways. I recognized one particular detail from after Mom died. We moved the following year, because my father never liked our house's floor plan. That's what I'd thought, at least. Too cramped, he always said; wherever you turned, a wall or closet blocked your path. In the story, though, the characters move because the father can't disassociate the house from his wife. Her presence is everywhere: in the bedroom, the bathroom, in the silverware pattern, the flowering jacaranda in the backyard.

She used to trim purple blooms from the tree and scatter them around the house, on bookshelves, on the dining room table, he wrote. *It seemed a perfectly attuned response to the natural world, a way of inviting the outside, inside.*

I remembered those blooms. I remembered how the house smelled with her in it, though I couldn't name the smell. I recalled her *presence,* vast ineffable thing.

I finished reading in the bath. I was no longer angry. I was a little jealous. Mostly I was sad. The story, which showed father and son

failing to connect again and again, ends in a motel room in Big
Pine Key (we used to go there in December), the father watching a
cop show on TV while the boy sleeps. He's having a bad dream, the
father can tell by the way his face winces and frowns. The father lies
down next to him, hesitant to wake him up, and tries to imagine
what he's dreaming about.

Don't wake up, the father tells him. *Nothing in your sleep can hurt
you.*

The boy was probably dreaming of a helicopter losing altitude. It
was a recurring nightmare of mine after Mom died. I'd be cutting
through the sky, past my house, past the hospital, when suddenly
the control panel starts beeping and the helicopter spins down,
down. My body fills with air as I yank the joystick. The noise is the
worst. Like a monster oncoming bee. My head buzzes long after I
wake up, shower, and sit down to breakfast. My father, who's just
begun enthusing about dreams, a hobby that even then I found ridiculous, asks what I dreamed about.

"Well," I say between bites of cereal. "I'm in a blue—no, no, a
golden suit. And all of a sudden I'm swimming in an enormous
fishbowl in a pet store filled with eager customers. And the thing is,
they all look like you. The other thing is, I *love* it. I want to stay in
the fishbowl forever. Any idea what that means?"

"Finish your breakfast," he says, eyes downcast.

I'd like to add a part where I say *just kidding,* then tell him my
dream. He could decide it's about anxiety, or fear. Even better: he
could just backhand me. I could walk around with a handprint on
my face. It could go from red to purple to brownish blue, poetic-
like. Instead, we sulked. It happened again and again, until mornings grew as joyless and choreographed as the interactions of people who worked among deafening machines.

In the bathroom I dried myself off and wrapped a towel around
my waist. I found Carrie in the kitchen eating oyster crackers. "So?"
she said.

Her expression was so beseeching, such a lidless empty jug.

I tossed the journal onto the table. "Awful," I said. "Sentimental,
boring. I don't know. Maybe I'm just biased against bad writing."

"And maybe," she said, "you're just jealous of good writing." She
dusted crumbs from her shirt. "I know it's good, you know it's
good. You aren't going anywhere till you admit that."

"And where am I trying to go?"

She regarded me with a look I recalled from Hodgett's class. Bemused amusement. The first day, while Hodgett asked each of us to name our favorite book, then explained why we were wrong, I was daydreaming about this girl in a white V-neck reading my work and timidly approaching me afterward to ask, What did the father's broken watch represent? and me saying *futility*, or *despair*, and then maybe kissing her. She turned out to be the toughest reader in class, far tougher than Hodgett, who was usually content to make vague pronouncements about *patterning* and *the octane of the epiphany*. Carrie was cold and smart and meticulous. She crawled inside your story with a flashlight and blew out all your candles. She said of one of my early pieces, "On what planet do people actually talk to each other like this?" And: "Does this character do anything but shuck peas?"

I knew she was right about my father's story. But I didn't want to talk about it anymore. So I unfastened my towel and let it drop to the floor. "Uh-oh," I said. "What do you think of this plot device?"

She looked at me, down, up, down. "We're not doing anything until you admit your father wrote a good story."

"*Good?* What's that even mean? Like, can it fetch and speak and sit?"

"Good," Carrie repeated. "It's executed as vigorously as it's conceived. It isn't false or pretentious. It doesn't jerk the reader around to no effect. It lives by its own logic. It's poignant without trying too hard."

I looked down at my naked torso. At some point during her litany, I seemed to have developed an erection. My penis looked all eager, as if it wanted to join the discussion, and unnecessary. "In that case," I said, "I guess he wrote one good story. Do I have to be happy about it?"

"Now I want you to call him and tell him how much you like it."

I picked up the towel, refastened it, and started toward the living room.

"I'm just joking," she said. "You can call him later."

Dejected, I followed Carrie to my room. She won, she always won. I didn't even feel like having sex anymore. My room smelled like the bottom of a pond, like a turtle's moistly rotting cavity. She lay on my bed, still talking about my father's story. "I love that little boy in the motel room," she said, kissing me, taking off her shirt. "I love how he's still frowning in his sleep."

I never called my father, though I told Carrie I did. I said I called and congratulated him. "What's his next project?" she asked. Project! As if he was a famous architect or something. I said he's considering a number of projects, each project more poignant-without-trying-too-hard than the project before it.

He phoned a week later. I was reading my students' paragraph essays, feeling my soul wither with each word. The paragraphs were in response to a prompt: "Where do you go to be alone?" All the students, except one, went to their room to be alone. The exception was Daryl Ellington, who went to his rom.

"You sound busy," my father said.

"Just getting some work done," I said.

We exchanged postcard versions of our last few weeks. I'm fine, Carrie's fine. He's fine, Lara's fine. I'd decided I would let him bring up the journal.

"Been writing," he said.

"Here and there. Some days it comes, some days it doesn't."

"I meant me," he said, then slowly he paddled through a summary of how he'd been writing stories since I sent him one of mine (I'd forgotten this), and of reading dozens of story collections, and then of some dream he had, then, *finally*, of having his story accepted for publication (and two others, forthcoming). He sounded chagrined by the whole thing. "I told them to publish it as Seth Moxley but lines must've gotten crossed," he said. "Anyway, I'll put a copy in the mail today. If you get a chance to read it, I'd love to hear what you think."

"What happened to scuba diving?" I asked.

"I still dive. Lara and I are going down to the Pennekamp next week."

"Right, but—writing's not some hobby you just dabble in, Dad. It's not like scuba diving."

"I didn't say it was. You're the one who brought up diving." He inhaled deeply. "Why do you always do this?"

"Do what?"

"Make everything so damn difficult. I had to drink two glasses of wine before I called, just to relax. You were such an easygoing kid,

232 KEVIN MOFFETT

you know that? Your mom used to call you Placido. I'd wake up panicked in the middle of the night and run to check on you, because you didn't make any noise."

"Maybe she was talking about the opera singer," I said.

Pause, a silent up-grinding of gears. "You don't remember much about your mother, do you?"

"A few things," I said.

"Her voice?"

"Not really."

"She had a terrific voice."

I didn't listen to much after that. Not because I'd already heard it, though I had—I wanted to collect a few things I remembered about her, instead of listening to his version again. Not facts or adjectives or secondhand details, but . . . qualities. Spliced-together images I could summon without words: her reaching without looking to take my hand in the street, the pockmarks on her wrist from the pins inserted when she broke her arm, her laughing, her crying, her warmth muted, her gone, dissolving room-by-room from our house. I'd never been able to write about her, not expressly. Whenever I tried she emerged all white-robed and beatific, floating around, dispensing wisdom, laying doomed hands on me and everyone. Writing about her was imperfect remembering; it felt like a second death. I was far happier writing about fathers making sons help drag a deer to the roadside, saying, "Look into them fogged-up eyes. Now that's death, boy."

"She always had big plans for you," my father was saying. It was something he often said. I never asked him to be more specific.

It occurs to me that I'm breaking two of Hodgett's laws here. Never write about writing, and Never dramatize phone conversations. Put characters in the same room, he always said. See what they do when they can't hang up. "We'd love to see Carrie again," my father said after a while. "Any chance you'll be home for Christmas?"

Christmas was two months away. "We'll try," I told him.

After hanging up, I returned to my students' paragraphs, happy to marinate for a while in their simple insight. *My room is the special place,* Monica Mendez wrote. *Everywhere around me are shelfs of my memory things.*

*

Imagine a time for your characters, Hodgett used to say, when things might have turned out differently. Find the moment a choice was made that made other choices impossible. Readers like to see characters making choices.

She died in May. A week after the funeral my father drives me and three friends to a theme park called Boardwalk and Baseball. He probably hopes it'll distract us for a few hours. All day long my friends and I ride roller coasters, take swings in the batting cage, eat hot dogs. I toss a Ping-Pong ball into a milk bottle and win a T-shirt. I can't even remember what kind of T-shirt it was, but I remember my glee after winning it.

My father follows us around and sits on a bench while we wait in line. He must be feeling pretty ruined but his son is doing just fine. His son is running from ride to ride, laughing it up with his friends. In fact, he hasn't thought about his mom once since they passed through the turnstiles.

My father is wearing sunglasses, to help with his allergies, he says. His sleeves are damp. I think he's been crying. "Having fun?" he keeps asking me.

I am, clearly I am. Sure, my mom died a week ago, but I just won a new T-shirt and my father gave each of us twenty dollars and the line to the Viper is really short and the sun is shining and I think we saw the girl from *Who's the Boss,* or someone who looks a lot like her, in line at the popcorn cart.

I cringe when I remember this day. I want to revise everything. I want to come down with food poisoning, or lose a couple of fingers on the Raptor, something to mar the flawless good time I was having. Now I have to mar it in memory, I have to remember it with a black line through it.

"I'm glad you had fun," my father says on the drive home.

Our house is waiting for us when we get back. The failing spider plants on the front porch, the powder-blue envelopes in the mailbox.

November was a smear. Morning after morning I tried writing but instead played Etch-a-Sketch for two hours. I wrote a sentence. I waited. I stood up and walked around, thinking about the sentence. I leaned over the kitchen sink and ate an entire sleeve of graham crackers. I sat at my desk and stared at the sentence. I deleted it and wrote a different sentence. I returned to the kitchen and ate a handful of baby carrots. I began wondering about the carrots, so I dialed the toll-free number on the bag and spoke to a woman in Bakersfield, California.

"I would like to know where baby carrots come from," I said.

"Would you like the long version or the short version?" the woman asked.

For the first time in days I felt adequately tended to. "Both," I said.

The short version: baby carrots are adult carrots cut into smaller pieces.

I returned to my desk, deleted my last sentence, and typed, "Babies are adults cut into smaller pieces." I liked this. I knew it would make an outstanding story, one that would win trophies and change the way people thought about fathers and sons if only I could find another three hundred or so sentences to follow it. But where were they?

A few weeks after my father sent me his first story, I received the winter issue of the *Longboat Quarterly* with a note: *Your father really wants to hear back from you about his story. He thinks you hated it. You didn't hate it, did you? XO, Lara.* No, Lara, I didn't. And I probably wouldn't hate this one, though I couldn't read past the title, "Blue Angels," without succumbing to the urge to sidearm the journal under my sofa (it took me four tries). I already knew what it was about.

Later, I sat next to Carrie on the sofa while she read it. Have you ever watched someone read a story? Their expression is dim and tentative at the beginning, alternately surprised and bewildered during the middle, and serene at the end. At least Carrie's was then.

"Well," she said when she was done. "How should we proceed?"

"Don't tell me. Just punch me in the abdomen. Hard."

I pulled up my shirt, closed my eyes, and waited. I heard Carrie close the journal, then felt it lightly smack against my stomach.

I read the story in the tub. Suffice it to say, it wasn't what I expected.

As a kid I was obsessed with fighter planes. Tomcats, Super Hornets, anything with wings and missiles. I thought the story was going to be about my father taking me to see the Blue Angels, the U.S. Navy's flight team. It wouldn't have been much of a story: miserable heat, planes doing stunts, me in the autograph line for an hour, getting sunburned, and falling asleep staring at five jets on a poster as we drove home.

The story is about a widowed father drinking too much and deciding he needs to clean the house. He goes from room to room dusting, scrubbing floors, throwing things away. The blue angels are a trio of antique porcelain dolls my mother held on to from childhood. The man throws them away, then regrets it as soon as he hears the garbage truck driving off. The story ends with father and son at the dump, staring across vast hillocks of trash, paralyzed.

I remembered the dump, hot syrup stench, blizzard of birds overhead. He told me it was important to see where our trash ended up.

When I finished, I was sad again, nostalgic, and wanting to call my father. Which I did after drying off. Carrie sat next to me on the sofa with her legs over mine. "What are you doing?" she asked. I dialed the number, waited, listened to his answering machine greeting—*Fred and Lara can't believe we missed your call*—and then hung up.

"Have I ever told you about when I saw the Blue Angels?" I asked Carrie.

"I don't think so."

"Well, get ready," I said.

I quit writing for a few weeks and went out into the world. I visited the airport, the beach, a fish camp, a cemetery, a sinkhole. I collected evidence, listened, tried to see past my impatience to the blood-radiant heart of things. I saw a man towing a woman on the handlebars of a beach cruiser. They were wearing sunglasses. They were poor. They were in love. I heard one woman say to another: *Everyone has a distinct scent, except me. Smell me, I don't have any scent.*

At the cemetery where my mother was buried, I came upon an old man lying very still on the ground in front of a headstone. When I walked by, I read the twin inscription. RUTH GOODINE 1920–1999, CHARLES GOODINE 1923–. "Don't mind me," the man said as I passed.

At my desk, I struggled to make something of this. I imagined what happened before and after. What moment made other moments impossible. He had come to the cemetery to practice for

eternity. I could still picture him lying there in his gray suit, but the
before and after were murky. Before, he'd been on a bus, or in a
car, or a taxi. Afterward he would definitely go to . . . the supermarket to buy . . . lunch meat?

"Anything worth saying," Hodgett used to declare, "is unsayable.
That's why we tell stories."

I returned to the cemetery. I walked from one end to the other,
from the granite cenotaphs to the unmarked wooden headstones.
Then I walked into the mausoleum and found my mother's placard, second from the bottom. I had to kneel down to see it. Another of Hodgett's six laws: Never dramatize a funeral or a trip to
the cemetery. Too melodramatic, too obvious. I sat against something called the Serenity Wall and watched visitors mill in and out.
They looked more inconvenienced than sad. My father and I used
to come here, but at some point we quit. Afterward we'd go to a
diner and he would say, "Order anything you want, anything," and
I would order what I always ordered.

A woman with a camera asked if I could take her picture in front
of her grandmother's placard. I said, "One, two, three, smile," and
snapped her picture.

When the woman left, I said some things to my mom, all melodramatic, all obvious. In the months before she died, she talked
about death like it was a long trip she was taking. She would watch
over me, she said, if they let her. "I'm going to miss you," she said,
which hadn't seemed strange until now. Sometimes I hoped she
was watching me, but usually it was too terrible to imagine. "Here I
am," I told the placard. I don't know why. It felt good so I said it
again.

"Why don't you talk about your mom?" Carrie asked me after I
told her about going to the cemetery.

"You mean in general, or right now?"

Carrie didn't say anything. She had remarkable tolerance for
waiting.

"What do you want to know?" I asked.

"Anything you tell me."

I forced a laugh. "I thought you were about to say, 'Anything you
tell me is strictly confidential.' Like in therapy. Isn't that what they
tell you in therapy?"

For some reason I recalled my mother at the beach standing in the knee-deep water with her back to me. Her pants are wet to the waist and any deeper and her shirt will be soaked, too. I wondered why I needed to hoard this memory. Why did this simple static image seem like such a rare coin?

"Still waiting," Carrie said.

My father published two more stories in November, both about a man whose wife is dying of cancer. He had a weakness for depicting dreams, long, overtly symbolic dreams, and I found that the stories themselves read like dreams, I suffered them like dreams, and after a while I forgot I was reading. Like my high school band teacher used to tell us, "Your goal is to stop seeing the notes." This never happened to me, every note was a seed I had to swallow, but now I saw what he meant.

Toward the end of the month, I was sick for a week. I canceled class and lay in bed, frantic with half-dreams. Carrie appeared, disappeared, reappeared. I picked up my father's stories at random and reread paragraphs out of order. I looked for repeated words, recurring details. One particular sentence called to me, from "Under the Light."

That fall the trees stingily held on to their leaves.

In my delirium, this sentence seemed to solve everything. I memorized it. I chanted it. *I* was the tree holding on to its leaves, but I couldn't let them go, because if I did I wouldn't have any more leaves. My father was waiting with a rake because that was his *job* but I was being too stingy and weren't trees a lot like people?

I got better.

The morning I returned to class, Jacob Harvin from Prep Writing set a bag of Cheetos on my desk. "The machine gave me two by accident," he said.

I thanked him and began talking about subject-verb agreement. Out of the corner of my eye, I kept peeking at the orange Cheetos bag and feeling dreadful gratitude. "Someone tell me the subject in this sentence," I said, writing on the board. "*The trees of Florida hold on to their leaves.*"

Terrie Inal raised her hand. "You crying, Mr. Moxley?" she asked.

"No, Terrie," I said. "I'm allergic to things."

"Looks like you're crying," she said. "You need a moment?"

The word *moment* did it. I let go. I wept in front of the class while they looked on horrified, bored, amused, sympathetic. "It's just, that was so *nice*," I explained.

Late in the week, my father called and I told him I was almost done with one of his stories. "Good so far," I said. Carrie suggested I quit writing for a while, unaware that I already had. I got drunk and broke my glasses. Someone wrote *Roach* with indelible marker on the hood of my car.

One day, I visited Harry Hodgett in his office. I walked to campus with a bagged bottle of Chivas Regal, his favorite, practicing what I'd say. Hodgett was an intimidating figure. He enjoyed playing games with you.

His door was open, but the only sign of him was an empty mug next to a student story. I leaned over to see *S.B.N.I.* written in the margin in Hodgett's telltale blue pen — it stood for *Sad But Not Interesting* — then I sat down. The office had the warm, stale smell of old books. Framed pictures of Hodgett and various well-known degenerates hung on the wall.

"This ain't the petting zoo," Hodgett said on his way in. He was wearing sweatpants and an Everlast T-shirt with frayed cut-off sleeves. "Who are you?"

Hodgett was playing one of his games. He knew exactly who I was. "It's me," I said, playing along. "Moxley."

He sat down with a grunt. He looked beat-up, baffled, winded, which meant he was in the early days of one of his sober sprees. "Oh yeah, Moxley, sure. Didn't recognize you without the . . . you know."

"Hat," I tried.

He coughed for a while, then lifted his trash can and expectorated into it. "So what are you pretending to be today?" he asked, which was Hodgett code for "So how are you doing?"

I hesitated, then answered, "Bamboo," a nice inscrutable thing to pretend to be. He closed his eyes, leaned his head back to reveal the livid scar under his chin, which was Hodgett code for "Please proceed." I told him all about my father. Knowing Hodgett's predilections, I exaggerated some things, made my father sound more abusive. Hodgett's eyes were shut, but I could tell he was listening by the way his face ticced and scowled. "He sends the stories out under my name," I said. "I haven't written a word in over a month."

To my surprise, Hodgett opened his eyes, looked at me as if he'd just awoken, and said, "My old man once tried to staple-gun a dead songbird to my scrotum." He folded his arms across his chest. "Just facts, not looking for pity."

I remembered reading this exact sentence — *staple-gun, songbird, scrotum* — then I realized where. "That happened to Moser," I said, "at the end of your novel *The Hard Road*. His dad wants to teach him a lesson about deprivation."

"That wasn't a novel, Chief. That was first-person *life*." He huffed hoarsely. "All this business about literary journals and phone calls and hurt feelings, it's just not compelling. A story needs to sing like a wound. I mean, put your father and son in the same room together. Leave some weapons lying around."

"It isn't a story," I said. "I'm living it."

"I'm paid to teach students like you how to spoil paper. Look at me, man — I can barely put my head together." His face went through a series of contortions, like a ghoul in a mirror. "You want my advice," he said. "Go talk to the old man. Life ain't an opera. It's more like a series of commercials for things we have no intention of buying."

He narrowed his eyes, studying me. His eyes drooped; his mouth had white film at the corners. His nose was netted with burst capillaries.

"What happened to the young woman, anyway?" Hodgett asked. "The one with the nasty allure."

"You mean Carrie? My girlfriend?"

"Carrie, yeah. I used to have girlfriends like Carrie. They're fun." He closed his eyes and with his right hand began casually kneading his crotch. "She did that story about the burn ward."

"Carrie doesn't write anymore," I said, trying to break the spell.

"Shame," Hodgett said. "Well, I guess that's how it goes. Talent realizes its limitations and gives up while incompetence keeps plugging away until it has a book. I'd take incompetence over talent in a street fight any day of the week."

I picked up the Chivas Regal bottle and stood to leave. I studied the old man's big noisy battered redneck face. He was still fondling himself. I wanted to say something ruthless to him. I wanted my words to clatter around in his head all day, like his words did in mine. "Thanks," I said.

He nodded, pointed to the bottle. "You can leave that anywhere," he said.

Another memory: my mother, father, and me in our living room. I am eight years old. In the corner is the Christmas tree, on the wall are three stockings, on the kitchen table is a Styrofoam-ball snowman. We're about to open presents. My father likes to systematically inspect his to figure out what's inside. He picks up a flat parcel wrapped in silver paper, shakes it, turns it over, holds it to his ear, and says, "A book." He sets it on his lap and closes his eyes. "A . . . autobiography."

He's right every time.

My mother wears a yellow bathrobe and sits under a blanket. She's cold again. She's sick but I don't know this yet. She opens her presents distractedly, saying *wow* and *how nice* and neatly folding the wrapping paper in half, then in quarters, while I tear into my gifts one after another. I say thanks without looking up.

That year, she and I picked out a new diver's watch for my father, which we wait until all the presents have been opened to give him. We've wrapped it in a small box and then wrapped that box inside a much larger one.

I set it in front of him. He looks at me, then her. He lifts the box. "Awfully light." He shakes it, knocks on each of the box's six sides. "Things are not what they seem."

My mother begins coughing, softly at first—my father pauses, sets his hands flat atop the box—then uncontrollably, in big hacking gusts. I bring her water, which she drinks, still coughing. My father helps her to the bathroom and I can hear her in there, gagging and hacking. For some reason I'm holding the remote control to the television.

The box sits unopened in the living room for the rest of the day. At night, with Mom in bed and me brushing my teeth, he picks it up, says "Diver's watch, waterproof up to a hundred meters," then opens it.

Carrie and I drove to Vero Beach the day before Christmas Eve. There seemed to be a surplus of abandoned cars and dead animals on the side of the road and, between this and the gray sky and the homemade signs marking off the fallow farms—PREPARE FOR THE RAPTURE; PRAISE HIM—I began to daydream about the apocalypse. I was hoping it would arrive just like this, quietly, without much warning or fanfare.

"I know it's fiction," Carrie was saying, referring to my father's most recent story, "but it's hard not to read it as fact. Did you actually tape pictures of your mom to the front door when Lara came over the first time?"

"Maybe," I said. "Probably. I don't really remember."

I taped the pictures in a circle, like the face of a clock. I waited at the top of the stairs for the doorbell to ring.

Carrie pointed to a billboard featuring the likeness of a recently killed NASCAR driver's car, flanked by white angel wings. "I hope they haven't started letting race cars into heaven," she said.

I finally talked to my father about his writing while we were in the garage looking for the Styrofoam-ball snowman. We were searching through boxes, coming across yearbooks, macramé owls, clothes, and my oboe, snug in purple velvet. I always forgot how fit and reasonable-looking my father was until I saw him in person. His hair was now fully gray and his silver-rimmed reading glasses sat low on his nose.

"I didn't know we went to the dump to hunt for those dolls," I said. It sounded more reproachful than I meant it to.

He looked up from the box, still squinting, as if he'd been searching dark, cramped quarters. "You mean the story?"

"'Blue Angels,'" I said. "I read it. I read all of them, actually."

"That's surprising," he said, folding the flaps of the box in front of him. "Best not to make too much out of what happens in stories, right?"

"But you were looking for those dolls."

"I didn't expect to find them. I wanted to see where they ended up." He shook his head. "It's hard to explain. After your mom died —I'd be making breakfast and my mind would wander to Annie and I'd start to lose it. The only time I relaxed was when I slept. That's why I started studying dreams. I found that if I did a few exercises before falling asleep, I could dictate what I dreamed about.

I could remember. I could pause and fast-forward and rewind. You're giving me a 'how pitiful' look."

"It's just strange," I said. "The dreams, the stories, it feels like I haven't been paying attention. I had no idea you were being all quietly desperate while I was waiting for my toast."

"It wasn't all the time." He pushed his glasses up on his nose and looked at me. "You should try writing about her, if you haven't already. You find yourself unearthing all sorts of things. Stories are just like dreams."

Something about his advice irritated me. It brought to mind his casually boastful author's note, *This is his first published story.* "Stories aren't dreams," I said.

"They're not? What are they, then?"

I didn't know. All I knew was that if he thought they were dreams, then they had to be something else. "They're jars," I said. "Full of bees. You unscrew the lid and out come the bees."

"All right," he said, moving the box out of his way. "But I still think you should try writing about her. Even if it means the bees coming out."

We searched until I found the snowman resting face-down in a box of embroidered tablecloths. A rat or weasel had eaten half of his head, but he still smiled his black-beaded smile.

"I remember when you made that," my father said.

I did, too. That is, I remembered *when* I made it, without remembering the actual making of it. I made it with my mom when I was three. Every year it appeared in the center of the kitchen table and every year she would say, "You and I made that. It was raining outside and you kept saying, 'Let's go stand in the soup.'" Maybe she thought that if she reminded me enough, I'd never forget the day we made it, and maybe I didn't, for a while.

I brought the snowman into the house and showed it to Carrie, who was sitting in the living room with Lara. "Monstrous," Carrie said.

Lara was looking at me significantly. An unfinished popcorn string dangled from her lap. "Carrie was sharing her thoughts on your dad's stories," she said. "Do you want to add anything?"

My father walked into the living room holding two mismatched candlesticks.

"They," I said slowly, looking at Carrie, waiting for her to mouth the words, "were," she really was lovely, not just lovely looking, but lovely, "good." I breathed and said, "They were good."

Carrie applauded. "He means it, too," she said. "That slightly nauseous look on his face, that's sincerity." Then to me: "Now that wasn't so hard. Don't you feel light now, the weight lifted?"

I felt as if I'd swallowed a stone. I felt it settling and the moss starting to cover it.

"Frederick here's the real writer," my father said. "I'm just dabbling."

How humble, right? How wise and fatherly and kind. But I know what he meant: Frederick here's the fraud. He's the hack ventriloquist. I'm just dabbing at his wounds.

What more should be said about our visit? I want to come to my father's Mexico story without too much flourish. I hear Hodgett's voice: Never end your story with a character realizing something. Characters shouldn't realize things: readers should. But what if the character is also a reader?

We decorated the tree. We strung lights around the sago palms in the front yard. We ate breakfast in an old sugar mill and, from the pier, saw a pod of dolphins rising and rolling at dawn. I watched my father, tried to resist the urge to catalog him. His default expression was benign curiosity. He and Lara still held hands. They finished each other's sentences. They seemed happy. Watching my father watch the dolphins, I felt like we were at an auction, bidding on the same item. It was an ugly, miserly feeling.

I couldn't sleep on Christmas Eve. Carrie and I shared my old bedroom, which now held a pair of single beds separated by my old tricolor nightstand. All the old anxieties were coming back, the deadness of a dark room, the stone-on-stone sound of a crypt top sliding closed as soon as I began drifting to sleep.

I heard Carrie stir during the night. "I can't sleep," I said.

"Keep practicing," she said groggily. "Practice makes practice."

"I was wondering why you quit writing. You had more talent than all of us. You always made it look so easy."

She exhaled through her nose and moved to face me. I could just barely see her eyes in the dark. "Let's pretend," she said.

I waited for her to finish. When she didn't I said, "Let's pretend what?"

"Let's pretend two people are lying next to each other in a room. Let's pretend they're talking about one thing and then another. It got too hard to put words in their mouths. They stopped cooperating." She rolled over, knocked her knee against the wall. "They started saying things like, I'm hungry, I'm thirsty, I need air. I'm tired of being depicted. I want to live."

I thought about her burn ward story, the way boys were on one side of the room and girls were on the other. Before lights-out the nurse came in and made everyone sing and then closed a curtain to separate the boys from the girls. After a while I said, "You sleeping?" She didn't answer so I went downstairs.

I poured a glass of water, and looked around my father's office for something to read. On his desk were a dictionary, a thesaurus, and something called *The Yellow Emperor's Classic of Internal Medicine,* which I flipped through. *When a man grows old his bones become dry and brittle like straw and his eyes bulge and sag.* I opened the top drawer of his filing cabinet and searched through a stack of photocopied stories until I found a stapled manuscript titled "Mexico Story." I sat down on his loveseat and read it.

In Mexico, it began, *some men still remember Pancho Villa.* I prepared for a thinly veiled account of my father's and Lara's vacation, but the story, it turned out, followed a man, his wife, and their son on vacation in Mexico City. They've traveled there because the mother is sick and their last hope is a healer rumored to help even the most hopeless cases. The family waits in the healer's sitting room for their appointment. The son, hiding under the headphones of his new Walkman, just wants to go home. The mother tries to talk to him but he just keeps saying *Huh? Huh?*

The three of us go into a dim room, where the healer asks my mother what's wrong, what her doctors said, why has she come. Then he shakes his head and apologizes. "Very bad," he says. He tells a rambling story about Pancho Villa, which none of us listens to, then reaches into a drawer and pulls out a wooden backscratcher. He runs it up and down along my mother's spine.

"How's that feel?" he asks.

"Okay," the mother says. "Is it doing anything?"

"Not a thing. But it feels good, yes? It's yours to keep, no charge." I must have fallen asleep while reading, because at some point the threads came loose in the story and mother, father, and son leave

Mexico for a beach that looks a lot like the one near our house. Hotels looming over the sea oats. The inlet lighthouse just visible in the distance. I sit on a blanket next to my father while my mother stands in knee-deep water with her back to us.

"She's sick," my father says. "She doesn't want me to say anything, but you're old enough to know. She's really . . . sick."

If she's sick she shouldn't be in the water, I think. Her pants are wet to the waist and if she wades in any deeper her shirt will be soaked, too. I pick up a handful of sand and let it fall through my fingers.

"So it's like a battle," he's saying. "Good versus bad. As long as we stick together, we'll get through it okay."

My mother walks out of the water. She is bathed in light and already I can barely see her. She sits next to us, puts her hand on my head, and, in the dream, I realize this is one of those moments I need to prolong. I put my hand over hers and hold it there. I push down on her hand until it hurts and I keep pushing.

"You can let go," she says. "I'm not going anywhere."

The next morning I found my father in checked pajamas near the Christmas tree. He carefully stepped over a stack of presents onto the tree skirt and picked up a gift from Carrie and me. He shook it and listened. He tapped on it with his finger.

"It's not a watch," I said.

He turned to me and smiled. "I've narrowed it down to two possibilities," he said. "Here." He waved me over. "Sit down, I've got something for you."

I sat on the couch and he handed me a long, flat package wrapped in red and white paper. "Wait, wait," he said when I started to unwrap it. "Guess what it is first."

I looked at it. All that came to mind was a pair of chopsticks.

"Listen," he said, taking it from me. He held it up to my ear and shook it. "Don't think, just listen. What's that sound like to you?"

I didn't hear anything. "I don't hear anything," I said.

He continued shaking the gift. "It's trying to tell you what it is. Hear it?"

I waited for it, I listened. "No."

He tapped the package against my head. "Listen harder," he said.

TÉA OBREHT

The Laugh

FROM *The Atlantic*

THEY WERE TALKING about the funeral when the lights went out. They had been sitting on the porch for almost two hours, and Neal, still on his first gin and tonic, was telling Roland about the priest he had found in Longido to do the services. He was telling Roland about how the priest, Father Abasi, had once been watering the garden in shorts and clogs when a man came by from the village and asked to see his boss, and how Father Abasi said, "I'll go get him," and turned off the hose and went inside and changed into his cassock and came back out and then went to bury the man's daughter.

Neal was talking, and Roland had his hat on his knees and was pouring himself another gin. They had brought Femi's coffin back from Longido around noon, and Roland had been drinking steadily since then, except for the twenty minutes before dinner when he had gone upstairs to bottle-feed Nyah and put her to bed.

"I think Femi would have liked this priest," Neal was saying. "I think she would have tolerated him." Then the porch went dark.

Neal needed a moment to realize what had happened. He was already turning in his seat to call for Mrs. Halima, the housekeeper, to tell her she'd turned the porch lights off by mistake, when he realized that he couldn't see the house behind him, couldn't see the tourist bungalows or the gate lamps. The generator, he realized. The generator had blown in the heat. A bright half-moon clung to the side of the main house like something unfinished, and Neal could see the fever trees that lined the drive, thick with roosting vultures, baldheaded and silent, and the rolling tilt of the hills that clustered on the horizon and then dropped off into Ngorongoro.

The darkness, the sudden crippling of his senses, brought back his awareness of the wildebeest. They had been on the move since last week, and now the smell of them on the dry wind made the air rancid and dense. He could hear them on the plain beyond the lodge gate, hundreds of stragglers from the main herd spread out on the veldt, swarming the dirt trail that led down to the water hole. The light, he realized, had given him the illusion of distance, and now that it was gone the night felt crowded with soft grunts, the insistent, rubber-soled scraping of their voices. Last night, lions had brought down a bull by the water, and the screaming before the windpipes gave way had been extraordinary. In the morning, Neal had found the red domes of the rib cage swarming with vultures. In large part this was why he had relocated his tourists. He was glad, more than ever, that he had.

Roland hadn't moved at all, but now Neal heard him say, "Where's the dog?"

"Upstairs," Neal said. "With the baby."

"Where's Simon?"

"I sent him home," Neal said. "We don't have any tourists to guard." He heard Roland lower his feet from the porch railing and push the chair back. "Let's wait for the generator," Neal said. "Let's wait and see what it does."

Roland was leaning forward in his chair. Neal could hear him drinking the gin, the ice in the glass clinking. Neal's eyes were adjusting now, and the moon seemed brighter. He was beginning to make out the slope of the trail leading down from the lodge, the grass shuddering over the hills, the distant glassy surface of the water hole. Roland groped for the end table and put the glass down. Neal heard shuffling footsteps, and then Mrs. Halima came out onto the porch, carrying a large square candle. She put it on the table, picked up Roland's empty glass, then reached for the gin bottle beside the chair. She was a thin Swahili woman with a serious face, a widow. She had been working for the previous owners of Harper's Lodge when Neal bought the place three years ago, and the first day he met her, she'd said to him: "Breakfast is at seven, and I told the staff they'll be turning the sheets down same as they always have." He'd realized then she wasn't going anywhere.

He was more grateful for her than ever now. Mrs. Halima had

carried out all the preparations for Femi's wake herself. All morning he had allowed himself to be mesmerized by the methodical necessity of what she was doing, the way she boxed up the tinsel and ribbons that had been up around the fireplace, the velvet mistletoe above the door. She found some comfort in taking last week's celebration out of the house, some quiet reverie he could not find for himself. He had sat in the living room, watching her prepare the table for the casket, watching her line up candles on the mantelpiece, trying to absorb some of that stoicism until it was time for him to go and pick up the coffin. She had shown emotion only once, briefly, when he had been halfway out the door. She had grabbed his sleeve and said: "You tell Mr. Roland everything's ready, you tell him we'll take good care of him and his little girl." He had promised to, and then she'd looked at him with something he couldn't name in her eyes and said, "Do you think it will be terrible—what's in that coffin?" He hadn't been able to answer.

But now, on the porch, in the darkness, she was back to her old self. "Nyah's still asleep," Mrs. Halima said. "Egg sandwiches are in the kitchen." She stood there, behind them, for a few minutes, while the sounds beyond the gate rolled up the slope and across the porch: a zebra's yelp, the wings of some large bird passing by, the sandpaper hum of the cicadas in the long grass. Mrs. Halima said, "I think the electricity is out down in Longido, too."

"We may be the only ones," Neal said. "Our generator may be out. This heat is too much, even for January."

"I think I'll go down and check on it anyway," Roland said.

Neal said, "Give it a few more minutes, it'll come back on. This has happened before, it'll come back on." He didn't want to mention that the last time they'd had a power failure, it had been the fault of some idiot teenagers from San Diego who had wandered out in the middle of the night and found their way into the generator shed with the brilliant plan of ruining the night for their parents back at the lodge. Neal remembered how they'd looked, those teenagers, after spending the night in the generator shed, afraid to cross back in the dark, their faces red with tears, when he'd driven out in the Jeep to find them. And Femi—Femi had a place in that memory. She had come in from Vibanda to look them over, to check for injuries, to give them sedatives. He remembered her bedside manner, the way she had smiled at them to make them believe she sympathized, when, in fact, she was furious. Then Neal remembered the hot-air balloon, felt the blood rush to his face, and he rubbed his forehead with his knuckles. "I can't see anything with this on," he said, and blew out the candle. Some melted ice water was in his glass, and he drank it down.

"I'm going," Roland said, and stood up.

"Mr. Roland, I don't think you should," Mrs. Halima said. "These last few days have been too much. Just stay here."

"Don't worry," Neal said to her. "We'll take the Jeep."

"I'm walking," Roland said.

Neal looked at the bald outline of Roland's head. "We should drive," Neal said, after a minute.

"I'm going to walk."

"Mr. Roland," Mrs. Halima said, "stay here."

But Neal could already hear Roland's footsteps moving to the back of the porch, the sound of Roland picking up his rifle, the sliding sound of the strap going over his shoulder. Neal felt his way over to the porch bench and opened the seat. He rummaged around inside until he found two flashlights. He heard Roland go down the porch steps. "Don't worry," Neal said to Mrs. Halima. "Just stay inside. We'll only be a minute." At the bottom of the stairs, Roland was holding a rifle out to Neal.

The generator stood at the water's edge, in a shed where the previous lodge owners had kept their boat during the rainy season, when the water hole, usually a turbid, red-brown dent in the plain, filled up and spilled leisurely into a small stream that fed the savanna. The shed lay almost a half-mile down the slope of the lawn, past the gate, in a long thicket of umbrella thorns, where the trail tapered out around the water hole.

Roland walked ahead, the rifle on his shoulder, and Neal followed him with a flashlight. They went down the trail along the twisting avenue of acacias, past the fire pit where the evening buffet was normally held, past the now deserted croquet lawn. Neal was sweating. A film of moist salt gathered above his mouth, and he licked it off every few seconds. But it appeared and reappeared, and eventually he just gave up and let it run down his face. Femi would not approve of this, he thought, she would never have let the two of them come out in the dark without a vehicle, not with the herd roaming about just outside. Roland was drunk. He was being careless. But Roland, Neal thought, had the right to do what he wanted—just as he had the right to have the wake at Neal's lodge, even though that meant losing a week's worth of profits. Because the thought of Roland sitting over the casket alone the night before the funeral—rocking Nyah to sleep, and then, with the lights dimmed and the mounted heads in the parlor for company, sitting up with his wife's coffin until he finally gave in and opened the lid to look inside—made Neal sick. It made him sick, and made him think of Femi in the hot-air balloon before she died, and he walked behind Roland wiping the sweat off his forehead.

"Slow down," he said to Roland, but Roland said nothing. Halfway down the trail, still hoping that the lights would come back on, Neal stopped and looked back at the lodge, the moon crawling up the dim gables of the main house, the squat bungalows behind it. He could see a dim flicker of something—a candle—and he thought, *Good, she's gone upstairs to be with the baby.* But the more he looked, the more he realized that the light was coming from the wrong place.

"Wait," he said to Roland. "Where's that candle lit?"

He heard Roland's footsteps stop in the darkness ahead of him, and then Roland came back. He was breathing hard, and he smelled faintly of gin and sweat. Neal heard him take off his hat and rub his head.

"I think she's still on the porch," Neal said.

Roland was rummaging in his pockets. "She's gone inside, she's probably in the kitchen." In a momentary flash of fire, he saw Roland's face, and then the bright red tip of a cigarette.

"I'm telling you, she's still outside," Neal said. Bats were in the glade behind him, and he could hear the strange, persistent sound of their flight. He thought of the first time he had met Femi, the first time Roland had introduced Neal to her in the neon heat of her family convenience store at Vibanda. She had closed up shop, and the three of them had sat on plastic chairs in the dirt yard outside, sipping sweet tea, chickens scratching around at their feet, blue rain clouds filling the horizon in the east, until the sun dipped and bats swarmed out of the scrubland trees, rising like fog.

His shirt was soaked with sweat, and he shifted around in it. He suddenly realized that Roland was looking at him. The light from the cigarette tip was spilling out over the creases under Roland's eyes, the big bridge of Roland's nose. Roland looked haggard, more haggard than he had looked after he came back from volunteering at that malaria hospital in Zimbabwe, where he had first met Femi.

"I don't like this," Neal said.

"I don't either," Roland said. Then he turned around and kept walking, out from under the acacias and toward the gate.

Neal stood there for a few moments, while Roland's footsteps receded away and away, the trill of the cicadas following him in waves of silence and sound. The widening darkness tugged at Neal's gut. He put his flashlight between his teeth and brought up the rifle from where it rested against his thigh. He lifted the bolt pin, opened the chamber, and looked inside. The chamber was empty.

"Roland!" he said. "This gun's not loaded, we have to go back."

But Roland said nothing, so Neal shouldered the gun and pressed on after him.

Since Femi's death, Neal had found himself thinking about her more often than usual, but most often in the long moments before sleep. The nights were quiet then, and he would find himself in a kind of waking dream, subdued by the mosquito net draped above him, the rhythm of the savanna sounds and the fan, and the dull thumping of Baviaan's tail on the rug under the bed.

He would think about her as she was at the Christmas party. He would think about that because he tried hard not to think about anything else, about how his memories seemed stupid, pointless, wasted, because he had not known that they would be memories. He thought about the white dress she had worn and the stew she had brought from home, about how she had sat on the couch with Roland's arm around her, glowing with enjoyment and wine, laughing with Mrs. Halima in Swahili. He thought about how he'd gotten drunk and drifted off only to wake up hours later, the house still, the lodge staff gone, and Femi awake and smiling at him from where she and Roland had fallen asleep on the rug in front of the fire. He thought about that: he and Femi, the only ones awake, even the tourists in the lodge bungalows sound asleep; and he thought about how they had stolen away into the kitchen and made cucumber sandwiches together.

Or he would think about other things, about when he went to visit her for the first time at the convenience store at Vibanda—but in those memories everything was vivid, except for Femi herself.

He could remember the number of meat cans he dropped off, the price of the gas, the feel of the paper bills in his hand. The paraffin stove in the corner where she made coffee. How he'd realized she was probably just being polite, but how he had sat down anyway on the mattress in her one-room bungalow behind the store. How Femi had talked about the weather and the crops and the low number of kudu out on the plains, and how he had looked around, feeling sheepish. He remembered how Femi had told him not to worry, that he had done a great job fixing up that little lodge, that the money would come soon enough. He remembered the spice rack and the steel mini-fridge, the chest of drawers, the desk where several binders were neatly stacked against the rear wall of the hut. Nyah, much smaller then, dozing in her crib by the bed. The fact that Roland wasn't there.

He remembered that the bed was small but clean, and he remembered thinking about Femi lying there with Roland, even while she was handing Neal a plate of fruit and making fun of him for his inability to cope with what she called "real coffee." He remembered wondering, while she talked about the tourists who had stopped by on their way to Kilimanjaro, what she had been like before she'd met Roland.

He would remember all these things, and then he would begin to drift. He tried not to, but he found himself doing it anyway, drifting into sleep and watching Femi walk home across the plain in the yellow hush of twilight, dust-filtered air rising slowly, and his eyes on her from some place low to the ground. He would watch her for what seemed like a long time, and then, slowly, without even realizing it, move closer and closer to her, until he started awake, sweating, almost on top of her, flush against the hem of her skirt, and then he would sit up and rub his face until the blood came back to it, the hum of the fan above him useless and far away, Baviaan's tail on the floor steady and uninterrupted. He wondered, in those moments, whether Roland ever had the same dream, and if he did, whether he got up to check on Nyah, asleep in her crib, padded with pillows on either side.

For hours after those dreams, while he made breakfast or did paperwork, going over bookings in the study overlooking the yard, Neal would think of Roland: Roland on the veldt when he got the call, Roland in the Jeep on the way to the police station. He had known Roland for years. He had seen Roland stand his ground and fire, systematically and without flinching, into a charging male hippo. He had seen Roland help a mother whose baby had been half-eaten by a rogue baboon bury her child. But the image of him arriving at the coroner's office, hat in his fist, refusing to take Nyah from Mrs. Halima, would stay with Neal forever.

By the time Neal reached the gate, Roland had already opened it and was walking into the herd. Neal brought up the flashlight, which blazed a trail through the grass, catching eye-shine from the wildebeest. They turned away from it, opening and closing around him. He could see the dim outline of Roland's back, his legs lost somewhere in the grass. The air was thick and humid, moist with the privacy of savanna darkness, the smells of birth and death and shit. Neal was running now, and all around him the herd was making its low, incessant calls, the night as resonant as the inside of a shell.

"Roland, stop!" Neal shouted. "Don't be an idiot—slow down."

He swung the light back and forth into the confused, black faces of the wildebeest. He couldn't see Roland anymore, but he had a strange and terrible sense that the two of them had walked into some infinite kind of closed space, and that out here, with the night on them, with Roland drunk and half-crazy, they could no longer rely on even themselves. And Femi's face, the last time he had seen it—perhaps the last time anyone had seen it—in the hot-air balloon, her eyes wide and soft. The heat, the closeness of the herd, was suddenly overwhelming. He stopped and put a hand to his ribs in the dark and just stood there, the useless weight of the rifle on his shoulder and the sound of Roland's labored breaths filling the air to his right.

He could smell something dead close by, or maybe far away. He raised his flashlight again. He could see the first of the umbrella thorn trees that made up the little grove where the shed stood, opening up some twenty yards ahead.

"My gun is empty" he said to the darkness.

"Mine's not," Roland said.

Neal's scalp felt strange. "It's all right," he said. "The shed's only a little way. We'll make it back with just one."

"I know," Roland said.

Neal let the silence stretch between them. Then he said, "I'm sorry." He realized a moment later that he shouldn't have said it, so he said: "Don't—don't do that anymore, please. Don't run off like that. I don't know what you were thinking. It's so dark, and we only have one gun. Please."

"My wife is dead," Roland said.

"I know," Neal said. "I'm sorry." Then he said, "But you still have Nyah." Roland didn't say anything, so Neal said, "You have to tell Nyah about her. You loved her very much, everyone loved her."

"I know," Roland said. Neal rubbed his hand over his mouth.

"We have to go forward or back," Neal said. "We shouldn't just stand around here."

"With your gun empty," Roland said, in what sounded like agreement.

"To the house?"

"To the generator."

"I don't know," Neal said. "I think we should go home."

Silence, then chortling from the zebras somewhere on the endless plain. Roland said, "I need a minute." And he heard Roland crouch down in the grass. Neal stood by dumbly with his hand in his pocket, waiting for the thump of the rifle butt hitting the dirt. It didn't come.

"Are you throwing up?"

"No."

"What are you doing?" Neal said. No answer. Neal fumbled for his flashlight. He turned it on again and found Roland with it. Roland was crouching in the trampled dirt of the trail, his bald head clenched in his hands like some kind of buffed fruit. The rifle lay across his knees. He looked up at Neal, and Neal turned the flashlight off.

"I'd want you to take Nyah," Roland said suddenly, "if anything happened."

"Don't say that," Neal said. He felt a new wave of heat on his face, and he put his fist up to his forehead and pressed it there.

"I keep thinking," Roland said. Neal heard him thrum his fingers on the rifle butt. "I keep thinking about that coffin." The sound of him dusting the hat off, putting it back on his head again. "It's light." Standing up. "The coffin—don't you think it's light?"

Neal said, "I don't know." He didn't want to think about it.

"I keep thinking maybe I should have had her cremated," Roland said. "Maybe she would have liked that."

"Maybe," Neal said. He wanted to say something comforting,

something generous, something that would have meaning. But he couldn't think of anything to say.

Suddenly Roland said: "Do you hear that?"

"No," Neal said.

"Listen."

A warthog family was rooting around in the dirt somewhere nearby, snorting softly—the sound, like everything else in the bush, muted by a coarse layer of dust. Wildebeest grunts. Somewhere far behind them, a heron was calling from the riverbank, a strange, echoing cry that made Neal feel exposed.

"I don't hear anything," Neal said.

Roland was still listening, so Neal listened too.

The cicadas went quiet, and then came back in again, louder than ever, hissing like a current through the grass. He heard the muffled clamor of the herd, the indistinct click of hooves in the dirt. Moments later, he heard a low moaning rumble over the hills, a sound like a foghorn.

"Lions?" he said. "They're miles away."

He suddenly realized that he had underestimated his own anxiety. He wanted a cigarette, water, something to calm his nerves, anything, because Roland was saying, "No, not that—listen," and Neal still couldn't hear what he was being told to listen for.

He closed his eyes and thought of Femi. He listened. Then he heard it, a high-pitched singsong, melancholy, almost human, almost too indistinct. "What is that?" he said. Again. Low, then rising.

Roland's voice was quiet. "Hyena."

"Are you sure?" he said. The cry sounded like something else to him, something closer, like the creak of the porch swing at the house, or the wind, maybe, the wind whining in the branches of the jackalberry trees outside his window. He could feel the sweat gathering on his back, the coarse feel of his shirt where it clung to his skin in wet patches.

Roland's breathing in the darkness had grown fast and shallow.

"Where's it coming from?" Neal said.

"I'm not sure," Roland told him, and started walking back up the trail through the grass. He could hear Roland's boots on the dirt, and he ran to catch up. They entered the thick of the grove at the bottom of the hill and started up, through the trees, toward the gate. The smell of the wildebeest was sour. At the top of the slope, the house was still dark. He wanted to see candles, he wanted to see that Mrs. Halima had gone back inside. But now he saw nothing, and that empty feeling, the empty feeling of the house and the dark and the long drive winding up the slope, jolted him, and then he heard it—up ahead of them, somewhere close, certain and loud: the laugh.

One late afternoon, a year after Neal had bought the lodge, while he sat on the wicker swing with a book across his knees, comfortable in the knowledge that his first group of tourists was out on safari somewhere with Roland, he had seen Baviaan stand up, apparently unprovoked, and trot out to the gate, where the dog stood perfectly still for a long time watching the plain mist over. Mrs. Halima had come out with the laundry and she, too, noticed Baviaan there.

"*Kingugwa,*" she'd said.

"I'm sorry?" Neal said.

"*Kingugwa,*" said Mrs. Halima, resettling the laundry basket on her hip. "Hyena."

Neal remembered taking offense at this. "He's a bloodhound," he told her gently.

But she only laughed at him. "No. It means hyena," she said, and pointed. "He's standing at the gate to listen. You can't hear them, but look—they're calling his name."

It had taken him a long time to get used to almost everything: strangled lion cubs by the gate at dawn, drowned wildebeest damming the river, baboons in the kitchen stealing dog food and granola, scattering coffee grounds, making off with cans of Pringles and, when they could get their hands on it, toilet paper, which he would afterward pick out of the acacia groves for days.

But he had never gotten used to the hyenas. He hadn't seen them when he first came to Africa. He had been a photojournalist then, charged with the unhappy task of filming the mating rituals of hippos. He had often thought since that if he had seen hyenas he might not have bought the lodge and moved out here in the first place, not the way he had, anyway, or the way most people did: on a romantic whim, like a fool. He got to know them during the first migration he spent at Longido, when they followed the wildebeest up from Ngorongoro and onto the plain. He remembered mistaking them briefly for wild dogs—he was still picking animals out of the manual he kept in his pocket at the time—but then he had recognized, even at a distance, the stooped haunches and the low-slung head with the mane curving back over the rift between the shoulder blades. Like everyone he had ever known, he had been perfectly happy to believe the myths he'd heard about them. He believed they were cowards until he saw them fight, scavengers until he saw them kill, and after the first few times they cornered him in the Jeep while Roland was out tagging elephants in the bush, he began to take more notice of the local stories about them: their big-eyed curiosity and unnerving persistence, the relative ease with which they let themselves into gated villages and made off with children and young mothers.

What he noticed most was not the eyes or the hunchbacked lope, not even the smell: it was the sound they made, that whining yelp, like a child's voice rising. It was the laugh that made his stomach turn, and they laughed all the time, every night they were there, as if they knew their laugh made him wonder, made him want to come outside to them in the dark, or, otherwise, put a gun in his mouth. Whenever he heard it he remembered those stories Roland had told him about ancient travelers huddling in their camps while the wailing night rose around them, until they folded to the sound and drifted from the fire, one by one, into the range of the stilling gaze.

He had been thinking about the laugh while he was ignoring the warning signs the month before Femi's death. Afterward, he blamed it on transportation limits, the postboy, the fact that the newspapers were three or four days old by the time he read them over toast and coffee. But he'd been aware, all along, of the attacks that had started just ninety miles away in Ngorongoro and moved slowly toward them, following the herd east—he had read first about the teenage cowherd who had been found at the bottom of the mountain with most of his abdomen missing, and then about the *daladala* driver and his companion who had stopped at a watering hole to cool off in the unseasonably hot weather, and finally about the rhino poachers who had risked arrest to bring one of their own, torn open from the midsection up, into an Arusha hospital—so that, when the call came a few days after Christmas, he knew, felt in the deepest part of his gut, what had happened even before Mrs. Halima handed him the phone.

Roland was running, the sound of his footfalls frantic, pounding through the darkness ahead of him. Neal tucked the gun into the

crook of his arm so he could hold up the flashlight, and the wildebeest, dumb-eyed, bearded, startled by the light, darted across the
trail around them and bellowed. They jumped the gate and ran
on, up the path toward the sound. A hundred yards from the house
the smell was unbearable, the garbage-heap stench of hyenas, and
he felt it tear into his lungs. And then he saw her, Mrs. Halima,
running toward them across the plain, and Roland stopped instantly. Neal swung the flashlight up, streaking the field behind her
with light, and out of the corner of his eye he saw Roland raise the
gun to his shoulder and aim, and he thought, *My God, not really?*,
unable to imagine Roland taking the shot with Mrs. Halima in his
line of fire. But seconds passed and nothing happened, and he
watched the distance between them close as she ran, her skirt wrapping around her ankles, her face drawn and desolate. At twenty
yards, he saw the baby in her arms, and by the time she reached
them, Roland was already holding his hands out for Nyah, and Mrs.
Halima was shrieking: "It came in! It came in! It came in the house!"

"What?"

"*Kingugwa,*" Mrs. Halima said. "It came in, it came in to take
her!"

He thought of the coffin, and it hit him all at once—the dark
and the stupid helplessness he felt. The plain fell silent, and his
knees felt strange. The light he held up shook with the force of his
breath where it fell on Roland and Nyah, and on Mrs. Halima, who
was bent at the waist and sobbing.

"I knocked it down," Mrs. Halima was saying. She squatted in the
grass and began to rock back and forth, sobbing with her head in
her hands. "I knocked it down, I knocked it down, I'm so sorry I
knocked it down."

"What?" Roland said. "What?"

"*Her,*" Mrs. Halima said. "I knocked it down—I knocked down
the coffin when I ran out."

Roland put an arm around her, and Nyah, pressed between
them, began to whimper. Neal rubbed his eyes, his stomach wad-
ded up against the bottom of his ribs.

"I'll go," Neal said.

"You mustn't," Mrs. Halima said, grabbing his leg. "It came in to
take her, it'll kill you." Her eyes were wide.

"I'll be all right," Neal said, and he turned the flashlight on the
dark porch of the house.

"You shouldn't," Roland said, but he didn't move. Nyah's shrill, throbbing wail rose like a siren. "I'll do it."

"Don't be stupid," Neal told him. "The coffin fell—think of what you'll see." He turned and strode through the grass, the sound of Nyah's screams fading behind him and the light ahead shifting in lines over the carved banister of the veranda, the throw cushions on the swing, Baviaan's bowl and plastic chew toys underfoot as he climbed the stairs, the porch swing creaking.

Neal stood near the door for a moment, resting the muzzle of the gun against the handle, and then he pushed it open.

She had been walking home at twilight. The ranger who found her told Neal what he could read from the ground, that she had cut straight through the herd, a terrible mistake, because the topi antelope were nearing the end of their rut and the hyenas, there to pick off the weaker males as they collapsed from exhaustion, were waiting for her at the crest of the hill. There had been a chase—she was small enough, and the whole clan had been on the hunt. They had her within forty yards of the convenience store. Then they dragged her out onto the open plain, where the matriarch and her daughters fed first, and the jackals waited their turn for more than an hour before a ranger on patrol found her. It was at that moment—while the police captain was giving this gravely overdrawn narrative, before Roland arrived at the station—that Neal thought of his tourists and the safaris he had led, and remembered, in absolute detail, the outspread ring of blood that tinged the top of the grass, the reddened jowls, eyes that looked straight ahead while the jaw descended on bone, and he turned in place and threw up all over the police captain's desk, which he afterward volunteered to clean, but was dissuaded by a mild-mannered deputy who escorted him outside before he could do any more damage.

At the mortuary that morning, the coffin had already been closed.

Neal stood in the doorway for a minute, then two.

He called for the dog. "Baviaan," he said, then louder: "Baviaan!" There was no sign of him.

The flashlight beam darted around the room and caught the edges of furniture—the table legs, the vintage telescope and tripod they kept in the parlor for the amusement of guests, a broken

lamp and, several feet later, its rose-printed shade. The tabletop
was empty, that much was certain, and when he swung the light
onto the floor and followed the dim outline of the wood he found
it, the coffin, upturned and resting on its half-open lid in the middle of the room. The moment he recognized it, he thought he saw
something—a hand, a piece of cloth, anything that may have been
left of her—and his stomach lurched forward. He stumbled back
against the wall and dropped the flashlight. It rolled away from
him and the beam settled on the hallway leading into the kitchen,
the bags of flour, delivered that morning, standing in rows by the
oven.

"God," he said, and waited for the laugh.

It didn't come. He couldn't see the hyena, but the stench of it
was there, the stagnant reek of meat and sweat and piss. He thought
he felt it move closer, but minutes went by and the faint sound of
Nyah's distant shrieking receded. He got up slowly and, with his
eyes on the floor, inched to where the flashlight had fallen and
picked it up. He aimed it at the shadows of the fireplace and sideboard, and finally at the screen door, which had been wrenched
open and now hung precariously on its hinges over the stairs leading to the back porch. He got to his feet and went over to it, tried
to close it, but it just shuddered and creaked, and he eventually
gave up and moved back toward the middle of the room, where
the coffin was.

He touched one corner of it with his foot, and it made a hollow
sound. He raised the light again and passed it over the room one
more time, searching for eye-shine. Then he squatted and, with
the thought of Femi—bright-eyed and smiling, brewing sweet tea
with her glasses high on her nose, rocking Nyah to sleep in the
porch swing before the Christmas party, the jasmine in the window
box in bloom—pushed to the forefront of his mind, he pulled up
the coffin and turned it over. It was empty.

"Oh my God," he said, and turned, but there was nothing, just
the empty room and the staircase leading up to the landing, and
the big African moon in the window. He put the gun and the flashlight down on the end table. The yellow ring of light trembled
against the back of the brick fireplace.

He tried to remember how heavy the coffin had been that morning, the weight of it spread out over his left shoulder as he helped
Roland carry it up the stairs and into the parlor, the shape of Ro-

land's back, hunched in front of him when they set it down on the table. How heavy had it been, the coffin? He thought of Roland's hands, patient and callused, clasped around the waist of the little white dress that was laid out for Nyah in the guest nursery, the little white dress and the little white shoes sitting on Roland's lap at the funeral tomorrow, and the empty velvet in the pine box going into the ground; Mrs. Halima's words, *It came in to take her,* no blood anywhere, anywhere at all, and the stagnant heat of the African night coming in through the windows and doors and the cracks in the floor. He went into the kitchen and dragged one of the flour bags out.

That was when the light came back on. He heard, almost felt, the distant hum of it pulling through all the wires and cables in the house, and when it blazed on, illuminating the chandelier above the parlor table and the yellow sconces in the kitchen, he stopped and covered his eyes with his hand, the weight of the flour bag resting against his leg. When he finally looked up, he noticed the face in the window.

He knew what was there even before he looked at it, and he leaned forward and reached for the gun. The gun. The gun was empty. He'd come in with an empty gun. His gun was empty, and Roland had watched him walk in with it empty—even though he couldn't have known, how could he have known any of it?

Femi had never been in a balloon before, and Neal had offered to take her up that evening—because the wind was pleasant, because he had just brought the tourists back and the launching crew was still there to help, because Mrs. Halima had the baby and Roland had gone on a game count and wouldn't be back for days. Femi had stood aside and watched him pump up the burners before the canvas envelope filled and the blue and white drape lifted out of the grass, swollen with air. It was late afternoon and the sun was melting into the red haze over the savanna when he helped her into the basket and fired the jets and tossed the sandbags over the side. He wondered if she had been afraid at first, going up in that little wicker basket with the hills falling away. He wondered if the sight of the crowded rivers of wildebeest below had instilled in her the same feelings of exhilarated panic he had felt on his first visit there, that vitality of the cradle he had searched for all his life, the push and pull of the wind, the birthing grounds and killing grounds, endless and unyielding, that allowed him to somehow reassemble himself. He couldn't remember quite what had happened, but he knew he had reached for her. He had put his hand on the small of her back, or pressed himself against her where she stood holding the ropes, and she had indulged him, for a moment or two, perhaps out of kindness, or because it was unexpected and she didn't quite know how to react. But then she had stepped away with a forgiving smile, the laugh that came with it embarrassed, and she had stayed against the opposite end of the basket while they sailed on and eventually came down in a stretch of grassland where the antelope were in summer rut. She had climbed out by herself and walked home.

He finally made himself look through the window at the face outside on the porch, and when the lamplight eyes caught his look, the black lips pulled away from the teeth, grinning, and the hyena laughed. For a long time, Neal stood there thinking he would raise the empty gun, turn it in his hands, reach for a knife from the block. But the face that stilled him did not move, and the hyena did not come back inside.

He would think about it afterward, at the funeral, and then again after the service in the parlor, where Mrs. Halima would put out pictures of Femi and serve wine and tea until everyone was finished and had gone away; he would think about it that night, as he took Roland and Nyah home. He would think about the flour bags and how he had laid them there, in the coffin, and he would think about the coffin, with earth smoothed over it, lying near the church in a plot overlooking Mount Longido, with the flour bags inside. And when he set off that evening from Roland's place, the lights disappearing behind him, the gun over his shoulder, all the forward-facing eyes in the darkness coming on, pair by pair, while the moon came up over the wind-rubbed plain, the laugh—her laugh—would follow him all the way home.

LORI OSTLUND

All Boy

FROM *New England Review*

LATER, WHEN HAROLD FINALLY LEARNED that his parents
had not fired Mrs. Norman, the babysitter, for locking him in the
closet while she watched her favorite television shows, he could not
imagine why he had ever attributed her firing to this in the first
place, especially since his parents had not seemed particularly upset by the news of his confinement. His father had said something
vague about it building character and teaching inner resources,
and his mother, in an attempt to be more specific, said that it could
not hurt to learn how the sightless got by. Nor had Harold minded
being in the closet, where he kept a *survival kit* inspired by the one
that his parents, indeed all Minnesotans, stored in their cars in
winter, though his contained only a small flashlight, several books,
water, and a roll of Life Savers, chosen because he liked the surprise — there in the dark — of not knowing which flavor was next.

Furthermore, he understood Mrs. Norman's motivations, which
had to do with the fact that if he were allowed to watch television
with her, he would inevitably ask questions, which she would feel
obligated to answer, thus diminishing her concentration and so
her pleasure. Her concerns seemed to him reasonable: he had a
tendency to ask questions, for he was a curious child (though awkwardly so), a characteristic that his teachers cited as proof in making comments both positive and negative.

Mrs. Norman, it turned out, had been fired because she sometimes wore his father's socks while she watched television, slipping
them on over her own bare feet. It was the "bare" part that completely unhinged his father, who did not like to drink from other

people's glasses or sit in the dentist's chair while the dentist stood close to him smelling of metal. One night, Mrs. Norman left a pair of his father's socks on the sofa instead of putting them back in his father's drawer, and when his father asked her about it, she said, "Oh my, I took them off when my toes got toasty and forgot all about them," apologizing as though the issue were the forgetting and not the wearing. This had further angered Harold's father, who considered the sharing of socks—his naked feet where hers had been—an intimacy beyond what he could bear, and after he talked about it "morning, noon, and night for two days," as Harold's mother later put it, they fired Mrs. Norman.

Harold was quite familiar with Mrs. Norman's feet. They were what old people's feet should look like, he thought, with nails so yellow and thick that she could not cut them by herself, not even with his assistance. Instead, her daughter, who occasionally stopped by on one of the two nights each week that Mrs. Norman stayed with Harold, cut them using a tool with long handles and an end that looked like the beak of a parrot.

"May I watch?" Harold asked because he was the sort of child who differentiated between "may" and "can" and found that adults often responded favorably to this, granting him privileges that they might not otherwise have. He did not feel that he was being dishonest because he cared deeply about grammar and would have gone on using "may" even without such incentives.

"You may," replied Mrs. Norman, inclining her head toward him as though she were a visiting dignitary granting him an audience, and Harold sat down next to her. Her daughter, a powerful-looking woman in her thirties, stood over them with the device, holding it in a way that suggested that she enjoyed tools and was looking forward to using it. Harold did not like tools, which he thought of as destructive, even though his father told him that he needed to learn to view the bigger picture: it was true that tools were used to cut and bore and pound, but these small acts of destruction generally resulted in a much bigger act of creation. "Like our house," his father said, as though their house were an obvious example of the way that creation came out of destruction.

Mrs. Norman's daughter was what his parents called "jolly." There were other words that they used, words that he did not yet know despite his extensive vocabulary, but he knew "jolly" and felt

that she was. She drove a very old motorcycle, which she had to roll
to start, and once when his father, who knew nothing about motorcycles, made polite conversation, asking, "Is it a Harley?," she replied, "More like a Hardly," and then she thumped his father on
the shoulder and laughed. His father had also laughed, surprising
Harold because being touched by people he didn't really know was
another thing his father considered too intimate.

Mrs. Norman's daughter grasped her mother's foot and positioned it on her thigh, but this gave her no room to wield the device properly, so she helped her mother onto the floor, where Mrs.
Norman sat with her back braced against the sofa while her daughter squeezed the ends of the cutting device together and the tips of
the nails broke free with a loud snap and flew into the air like Tid-
dlywinks.

"Can you please pick those up, Harold?" said Mrs. Norman.
"They're sharp, and I don't want anyone stepping on them."

Harold crouched on the floor around Mrs. Norman's newly
trimmed feet and began to collect the nails, gathering them in his
cupped left hand. He studied one of them, flexing it between his
fingers, surprised at its sturdiness. "May I keep it?" he asked, thinking that it would make a welcome addition to the contents of his
pocket, which already included a small snail shell, an empty bullet
casing, a strip of birch tree parchment, and several dried lima
beans, items chosen because they offered a certain tactile reassur-
ance.

"Ish, no," said Mrs. Norman. "I want you to throw them away this
minute and then scrub your hands. You too," she admonished her
daughter, who was using the hem of her shirt to brush away the
chalky residue that clung to the tool's beak.

Harold went into the kitchen and emptied Mrs. Norman's toenails into the milk carton filled with compost—all except the large
one, which he slipped into his pocket. As he scrubbed his hands at
the sink, Mrs. Norman's daughter came and stood beside him, so
close that he could smell her, an oily smell that he suspected came
from the Hardly. Harold did not like to be this close to people,
close enough to smell them, though his mother said that this was
simply his father rubbing off on him and that he needed to focus
on the positive aspects of smell, the way that it enhanced hunger
and rounded out memory. Harold tried to embrace his mother's

perspective, but he could not get over the way that odor disregarded boundaries, wrapping him, for example, in the earthy, almost tuberish smell that hung in the air after Mrs. Norman had spent time in the bathroom.

"How old are you these days?" asked Mrs. Norman's daughter as she scrubbed vigorously at her hands.

"Ten," he said. "Well, eleven."

"Which is it?" asked Mrs. Norman's daughter, still scrubbing. "Ten or eleven? Age is a very clear-cut thing, you know. When you become eleven, you lose all rights to ten." She said this in a serious tone, looking him in the eye rather than down at her soapy hands, but then she laughed the way she had when she said "more like a Hardly" to his father, and Harold instinctively stepped away from her.

"Eleven." This was true. He had turned eleven just two weeks earlier.

"And what sorts of things do eleven-year-old boys like to do these days?"

"I'm not sure." He knew what *he* liked to do. Besides reading, which was his primary interest and one that he would not belittle by calling a hobby, he liked very specific things: he enjoyed making pancakes but not waffles; he took pleasure in helping his mother dust but could not be persuaded to vacuum; he kept lists of words that he particularly liked or disliked the sound of. At the moment, he thought that "vaccination" and "expectorate" were beautiful but could not bear the word "dwindle."

He did not, however, know what boys his age liked to do, for he had no friends. At school, he interacted only with adults, who, he had learned, were subject to many of the same foibles he witnessed in his classmates, especially Miss Jamison, his homeroom teacher, who cared deeply about having the approval of her students and found ways to ridicule Harold in front of them, not overtly as his classmates did but making clear her intention nonetheless.

For example, after he had been home with a cold for two days, she asked, "Harry, how are you feeling?" She was the only teacher who called him Harry, though all of his classmates did, and he hated it, convinced that they were really saying "hairy," but when he complained to his mother, she told him to explain that he "did not care for the diminutive," and so he did not mention the problem to her again.

"I'm better," he said.

"Better?" Miss Jamison repeated loudly. "So you're feeling *better*?" She said this with a smirk, exaggerating "better" as though it were wrong in some fundamental and obvious way, and his classmates all laughed knowingly. He spent the rest of the morning thinking about it: hadn't she been asking him to compare how he felt today with how he felt yesterday? Ultimately, he decided that there was nothing wrong with saying "better," but that night at dinner when his father asked how he was feeling, he said, "Well," just to be safe.

Shortly after Mrs. Norman's firing, it seemed that Harold might acquire a friend, a boy named Simon, who transferred into his class just after Thanksgiving. When Simon came over to his house to play, however, he announced to Harold that his mother had a lustful look.

"I don't know what that means," Harold replied grudgingly, for he was used to being the one who knew words that his classmates did not.

"You know. Like she wants sex," Simon said matter-of-factly, as though this were a perfectly normal observation to make about a potential friend's mother. Harold did not reply, and the two boys sat on the floor in his room chewing summer sausage sandwiches, made for them by his mother, who had chatted away with Simon as she cut and buttered the bread, trying, Harold knew, to be overly gay as a way of making up for his inability to say and do the sorts of things that would make Simon want to visit again. This is what her hard work had earned her, Harold thought sadly, the indignity of being described as lustful by an eleven-year-old boy who then gobbled up the sandwiches that she had so lustfully prepared.

Simon's comment struck him as particularly unfair because he knew that his parents did not have sex. He had heard his mother telling Aunt Elizabeth as much on the telephone. His aunt lived in Milwaukee, and because it was a long-distance call, she and his mother talked just once a month, generally when his father was at work, though lately they had begun to talk more often, and his father had started to complain about the higher bills. "Why doesn't she ever call you?" asked his father, adding, "Goddamn hippies."

Harold did not know what hippies were, not exactly, but his aunt had spent two days with them in August, and so he had his theories. Prior to this visit, he had not seen his aunt since he was six because she and his father did not get along, and throughout the visit, he felt his father's unspoken expectation of loyalty, but he could not help himself: he had liked his aunt, who wore fringe and waited until both of his parents were out of the room to say, "Harold, I'm deeply sorry about your name. I should have tried to stop them."

Harold didn't know how to respond, for he thought of his name as who he was, a feature that could not be changed without altering everything else. Still, he liked the earnest, conspiratorial way in which his aunt addressed him.

"What do your friends call you?" she asked. "Harry?"

He did not tell her that he had no friends. "No, I don't really care for diminutives," he said instead.

She laughed. "Well. Now I can certainly see why they chose Harold."

He smiled shyly then and offered to make her iced tea.

"Groovy," she said. "I like a man who can cook," and when he explained that iced tea did not actually involve cooking, she laughed her throaty, pleasant laugh yet again.

Eventually, Harold understood that his mother called his aunt more frequently because she and his father argued more frequently, their arguments sometimes taking root right in front of him but over things so small that he did not understand how they had been able to make an argument out of it. Thanksgiving was a perfect example. As the turkey cooked, his parents sat together in the kitchen drinking wine and chatting, their faces growing flushed from the heat and the alcohol, and when everything was ready, his father seated his mother and then placed the turkey in front of her with a flourish.

"Le turkey, Madame," he declared, pronouncing "turkey" as though it were French.

His mother giggled and picked up the carving knife. "Harold, what part would you like?" she asked.

"White meat, please."

"I'll give you breast meat," his mother said, adding with a small chuckle, "God knows your father has no interest in breast."

For the rest of the meal, Harold's father spoke only to Harold, asking *him* for the gravy when it actually sat in front of his mother. His mother was also silent, and when the meal was nearly over, she dumped the last of the cranberries onto Harold's plate even though all three of them knew that cranberries were his father's favorite part of Thanksgiving. Later, as Harold sat reading in his room, he heard his parents yelling, and he crept down the hallway and perched at the top of the stairs, letting their voices funnel up to him.

"You know *exactly* what I'm talking about," his father yelled.

"Come on, Charles. Lighten up." Harold heard a small catch in his mother's voice, which meant she wanted to laugh. "He thought I was talking about the turkey breast." She paused. "Which, of course, I was."

There were five words that were forbidden in their household, words that, according to his father, were not only profane but aesthetically unappealing. Harold heard his father say one of these words to his mother, his voice becoming low and precise as it did when he was very angry. His mother did not reply, and a moment later, Harold heard his father open the front door and leave.

When his mother came to tuck him in, her eyes red from crying, he asked where his father had gone. "To the pool hall," she said, which made her start crying again because this was an old joke between them. When his father occasionally disappeared after dinner, slipping out unannounced, Harold's mother always said, "I guess he's gone to the pool hall." She had explained to Harold what a pool hall was, and they both laughed at the notion of his neat, serious father in such a place, there among men who smoked cigars and sweated and made bets with their hard-earned money.

"You have a lot of books," Simon said after he had proclaimed Harold's mother lustful and they had finished their sandwiches, and there seemed nothing left to do.

"Yes," said Harold. He almost added that he was a "voracious reader," but remembering what his father always said, that words were meant to be tools of communication but just as often drove wedges between people, he opted for triteness instead. "I love reading," he mumbled.

"Have you read all of these books?" asked Simon with a shrug.

"Yes. Now, I mainly check them out of the library. The limit is three at a time, but Mr. Tesky lets me take five." Mr. Tesky was his favorite librarian because, in making recommendations, he never relied on expressions like "the other boys" or "kids your age."

"Yes," replied Simon. "That's because he's a fag."

Harold had no idea what "fag" meant, but he regretted terribly not using "voracious." "Figure it out from context," his mother always told him after he had bothered her one too many times to explain words. He considered the context and decided that "fag" had to do with being helpful.

"Yes," he agreed. "He is."

Simon laughed and threw a pillow at him. "You're a fag also," Simon said.

It turned out that "fag" meant to work really hard: "toil," said his dictionary. Which made sense, for Mr. Tesky did work very hard. Of course, Harold normally would have noticed that this "fag" was a verb while Simon had used it as a noun, but Simon's visit had left him feeling tired and unmoored, and so he overlooked this obvious distinction. He set the dictionary back on the shelf in the spot that it always occupied and surveyed his room, looking for something out of place, something to explain his uneasiness. Finally, he decided to calm himself by slipping into his kimono.

Harold had purchased the kimono that summer at a yard sale at which his mother had been persuaded to stop only because there were books for sale. Overall, his parents did not approve of yard sales, for they felt that there was something *unsavory* about putting one's personal belongings outside for strangers to see, and not just to see but to handle and even buy. Harold, however, liked wandering amid carpets with dark, mysterious stains and mismatched cutlery and stacks of clothing that had presumably once fit the people selling them, people who seemed in no way embarrassed to be associated with these dingy socks and stretched-out waistbands.

The kimono, by contrast, was the most beautiful piece of clothing he had ever seen, black with a crane painted across the back, and his mother, who lent him the two dollars to purchase it, told him that it was from Japan and that in Japan everyone wore such things, and though he found this hard to believe, Mr. Tesky later showed him a book from his personal collection with pictures of Japanese people wearing kimonos as they walked in the streets and sat around drinking tea. Harold wore his kimono only at home, but he felt different when he slipped it on, more graceful and at ease, though whether this meant that he felt more himself or less, he could not say.

He stopped wearing the kimono quite abruptly when he overheard his father referring to it as his "dress," though there had been issues before that: as he ate, the sleeves dragged across his food and became sullied with red spaghetti sauce and pork chop grease, and as he descended the stairs one night, he tripped on the hem, toppling down the last three steps and wrenching his ankle. For days afterwards, he worried that he had inherited his mother's clumsiness, though she tended to fall only in public, usually on special occasions. On his first day of school this year, for example, she turned to wave at him and caught her foot where the tile became carpeting. She flew forward, upsetting an easel at which one of his classmates stood painting, and landed face down on the floor, her skirt hiked up along her thigh. Miss Jamison rushed to help, and his classmates gathered around her in awe, shocked and excited to see an adult splayed out on the floor. His mother always attended carefully to his cuts and fevers and upset stomachs, and he knew that he should go to her, but he did not because he could not bear being regarded as the boy whose mother fell. Instead, he stayed at his desk with the top up against the sight of her, arranging his books. When he got home that afternoon, his mother teased him about it so relentlessly that he knew he had hurt her deeply.

His mother knocked at his door and came in. If she was surprised to see him wearing his kimono again, she did not say so. Instead, she got right to her point, which was that she felt he should invite Simon for a sleepover.

"I don't think that's a good idea," said Harold.

"Why not?" asked his mother, ready, he knew, to tell him yet again that he would have more friends (using "more" as though he actually had some) once he learned not to be so hard on people. "He seemed like an affable fellow."

"Yes," agreed Harold, trying to think of a way to turn his mother against Simon without having to use the word "lustful." "He is affable, but he's also a Democrat."

His mother sighed loudly and stood up. "I thought you'd had enough of that thing," she said, meaning his kimono, and she went downstairs to make dinner.

Harold's parents were Republicans. For Halloween, they had insisted that he go as the Gallup Poll, a costume requiring two people, one to be Jimmy Carter and the other, Gerald Ford. He wanted to be Carter because he liked the slow, buttery way that Carter spoke, but his parents had forbidden it, instead phoning the parents of a girl in his class whose father was his father's subordinate at the bank. The girl, whose name was Molly, had been dropped off the afternoon before Halloween, and the two of them sat in his living room, where, with the help of his mother and several newspaper photos, they sketched the two candidates. He was surprised at how well the masks captured the two men—Carter's sheepish smile and Ford's large, bland forehead—and after cutting small slits for the eyes and stapling elastic bands to the sides, he and Molly slipped them on and practiced trotting around the living room side by side, pretending to jockey for position and calling out, "We're the Gallup Poll."

Later, after Molly had gone home, his mother told him that he needed to be sure to finish ahead, and so, as they paraded in front of the judges the next afternoon, he made a halfhearted surge at the very end, nosing ahead of Jimmy Carter. After the prizes had been given, predictably, to a witch, a robot, and a farmer, Mr. Tesky came up to Harold and complimented him on his costume. "Do you follow politics?" Mr. Tesky asked, his Adam's apple bobbing playfully. As usual, he wore corduroy pants with a belt so long that it actually made another half turn around his body. Harold wondered whether Mr. Tesky had once been fat, a man better suited for this belt, but he did not ask because he knew that it was impolite to ask questions about health. Actually, his parents included money, religion, and politics on this list as well, so Harold did not know how to respond to Mr. Tesky's question.

"No," he said finally. "I'm too young to follow politics."

Mr. Tesky laughed and reached out as though to ruffle his hair, then seemed to think better of it and retracted his hand, thrusting it into his back pocket as though putting the gesture literally behind him.

At dinner, Harold's father asked nothing about Simon's visit, which Harold took as an indication that his mother had been sufficiently convinced of Simon's unsuitability. Instead, the conversation centered on back-to-school night, which they would all three be attending the next evening. Harold did not understand why his parents required him to participate, but the one time that he had protested, explaining that none of his classmates would be going, his father berated him for his apathy. As his parents chewed their roast beef, Harold went through the list of his teachers again, making sure that they understood that Mrs. Olson taught science and Miss Olson, social studies, because his parents tended to mix up the two women, expecting Miss Olson to be young when, in fact, she was just a few years from retirement.

"You should also meet Mr. Tesky," he said, and then because it was his habit to utilize new words immediately, he added, "He's a fag."

"Harold," said his mother in her severe voice. "I don't want to hear you ever talking that way about people. That's a terrible accusation." His father said nothing. Harold did not reply because he had found that when his mother became angry like this, it was best to remain silent and let the moment pass, even when he did not understand what had caused her outburst, for his confusion often provoked her more.

The next night, as his mother stood in his homeroom talking to a group of other mothers, his father announced, "I think I will have a talk with your Mr. Tesky. Perhaps you can escort me to the library, Harold."

Mr. Tesky was on a ladder when they arrived, wearing his belt and a half, the tip of it sticking out at them from behind like a tongue. He did not seem to realize at first that they had come to talk to him, and so while they stood looking up at him, he continued to shelve books, sliding himself nervously along on his rolling ladder. When he finally came down and shook hands with Harold's father, Harold saw that his collar was twisted inward on one side; it occurred to him that Mr. Tesky's collars were always askew but that he had never thought to note it until now, now that he was viewing Mr. Tesky through his father's eyes.

For nearly ten minutes, they discussed Harold and his reading habits, his father comporting himself as though he were gathering information on a new hire at the bank, revealing nothing about himself while asking questions that sought to lay bare gaps in Harold's knowledge or abilities, weaknesses in his approach to reading. Then, shifting the conversation suddenly away from Harold, his father asked, "Say, what do you make of these speed-reading courses?"

"Speed-reading?" repeated Mr. Tesky.

"I've been doing some research," said his father. "Apparently the Carters are big fans and so was Kennedy," adding with a snort, "for what that's worth," as though speed-reading, like opinions on communism or the economy, must be discussed along party lines. "I'm thinking about holding a seminar at the bank, maybe bringing in a specialist."

Mr. Tesky sawed his index finger vigorously back and forth beneath his nose.

"Did you know that the average person reads just two words a second?" his father continued. "But with training, that can be increased to five, even seven. I've just been reading about the Wood Method. Ever heard of it? You move your hand across the page as you read, and apparently the motion catches the eye's attention and stimulates it to work faster." He opened a book and demonstrated, sweeping his hand across the page as though blessing it or driving out demons.

Mr. Tesky regarded him the way that Harold's mother regarded guests who added salt to the food before tasting it. "Mr. Lundstrom," he began, his neck growing blotchy. "The point of reading is to luxuriate in the words, to appreciate their beauty and nuance, to delve fully into their meaning."

"Speed-reading maintains comprehension," insisted Harold's father.

"Understanding has its own rhythm, Mr. Lundstrom," said Mr. Tesky. "Waving your hand about? Well. That is merely a distraction."

Harold had never heard Mr. Tesky speak with such severity, not even when children ignored basic library rules, laughing loudly or moving books around so that others would have trouble finding them. In turn, he had always been impressed with his father's ability to make conversation with all sorts of people: when the electrician came to update the wiring in their kitchen, his father asked him why electricians made less than plumbers when their work was so much more dangerous, and when the plumber came the next week to unclog the toilet, he told the plumber that he deserved every penny he charged and then some, given what he had to endure. His father deftly calculated people's interests and needs, drawing them out by soliciting their advice, by making them feel knowledgeable and competent, yet with Mr. Tesky, he had failed. He had asked him about speed-reading but said nothing about the stacks of books that he kept on his nightstand and read faithfully from each night.

Harold and his father made their way back down the half-lit hallway to his classroom, where his mother was still deep in conversation with the other mothers, standing in a circle near the bulletin board on which Miss Jamison had placed examples of what she considered their best work. In Harold's case, she had tacked up an uninspired summary of the process of photosynthesis, something he had dashed off one morning before school. Harold knew that people would assume that science was his favorite subject, particularly given the correctness of the writing, but the truth was that he hated science and had written about it correctly only because it would have required more effort to write incorrectly, to misplace commas or choose less exact words.

His mother, unaware that he and his father had returned, was indeed pointing to his paragraph as she described a boy fascinated by earthquakes, the solar system, and creatures without legs, speaking for several minutes but never mentioning that his fascination was a function not of curiosity but of fear. The other mothers chuckled politely, and then, her voice rising toward closure, his mother announced, "I guess Harold's just all boy," invoking his name to refer to a boy who seemed to him as unknowable as God. His mother turned and saw Harold behind her, and her words became a door shutting between them.

By Minnesota standards, the winter was mild, meaning that the temperature hovered just above zero rather than dipping precipitously below. Still, as they drove home, the road stretched before them treacherously, the icy patches more difficult to detect at night. His mother, who was better on ice, was behind the wheel, Harold beside her because his father had climbed into the back, indicating his wish to be left alone. His mother did not take heed of this, however, instead offering comments about the other mothers that would normally have made his father laugh. Harold wondered whether he would some day grow to care about the sorts of things that his parents did, things like whether a person was missing a button or had applied slightly more mascara to the right eye than the left.

"Oh," she blurted out, as though suddenly remembering a missed appointment or forgotten birthday. "The librarian. How was he?"

"Ichabod Crane," said his father tiredly. "Skinny. Bookish. Disheveled."

Harold's father did not approve of skinniness in men. He believed that men should be muscular, and though he himself was not, he had established a workout space in a small room at the back of the house, filling it with variously sized barbells and two weight machines and covering the walls with pictures of men flexing their muscles. Harold knew that his father had taped up the pictures to provide inspiration, but the men frightened Harold because they had a hard, geometric quality: they wore V-shaped swimming suits, and their torsos—small waists and broad shoulders—were inverted triangles topped off by square heads. Often, his father came home from work and went directly into this room without even changing out of his suit and tie, and when Harold was sent to call him for dinner, he always paused at the door and then left without knocking because he could hear his father inside, groaning.

A week later, Harold entered the house to the now familiar sound of his mother speaking to Aunt Elizabeth on the telephone. School had been dismissed an hour early because it was the start of Christmas break, but his mother seemed to have forgotten this, and Harold set about quietly preparing his favorite snack, Minute Rice with butter. "Before we even met, apparently," he heard his mother say as he waited for the water to boil, "but do you suppose he thought to tell me about it? I'm just the wife—the blind, convenient little banker's wife."

She listened a moment, then cut in sharply. "Don't patronize me, Elizabeth. I know that." She snorted. "In the closet," she said derisively. "Where do you even get these terms?" She slammed down the receiver, and as Harold ate his Minute Rice with butter, he could hear his mother sobbing in her bedroom upstairs.

When she came down an hour later, she looked surprised to find him sitting at the kitchen table. He had washed his rice bowl and pot and put everything away, and he let her believe that he had just arrived.

"Should I make you a snack?" she asked.

"No," Harold said. "I'm not really hungry." He waited until she took out the cutting board and began cutting up apples for a crisp. "Remember when you fired Mrs. Norman for putting me in the closet?" he said in what he hoped was a casual voice.

His mother turned toward him quickly. "That's not why we fired Mrs. Norman," she said, and she explained in great detail about the socks. "He's always been like that. So particular." She paused. "Harold, your father is leaving. I'll let him explain it to you." She turned back around and continued cutting.

That night, after the three of them had eaten dinner in silence, Harold walked outside with his father, who was carrying two suit-cases and a garment bag. His father stowed the luggage in the trunk of his car and then told Harold that he had something to say.

"Okay," said Harold.

His father cleared his throat several times, sounding like a lawn-mower that would not turn over. "According to basic economic theory," he began, "human beings always work harder to avoid los-ing what they already have rather than to acquire more. You see, loss is always more devastating than the potential for gain is moti-vating. I want you to remember that, Harold."

Harold nodded and thrust his hands deep into his pockets, seek-ing out Mrs. Norman's toenail, which he flexed between his thumb and index finger.

"I have a new friend," his father said, "and I'm moving in with" —he hesitated—"him."

"Does that mean that you won't be checking the windows and doors anymore?" Harold asked. Every night before shutting off the lights, his father walked through the house, staring at each window and each door, checking to make sure that they were properly closed. His mother had always been annoyed by the practice, by the time it took his father to inspect the entire house, but it was something that he had done every night of Harold's life and so Harold considered it as much a part of bedtime as brushing his teeth and closing his eyes.

"I guess not," his father said, sounding disappointed at Harold's question. He reached out and placed his hand on his car door, and Harold knew what this meant: that his father was ready, even impatient, to leave, that as he stood there explaining himself to Harold, he really wanted to be in his car driving away, away toward his new friend and his new house—while Harold stayed behind in this house, where he would continue to brush his teeth and close his eyes as he always had, except from now on he and his mother would sleep with the windows and doors unchecked all around them. The thought of this filled him with terror, and as he stood there in the driveway watching his father leave, Harold found himself longing for the dark safety of the closet: the familiar smells of wet wool and vacuum cleaner dust; the far-off chatter of Mrs. Norman's television shows; the line of light marking the bottom of the locked door, a line so thin that it made what lay on the other side seem, after all, like nothing.

RON RASH

The Ascent

FROM *Tin House*

JARED HAD NEVER BEEN THIS FAR BEFORE, over Sawmill
Ridge and across a creek glazed with ice, then past the triangu-
lar metal sign that said GREAT SMOKY MOUNTAINS NATIONAL
PARK. If it had still been snowing and his tracks were being covered up, he'd have turned back. People had gotten lost in this
park. Children wandered off from family picnics, hikers strayed off
trails. Sometimes it took days to find them. But today the sun was
out, the sky deep and blue. No more snow would fall, so it would
be easy to retrace his tracks. Jared heard a helicopter hovering
somewhere to the west, which meant that after a week they still
hadn't found the airplane. They'd been searching all the way from
Bryson City to the Tennessee line, or so he'd heard at school.

The land slanted downward and the sound of the helicopter disappeared. In the steepest places, Jared leaned sideways and held
on to trees to keep from slipping. As he made his way into the
denser woods, he wasn't thinking of the lost airplane or if he would
get the mountain bike he'd asked for as his Christmas present. Not
thinking about his parents either, though they were the main reason he was spending his first day of Christmas vacation out here
—better to be outside on a cold day than in the house where everything, the rickety chairs and sagging couch, the gaps where the
TV and microwave had been, felt sad.

He thought instead of Lyndee Starnes, the girl who sat in front
of him in fifth-grade homeroom. Jared pretended she was walking
beside him and he was showing her the tracks in the snow, telling
her which markings were squirrel and which rabbit and which

deer. Pointing out a bear's tracks too and Lyndee telling him she was afraid of bears and Jared saying he'd protect her.

Jared stopped walking. He hadn't seen any human tracks, but he looked behind him to be sure no one was around. He took out the pocketknife and raised it, making believe that the pocketknife was a hunting knife and that Lyndee was beside him. If a bear comes, I'll take care of you, he said out loud. Jared imagined Lyndee reaching out and taking his free arm. He kept the knife out as he walked up another ridge, one whose name he didn't know. Lyndee still grasped his arm as they walked up the ridge. Lyndee told him how sorry she was that at school she'd said his clothes smelled bad.

At the ridge top, Jared pretended a bear suddenly raised up, baring its teeth and growling. He slashed at the bear with the knife and the bear ran away. Jared held the knife before him as he descended the ridge. Sometimes they'll come back, he said aloud.

He was halfway down the ridge when the knife blade caught the midday sun and the steel flashed. Another flash came from below, as if it was answering. At first Jared saw only a glimmer of metal in the dull green of rhododendron, but as he came nearer he saw more, a crumpled silver propeller and white tailfin and part of a shattered wing.

For a few moments Jared thought about turning around, but then told himself that someone who'd just fought a bear shouldn't be afraid to get close to a crashed airplane. He made his way down the ridge, snapping rhododendron branches to clear a path. When he finally made it to the plane, he couldn't see much because snow and ice covered the windows. He turned the passenger-side door's outside handle, but the door didn't budge until Jared wedged in the pocketknife's blade. The door made a sucking sound as it opened.

A woman was in the passenger seat, her body bent forward like a horseshoe. Long brown hair fell over her face. The hair had frozen and looked as if it would snap off like icicles. She wore blue jeans and a yellow sweater. Her left arm was flung out before her and on one finger was a ring. The man across from her leaned toward the pilot window, his head cocked against the glass. Bloodstains reddened the window and his face was not covered like the woman's. There was a seat in the back, empty. Jared placed the knife in his pocket and climbed into the back seat and closed the passenger door. Because it's so cold, that's why they don't smell much, he thought.

For a while he sat and listened to how quiet and still the world was. He couldn't hear the helicopter or even the chatter of a gray squirrel or caw of a crow. Here between the ridges not even the sound of the wind. Jared tried not to move or breathe hard, to make it even quieter, quiet as the man and woman up front. The plane was snug and cozy. After a while he heard something, just the slightest sound, coming from the man's side. Jared listened harder, then knew what it was. He leaned forward between the front seats. The man's right forearm rested against a knee. Jared pulled back the man's shirtsleeve and saw the watch. He checked the time, almost four o'clock. He'd been sitting in the back seat two hours, though it seemed only a few minutes. The light that would let him follow the tracks back home would be gone soon.

As he got out of the back seat, Jared saw the woman's ring. Even in the cabin's muted light, it shone. He took the ring off the woman's finger and placed it in his jeans pocket. He closed the passenger door and followed his boot prints back the way he came. Jared tried to step into his earlier tracks, pretending that he needed to confuse a wolf following him.

It took longer than he'd thought, the sun almost down when he crossed the park boundary. As he came down the last ridge, Jared saw that the blue pickup was parked in the yard, the lights on in the front room. He remembered it was Saturday and his father had gotten his paycheck. When Jared opened the door, the small red glass pipe was on the coffee table, an empty baggie beside it. His father kneeled before the fireplace, meticulously arranging and rearranging kindling around an oak log. A dozen crushed beer cans lay amid the kindling, balanced on the log itself three red and white fishing bobbers. His mother sat on the couch, her eyes glazed, as she told Jared's father how to arrange the cans. In her lap lay a roll of tinfoil she was cutting into foot-long strips.

"Look what we're making," she said, smiling at Jared. "It's going to be our Christmas tree."

When he didn't speak, his mother's smile quivered.

"Don't you like it, honey?"

His mother got up, strips of tinfoil in her left hand. She knelt

beside his father and carefully draped them on the oak log and
kindling.

Jared walked into the kitchen and took the milk from the refrigerator. He washed a bowl and spoon left in the sink and poured
some cereal. After he ate, Jared went into his bedroom and closed
the door. He sat on his bed and took the ring from his pocket and
set it in his palm. He held the ring under the lamp's bulb and
swayed his hand slowly back and forth so the stone's different colors flashed and merged. He'd give it to Lyndee when they were on
the playground, on the first sunny day after Christmas vacation, so
she could see how pretty the ring's colors were. Once he gave it to
her, Lyndee would finally like him, and it would be for real.

Jared didn't hear his father until the door swung open.

"Your mother wants you to help light the tree."

The ring fell onto the wooden floor. Jared picked it up and
closed his hand.

"What's that?" his father asked.

"Nothing," Jared said. "Just something I found in the woods."

"Let me see."

Jared opened his hand. His father stepped closer and took the
ring. He pressed the ring with his thumb and finger.

"That's surely a fake diamond, but the ring looks to be real
gold."

His father tapped it against the bedpost as if the sound could
confirm its authenticity. His father called his mother and she came
into the room.

"Look what Jared found," he said, and handed her the ring. "It's
gold."

His mother set the ring in her palm, held it out before her so
they all three could see it.

"Where'd you find it, honey?"

"In the woods," Jared said.

"I didn't know you could find rings in the woods," his mother
said dreamily. "But isn't it wonderful that you can."

"That diamond can't be real, can it?" his father asked.

His mother stepped close to the lamp. She cupped her hand and
slowly rocked it back and forth, watching the different colors flash
inside the stone.

"It might be," his mother said.

"Can I have it back?" Jared asked.

"Not until we find out if it's real, son," his father said.

His father took the ring from his mother's palm and placed it in his pants pocket. Then he went into the other bedroom and got his coat.

"I'm going down to town and find out if it's real or not."

"But you're not going to sell it," Jared said.

"I'm just going to have a jeweler look at it," his father said, already putting on his coat. "We need to know what it's worth, don't we? We might have to insure it. You and your momma go ahead and light our Christmas tree. I'll be back in just a few minutes."

"It's not a Christmas tree," Jared said.

"Sure it is, son," his father replied. "It's just one that's chopped up, is all."

He wanted to stay awake until his father returned, so he helped his mother spread the last strips of tinfoil on the wood. His mother struck a match and told him it was time to light the tree. The kindling caught and the foil and cans withered and blackened. The fishing bobbers melted. His mother kept adding kindling to the fire, telling Jared if he watched closely he'd see angel wings folding and unfolding inside the flames. Angels come down the chimney sometimes, just like Santa Claus, she told him. Midnight came and his father still wasn't back. Jared went to his room. I'll lay down just for a few minutes, he told himself, but when he opened his eyes it was light outside.

As soon as he came into the front room, Jared could tell his parents hadn't been to bed. The fire was still going, kindling piled around the hearth. His mother sat where she'd been last night, wearing the same clothes. She was tearing pages out of a magazine one at a time, using scissors to make ragged stars she stuck on the walls with tape. His father sat beside her, watching intently.

The glass pipe lay on the coffee table beside four baggies, two with powder still in them. There'd never been more than one before.

His father grinned at him.

"I got you some of that cereal you like," he said, and pointed to a box with a green leprechaun on its front.

"Where's the ring?" Jared asked.

"The sheriff took it," his father said. "When I showed it to the jeweler, he said the sheriff had been in there just yesterday. A woman had reported it missing. I knew you'd be disappointed, that's why I bought you that cereal. Got something else for you too."

His father nodded toward the front door where a mountain bike was propped against the wall. Jared walked over to it. He could tell it wasn't new, some of the blue paint chipped away and one of the rubber handle grips missing, but the tires didn't sag and the handlebars were straight.

"It didn't seem right for you to have to wait till Christmas to have it," his father said. "Too bad there's snow on the ground, but it'll soon enough melt and you'll be able to ride it."

Jared's mother looked up.

"Wasn't that nice of your daddy," she said, her eyes bright and gleaming. Go ahead and eat your cereal, son. A growing boy needs his breakfast."

Jared ate as his parents sat in the front room passing the pipe back and forth. He looked out the window and saw the sky held nothing but blue, not even a few white clouds. He wanted to go back to the plane, but as soon as he laid his bowl in the sink his father announced that the three of them were going to go find a real Christmas tree.

"The best Christmas tree ever," his mother told Jared.

They put on their coats and walked up the ridge, his father carrying a rusty saw. Near the ridge top, they found Fraser firs and white pines.

"Which one do you like best?" his father asked.

Jared looked over the trees, then picked a Fraser fir no taller than himself.

"You don't want a bigger one?" his father asked.

When Jared shook his head no, his father knelt before the tree. The saw's teeth were dull but his father finally broke the bark and worked the saw through. They dragged the tree down the ridge and propped it in the corner by the fireplace. His parents smoked the pipe again and then his father went out to the shed and got a hammer and nails and two boards. While his father built the makeshift tree stand, Jared's mother cut more stars from a magazine.

"I think I'll go outside a while," Jared said.

"But you can't," his mother replied. "You've got to help me tape the stars to the tree."

By the time they'd finished, the sun was falling behind Sawmill Ridge. I'll go tomorrow, he told himself.

On Monday morning the baggies were empty and his parents were sick. His mother sat on the couch wrapped in a quilt, shivering. She hadn't bathed since Friday and her hair was stringy and greasy. His father looked little better, his blue eyes receding deep into his skull, his lips chapped and bleeding.

"Your momma, she's sick," his father said.

Jared watched his mother all morning. After a while she lit the pipe and sucked deeply for what residue might remain. His father crossed his arms, rubbing his biceps as he looked around the room, as if expecting to see something he'd not seen moments earlier. The fire had gone out, the cold causing his mother to shake more violently.

"You got to go see Wesley," she told Jared's father.

"We got no money left," he answered.

Jared watched them, waiting for the sweep of his father's eyes to stop beside the front door where the mountain bike was. But his father's eyes went past it without the slightest pause. The kerosene heater in the kitchen was on, but its heat hardly radiated into the front room.

His mother looked up at Jared.

"Can you fix us a fire, honey?"

He went out to the back porch and gathered an armload of kindling, then placed a thick oak log on the andirons as well. Beneath it he wedged newspaper left over from the star cutting. He lit the newspaper and watched the fire slowly take hold, then watched the flames a while longer before turning to his parents.

"You can take the bike to town and sell it," he said.

"No, son," his mother said. "That's your Christmas present."

"We'll be all right," his father said. "Your momma and me just did too much partying yesterday is all."

But as the morning passed, they got no better. At noon Jared went to his room and got his coat.

"Where you going, honey?" his mother asked as he walked toward the door.

"To get more firewood."

Jared walked into the shed but did not gather wood. Instead, he took a length of dusty rope off the shed's back wall and wrapped it around his waist and then knotted it. He left the shed and followed his own tracks west into the park. The snow had become harder, and it crunched beneath his boots. The sky was gray, darker clouds farther west. More snow would soon come, maybe by afternoon. Jared told Lyndee it was too dangerous for her to go with him. He was on a rescue mission in Alaska, the rope tied around him dragging a sled filled with food and medicine. The footprints weren't his but of the people he'd been sent to find.

When he got to the airplane, Jared pretended to unpack the supplies and give the man and woman something to eat and drink. He told them they were too hurt to walk back with him and he'd have to go and get more help. Jared took the watch off the man's wrist. He set it in his palm, face upward. I've got to take your compass, he told the man. A blizzard's coming, and I may need it.

Jared slipped the watch into his pocket. He got out of the plane and walked back up the ridge. The clouds were hard and granite-looking now, and the first flurries were falling. Jared pulled out the watch every few minutes, pointed the hour hand east as he followed his tracks back to the house.

The truck was still out front, and through the window Jared saw the mountain bike. He could see his parents as well, huddled together on the couch. For a few moments Jared simply stared through the window at them.

When he went inside, the fire was out and the room was cold enough to see his breath. His mother looked up anxiously from the couch.

"You shouldn't go off that long without telling us where you're going, honey."

Jared lifted the watch from his pocket.

"Here," he said, and gave it to his father.

His father studied it a few moments, then broke into a wide grin.

"This watch is a Rolex," his father said.

"Thank you, Jared," his mother said, looking as if she might cry. "How much can we get for it?"

"I bet a couple of hundred at least," his father answered.

His father clamped the watch onto his wrist and got up. Jared's mother rose as well.

"I'm going with you. I need something quick as I can get it." She turned to Jared. "You stay here, honey. We'll be back in just a little while. We'll bring you back a hamburger and a Co-Cola, some more of that cereal too."

Jared watched as they drove down the road. When the truck had vanished, he sat down on the couch and rested a few minutes. He hadn't taken his coat off. He checked to make sure the fire was out and then went to his room and emptied his backpack of schoolbooks. He went out to the shed and picked up a wrench and a hammer and placed them in the backpack. The flurries were thicker now, already beginning to fill in his tracks. He crossed over Sawmill Ridge, the tools clanking in his backpack. More weight to carry, he thought, but at least he wouldn't have to carry them back.

When he got to the plane, he didn't open the door, not at first. Instead, he took the tools from the backpack and laid them before him. He studied the plane's crushed nose and propeller, the broken right wing. The wrench was best to tighten the propeller, he decided. He'd straighten out the wing with the hammer.

As he switched tools and moved around the plane, the snow fell harder. Jared looked behind him and on up the ridge and saw his footprints were growing fainter. He chipped the snow and ice off the windshields with the hammer's claw. Finished, he said, and dropped the hammer on the ground. He opened the passenger door and got in.

"I fixed it so it'll fly now," he told the man.

He sat in the back seat and waited. The work and walk had warmed him but he quickly grew cold. He watched the snow cover the plane's front window with a darkening whiteness. After a while he began to shiver but after a longer while he was no longer cold. Jared looked out the side window and saw the whiteness was not only in front of him but below. He knew then that they had taken off and risen so high that they were enveloped inside a cloud, but still he looked down, waiting for the clouds to clear so he might look for the blue pickup, making its way through the snow, toward the place they were all headed.

KAREN RUSSELL

The Seagull Army Descends on Strong Beach

FROM *Tin House*

THE GULLS LANDED IN ATHERTOWN on July 10, 1979. Clouds
of them, in numbers unseen since the ornithologists began keeping records of such things. Scientists all over the country hypothe-
sized about climate change and migratory routes. At first sullen
Nal barely noticed them. Lost in his thoughts, he dribbled his
basketball up the boardwalk, right past the hundreds of gulls on
Strong Beach, gulls grouped so thickly that from a distance they
looked like snow banks. Their bodies capped the dunes. If Nal had
looked up, he would have seen a thunderhead of seagulls in the
well of the sky, rolling seaward. Instead, he ducked under the dirty
turquoise umbrella of the Beach Grub cart and spent his last dollar
on a hamburger; while he struggled to open a packet of yellow
mustard, one giant gull swooped in and snatched the patty from its
bun with a surgical jerk. Nal took two bites of bread and lettuce before he realized what had happened. The gull taunted him, wings
akimbo, on the Beach Grub umbrella, glugging down his burger.
Nal went on chewing the greasy bread, concluding that this was
pretty much par for his recent course.

All summer long, since his mother's termination, Nal had begun to sense that his life had jumped the rails—and then right at
his nadir, he'd agreed to an "avant" haircut performed by Cousin
Steve. Cousin Steve was participating in a correspondence course
with a beauty school in Nevada, America, and to pass his Radical
Metamorphosis II course, he decided to dye Nal's head a vivid blue
and then razor the front into tentacle-like bangs. "Radical," Nal

said dryly as Steve removed the foil. Cousin Steve then had to air-mail a snapshot of Nal's ravaged head to the United States desert, $17.49 in postage, so that he could get his diploma. In the photograph, Nal looks like he is going stoically to his death in the grip of a small blue octopus.

Samson Wilson, Nal's brother, took his turn in Cousin Steve's improvised barber chair—a wrecked church pew that Steve had carted into his apartment from off the street. Cousin Steve used Samson as a guinea pig for "Creative Clippers." He gave Samson a standard buzz cut to start, but that looked so good that he kept going with the razor. Pretty soon Samson had a gleaming cue ball head. He'd cracked jokes about the biblical significance of this, and Nal had secretly hoped that his brother's power over women would in fact be diminished. But to Nal's dismay, the ladies of Athertown flocked to Samson in greater multitudes than before. Girls trailed him down the boardwalk, clucking stupidly about the new waxy sheen to his head. Samson was seventeen and had what Nal could only describe as a bovine charm: he was hale and beefy, with a big laugh and the deep serenity of a grazing creature. Nal loved him too, of course—it was impossible not to—but he was baffled by Sam's ease with women, his ease in the world.

That summer Nal was fourteen and looking for excuses to have extreme feelings about himself. He and Samson played a lot of basketball on summer nights and weekends. Nal would replay every second of their games until he was so sick of his own inner sportscaster that he wanted to puke. He actually had puked once—last September he had walked calmly out of the JV tryouts and retched in the frangipani. The voice in his head logged every on-court disaster, every stolen ball and missed shot, the unique fuckups and muscular failures that he had privately termed "Nal-fouls." Samson had been on the varsity team since his freshman year, and he wasn't interested in these instant replays—he wanted the game to move forward. Nal and his brother would play for hours, and when he got tired of losing, Nal would stand in the shade of a eucalyptus grove and dribble in place.

"It's just a pickup game, Nal," Samson told him.

"Quit eavesdropping on me!" Nal shouted, running the ball down the blacktop. "I'm talking to myself."

Then he'd take off sprinting down the road, but no matter how punishing the distance he ran—he once dribbled the ball all the way down to the ruined industrial marina at Pier 12, where the sea rippled like melted aluminum—Nal felt he couldn't get away from himself. He sank hoops and it was always Nal sinking them; he missed, and he was Nal missing. He felt incapable of spontaneous action: before he could do anything, a tiny homunculus had to generate a flowchart in his brain. If *p*, then *q*; If *z*, then back to *a*. This homunculus could gnaw a pencil down to a nub, deliberating. All day, he could hear the homunculus clacking in his brain like a secretary from a 1940s movie: Nal shouldn't! Nal can't! Nal won't! and then hitting the bell of the return key. He pictured the homunculus as a tiny, blankly handsome man in a green sweater, very agreeably going about his task of wringing the life from Nal's life.

He wanted to get to a place where he wasn't thinking about every movement at every second; where he wasn't even really Nal any longer but just weight sinking into feet, feet leaving the pavement, fingers fanning forcelessly through air, the *swish!* of a made basket and the net birthing the ball. He couldn't remember the last time he had acted without reservation on a single desire. Samson seemed to do it all the time. Once, when Nal returned home from his miles-long run with the ball, sweating and furious, they had talked about his aspiration for vacancy—the way he wanted to be empty and free. He'd explained it to Samson in a breathless rush, expecting to be misunderstood.

"Sure," Samson said. "I know what you're talking about."

"You do?"

"From surfing. Oh, it's wild, brother." Why did Samson have to know him so well? "The feeling of being part of the same wave that's lifting you. It's like you're coasting outside of time, outside your own skin."

Nal felt himself redden. Sometimes he wished his brother would simply say, "No, Nal, what the hell do you mean?" Samson had a knack for this kind of insight: he was like a grinning fisherman who could wrench a secret from the depths of your chest and dangle it in front of you, revealing it to be nothing but a common, mud-colored fish.

"You know what else can get you there, Nal, since you're such a shitty athlete?" Samson grinned and cocked his thumb and his pinky, tipped them back. "Boozing. Or smoking. Last night I was out with Vanessa and we were maybe three pitchers in when the feeling happened. All night I was in love with everybody."

So Samson was now dating Vanessa Grigalunas? Nal had been infatuated with her for three years and had been so certain, for so long, that they were meant to be together, he was genuinely confused by this development, as if the iron of his destiny had gone soft and pliant as candle wax. Vanessa was in Nal's grade, a fellow survivor of freshman year. He had sat behind her in Japanese class and it was only in that language—where he was a novice and felt he had license to stammer like a fool—that he could talk to her. "K-k-k," he'd say. Vanessa would smile politely as he revved his stubborn engine syllable, until he was finally able to sputter out a "Konnichiwa."

Nal had never breathed a word about his love for Vanessa to anyone. And then in early June, out of the clear blue, Samson began raving about her. "Vanessa Grigalunas? But . . . why her?" Nal asked, thinking of all the hundreds of reasons that he'd by now collected. It didn't seem possible that the desire to date Vanessa could have co-evolved in Samson. Vanessa wasn't his type at all; Samson usually dated beach floozies, twenty-somethings with hair like dry spaghetti, these women he'd put up with because they bought him liquor and pot, who sat on his lap in Gerlando's, Athertown's only cloth-napkin restaurant, and cawed laughter. Vanessa's hair shone like a lake. Vanessa read books and moved through the world as if she were afraid that her footsteps might wake it.

"I can't stop thinking about her." Samson grinned, running a paw over his bald head. "It's crazy, like I caught a Vanessa bug or something."

Nal nodded miserably—now he couldn't stop thinking about the two of them together. He sketched out interview questions in his black composition notebook that he hoped to one day ask her:

1. What is it that you like about my brother? List three things (not physical).
2. What made you want to sleep with my brother? What was your thought in the actual moment when you decided? Was it a conscious choice, like, Yes, I will do this! or was it more like collapsing onto a sofa?
3. Under what circumstances can you imagine sleeping with me? Global apocalypse? National pandemic? Strep throat shuts down the high school? What if we were to do it immediately after I'd received a lethal bite from a rattlesnake so you could

feel confident that I would die soon and tell no one? Can you just quantify for me, in terms of beer, what it would take?

It made Nal sadder still that even Vanessa's mom, Mrs. Grigalunas—a woman who had no sons of her own and who treated all teenage boys like smaller versions of her husband—even kindly, delusional Mrs. Grigalunas recognized Nal as a deterrent to love. One Saturday night Samson informed him that the *three* of them would be going on a date to Strong Beach together; they needed Nal's presence to reassure Mrs. Grigalunas that nothing dangerous or fun would happen.

"Yes, you two can go to the beach," she told Vanessa, "but bring that Nal along with you. He's such a nice boy."

What were all these seagulls doing out flying at night? Usually Nal came out here to Strong Beach solo, dribbling his ball past these dunes in a fog of fantasies about Vanessa—anatomically vague, excruciatingly arousing fantasies, wherein she spontaneously lost her top. But now that he was here with Vanessa and Sam he finally noticed them. They were kelp gulls, big ones. He was shocked to see how many of the birds now occupied Strong Beach. Where'd they all come from? He hoped they'd leave soon, anyway. He was trying to finish a poem. White globs of gull shit kept falling from the sky, a cascade that Nal found inimical to his writing process. The poem that Nal was working on had nothing to do with his feelings—poetry, he'd decided, was to honor remote and immortal subjects, like the moon. "Lambent Planet, Madre Moon" was the working title of this one, and he'd already jotted down three sestets. *Green nuclei of fireflies,* Nal wrote. *The red commas of two fires.* A putrid, stinky blob fell from above and put out his word. "Shoo, you shit balloons!" he yelled as the gulls rained on.

There were no fireflies on the beach that night, but there were plenty of spider fleas, their abdomens pulsing with low-grade toxins. The air was tangy and cold. Between two lumps of sand about a hundred yards behind him, Vanessa and Nal's brother, Samson, were . . . Nal couldn't stand to think about it. In five minutes' time they had given up on keeping their activities a secret from him, or anybody. Vanessa's low moan was rising behind him, rich and feral and nothing like her classroom whisper.

Nal felt a little sick.

What on earth was the moon like? he wondered, squinting. What did the moon most resemble to him? Nal wiped at his dry eyes and dug into the paper. One of the seagulls had settled on an auburn coil of seaweed a few feet away from his bare foot. He tried to ignore it, but the gull was making a big production out of eviscerating a cigarette. It drew out red flakes of tobacco with its pincerlike bill and ate them. Perfect, Nal thought. Here I am trying to eulogize Mother Nature and this is the tableau she presents me with.

Behind him, Samson growled Vanessa's name. Don't look back, you asshole! he thought. Good advice, from Orpheus to Lot. But Nal couldn't help himself. He lacked the power to look away, but he never worked up the annihilating courage to look directly at them either; instead, he angled his body and let his eyes slide to the left. This was like taking dainty sips of poison. Samson's broad back had almost completely covered Vanessa—only her legs were visible over the dune, her pink feet twitching as if she were impatient for sleep. "Oh!" said Vanessa, over and over again. "Oh!" She sounded happy, astonished.

Nal was a virgin. He kicked at a wet clump of sand until it exploded. He went on a rampage, doing whirling jujitsu kicks into a settlement of abandoned sand castles along the beach for a full minute before he paused, panting, to recover himself. The tide rushed icy fingers of water up the beach and covered Nal's foot.

"Ahh!" Nal cried into one of the troughs of silence between Samson and Vanessa's moans. He had wandered to the water's edge, six or seven dunes away from them. His own voice was drowned out by the ocean. The salt water sleuthed out cuts on his legs that he had forgotten about or failed to feel until now, and he almost enjoyed the burning, which felt to him like a violent reanimation. His heartbeat hadn't slowed yet. He looked around for something else to kick but only one turret remained on the beach, a bucket-shaped stump in the middle of damp heaps. The giant seagull was standing beside it. Up close the gull seemed as large as a house cat. Its white face was luminous, its wings ink-dipped; its beak was fixed in that perennial shit-eating grin of all shearwaters and frigate birds.

"What are you grinning at?" Nal muttered. As if in response, the gull spread its wings and opened its shadow over the miniature ruins of the castle—too huge, Nal thought, and vaguely humanoid in shape—and then it flew off, laboring heavily against the wind. In the soft moonlight this created the disturbing illusion that the bird had hitched itself to Nal's shadow and was pulling his darkness from him.

Nal wasn't supposed to be in town that summer. He had been accepted to LMAS, the Lake Marion Achievement Summer Seminars: a six-week precollege program for the top three percent of the country's high school students. It was a big deal—seniors who completed all four summers of the program were automatically admitted to Lake Marion College with a full scholarship package. "Cream Rises" was the camp's motto; their mascot was an oblong custard-looking thing, the spumy top layer of which Nal guessed was meant to represent the gifted. In March a yellow T-shirt with this logo had arrived in the mail, bundled in with his acceptance letter. Nal tried to imagine a hundred kids wearing the same shirt in the Lake Marion dormitories, kids with overbites and cowlicks and shy, squint-eyed ambitions—LMAS! he thought, a kind of heaven. Had he worn the shirt with the custard-thing to his own school, it would have been a request for a punch in the mouth.

But then one day his mom came home from work and said she was being scapegoated by the Paradise Nursing Facility for what management was calling "a distressing oversight." Her superiors recommended that she not return to work. But for almost two weeks Nal's mother would set her alarm for five o'clock, suit up, take the number 14 bus to Paradise. Only after she was officially terminated did she file for unemployment, and so far as Nal could tell this was the last real action she had taken; she'd been on their couch for three months now and counting. Gradually she began to lose her old habits, as if these too were a uniform that she could slip out of: she stopped cooking entirely, slept at odd hours, mummied herself in blankets in front of their TV. What was she waiting for? There was something maddening about her posture—the way she sat there with one ear cocked sideways as if listening for a break in the weather. Nal had been forced to forfeit his deposit at Lake Marion and interview for a job behind the register at Penny's Grocery. He took a pen to the Help Wanted ads and papered their fridge with them. This was back in April, when he'd still believed his mom might find another job in time to pay the Lake Marion fee.

"Mom, just look at these, okay?" he'd shout above the surf roar of their TV, "I circled the good ones in green," and she'd explain again without looking over that the whole town was against her. Nobody was going to hire Claire Wilson *now*. All of these changes came about as the result of a single failed mainstay. The windows at Paradise were supposed to be fitted with a stop screw, to prevent what the Paradise manual euphemistically referred to as "elopement." Jailbreak was another word for this, suicide, accidental defenestration—as Nal's mom put it, many of the residents were forty-eight cards to a deck and couldn't be trusted with their own lives. With the stop screws in place, no window opened more than six inches. But as it happened, a stop screw was missing from a sixth-floor window—one of the hundred-plus windows in Paradise—an oversight that was discovered when a ninety-two-year-old resident shoved it open to have a smoke. A visitor found the old woman leaning halfway out the window and drew her back inside the frame. The visitor described the "near fatal incident" to Nal's mother while the "victim" plucked ash from her tongue. According to Nal's mom, the Paradise administrators came to the sudden agreement that it had always been Claire Wilson's responsibility to check the window locks. She came home that night babbling insincere threats: "They try to pin this on me, boys, you watch, I will quit in a heartbeat." But then the resident's daughter wrote a series of histrionic letters to the newspaper, and the sleepy Athertown news station decided to do an "exposé" of Paradise, modeled on the American networks, complete with a square-jawed black actress to play the role of Nal's mother.

Only Nal had watched the dramatization through to its ending. They'd staged a simulation of a six-story fall using a flour sack dummy, the sack splitting open on the gates and spilling flour everywhere, powdering the inscrutable faces of the stone angels in the garden below. Lawsuits were filed, and, in the ensuing din of threats and accusations, Nal's mother was let go.

Nal had expected his mom to react to this with a froth and vengeance that at least matched his own, perhaps even file a legal action. But she returned home from her final day at work exhausted. Her superiors had bullied her into a defeated sort of gratitude: "They said it was my job, who knows? I'm not perfect. I'm just glad they caught the problem when they did," she kept saying.

"Quit talking like that!" Nal moaned. "It wasn't your fault, Mom. You've been brainwashed by these people. Don't be such a pushover."

"A pushover!" she said. "Who's pushing me over? I know it wasn't my fault, Nal. I can't be grateful that nobody got killed?" She described the "averted tragedy" in the canned language of the Paradise directors: the chance of one of her charges flailing backwards out the window and onto the gate's tiny spears. In her dreams the victim wasn't a flour sack dummy but a body with no face, impaled on the spikes.

"That's your body, Ma!" Nal cried. "That's you!" But she didn't see it that way.

"Let's just be thankful nobody was hurt," she mumbled.

Nal didn't want his mom to relinquish her first fury. "How can you say that? They fired you, mom! Now everything's . . . off course."

His mom stroked a blue curl of Nal's hair and gave him a tired smile. "Ooh, we're off course, right. I forgot. And what course was that?"

Nal picked up more shifts at the grocery store. He ran eggs and pork tenderloins down the register, the scanner catching his knuckles in a web of red light. Time felt heavy inside Penny's. Beep! he whimpered along with the machine, swiping a tin of tomatoes. Beep! Sometimes he could still feel the progress of his lost future inside him, the summer at Lake Marion piping like a vacant bubble through his blood.

"Mom, can I still go away to college, though?" he asked her one Sunday, when they were sitting in the aquarium light of the TV. He'd felt the bubble swell to an unbearable pressure in his lungs. "Sure," she said, not looking over from the TV. Her eyes were like Samson's, bright splashes of blue in an oak-stained face. "You can do whatever you want."

When the bubble in him would burst, Nal would try to start a fight. He shouted that what she called his "choices" about college and LMAS and Penny's Grocery were her consequences, a domino run of misfortune. He told her that he wouldn't be able to go to college if she didn't find another job, that it was lying to pretend like he could.

"I heard you guys going at it," Samson said later in the kitchen, clapping mayonnaise onto two slices of bread. "Give Mom a break, kid. I think she's sick."

But Nal didn't think that his mom had contracted any particular illness—he was terrified that she was more generally dying, or dis-

integrating, letting her white roots grow out and fusing her spine
to their couch. She was still sitting in the champagne shadows of
the blinds when he got off his shift at six thirty.

Nal wrote a poem about how his mother had become the sea
hum inside the conch shell of their living room. He thought it
must be the best poem he'd ever written because he tried to recite
it to his bathroom reflection and his throat shut, and his eyes stung
so badly he could barely see his own face. She was sitting out there
now, watching TV reruns and muttering under her breath. Samson
was out drinking that night with Vanessa. Nal gave his mother the
poem to read and it was still sitting under a dirty mug, accumulat-
ing rings, when he came back to check on her that Friday.

Nal got a second job housesitting for his high school science
teacher, Mr. McGowen, who was going to Lake Marion to teach an
advanced chemistry course. Now Nal spent his nights in the shell
of Mr. McGowen's house. Each week Mr. McGowen sent him a
check for fifty-six dollars, and his mom lived on this income plus
the occasional contribution from Samson, wads of cash that Sam
had almost certainly borrowed from someone else. "It helps," she
said, "it's such a help," and whenever she said this Nal felt his guts
twist. Mr. McGowen's two-room rental house was making slow progress down the cliffs; another hurricane would finish it. The move
there hadn't mattered in any of the ways that Nal had hoped it
would. Samson had buffaloed him into giving him a spare key, and
now Nal would wake up to find his brother standing in the umbili-
cal hallway between the two rooms at odd hours:

SUNDAY: "How you living, Nal? Living easy? Easy living? You get
paid yet this week? I need you to do me a solid, brotherman . . ."
He was already peeling the bills out of Nal's wallet.

MONDAY: "Cable's out. I want to watch the game tonight, so I'll
probably just crash here . . ."

TUESDAY: "You're out of toilet paper again. I fucking swear, I'm
going to get a rash from coming over here! Some deadly fucking
disease . . ."

WEDNESDAY: "Shit, kid, you need to get to the store. Your fridge
is just desolate. What have you been eating?"

For three days, Nal hadn't ingested anything besides black coffee and a pint of freezer-burned ice cream. Weight was tumbling
from his body. Nal was living on liquid hatred now.

"Hey, Nal," said Samson, barging through the door. "Listen, Vanessa and I were sort of hoping we could spend the night here? She lied and told Mrs. Griga-looney that she's crashing at a friend's spot. Cool? Although you should really pick up before she gets here, this place is gross."

"Cool," Nal said, his blue hair igniting in the flashing light of the TV. "I just did laundry. Fresh sheets for you guys." Nal left Samson to root around the empty fridge and fished clean sheets out of Mr. McGowen's dryer. He made the twin bed with hospital corners, pushed his sneakers and sweaty V-necks under the frame, filled two glasses at the sink faucet and set them on the nightstand. He lit Mr. McGowen's orange emergency candles to provide a romantic accent. Nal knew this was not the most excellent strategy to woo Vanessa—making the bed so that she could sleep with his brother—but he was getting a sick pleasure from this seduction by proxy. The bedroom was freezing, Nal realized, and he reached over to shut the window—then screamed and leapt a full foot back.

A giant seagull was strutting along Nal's sill, a bouquet of eelgrass dangling from its beak. Its crown feathers waggled at Nal like tiny fingers. He felt a drip of fear. "What are you doing here?" He had to flick at the webbing of its slate feet before it moved and he could shut the window. The gull cocked its head and bored into Nal with its bright eyes; it was still looking at him as he backed out of the room.

"Hey," Vanessa greeted him shyly in the kitchen. "So this is McGowen's place." She was wearing thin silver bracelets up her arm and had blown out her hair. She had circled her eyes in lime and magenta powder; to Nal it looked as if she'd allowed a bag of candy to melt on her face. He thought she looked much prettier in school.

"Do you guys want chips or anything?" he asked stupidly, looking from Samson to Vanessa. "Soda? I have chips."

Vanessa kept her eyes on the nubby carpet. "Soda sounds good."

"He's just leaving," Samson said. He squeezed Nal's shoulder as he spun him toward the door. "Thank you," he said, leaning in so close that Nal could smell the spearmint and vodka mix on his breath, "Thank you *so much*"—which somehow made everything worse.

*

"Nal drives the lane! Nal brings the ball upcourt with seconds to play!" Nal whispered, dribbling his ball well past midnight. He dribbled up and down the main street that led to Strong Beach, and kept spooking himself with his own image in the dark store-front windows. "Nal has the ball . . ." he continued down to the public courts. "Jesus! Not you again!" A giant seagull had perched on the backboard and was staring opaquely forward. "Get out of here!" Nal yelled. He threw the ball until the backboard juddered, threw it again and again, but the bird remained. Maybe it's sick, Nal thought. Maybe it has some kind of neurological damage. He tucked the ball under his arm and walked farther down Strong Beach. The seagull flew over his head and disappeared into a dark thicket of pines, the beginnings of the National Reserve forest that lined Strong Beach. Nal was surprised to find himself jogging after it, following the bird into those shadows.

"Gull?" he called after it, his sneakers sinking into the dark leaves.

He found it settled on a low pine branch. The giant seagull had a sheriff's build—distended barrel chest, spindly legs splayed into star-shaped webbed feet. Nal had a sudden presentiment: "Are you my conscience?" he asked, reaching out to stroke the vane of one feather. The gull blatted at Nal and began digging around the underside of one wing with its beak like a tiny man sniffing his armpits. Okay, not my conscience, then, Nal decided. But maybe some kind of omen? Something was dangling from its lower beak—another cigarette, Nal thought at first, then realized it was a square of glossy paper. As he watched, the gull lifted off the branch and soared directly into one of the trees. In the moonlight, Nal saw a hollow there about the size of his basketball: gulls kept disappearing into this hole. Dozens of them were flying around the moon-bright leaves—they moved with the organized frenzy of bees or bats. How deep was the hollow, Nal wondered? Was this normal nocturnal activity for this kind of gull? The birds flew in absolute silence. Their wingtips sailed as softly as paintbrushes across the night sky; every so often single birds descended from this cloud. Each gull flapped into the hollow and didn't reemerge for whole minutes.

Nal chucked his basketball at the hollow to see if it would disappear like in that terrible TV movie that he secretly loved, *Magellan*

Maps the Black Hole, winking into another dimension. The basketball bounced back and caught Nal hard against his jaw. He winced
and shot a look up and down Strong Beach to make sure that nobody had seen. The hollow was almost a foot above Nal's head, and
when he pushed up to look inside it he saw nothing: just the pulpy
reddish guts of the tree. No seagulls, and no passage through that
he could divine. There was a nest in the tree hollow, though, a dark
wet cup of vegetation. The bottom of the nest was lined with paper
scraps—a few were tickets, Nal saw, not stubs or fragments but
whole squares, some legible: Mary Gloster's train tickets to Florence, a hologram stamp for a Thai *Lotus Blossom* day cruise, a roll
of carnival-red ADMIT ONES. Nal riffled through the top layer.
Mary Gloster's tickets, he noticed, were dated two years in the future. He saw a square edge with the letters WIL beneath a wreath
of blackened moss and tugged at it. My ticket, Nal thought wonder-
ingly. WILSON. How did you get that? It was his pass for the rising
sophomore class's summer trip to Whitsunday Island, a glowing
ember of volcanic rock that was just visible from the Athertown marina. He was shocked to find it here; his mother hadn't been able
to pay the fee back in April, and Nal's name had been removed
from the list of participants. The trip was tomorrow.

Nal was at the marina by 8 AM. He was sitting on a barrel when his
teacher arrived, and he watched as she tore open a sealed envelope
and distributed the tickets one by one to each of his classmates. He
waited until all the other students had disappeared onto the ferry
to approach her.

"Nal Wilson? Oh dear. I wasn't aware that you were coming . . ."
She gave him a tight smile and shook out the empty manila envelope, as if trying to convince him that his presence here was a
slightly embarrassing mistake.

"'S okay, I have my ticket here." Nal waved the orange ticket,
which was shot through with tiny perforations from where the
gull's beak had stabbed it. He lined up on the waffled copper of
the ferry ramp. The boat captain stamped his ticket REDEEMED,
and Nal felt that he had won a small but significant battle. On the
hydrofoil, Nal sat next to Vanessa. "That's my seat," grumbled a
stout Fijian man in a bolo tie behind him, but Nal shrugged and
gestured around the hold. "Looks like there are plenty of seats
to go around, sir," he said, and was surprised when the big man

floated on like some bad weather he'd dispelled with native magic. He could feel Vanessa radiating warmth beside him and was afraid to turn.

"Hey, you," Vanessa said. "Thanks for letting me crash in your bed last night."

"Don't mention it. Always fun to be the maid service for my brother."

Vanessa regarded him quietly for a moment. "I like your hair."

"Oh," Nal said miserably, rolling his eyes upward. "This blue isn't really me —" and then he felt immediately stupid, because just who did he think he was, anyway? Cousin Steve refused to shave it off, saying that to do so would be a "violation of the Hippocratic Oath of Beauty Professionals." "Unfortunately you have an extremely lumpy head," Cousin Steve had informed him, stern as a physician. "You need that blue to hide the contours. It's like you've got golf balls buried up there." But Vanessa, he saw with a rush of gratitude, was nodding at him.

"I know it's not you," she said. "But it's a good disguise."

Nal nodded, wondering what she might be referring to. He was thrilled by the idea that Vanessa saw past this camouflage to something hidden in him, so secret that even he didn't know what she was seeing there.

On the long ride to Whitsunday, they talked about their families. Vanessa was the youngest of five girls, and, from what she was telling Nal, it sounded as if her adolescence had been both accelerated and prolonged. She was still playing with dolls when she watched her eldest sister, Rue Ann, guide her boyfriend to their bedroom. "We have to leave the lights on, or Vanessa will be scared. It's fine, she's still tiny. She doesn't understand." The boyfriend grinning into her playpen, twaddling his fingers. Vanessa watched with eyes round as moon pies as her sister disrobed, draping her black T-shirt over the lampshade to dim it. But she had also been babied by her four sisters, and her questions about their activities got smothered beneath a blanket of care. Her parents began treating her like the baby of the family again once the other girls were gone. Her father was a Qantas mechanic and her mother worked a series of housekeeping jobs even though she didn't strictly need to, greeting Vanessa with a nervous "hello!" at the end of each day.

"Which is funny, because our own house is always a mess now . . ."

Nal watched the way her mouth twitched; his heart and his stomach were staging some weird circus inside him.

"Yeah, that's pretty funny." Nal frowned. "Except that, I mean, it sounds really awful too . . ."

He tried to get one arm around Vanessa's left shoulder but felt too cowardly to lower it all the way; he stared in horror at where his arm had stopped, about an inch above Vanessa's skin, like a malfunctioning bar in a theme park ride. When he lifted his arm again he noticed a gauzy stripe peeking out of Vanessa's shirt.

"I'm sorry," Nal interrupted, "Vanessa? Uh, your shirt is falling down . . ."

"Yeah," she tugged at it, unconcerned. "This was Brianne's, and she was never what you'd call petite. She's an air hostess now and my dad always jokes that he doesn't know how she maneuvers the aisles." Vanessa hooked a clear nail under her neckline. "My dad can be pretty mean. He's mad at her for leaving."

Nal couldn't take his eyes off the white binding. "Is that . . . is that a bandage?"

"Yes," she said simply. "It's my disguise."

Vanessa said she still held onto some childlike habits because they seemed to calm her parents. "I had to pretend I believed in Santa Claus until I was twelve," she said. "Did Sam tell you that I was accepted to LMAS, too?"

"Oh, wow. Congratulations. When do you leave?"

"I'm not going. I mentioned that the dorms at Lake Marion were coed and my father didn't speak to me for days." Why her development of breasts should terrify her parents Vanessa didn't understand, but she began wearing bulky, loose shirts and wrapping Ace bandages over her bras all the same. "I got the idea from English class," she said. "Shakespeare's Rosalind." Her voice changed when she talked about this—she let out a hot, embarrassed laugh and then dove into a whisper, as if she'd been trying to make a joke and suddenly switched gears.

"Isn't that a little weird?"

Vanessa shrugged. "Less friction with my parents. The tape doesn't work as good as it did last year but it's sort of become this habit?"

Nal couldn't figure out where he was supposed to look; he was having a hard time staying focused in the midst of all this overt discussion of Vanessa's breasts.

"So you're stuck there now?"

"I don't see how I could leave my folks. I'm their last."

Vanessa wanted out but said she felt as though the exits had vanished with her sisters. They'd each schemed or blundered their way out of Athertown—early pregnancy, nursing school, marriage, the Service Corp. Now Vanessa rumbled around the house like its last working part. Nal got an image of Mr. and Mrs. Grigalunas sitting in their kitchen with their backs to the whirlwind void opened by their daughters' absence: reading the paper; sipping orange juice; collecting these old clothes like the shed skins of their former daughters and dressing Vanessa in them. He thought about her gloopy makeup and the urgency with which she'd kissed his brother, her thin legs knifing over the dune. Maybe she doesn't actually like my brother at all, Nal thought, encouraged by a new theory. Maybe she treats sex like oxidizing air. Aging rapidly wherever she can manage it, like a cut apple left on a counter.

"That's why it's easy to be with your brother," she said. "It's a relief to . . . to get out of there, to be with someone older. But it's not like we're serious, you know?" She brightened as she said this last part, as if it were a wonderful idea that had just occurred to her.

What do I say now? Nal wondered. Should I ask her to explain what she means? Should I tell her Samson doesn't love her, but I do? The homunculus typed up frantic speeches, discarded them, tore at his green sweater in anguish, gnashed the typewriter ribbon between his buckteeth. Nal could hear himself babbling—they talked about the insufferable stupidity of this year's ninth-graders, his harem of geezers at Penny's, Dr. J's jump hook, Cousin Steve's bewildering mullet. More than once, Nal watched her tug her sister's tentlike shirt up. They spent the rest of the afternoon exploring Whitsunday Island together, cracking jokes as they filed past the flowery enclosure full of crocodiles; the dry pool of Komodo dragons with their wispy beards; and finally, just before the park's exit, the koala who looked like a raddled veteran of war, gumming leaves at twilight. They talked about how maybe it wasn't such a terrible thing that they'd both missed out on Lake Marion, and on the way back up the waffled ramp to the hydrofoil Vanessa let her hand slide inside Nal's sweating palm.

That night Nal had a nightmare about the seagulls. Millions of them flew out of a blood red sunset and began to resettle the town, snapping telephone wires and sinking small boats beneath all their weight. Gulls covered the fence posts and rooftops of Athertown, drew a white caul over the marina, muffled every window with the static of their bodies—and each gull had a burgled object twinkling in its split beak. Warping people's futures into some new and terrible shape, just by stealing these smallest linchpins from their presents.

The next day, Nal went to the Athertown library to research omen birds. He was the only patron in the reading room. Beneath the painting of the full orange moon and the plastic bamboo, he read a book called *Avian Auspices* by Dr. Carlos Ramirez. Things looked pretty grim:

CROW: AN OMEN OF DEATH, DISEASE
RAVEN: AN OMEN OF DEATH, DISEASE
ALBATROSS: AN OMEN OF DEATH AT SEA

Screech owls, Old World vultures, even the innocuous-sounding cuckoo, all harbingers of doom. Terrific, Nal thought, and if an enormous seagull followed you around and appeared to be making a blithe feast of your life, pecking at squares of paper and erasing whole futures, what did that mean? Coleridge and Audubon were no help here, either. Seagulls were scavengers, kleptoparasites. And, according to the books he found, they didn't portend a thing.

Nal began going to the nest every day. He woke at dawn and walked barefoot on the chilly sand down to the hollow. By the second week he'd collected an impressive array of objects: a tuxedo button, a scrap of paper with a phone number (out of service—Nal tried it), a penny with a mint date one year in the future. On Friday, he found what appeared to be the disgorged, shimmering innards of a hundred cassette tapes, disguised at first against the slick weeds. The seagulls had many victims, then—they weren't just stealing from Nal. He wondered if the gulls had different caches, in caves or distant forests. Whenever he swept his hand over the damp nest he found new stuff:

An eviction notice, neatly halved by the gull's beak.

Half a dozen keys of various sizes—car keys, big skeleton keys and tiny ones for safes and mailboxes, a John Deere tractor key, one jangling janitor's ring.

A cheap fountain pen.

A stamp from a country Nal didn't recognize.

An empty vial of pills, the label soaking and illegible.

Most disturbingly, on the soggy bottom of the nest, beneath a web of green eider, he found the disconnected wires of a child's gleaming retainer.

Nal lined these objects up and pushed them around on the sand. He felt like the paleontologist of some poor sod's stolen fate— somewhere a man or a woman's life continued without these tiny vertebrae, curving like a spine knocked out of alignment. Suddenly the ordinary shine of the plastic and aluminum bits began to really frighten him. He drew the tiny fangs of the tractor key through the sand and tried to imagine the objects' owners: A shy child without his retainer, with a smile that would now go unchaperoned. A red-head with pale eyelashes succumbing to fever. A farmer on his belly in a field of corn, hunting for this key. What new direction would their lives take? In Nal's imagination, dark stalks swayed and knit together, obliterating the stranger from view. Somewhere the huge tractor wheels began to groan and squeal backwards, trampling his extant rows of corn. A new crop was pushing into the spaces that the tractor had abandoned—husks hissing out of the earth, bristling and green, like the future sprouting new fur.

We have to alert the authorities, he decided. He zipped the future into his backpack and walked down to the police station.

"What do you want me to do with this sack of crap, son?" Sheila, the Athertown policewoman, wanted to know. "The pawnshop moved; it's down by the esplanade now. Why don't you take this stuff over there, see if Mr. Tarak will give you some quarters for it. Play you some video games."

"But it belongs to somebody." Nal hadn't found the courage to tell her his theory that the new seagulls were cosmic scavengers. He tried to imagine saying this out loud: "The seagulls are stealing scraps of our lives to feather this weird nest I found in a tree hollow on Strong Beach. These birds are messing with our futures." Sheila, who had a red lioness's mane of curls bursting from an alligator clip and bigger triceps than Nal's, did not look as if she suffered fools gladly. She was the kind of woman who would put DDT in the nest and call it a day.

"So leave it here then." She shrugged. "When somebody comes to report the theft of their number two pencil, I'll let you know."

On Saturday he found a wedding invitation for Bruce and Nancy, in an envelope the color of lilac icing. There was no return address. On Tuesday he checked the nest and found the wrinkled passport of one Dodi Watts. Did that mean he was dead, or never was? Nal shuddered. Or just that he'd missed his flight?

His guesswork was beginning to feel stupid. Pens and keys and train tickets, so what? Now what? Sheila was right. How was he supposed to make anything out of this sack of crap?

The giant seagull, who Nal now thought of as his not-conscience, appeared to be the colony's dominant gull. Today it was screaming in wide circles over the sea. Nal sat on a canted rock and watched something tiny fall from its beak into the waves, glinting all the way down. Beneath him the waves had turned a foam-blistered violet, and the sky growled. The whole bowl of the bay seethed around the rocks like a cauldron. Nal shuddered; when he squinted he could see something fine as salt shaking into the sea. Rain, he thought, watching the seagull ride the thermals, maybe it's only raining . . .

Later, when the sky above Strong Beach was riddled with stars, Nal got up on shaky legs and entered the woods. The gulls had vanished, and it was hard for him to find the tree with the hollow. He stumbled around with his flashlight for what felt like hours looking for it, growing increasingly frantic until he felt near-hysterical, his heart drumming. Even after he'd found what he thought was the right tree Nal couldn't be sure, because the nest inside was damp and empty. He sunk his hands into the old leaves and at first felt nothing, but digging down he began to find an older stratum of plunder: a leather bookmark, a baby's rusting spoon. The gulls must have stolen this stuff a while ago, Nal thought, from a future that was now peeling away in ribbons, a future that had already been perverted or lost, a past. At the very bottom of the nest he saw a wink of light. Nal pinched at the wink, pulled it out.

"Oh God," he groaned. When he saw what he was holding he almost dropped it. "Is this some kind of joke?"

It was nothing, really. It was just a dull knuckle of metal. A screw.

Nal closed his fist around the screw, opened it. Here was something indigestible. It was a stop screw—he knew this from the diagram that had run with the local paper's story "Allegations of Nursing Home Negligence," next to a photograph of the two-inch chasm in the Paradise window made lurid by the journalist's ink. They'd also run a bad photo of his mother. Her face had been washed out by the fluorescent light. She was old, Nal realized. It looked like the "scandal" had aged her. Nal had stared at his mother's gray face and seen a certain future, something you didn't need a bird to augur.

He wouldn't even show her, he decided. What was the point of coming back here? The screw couldn't shut that window now.

Nal was shooting hoops on the public court half a mile from Mr. McGowen's house when Samson found him. A fine dust from the nearby construction site kept blowing over in clouds whenever the wind picked up. Nal had to kick a crust of gravel off the asphalt so that he could dribble the ball.

"Hey, buddy, I've been looking everywhere for you. Mom says you two had a fight?"

Nal shoots, whispered the homunculus. He turned away from Samson and planted his feet on the asphalt. Shooter's roll—the ball teetered on the edge and at the last moment fell into the basket. "It was nothing; it was about college again. What do you need?"

"Just a tiny loan so I can buy Vanessa a ring. Mr. Tarak's going to let me do it in installments."

"Mr. Tarak said that?" Nal had always thought of Mr. Tarak as a CASH ONLY!!! sort of merchant. He had a spleeny hatred of everyone under thirty-five and liked telling Nal his new haircut made him look like the Antichrist.

Samson laughed. "Yeah, well, he knows I'm good for it." He was used to the fact that people went out of their way for him. It made strangers happy to see Samson happy and so they'd give him things, let him run up a tab with them, just to buoy that feeling.

"What kind of ring? A wedding ring?"

"Nah, it's just . . . I dunno. She'll like it. Tiny flowers on the inside part, what do you call that . . ."

"The band." Nal's eyes were on the red square on the backboard; he squatted into his thin calves. "Are you in love?"

Samson snorted. "We're having fun, Nal. We're having a good time." He shrugged. "It's her birthday, help me out."

"Sorry," Nal said, shooting again. "I got nothing."

"You've got nothing, huh?" Samson leaned in and made a playful grab for the ball, and Nal slugged him in the stomach.

"Jesus! What's wrong with you?"

Nal stared at his fist in amazement. He'd had no idea that swing was in the works. Wind pushed the ball downcourt and he flexed his empty hands. When his brother took a step toward him he swung wide and slammed his fist into the left shoulder—pain sprang into his knuckles and Nal had time to cock his fist back again. He thought, *I am going to really mess you up here,* right before Samson shoved him down onto the gravel. He stared down at Nal with an open mouth, his bare chest contracting. No visible signs of injury there, he saw with something close to disappointment. The basket craned above them. Blood and pebbled pits colored Nal's palms and raked up the sides of his legs. He could feel, strangest of all, a grin spreading on his face.

"Did I hurt you?" Nal asked. He was still sitting on the blacktop. He noticed that Samson was wearing his socks.

"What's your problem?" Samson said. He wasn't looking at Nal. One hand shielded his eyes, the sun pleating his forehead, and he looked like a sailor scouting for land beyond the blue gravel. "You don't want to help me out, just say so. Fucking learn to behave like a normal person."

"I can't help you," Nal called after him.

Later that afternoon, when Strong Beach was turning a hundred sorbet colors in the sun, Nal walked down the esplanade to Mr. Tarak's pawnshop. He saw the ring right away—it was in the front display, nested in a cheap navy box between old radios and men's watches, a quarter-full bottle of Chanel.

"Repent," said Mr. Tarak without looking up from his newspaper. "Get a man's haircut."

"I'd like to buy this ring here," Nal tapped on the glass.

"On hold."

"I can make the payment right now, sir. In full."

Mr. Tarak shoved up off his stool and took it out. It didn't look like a wedding band; it was a simple, wrought-iron thing with a floral design etched on the inside. Nal found he didn't care about the first woman who had pawned or lost it, or Samson who wanted to buy it. Nal was the owner now. He paid and pocketed the ring.

Before he went to catch the 3:03 bus to Vanessa's house, Nal walked back to the pinewoods. If he was really going through with this, he didn't want to take any chances that these birds would sabotage his plan. He took his basketball and fitted it in the hollow.

The gulls were back, circumnavigating the pine at different velocities, screeching irritably. He watched with some satisfaction as one scraped its wing back against the ball. He patted the ring in his pocket. He knew this was just a temporary fix. There was no protecting against the voracity of the gulls. If fate was just a disintegrating blanket—some fraying skein that the gulls were tearing right this second—then Nal didn't see why he couldn't also find a loose thread, and pull.

Vanessa's house was part of a new community on the outskirts of Athertown. The bus drove past the long neck of a crane rising out of an exposed gravel pit, the slate glistening with recent rain. A summer shower had rolled in from the east and tripped some of the streetlights prematurely. The gulls had not made it this far inland yet; the only birds here were sparrows and a few doll-like cockatoos along the fences.

Vanessa seemed surprised and happy to see him. "Come in," she said, her thin face filling the doorway. She looked scrubbed and plain, not the way she did with Samson. "Nobody's home but me. Is Sam with you?"

"No," said Nal. For years he'd been planning to say to her, "I think we're meant to be," but now that he was here he didn't say anything; his heart was going, and he almost had to stop himself from shoving his way inside.

"I brought you this," he said, pushing the ring at her. "I've been saving up for it."

"Nal!" she said, turning the ring over in her hands. "But this is really beautiful . . ."

It was easy. What had he worried about? He just stepped in and kissed her, touched her neck. Suddenly he was feeling every temperature at once, the coolness of her skin and the wet warmth of her mouth and even the tepid slide of sweat over his knuckles. She kissed him back, and Nal slid his hand beneath the neckline of her blouse and touched the bandage there. The Grigalunases' house was dark and still inside, the walls lined with framed pictures of dark-haired girls who looked like funhouse images of Vanessa, her sisters or her former selves. An orange cat darted under the stairwell.

"Nal? Do you want to sit down?" She addressed this to her own face in the foyer mirror, a glass crescent above the door, and when she turned back to Nal her eyes had brightened, charged with some anticipation that almost didn't seem to include him. Nal kissed her again and started steering her toward the living room. A rope was pulling him forward, a buried cable, and he was only able to relax into it now because he had spent his short lifetime doing up all the knots. Perhaps this is how the future works, Nal thought —nothing fated or inevitable but just these knots like fists that you could tighten or undo.

Nal and Vanessa sat down on the green sofa, a little stiffly. Nal had never so much as grazed a girl's knee but somehow he was kissing her neck, he was sliding a hand up her leg, beneath the elastic band of her underwear . . .

Vanessa struggled to undo Nal's belt and the tab of his jeans and now she looked up at him; his zipper was stuck. He was trapped inside his pants. Thanks to his recent weight loss, he was able to wriggle out of them, tugging furiously at the denim. At last he got them off with a grunt of satisfaction and, breathless and red-faced, flung them to the floor. The zipper liner left a nasty scratch down his skin. Nal began to unroll his socks, hunching over and angling his hipbones. It was strange to see the splay of his dark toes on the Grigalunases' carpet, Vanessa half-naked beyond it.

She could have whinnied with laughter at him; instead, with a kindness that you can't teach people, she had walked over to the windows while Nal hopped and writhed. She had taken off her shirt and unwound the bandage and was shimmying out of her bra. The glass had gone dark with thunderheads. The smell of rain had crept into the house. She drew the curtains and slid out of the rest of her clothes. The living room was a blue cave now—Nal could see the soft curve of the sofa's back in the dark. Was he supposed to turn the light on? Which way was more romantic? "Sorry," he said as they both walked back to the sofa, their eyes flicking all over one another. Vanessa slid a hand over Nal's torso.

"You and Samson have the same boxer shorts," she said.

"Our mother buys them for us."

Maybe this isn't going to happen, Nal thought.

But then he saw a glint of silver and felt recommitted. Vanessa had slipped the pawnshop ring on—it was huge on her. She caught him looking and held her hand up, letting the ring slide over her knuckle, and they both let out jumpy laughs. Nal could feel sweat collecting on the back of his neck. They tried kissing again for a while. Vanessa's dark hair slid through his hands like palmfuls of oil as he fumbled his way inside her, started to move. He wanted to ask: Is this right? Is this okay? It wasn't at all what he'd imagined. Nal, moving on top of Vanessa, was still Nal, still cloaked with consciousness and inescapably himself. He didn't feel invincible—he felt clumsy, guilty. Vanessa was trying to help him find his rhythm, her hands just above his bony hips.

"Hey," Vanessa said at one point, turning her face to the side. "The cat's watching."

The orange tabby was licking its paws on the first stair, beneath the clock. The cat had somehow gotten hold of the stop screw—it must have fallen out of his pocket—and was batting it around.

The feeling of arrival Nal was after kept receding like a charcoal line on bright water. This was not the time or the place but he kept picturing the gulls, screaming and wheeling in a vortex just beyond him, and he groaned and sped up his motions. "Don't stop," Vanessa said, and there was such a catch to her voice that Nal said, "I won't, I won't," with real seriousness, like a parent reassuring a child. Although very soon, Nal could feel, he would have to.

JIM SHEPARD

The Netherlands Lives with Water

FROM *McSweeney's*

A LONG TIME AGO a man had a dog that went down to the shoreline every day and howled. When she returned the man would look
at her blankly. Eventually the dog got exasperated. "Hey," the dog
said. "There's a shitstorm of biblical proportions headed your way."
"Please. I'm busy," the man said. "Hey," the dog said the next day,
and told him the same thing. This went on for a week. Finally the
man said, "If you say that once more I'm going to take you out to
sea and dump you overboard." The next morning the dog went
down to the shoreline again, and the man followed. "Hey," the dog
said, after a minute. "Yeah?" the man said. "Oh, I think you know,"
the dog said.

"Or here's another one," Cato says to me. "Adam goes to God,
'Why'd you make Eve so beautiful?' And God says, 'So you would
love her.' And Adam says, 'Well, why'd you make her so stupid?'
And God says, 'So she would love you.'"

Henk laughs. "Well, he thinks it's funny," Cato says.

"He's eleven years old," I tell her.

"And very precocious," she reminds me. Henk makes an overly
jovial face and holds two thumbs up. His mother takes her napkin
and wipes some egg from his chin.

We met in the same pre-university track. I was a year older but
hadn't passed Dutch and so took it again with her.

"You failed Dutch?" she whispered from her seat behind me.
She'd seen me gaping at her when I'd come in. The teacher had
announced that that's what those of us who were older were doing
there.

"It's your own language," she told me later that week. She was holding my penis upright so she could run the edge of her lip along the shaft. I felt like I was about to touch the ceiling.

"You're not very articulate," she remarked later, on the subject of the sounds I'd produced.

She acted as though I were a spot of sun in an otherwise rainy month. We always met at her house, a short bicycle ride away, and her parents seemed to be perpetually asleep or dead. In three months I saw her father from behind once. She explained that she'd been raised by depressives, and that they'd left her one of those girls who'd sit on the playground with the tools of happiness all around her and refuse to play. Her last boyfriend had walked out on her the week before we'd met. His diagnosis had been that she imposed on everyone else the gloom her family had taught her to expect.

"Do I sadden you?" she'd ask me late at night before taking me in her mouth. "Will you have children with me?" I started asking her back.

And she was flattered and seemed pleased without being particularly fooled. "I've been thinking about how hard it is to pull information out of you," she told me one night when we'd pitched our clothes out from under her comforter. I asked what she wanted to know and she said that that was the kind of thing she was talking about. While she was speaking I watched her front teeth, glazed from our kissing. When she had a cold and her nose was blocked up, she looked a little dazed in profile.

"I ask a question and you ask another one," she complained. "If I ask what your old girlfriend was like you ask what anyone's old girlfriend is like."

"So ask what you want to ask," I told her.

"Do you think that someone like you and someone like me should be together?" she said.

"Because we're so different?" I wanted to know.

"Do you think that someone like you and someone like me should be together?" she repeated.

"Yes," I told her.

"That's helpful. Thanks," she responded. And then she wouldn't see me for a week. When I felt I'd waited long enough, I intercepted her on her way home and asked, "Was the right answer no?" And she smiled and kissed me as though hunting up some compensation for diminished expectations. After that it was as if we'd agreed to give ourselves over to what we had. When I put my mouth on her, her hands would bend back at the wrists as if miming helplessness. I disappeared for minutes at a time from my classes, envisioning the trancelike way her lips would part after so much kissing.

The next time she asked me to tell her something about myself I had some candidates lined up. She held my hands away from her and the result tented the comforter to provide some cooling air. I told her I still remembered the way my older sister replaced her indigo hair bow with an orange one on royal birthdays. I remembered the way I followed her, chanting that she was a pig, and the way I was always unjustly punished for that. How I fed her staggeringly complicated lies that went on for weeks and ended in disaster with my parents or teachers. How before she died of the flu epidemic I slept in her bed the last three nights.

Her cousins had died then as well, Cato told me. If somebody even just brought up 2015, her aunt still went to pieces. She didn't let go of my hands so I went on. I told her that, being an outsider as a little boy, I'd noticed that *something* was screwed up with me, but I couldn't put my finger on what. I probably wasn't as baffled by it as I sounded, but it was still more than I'd ever told anyone else.

She'd grown up right off the Boompjes; I'd been way out in Pernis, looking at the Caltex refinery through the haze. The little fishing village was still there then, huddled in the center of the petrochemical sprawl. My sister loved the lights of the complex at night and the fires that went hundreds of feet into the air like solar flares when the waste gases burned off. Kids from other neighborhoods always noticed the smell on our skin. The light was that golden sodium-vapor light, and my father liked to say about it that it was always Christmas in Pernis. At night I'd be able to read with my bedroom lamp off. In the mornings while we got ready for school the dredging platforms with their twin pillars would disappear up into the fog like Gothic cathedrals.

A week after I told her all that, I introduced her to Kees. "I've never seen him like this," he told her. We were both on track for one of the technology universities, maybe Eindhoven, and he hadn't failed Dutch. "Well, I'm a pretty amazing woman," she explained to him.

Kees and I both went on to study physical geography and got

into the water sector. Cato became the media liaison for the program director for Rotterdam Climate Proof. We got married after our third International Knowledge for Climate Research conference. Kees asked us recently which anniversary we had coming up and I said eleventh and she said one hundredth.

It didn't take a crystal ball to realize that we were in a growth industry. Gravity and thermal measurements by GRACE satellites had already flagged the partial shutdown of the Atlantic circulation system. The World Glacier Monitoring Service, saddled with having to release one glum piece of news after another, had just that year reported that the Pyrenees, Africa, and the Rockies were all glacier-free. The Americans had just confirmed the collapse of the West Antarctic ice sheet. Once-in-a-century floods in England were now occurring every two years. Bangladesh was almost entirely a bay and that whole area a war zone because of the displacement issues.

It's the catastrophe for which the Dutch have been planning for fifty years. Or really, for as long as we've existed: we had cooperative water management before we had a state. The one created the other: either we pulled together as a collective or got swept away as individuals. The real old-timers had a saying for when things fucked up: "Well, the Netherlands lives with water." What they meant was that their land flooded twice a day.

Bishop Prudentius of Troyes wrote in his annals that in the ninth century the whole of the country was devoured by the sea: that all the settlements disappeared and that the water was higher than the dunes. In the Saint Felix Flood, North Beveland was completely swept away. In the All Saints' Flood the entire coast was inundated between Flanders and Germany. In 1717 a dike collapse killed fourteen thousand on Christmas night.

"You like going on like this, don't you?" Cato sometimes asks.

"I like the way it focuses your attention," I told her once.

"Do you like the way it scares our son?" she wanted to know.

"It doesn't scare me," Henk told us.

"It *does* scare you," she told him. "And your father doesn't seem to register that." For the last few years when I've announced that the sky is falling she's answered that our son doesn't need to hear it. And that I always bring it up when there's something else to be discussed. I always concede her point but that doesn't get me off the hook. "For instance, I'm still waiting to hear how your mother's making out," she complains during a dinner when we can't tear Henk's attention away from the Feyenoord celebrations. If a team wins the Cup, the whole town gets drunk. If it loses, the whole town gets drunk.

My mother's now at the point at which no one can deny it's dementia. She's still in the little house on Polluxstraat, even though the rest of the Pernis she knew seems to have evaporated around her. Cato finds it unconscionable that I've allowed her to stay there on her own, without help. "Let me guess: you don't want to talk about it," she says whenever she brings it up.

She doesn't know the half of it. The day after my father's funeral my mother brought me into their bedroom and revealed to me the paperwork on what she called their Rainy Day Account, a staggering amount. Where had they gotten so much? "Your father," she told me unhelpfully. I went home that night and Cato asked what was new and I told her about my mother's regime of short walks.

Each step of the way in the transfer of assets, financial advisers or bank officers have asked if my wife's name would be on the account as well. She still has no idea it exists. It means that I now have a secret net worth more than triple my family's. What am I up to? Your guess is as good as mine.

"Have you talked to anyone about the live-in position?" Cato wants to know. I'd raised the idea with my mother and she'd started shouting that she never should have showed me the money. Since then I've been less bullish about bringing Cato and Henk around to see her.

I tell her that things are progressing the way we would hope.

"Things are progressing the way we would hope?" Cato repeats.

"That's it in a nutshell," I tell her, a little playfully, but her expression makes clear that she's waiting for a fuller explanation.

"Don't you have homework?" I ask Henk, and he and his mother exchange a look. I've always believed that I'm a master at hiding my feelings, but I seem to be alone in that regard.

Cato's been through this before in various iterations. When my mother was first diagnosed, I hashed through the whole thing with Kees, who'd been in my office when the call had come in, and then told Cato later that night that there'd been no change, so as not to have to trudge through the whole story again. The doctor had called the next day when I was out to see how I was taking the news.

Henk looks at me like he's using my face to attempt some long division. Cato eats without saying anything until she finally loses her temper with the cutlery.

"I told you before that if you don't want to do this, I can," she says.

"There's nothing that needs doing," I tell her.

"There's plenty that needs doing," she says. She pulls the remote from Henk and switches off the news. "Look at him," she complains to Henk. "He's always got his eyes somewhere else. Does he even know he shakes his head when he listens?"

Pneumatic hammers pick up where they left off outside our window. There's always construction somewhere. Why not rip up the streets? The Germans did such a good job of it in 1940 that it's as if we've been competing with them ever since. Rotterdam: a deep hole in the pavement with a sign telling you to approach at your own risk. Our whole lives, walking through the city has meant muddy shoes.

As we're undressing that night she asks how I'd rate my recent performance as a husband.

I don't know; maybe not so good, not so bad, I tell her.

She answers that if I were a minister, I'd resign.

What area are we talking about here, in terms of performance? I want to know.

"Go to sleep," she tells me, and turns off the lamp.

If climate change is a hammer to the Dutch, the hammer's coming down more or less where we live. Rotterdam's astride an estuarine area that absorbs the Scheldt, Meuse, and Rhine outflows, and what we're facing is that troika of sea-level rise, peak river discharges, and extreme weather events. We've got the jewel of our water defenses—the massive water barriers at Maeslant and Dordrecht, and the rest of the Delta Works—ready to shut off the North Sea during the next cataclysmic storms, but what are we to do when that coincides with the peak river discharges? Sea levels are leaping up, our ground is subsiding, it's raining harder and more often, and our program of managed flooding—Make Room

for the Rivers—was overwhelmed long ago. The dunes and dikes
at eleven locations from Ter Heijde to Westkapelle no longer meet
what we decided would be the minimum safety standards. Temporary emergency measures are starting to be known to the public as
Hans Brinkers.

And this winter's been a festival of bad news. Kees's team has
measured increased snowmelt in the Alps to go along with prolonged rainfall across northern Europe and steadily increasing
wind speeds during gales, all of which are leading to ominously increased winter flows, especially for the Rhine. He and I—known
around the office as The Pessimists—forecasted this winter's discharge at eighteen thousand cubic meters per second. It's now up
to twenty-one. What are those of us in charge of dealing with that
supposed to do? A megastorm at this point would overwhelm the
barriers from both sides and inundate Rotterdam and its surroundings—three million people—in twenty-four hours.

Which is quite the challenge for someone in media relations.
"Remember, the Netherlands will always be here," Cato likes to say
as her way of signing off with one of the news agencies. "Though
probably under three meters of water," she'll add after she's
hung up.

Before this most recent emergency, my area of expertise had to
do with the strength and loading of the Water Defense structures,
especially in terms of the Scheldt estuary. We'd been integrating
forecasting and security software for high-risk areas and trying to
get Arcadis to understand that it needed to share almost everything with IBM and vice versa. I'd even been lent out to work on
the Venice, London, and St. Petersburg Surge Barriers. But now all
of us were back home and thrown into the Weak Links Project, that
overeducated fire brigade composed to rush off to address new
vulnerabilities as they emerged.

And we all have our faces turned helplessly to the Alps. There's
been a series of cloudbursts on the eastern slopes: fourteen inches
of rain in the last two weeks. The Germans have long since raised
their river dikes to funnel the water right past them and into the
Netherlands. Some of that water will be taken up in the soil, some
in lakes and ponds and catchment basins, and some in polders
and farmland that we've set aside for flooding emergencies. Some
in water plazas and water gardens and specially designed under-

ground parking garages and reservoirs. The rest will keep moving downriver to Rotterdam and the closed surge barriers.

"Well, change is the soul of Rotterdam," Kees joked when we first looked at the numbers on the meteorological disaster ahead. We were given private notification that there would be vertical evacuation if the warning time for an untenable situation were under two hours, and horizontal evacuation if it were over two.

"What am I supposed to do—tell the helicopter that we have to pop over to Henk's school?" Cato wanted to know when I told her. He now has an agreed-upon code: when it appears on his iFuze, he's to leave school immediately and head to her office.

But in the meantime, we operate as though it won't come to that. We think: We'll come up with something. We always have. Where would New Orleans or the Mekong Delta be without Dutch hydraulics and Dutch water management? And where would the U.S. and Europe be if we hadn't led the way out of the financial Panic and Depression, just by being ourselves? E.U. dominoes from Iceland to Ireland to Italy came down around our ears but there we sat, having been protected by our own Dutchness. What was the joke about us, after all? That we didn't go to the banks to take money out; we went to put money in. Who was going to be the first, as economy after economy capsized, to pony up the political courage to nationalize their banks and work cooperatively? Well, who took more seriously the public good than the Dutch? Who was more in love with rules? Who tells anyone who'll listen that we're providing the rest of the world with a glimpse of what the future will be?

After a third straight sleepless night—"Oh, who gets any sleep in the water sector?" Kees answered irritably the morning I complained about it—I leave the office early and ride a water taxi to Pernis. In Nieuwe Maas the shipping is so thick that it's like kayaking through canyons, and the taxi captain charges extra for what he calls a piloting fee. We tip and tumble on the backswells while four tugs nudge a supertanker sideways into its berth. The tugs look like puppies snuffling at the base of a cliff. The tanker's hull is so high that we can't see any superstructure above it.

I hike from the dock to Polluxstraat, the traffic on the A4 above rolling like surf. "Look who's here," my mother says, instead of hello. She goes about her tea-making as though I dropped in unannounced every afternoon. We sit in the breakfast nook off the kitchen. Before she settles in, she reverses the pillow embroidered *Good Night* so that it now reads *Good Morning*.

"How's Henk?" she wants to know. I tell her he's got some kind of chest thing. "As long as they're healthy," she replies. I don't see any reason to quibble.

The bottom shelves of her refrigerator are puddled with liquid from deliquescing vegetables and something spilled. The bristles of her bottle scraper on the counter are coated with dried mayonnaise. The front of her nightgown is an archipelago of stains. "How's Cato?" she asks.

"Cato wants to know if we're going to get you some help," I tell her.

"I just talked with her. She didn't say anything like that," she says irritably.

"You talked with her? What'd you talk about?" I ask. But she waves me off. "Did you talk with her or not?" I ask again.

"That girl from up north you brought here to meet me, I couldn't even understand her," she tells me. She talks about regional differences as though her country's the size of China.

"We thought she seemed very efficient," I tell her. "What else did Cato talk with you about?"

But she's already shifted her interest to the window. Years ago she had a traffic mirror mounted outside on the frame to let her spy on the street unobserved. She uses a finger to widen the gap in the lace curtains.

What else should she do all day long? She never goes out. The street's her revival house, always showing the same movie.

The holes in her winter stockings are patched with a carnival array of colored thread. We always lived by that old maxim that a thing lasted longer mended than new. My whole life, I heard that with thrift and hard work I could build a mansion. My father had in his office at home a typewritten note tacked to the wall: *Let those with abundance remember that they are surrounded by thorns.* "Who said *that?*" Cato asked when we were going through his things. "Calvin," I told her. "Well, you would know," she said.

He hadn't been so much a conservative as a man whose life philosophy had boiled down to the principle of no nonsense. I'd noticed even as a tiny boy that whenever he'd liked a business associate or a woman, that's what he said about them.

My mother's got her nose to the glass at this point. "You think you're the only one with secrets," she remarks.

"What's that supposed to mean?" I ask, but she acts as though she's not going to dignify my response. Follow-up questions don't get anywhere, either. I sit with her awhile longer. We watch a Chinese game show. I soak her bread in milk, and walk her to the toilet. I tell her we have to at least think about moving her bed downstairs somewhere. The steps to her second floor are vertiginous even by Dutch standards, and the treads accommodate less than half your foot. She makes an effort to follow what I seem to be on about, puzzling out that she needs to puzzle out something. But then her expression dissipates. She complains that she spent half the night looking for the coffee grinder.

"Why were you looking for the coffee grinder?" I ask her. I have to repeat the question. Then I have to stop, for fear of frightening her.

Henk's class is viewing a presentation at the Climate Campus—*Water: Precious Resource and Deadly Companion*—so we have the dinner table to ourselves. Cato's day was even longer than mine so I prepared the meal: two cans of pea soup with pigs' knuckles and some Belgian beer. She's too tired to complain. She's dealing with both the Americans, who are always hectoring for clarification on the changing risk factors for our projects in Miami and New Orleans, and the Germans, who've publicly dug in their heels on the issue of accepting any spillover from the Rhine in order to take some of the pressure off the situation downstream.

It's the usual debate, as far as the latter argument's concerned. We take the high road—it's only through cooperation that we can face such monumental challenges, etc.—and another country scoffs at our aspirations toward ever more comprehensive safety measures. The German foreign minister last year accused us on a simulcast of being old women.

"Maybe he's right," Cato says wearily. "Sometimes I wonder what it'd be like to be in a country where you don't need a license to build a fence around your garden."

Exasperated, we indulge in a little Dutch bashing. No one complains about themselves as well as the Dutch. Cato asks if I remember that story about the manufacturers having to certify that each of the chocolate letters handed out by Santa Claus contained an

equal amount of chocolate. I remind her about the number-one
download of the year turning out to have been *fireworks sound effects,* for those New Year's revelers who found real fireworks too
worrisome.

After we stop, she looks at me, her mouth a little slack. "Why
does this sort of thing make us horny?" she wants to know.

"Maybe it's the pea soup," I tell her in the shower. She's examining little crescents of fingernail marks where she held me when she
came. She turns off the water and we wrap ourselves in the bed
sheet–size towel she had made in Surinam. Cocooned on the floor
in the tiny steamy bathroom, we discuss Kees's love life. He now
shops at a singles' supermarket, the kind where if you're taken, you
use a blue basket and if you're available, a yellow. When I asked
him how his latest fling was working out, he said, "Well, I'm back to
the yellow basket."

Cato thinks it's a funny story. "How'd *we* get to be so lucky?" I ask
her. We're spooning and she does a minimal grind against me that
allows me to grow inside her.

"The other day someone from BBC One asked my boss that
same question about how he ended up where he did," she says. She
turns her cheek so I can kiss it.

"What'd he say?" I ask when I've moved from her cheek to her
neck. She's not a big fan of her boss.

She shrugs comfortably, her shoulder blades against my chest. I
wrap my arms tighter so the fit is even more perfect. She tells me
that the gist of his answer was: Mostly by not asking too many questions.

My mother always had memory problems, and even before my sister died my father always said that he didn't blame her: she'd seen
her own brothers swept away in the 1953 flood and had been a
wreck for years afterward. The night after her sixth birthday, January 31, a storm field that covered the entire North Sea swept down
out of the northwest with winds that registered gale force 11 and
combined with a spring tide to raise the sea six meters over NAP.
The breakers overtopped the dikes in eighty-nine locations over a
hundred-and-seventy-kilometer stretch and hollowed them out on
their land sides so that the surges that followed broke them. My
mother remembered eating her soup alongside her brothers while
they listened to the wind increase in volume until her father went

out to see to the barn and the draft from the opened door blew their board game off the table. Her mother's Bible pages flapped in her hands like panicked birds. Water was seeping through the window casing and her brother touched it and held his finger for her to taste. She remembered his look when she realized that it was salty: not rain but spray from the sea.

Her father returned to tell them that they all had to leave, now. They held hands in a chain and he went first and she went second and once the door was opened the wind staggered him and blew her off her feet.

He managed to retrieve her, but by then they couldn't find the others in the dark and the rain. She was soaked in ice and the water was already up to their thighs and in the distance she could see breakers where the dike had been. They headed inland and found refuge in the open door of a neighbor's brick home and discovered the back half of the house already torn away by the water. He led her up the stairs to the third floor and through a trap onto the roof. Their neighbors were already there, and her mother, huddling against the force of the wind and the cold. The house west of them imploded but its roof held together and was pushed upright in front of theirs, diverting the main force of the flood around them like a breakwater. She remembered holding her father's hand so that their bodies would be found in the same place. Her mother shrieked and pointed and she saw her brothers beside a man with a bundle and a woman with a baby on the roof of the house beyond theirs to the east. Each wave that broke against the front drenched them with spray, and the woman kept turning her torso to shield the baby. And then the front of the house caved in and everyone on it became bobbing heads in the water that were swept around the collapsing walls and away.

She remembered the wind having finally died down by midmorning, and a mist continuing out of the gray sky, and a fishing smack way off to the north coasting between the rooftops, bringing people on board. She remembered a dog lowered on a rope, its paws flailing as it turned.

After their rescue, she remembered a telegraph pole slanted over, its wires tugged by the current. She remembered the water smelling of gasoline and mud. She remembered treetops uncovered by the waves and a clog between two steep roofs filled with floating branches and dead cattle. She remembered a vast plain of wreckage on the water. She remembered that sea-smell of dead fish that traveled along the wind. She remembered two older boys sitting beside her examining the silt driven inside an unopened bottle of soda by the force of the waves. She remembered her mother's animal sounds and the length of time it took to get to dry land, and her father's chin on her mother's bent back, his head bumping whenever they crossed the wakes of the other boats.

We always knew this was coming. Years ago the city fathers of Rotterdam thought: This is our big opportunity. We're no longer just the ugly port or Amsterdam without the attractions. The bad news was going to impact us first and foremost, so we put out the word: we were looking for people with the nerve to put into practice what was barely possible anywhere else. The result was Waterplan 4 Rotterdam, with all-new approaches to water storage and water safety: water plazas, super cisterns, water balloons, green roofs, and even traffic tunnels that doubled as immense drainage systems, would all siphon off danger. It roped in Kees and Cato and me and by the end of the first week had set Cato against us. Her mandate was to showcase Dutch ingenuity, so the last thing she needed was The Pessimists buzzing about clamoring for more funding because nothing anyone had come up with yet was going to work. As far as she was concerned, our country was the testing ground for all high-profile adaptive measures and practically oriented knowledge and prototype projects that would attract worldwide attention and become a sluice-gate for high-tech exports. She spent her days in the international marketplace hawking the notion that *Here we're safe because we have the knowledge and we're using that knowledge to find creative solutions.* We were all assuming a secure population to be a collective social good for which the government and private sector would remain responsible: a notion not universally embraced by other countries, we realized.

Sea-facing barriers are inspected by hand and laser imaging. Smart dikes schedule their own maintenance based on sensors that detect seepage or changes in pressure and stability. Satellites track ocean currents and water-mass volumes. The areas most at risk have been divided into dike-ring compartments in an attempt to make the country a system of watertight doors. Our road and infrastructure networks now function independently of the ground layer. Nine entire neighborhoods have been made amphibious: built on hollow platforms that will rise with the water but remain anchored to submerged foundations. And besides the giant storm barriers, atop our dikes we've mounted titanium-braced walls that unfold from concrete channels, leviathan-like inflatable rubber dams, and special grasses grown on plastic mat revetments to anchor the inner walls.

Is it all enough? Henk wants to know, whenever there's a day of unremitting rain. Oh, honey, it's more than enough, Cato tells him. And then she quizzes him on our emergency code.

"It's funny how this kind of work has been good for me," Cato says. She's asked to go for a walk, an activity she knows I'll find nostalgically stirring. We tramped all over the city before and after lovemaking when we first got together. "All of this end-of-the-world stuff apparently cheers me up," she remarks. "I guess it's the same thing I used to get at home. All those glum faces, and I had to do the song and dance that explained why they got out of bed in the morning."

"The heavy lifting," I tell her.

"Exactly," she says with a faux mournfulness. "The heavy lifting. We're on for another simulcast tomorrow and it'll be three Germans with long faces and Cato the Optimist."

We negotiate a herd of bicycles on a plaza and she veers toward the harbor. We walk a little ways in single file. When we cross the skylights of the traffic tunnels, giant container haulers shudder by beneath our feet. She has a beautiful back, accentuated by the military cut of her overcoat. "Except that the people you're dealing with now *want* to be fooled," I tell her.

"It's not that they want to be fooled," she corrects. "It's just that they're not convinced that they need to go around glum all the time."

"How'd that philosophy work with your parents?" I ask.

"Not so well," she says sadly.

We turn onto Boompjes, which is sure to add to her melancholy. A seven-story construction crane with legs curving inward perches like a spider over the river.

"Your mother called about the coffee grinder," she remarks. "I couldn't pin down what she was talking about."

Boys in bathing suits are pitching themselves off the high dock by the Strand, though it seems much too cold for that, and the river too dirty. Even in the chill I can smell tar and rope and, somewhere, fresh bread.

"She called you or you called her?" I ask.

"I just told you," Cato says.

"It seems odd that she would call you," I tell her.

"What *was* she talking about?" Cato wants to know.

"I assume she was having trouble working the coffee grinder," I tell her.

"Working it or finding it?" she asks.

"Working it, I think," I suggest. "She called you?"

"Oh my God," Cato says.

"I'm just asking," I tell her after a minute.

All of Maashaven is blocked from view by a giant Suction Dredger that's being barged out to Maasvlakte 2. It's preceded by six tugs in the parade and looks like a small city going by. The thing uses dragheads connected to tubes the size of railway tunnels, and harvests sand down to a depth of twenty meters. It'll be deepening the docking areas out at Yangtzehaven, Europahaven, and Mississippihaven. There's been some worry that all of this dredging has been undermining the water defenses on the other side of the channel, which is the last thing we need. Kees has been dealing with their horseshit for a few weeks now.

We stop on a bench in front of some law offices. Over the front entrance, cameras have been installed to monitor the surveillance cameras, which have been vandalized. Once the Dredger has passed, we can see a family of day campers across the way who've pitched their tent on a berm overlooking the channel.

"Isn't it too cold for camping?" I ask her.

"Wasn't it too cold for swimming?" she responds, about the boys we passed.

She says Henk keeps replaying the same footage on his iFuze of Feyenoord's MVP being lowered into the stadium beneath the team flag by a VSTOL. "So here's what I'm thinking," she continues, as though that led her to her next thought. She mentions a conservatory in Berlin, fantastically expensive, that runs a winter program in chamber music. She'd like to send Henk there during his winter break, and maybe longer.

This seems to me to be mostly about his safety, though I don't acknowledge that. He's a gifted cellist, but hardly seems devoted to the instrument.

She repeats the amount it will cost with her pitchman's good cheer, though we don't have it. It's the daily rate for a five-star hotel. But she believes that money can always be found for a good idea, and if it can't, it wasn't a good idea. And her husband is, after all, a hydraulic engineer, the equivalent of an atomic physicist in terms of technological prestige.

Atomic physicists don't make a whole lot of money, either, I remind her. And our argument proceeds from there. I can see her disappointment expanding as we speak, and even as the result contracts my inner organs, I sit on the information of my hidden nest egg and allow all of the unhappiness to unfold. It all takes forever. The word in our country for the decision-making process is the same as the word for what we pour over our pancakes. Our national mindset pivots around the word *but:* as in, *This, yes, but that, too.* Cato puts her fingers to her temples and sheaths her cheeks with her palms. Her arguments run aground on my tolerance, which has been elsewhere described as a refusal to listen. Passion in Dutch meetings is punished by being ignored. The idea is that it's the argument itself that matters, and not the intensity with which it's presented. Outright rejections of a position are rare; what you get instead are suggestions for improvement that if followed would annihilate the original intent. And then everyone checks their agendas to schedule the next meeting.

Just like that, we're walking back. We're single file again, and it's gotten colder.

From our earliest years, we're taught not to burden others with our emotions. A young Amsterdammer in the Climate Campus is known as the Thespian because he sobbed in public at a co-worker's funeral. "You don't need to eliminate your emotions," Kees reminded him when he complained about it. "You just need to be a little more economical with them."

Another thing I've never told Cato: my sister and I had been jumping into the river in the winter as well, the week before she caught the flu. That had been my idea. When she'd come out, her feet and lips had been blue. She'd sneezed all the way home. "Do you think I'll catch a cold?" she asked that night. "Go to sleep," I told her in response.

We take a shortcut through the sunken pedestrian mall they call
the Shopping Gutter. By the time we reach our street it's dark and
it's raining again, and the muddy pavement is shining in the lights
of the cafés. Along the new athletic complex in the distance, sap-
phire blue searchlights are lancing up into the rain at even intervals, like a landscape's harp strings. "I don't know if you *know*
what this does to me, or you don't," Cato says at our doorstep, once
she's stopped and turned. Her thick brown hair is beaded with
moisture where it's not soaked. "But either way, it's just so miserable."

I actually *have* the solution to our problem, I'm reminded as I
follow her up the stairs. The thought makes me feel rehabilitated,
as though I've told her instead of only myself.

Cato always said about her parents' marriage that they practiced a
sort of apocalyptic utilitarianism: on the one hand they were sure
everything was going to hell in a handbasket, while on the other
they continued to operate as though they could turn things around
with a few practical measures.

But there's always that moment in a country's history when it
learns that the earth is less manageable than was thought. Ten
years ago we needed to conduct comprehensive assessments of the
flood defenses every five years. Now safety margins are adjusted
every six months to take new revelations into account. For the last
year and a half we've been told to build into our designs for whatever we're working on features that restrict the damaging effects
after an inevitable inundation. There won't be any retreating back
to the hinterlands, either, because given the numbers we're facing
there won't be any hinterlands. It's gotten to the point that pedestrians are banned from the sea-facing dikes in the far west even on
calm days. At the entrance to the Haringvlietdam they've erected
an immense yellow CAUTION sign that features two tiny stick figures with their arms raised in alarm at a black wave three times
their size that's curling over them.

I watched Kees's face during a recent simulation as one of his
new designs for a smart dike was overwhelmed in half the time he
would have predicted. It had always been the Dutch assumption
that we would resolve what problems faced us from a position of
strength. But we passed that station long ago. At this point each of

us understands privately that we're operating under the banner of lost control.

The next morning we're crammed into Rotterdam Climate Proof's Smartvan heading west on N211, still not speaking. Cato's driving. At 140 kilometers an hour the rain fans across the windshield energetically, racing the wipers. Gray clouds seem to be rushing in from the sea in the distance. We cross some polders that are already flooded and there's a rocking buoyancy when we traverse that part of the road that's floating. Trucks sweep by backward and recede behind us in the spray.

The only sounds are the sounds of the tires and wipers and rain. Exploring the radio is like visiting the Tower of Babel: Turks, Berbers, Cape Verdeans, Antilleans, Angolans, Portuguese, Croatians, Brazilians, Chinese. Cato managed to relocate her simulcast with her three long-faced Germans to the Hoek van Holland; she told the Germans she wanted the Maeslant Barrier as a backdrop but what she really intends is to surprise them, live, with the state of the water levels already. Out near the Barrier it's pretty dramatic. Cato the Optimist with indisputable visual evidence that the sky is falling: Can the German position remain unshaken in the face of that? Will her grandstanding work? It's hard to say. It's pretty clear that nothing else will.

"Want me to talk about Gravenzande?" I ask her. "That's the sort of thing that would certainly jolt the boys from the Reich."

"That's just what I need," she answers. "You starting a panic about something that might not even be true."

Gravenzande's where she's going to drop me, a few kilometers away. Geologists there three days ago turned up crushed shell deposits seven meters higher on the dune lines inland than anyone believed floods had ever reached. The deposits look to be only about ten thousand years old. If that ends up confirmed, it's very bad news, given what it clarifies about how cataclysmic things could get even before the climate's more recent turn for the worse.

It's Saturday, and we'll probably put in twelve hours. Henk's getting more comfortable with his weekend nanny than with us. As Cato likes to tell him when she's trying to induce him to do his chores: around here, you work. By which she means that old joke

that when you buy a shirt in Rotterdam, it comes with the sleeves
already rolled up.

We pass poplars in neat rows lining the canals, a canary yellow
smudge of a house submerged up to its second-floor windows. Beyond a roundabout, a pair of decrepit rugby goalposts.

"You're really going to announce that if the Germans pull their
weight, everything's going to be fine?" I ask. But she ignores me.

She needs a decision, she tells me a few minutes later, as though
tired of asking. Henk's winter break is coming up. I venture that I
thought it wasn't until the twelfth, and she reminds me with exasperation that it's the fifth, the schools now staggering the vacation
times to avoid overloading the transportation systems.

We pass the curved sod roofs of factories. The secret account's
not a problem but a solution, I decide, and as I model to myself
ways of implementing it as such, Cato finally asserts as though she's
waited long enough that she thinks she's found the answer: she
could take that Royal Dutch Shell offer to reconfigure its regional
media relations and they could set her up in Wannsee and Henk
could commute.

They could stay out there and get a bump in income besides.
Henk could enroll in the conservatory.

We exit N211 northwest on an even smaller access road to the
coast. Within a kilometer it ends in a turnaround next to the dunes,
and she pulls the car about so that it's pointed back toward her simulcast, then turns off the engine and sits there beside me with
her hands in her lap.

"How long has this been in the works?" I ask. She wants to know
what I mean and I tell her that it doesn't seem like so obscure a
question; that she said no to Shell years ago, so where did this new
offer come from?

She shrugs, as if I asked if they'd be paying her moving expenses.
"They called. I told them I'd listen to what they had to say."

"They called you," I tell her.

"They called me," she repeats.

She's only trying to hedge her bets, I tell myself to combat the
panic. Our country's all about spreading risk around.

"Do people just walk into this conservatory?" I ask. "Don't you
have to apply?"

She doesn't answer, which I take to mean that she and Henk
have already applied, and that he's been accepted.

"How did Henk feel about his good news?" I ask.

"He wanted to tell you," Cato answers.

"And we would see each other every other weekend? Once a month?" I'm attempting a version of steely neutrality but can hear the terror working its way forward.

"This is just one option of many," she reminds me. "We need to talk about all of them." She adds that she has to go. And that I should see the option as being primarily about Henk, and not us. I answer that the Netherlands will always be here, and she smiles and starts the van.

"You sure there's nothing else you want to talk to me about?" she asks.

"Like what?" I say. "I want to talk to you about everything."

She jiggles the gearshift lightly, considering me. "You're going to let me drive away with your having left it at that," she says.

"I don't want you to drive away at all," I tell her.

"Well, there is that," she concedes bitterly. She waits another full minute and then a curtain comes down on her expression and she puts the car in gear. She honks when she's pulling out.

At the top of the dune I watch surfers in wetsuits wading into the breakers in the rain, the waves barely enough to keep them on their boards. The rain picks up so that the sea's surface is in constant agitation. Even the surfers keep low, as if to stay out of it. The wet sand's like brown sugar in my shoes.

Five hundred thousand years ago it was possible to walk from where I live to England. At that point the Thames was a tributary of the Rhine. Even during the Romans' occupation, the Zuider Zee was dry. But by the sixth century BC we were building artificial hills out of marsh grass mixed with manure and our own refuse to keep our feet out of the water. And then in the seventeenth century Hulsebos invented the Archimedes screw, and waterwheels could raise a flow four meters higher than where it began, and we started to make real progress at keeping what the old people called the Waterwolf from the door.

In the fifteenth century Philip the Good ordered the sand dike that constituted the original Hondsbossche Seawall to be restored, and another built behind it as a backup. He named the latter the Sleeper dike. For extra security, he had another constructed behind that, and called that one the Dreamer dike. Ever since, schoolchildren have learned as one of their first geography sentences *Between Camperduin and Petten lie three dikes: the Watcher, the Sleeper, and the Dreamer.*

We're raised with the double message that we have to address our worst fears, but that they'll also somehow domesticate themselves nonetheless. Fifteen years ago Rotterdam Climate Proof revived "The Netherlands Lives with Water" as a slogan, the poster accompanying it featuring a two-panel cartoon in which a towering wave, in the first panel, is breaking over a terrified little boy before its crest, in the second, separates into immense foamy fingers so that he can relievedly shake its hand.

When Cato told me about that first offer from Shell, I could *see* her flash of feral excitement about what she was turning down. Royal Dutch Shell! She would have been fronting for one of the biggest corporations in the world. We conceived Henk a few nights later. There was a lot of urgent talk about getting deeper and closer and I remember striving once she'd guided me inside her to have my penis reach the back of her throat. Periodically we slowed into the barest sort of movement, just to further take stock of what was happening, and at one point when we paused in our tremoring, I put my lips to her ear and reminded her of what she'd passed up. After winning them over, she could have picked her city: Tokyo, Los Angeles, Rio. The notion caused in her eyes a momentary lack of focus. Then she started moving along a contraction as a response, and Shell and other options and speech evanesced away.

If she were to leave me, where would I be? It's as if she was put here to force my interaction with humans. And still I don't pull it off. It's like that story we were told as children, of Jesus telling the rich young man to go and sell all he has and give it to the poor, and the rich man choosing to keep what he has, and going away sorrowful. Kees said when we talked about it that he always assumed that the guy had settled in Holland.

That Monday, more bad news: warm air and heavy rain have ventured many meters above established snow lines in the western Alps, and Kees holds up before me with both hands GRACE's latest printouts about a storm cell the potential numbers of which we keep rechecking because they seem so extravagant. He spends the rest of the morning on the phone trying to stress that we've hit another type of threshold here; that these are calamity-level numbers. It seems to him that everyone's *saying* that they recognize the urgency of the new situation but that no one's *acting* like it. During lunch a call comes in about the hinge-and-socket joint, itself five stories high, of one of the Maeslant doors. In order to allow the doors to roll with the waves, the joints are designed to operate like a human shoulder, swinging along both horizontal and vertical axes and transferring the unimaginable stresses to the joint's foundation. The maintenance engineers are reporting that the foundation block—all fifty-two thousand tons of it—is moving.

Finally Kees flicks off his phone receptor and squeezes his eyes shut in despair. "Maybe our history's just the history of picking up after disasters like this," he tells me. "Like the way the Italians do pasta sauce, we do body retrieval."

After a few minutes of waiting for updated numbers, I call Cato and fail to get through and then try my mother, who says she's soaking her corns. I can picture the enamel basin with the legend CONTENTED FEET around the rim. The image seems to confirm that we're all just naked in the world, and I tell her to get some things together, that I'm going to be sending someone out for her, that she needs to leave town for a little while.

It's amazing that I'm able to keep trying Cato's numbers, given what's broken loose in all the levels of water management nationwide. Everyone's shouting into headpieces and clattering away at laptops at the same time. At all of the Delta stations the situation has already triggered the automatic emergency procedures with their checklists and hour-by-hour protocols. Outside my office window the canal is lined with barges of cows, of all things, awaiting their river pilot and transportation to safety. In front of them the road is a gypsy caravan of traffic piled high with suitcases and furniture and roped-down plastic bags. The occasional dog hangs from a window. Those roads that can float should allow vehicular evacuation for six or seven hours longer than the other roads will. The civil defense teams at roundabouts and intersections are doing what they can to dispense biopacs and aquacells. Through the glass everyone seems to be behaving well, though with a maximum of commotion.

I've got the mayor of Ter Heijde on one line saying he's up to his

ass in ice water and wanting to know where the fabled Weak Links
Project has gone when Cato's voice finally breaks in on the other.

"Where are you?" I shout and the mayor shouts back "Where
do you *think?*" and I kill his line and ask again and Cato answers
"What?" and in just her inflection of that one-word question, I
know that she heard what I said. "Is Henk with you?" I shout, and
Kees and some of the others around the office look up even given
that everyone's shouting. I ask again and she says that he is. I ask
if she's awaiting evacuation and she answers that she's already in
Berlin.

I'm shouting other questions when Kees cups a palm over my
receptor and says, "Here's an idea. Why don't you sort out all of
your personal problems now?"

After Cato's line goes dead, I can't raise her again, or she won't
answer. We're all engaged in such a blizzard of calls that it almost
doesn't matter. "Whoa," Kees says, his hands dropping to his desk,
and a number of our co-workers go silent as well, because the windows facing west are now black with rain and rattling. I look out
mine, and bags and other debris are tearing free of the traffic caravan and sailing east. The rain curtain hits the cows in their barges
and their ears flatten like mules' and their eyes squint shut at the
gale's power.

"Our ride is here," Kees calls, shaking my shoulder, and I realize
that everyone's in a flurry of collecting laptops and flash drives.
There's a tumult heading up the stairs to the roof and the roar of
the wind every time the outer door is opened, and the scrabbling
sounds of one last person dragging something out before the door
slams shut. And then, with surprising abruptness, it's quiet.

My window continues to shake as though it's not double pane
but cellophane. Now that our land has subsided as much as it has,
when the water does come, it will come like a wall, and each dike
that stops it will force it to turn, and in its churning, it will begin to
spiral and bore into the earth, eroding away the dike walls, until
the pressure builds and that dike collapses and it's on to the next
dike, with more pressure piling up behind, and so on and so on
until all the barriers start falling together and the water thunders
forward like a hand sweeping everything from the table.

The lights go off, and then on and off again, and then the halo-
gen emergency lights in the corridors engage, with their irritated
buzzing.

It's easier to see out with the interior lights gone. Along the line of cars a man carrying a framed painting staggers at an angle, like a sailboat tacking. He passes a woman in a van with her head against the headrest and her mouth open in an *Oh* of fatigue.

I'm imagining the helicopter crew's negotiations with my mother, and their fireman's carry once those negotiations have fallen through. She told me once that she often recalled after the flood of 1953 the way they drifted through the darkness for so long without the sky getting lighter. She said that when the sunrise finally came they watched the navy drop food and blankets and rubber boats and bottles of cooking gas to people on roofs or isolated high spots, and when their boat passed a small body lying across an eave with its arms in the water, her father told her that it was resting. She remembered later that morning saying to her mother, who had grown calmer, that it was a good sign that they saw so few people floating, and her mother had answered before her father could stop her that the drowned didn't float straightaway, but took a few days to come up.

And she talked with fondness about the way her father had tended to her later, when she'd been blinded by some windblown grit, by suggesting she rub one eye to make the other weep, the way farmers did when bothered by chaff. And she remembered, too, a service a week or so later, and the strangeness of one of the prayers her village priest recited once they all were back in their old church, the masonry buttressed with steel beams and planking to keep the walls from sagging outward any further: *I sink into deep mire, where there is no standing; I come into deep waters, where the floods overflow me.*

The window's immense pane shudders and flexes before me from the force of what's pouring out of the North Sea. Water's beginning to run its fingers out from under the seal on the sash. Cato will send me text updates whether she receives answers or not, wry and brisk and newsy, and Henk will author a few, as well. Everyone in Berlin will track the goings-on on the monitors above them while they shop or travel or work. The teaser heading will be something like THE NETHERLANDS UNDER SIEGE. Some of the more sober will think, That could have been us. Some of the more perceptive will consider that it soon may well be.

My finger's on the Cato icon on the screen without exerting the additional pressure that would initiate another call. What sort of

person ends up with someone like me? What sort of person finds
that *acceptable*, year to year? We went on vacations and fielded each
other's calls and took turns reading Henk to sleep and let slip away
that miracle that was there between us when we first came together.
We hunkered down before the wind picked up. We modeled for
our son risk management when we could have been embracing the
free fall of that astonishing *Here. This is yours to hold.* We said to
each other *I think I know* when we should have said *Lead me farther
through your amazing, amazing interior.*

Cato was moved by all of my mother's flood memories, but was
only brought to tears by one. My mother's only cherished memory
from that year: the Queen's address to the nation afterward, and
her celebration of what the crucible of the disaster had produced:
the return, at long last, of that unity the country had displayed during the war. My mother had purchased a copy of the speech on LP,
all those years ago, and had had her neighbor transfer it to a digital format. She played it for us while Cato and I visited, and Henk
knelt at the window spying on whomever was hurrying by. And my
mother held Cato's hand and Cato held mine and Henk gave us
fair warning of anything approaching of interest, while the Queen's
smooth and warm voice thanked us all for the way we had worked
together in that one great cause, soldiering on without a thought
for care, or grief, or inner divisions, and without even realizing
what we were denying ourselves.

MAGGIE SHIPSTEAD

The Cowboy Tango

FROM *Virginia Quarterly Review*

WHEN MR. GLEN OTTERBAUSCH hired Sammy Boone she was sixteen and so skinny that the whole of her beanpole body fit neatly inside the circle of shade cast by her hat. For three weeks he'd had an ad in the Bozeman paper for a wrangler, but only two men had shown up. One smelled like he'd swum across a whiskey river before his truck fishtailed to a dusty stop outside the lodge, and the other was missing his left arm. Mr. Otterbausch looked away from the man with one arm and told him that the job was already filled. He was planning to get away from beef-raising and go more toward the tourist trade, even though he'd promised his Uncle Dex, as Dex breathed his last wheezes, that he would do no such thing. Every summer during his childhood Mr. Otterbausch's schoolteacher parents had sent him to stay with Uncle Dex, a man who, in both body and spirit, resembled a petrified log. He had a face of knurled bark and knotholes for eyes and a mouth sealed up tight around a burned-down Marlboro. He spoke rarely; his voice rasped up through the dark tubes of his craw only to issue a command or to mock his nervous, skinny nephew for being nervous and skinny. He liked to creep up on young Glen and clang the dinner bell in his ear, showing yellow crocodile teeth when the boy jumped and twisted into the air. So Dex's bequest of all forty thousand acres to Mr. Otterbausch, announced when a faint breeze was still rattling through the doldrums of his tar-blackened lungs, was a deathbed confession that Dex loved no one, had no one to give his ranch to except a disliked nephew whose one point of redemption was his ability to sit a horse.

It was true that Mr. Otterbausch rode well, and because he liked to ride more than anything else, he quit his job managing a ski resort, loaded his gray mare Sleepy Jean into a trailer, and drove up to pay his last respects. By the time the first rain came and drilled Dex's ashes into the hard earth, Mr. Otterbausch had sold off half the cattle and bought two dozen new horses, three breeding stallions among them. He bought saddles and bridles, built a new barn with a double-size stall for Sleepy Jean, expanded the lodge and put in a bigger kitchen. When construction was under way on ten guest cabins and a new bunkhouse, he fired the worst of the old wranglers and placed his ad. Sammy showed up two days after the man with one arm. She must have hitched out to the ranch because when he caught sight of her she was just a white dot walking up the dirt road from I-191. His first impulse when he saw that she was just a kid was to send her away, but he was sympathetic toward the too-skinny. Moreover, he thought the dudes who would be paying his future bills might be intrigued by a girl wrangler in a way they would not have been by a man with a pinned-up sleeve who tied knots with his teeth. Mr. Otterbausch maintained a shiny and very bristly mustache, and his fingers stole up to tug at it.

"Can you shoot?" he asked.

"Yeah," she said.

"How are you with a rope?"

"All right."

"Can you ride?"

"Yup."

"Let's see then."

He dropped a saddle and bridle in her arms and showed her a short-legged twist of a buckskin, a bitch mare who had nearly thrown Mr. Otterbausch. He had gotten off and kicked her once right on the ass. The buckskin kicked back, leaving him with a boomerang-shaped bruise on his right thigh. When Sammy pulled the cinch tight, the mare flattened her ears and lunged around, her square teeth biting the air until they met Sammy's hard-swung fist. The mare squealed and pointed her nose at the sky, but then she stood still. Sammy climbed up. The mare dropped her head and crowhopped off to the right. Sammy jerked the reins up, but not meanly, and kicked the mare through the gate into the home paddock. In five minutes, she had her going around like a show pony.

"Hang on there a sec," Mr. Otterbausch said. He went and threw some tack on Sleepy Jean. He climbed up, rode her back to the paddock, and pulled open the gate for Sammy. "Let's try you without a fence. Head down the valley." Mr. Otterbausch pointed Sammy westward toward a horizon of dovetailing hills. The buckskin cow-kicked once and then rocketed off with Sammy sitting up straight as a telephone pole. Her long braid of brown hair thumped against her back. Sleepy Jean was plenty fast but Mr. Otterbausch kept her reined in to stay behind and observe. Sammy rode further back on her hip than most women, giving her ride some roll and swagger. It was a gusty day and the buckskin was really moving, but she didn't even bother to reach up and tug her hat down the way Mr. Otterbausch did. By the time they got back to the home paddock, both the horses and Mr. Otterbausch were in a lather.

"You want the job?" he asked.

Sammy nodded.

"How old are you?"

She hesitated, and he guessed she was deciding whether or not to lie. "Sixteen."

This seemed like the truth. "You're not some kind of runaway, are you? You should tell me so I can decide if I want the trouble."

She was shaking her head. "No one's coming to look for me. I got a dad, but he said I could go."

"Where's your dad?"

"Wyoming."

"What's he do?"

"Chickens."

"He won't hunt me down for kidnapping?" Trying to set her at ease, Mr. Otterbausch chuckled. The girl did not smile.

"No sir."

"Just a joke," Mr. Otterbausch said. "Just joking."

Sammy lived in the lodge until Mr. Otterbausch had a cottage built for her in a stand of trees off the east porch, on the other side of the lodge from the guest cabins and the bunkhouse. He'd hoped when she was transplanted to another building she would be less on his mind, but no such luck. All day he was mindful that she might be watching him and considered each movement before he made it, choreographing for her eyes a performance of strength while he moved bales of hay or of grace as he rode out on Sleepy Jean in the evening. He tried to stop himself from wringing his hands while he talked to her because an old girlfriend had told him the habit was annoying. Every night his imagination projected flickering films of Sammy Boone onto his bedroom ceiling: Sammy riding, always riding, across fields and hills and exotic deserts, always on beautiful horses, horses that Mr. Otterbausch certainly didn't own. He liked to imagine what her hair might look like out of its braid, what it would feel like in his fingers. Sometimes he allowed himself to imagine making love to Sammy, but he did so in a state of distracting discomfort. The bottom line was that she was too young, and he wasn't about to mess around with a girl who had nowhere else to go, even though she had a stillness to her that made her seem older, old even. He told himself he loved her the way he loved the wind and the mountains and the horses, and it would be a crime to damage her spirit. Plus, she showed no interest. She treated Mr. Otterbausch and the wranglers with a detached man-to-man courtesy. Sometimes she could even be coarse. She called the stuck latch on a paddock gate a "cocksucker," and she told a table of breakfasting dudes that the stallions had gone "a-fucking" one Sunday in breeding season. When she ran into Mr. Otterbausch she never talked about anything beyond the solid world of trees, rocks, water, and animals. If he tried to ask her about herself, she gave the shortest answer possible and then made herself scarce.

"You have any brothers or sisters?"

"Some brothers."

"Where are they?"

"Don't know. Got to check on Big Bob's abscess. Night, boss."

Ten years passed this way. Sammy stayed skinny except for her shoulders, which muscled up and broadened out. She started to go a little bowlegged, and her forearms turned brown and wiry. The dude business worked out well. Mr. Otterbausch made enough money to keep improving the ranch a bit at a time and also to put away some every year. Out on a ride he found a hot spring bubbling out of a hillside, and he dug the pool out bigger, lined it with rocks, and put in a cedar platform for the dudes to sit on. Dudes, it turned out, loved to sit in hot water, and the sulfurous pond drew enough new business that he added three more cabins and built a rough shelter way out on the property's north edge for use on overnight treks. The guests called Sammy a tough cookie, which irked Mr. Otterbausch, like when anyone said the distant, magnificent mountains were like a postcard.

Since the beginning, Sammy had the job of taking the best old horses up to a hillside spot called the Pearly Gates when their times came and shooting them in the head. The place was named for two clusters of white-barked aspen trees that flanked the trail where it opened out into a clearing. Mr. Otterbausch guessed that Sammy talked a lot more to horses than to people, and he figured she gave them a proper good-bye. When the wranglers saw Sammy come walking back down out of the hills, they knew to keep out of her way for a while. She left each carcass out until it was picked clean enough, maybe a few months, and then she went back and nailed up the skull on one of the pines around the clearing. Nobody asked what she did with the rest of the bones. Not many horses were lucky enough to go to the Pearly Gates; most of the ones who came in from winter pasture too lame and rickety to be reliable were sold at auction and ended up going down to Mexico in silver trucks with cheese-grater sides. From there they mostly wound up in thirty-pound bags of cheap dog food. But worthy horses came and went over the years, and their skulls circled the clearing on Parachute Hill like a council of wise men. Mr. Otterbausch went up there sometimes to get away. He would sit for a while beneath the long white faces and look up through the aspens' trembling leaves at a patch of sky. The dudes paid the bills, and he knew they had as much right as anyone else to enjoy this country, but some days they were as much a blight on the land as oil derricks or Wal-Marts or neon billboards. They strutted around as purposeful and aimless as pigeons, staring at the mountains and the sky and the trees, try-ing to stuff it all into their cameras. Wherever he was, Uncle Dex must have been royally pissed off.

Usually Sammy rode out alone when she wasn't with the dudes, but Mr. Otterbausch was happiest when he could make up some excuse for the two of them to ride together. Around dusk, after the dudes and the horses had been fed, he would seek her out to check on this or that bit of trail or retrieve a few steers that he had pur-posely let loose the night before. Those evenings, when the sky was amethyst and Sleepy Jean's mane blew over his hands as he loped along behind Sammy, it seemed that his longing and the moment when day tipped over into night were made out of the same stuff, aching and purple. While they hunted around for lost steers, he talked to her, telling her all his stories, and she listened without complaint or much comment, though sometimes she would ask

"Then what?" and he would talk on with new flair. He worried that she would fall in love with a dude or with one of the wranglers, but she never seemed tempted.

He wanted to believe it was self-restraint that kept him from falling on his knees and begging her to love him, to marry him, at least to sleep with him, but, during the rare moments when he told himself he must, if he did not want to spend the rest of his life in agony, confess his feelings, he knew the truth was that he was afraid. She was a full-grown woman, not some helpless girl. He was afraid she would leave, afraid she would laugh at him, afraid he would not be able to survive all alone out on the blinding salt flats of her rejection. He might have gone on that way until he was old and gray, but then Mr. Otterbausch called the girlfriend he kept in Bozeman by Sammy's name one too many times. "God damn it!" she shouted, standing naked beside her bed while Mr. Otterbausch cowered beneath the sheets. "You have called me Sammy for the last fucking time, Glen Otterbausch! My name is LuAnn! Remember me?" She grabbed her breasts with both hands and shook them at him. "LuAnn!"

He drove home, tail between his legs, and took a bottle of whiskey out on the front porch. The sun was dropping toward the hilltops where he had first ridden with Sammy, and he sat and looked at it. He didn't like whiskey, but it seemed to fit the occasion and was all he could scrounge from the two guys who happened to be in the bunkhouse when he stopped by. The dudes came in for dinner and then were herded off to campfire. After the lodge felt quiet and the sky was fading from blue to purple, Mr. Otterbausch went over to Sammy's cottage and knocked on the door. Her dog, Dirt, barked once and fell silent when she said, from somewhere, "Dirt, you hush up." She answered the door in her usual clothes, except she was barefoot. After he realized he was staring at her pale toes, he looked up and stared over her shoulder. A rocking chair with a Hudson Bay blanket on it. A skillet on the stove. He caught the smell of fried eggs. Dirt sniffed around his boots. The dog had simply appeared one day, walking up the dirt road like Sammy had, and she had acted like she'd been expecting him all along. Because Dirt was shaped and bristled like a brown bottlebrush, the joke with the wranglers was that Mr. Otterbausch had turned one of his old mustaches into a dog for Sammy.

"Boss?" she said. One hand was up behind her head. She was holding back her hair.

"Sorry to disturb you, but I wanted to ask a favor. Mrs. Mullinax —you know her? the lady from Chicago?—says she left her camera up on the lookout rock. I said I'd ride up and look for it, and I was wondering if you'd come along. Two eyes better than one, and all. Or I guess it's four eyes. Better than two." He laughed.

"All the guys are busy?"

"It's campfire night, and C.J. and Wayne went to town." Still she hesitated, he hoped not because she sensed his nervousness or smelled whiskey on him. "I thought you could take Hotrod. Give him some exercise."

"He don't get enough exercise with all that fucking he does?" But she shut the door on his face, and when she came back out her hair was in its braid and she had on her corduroy jacket with a wooly collar. "Dirt, you stay," she said.

Mr. Otterbausch was drunker than he thought and had to hop around with his foot in the rawhide stirrup before he could pull himself up in the saddle. As soon as he did, Sleepy Jean spread her back legs and lifted her tail to squirt some pee for Hotrod, who flipped his upper lip up over his nostrils and let the scent bounce around his cavernous sinuses.

"Slut," Sammy said to Sleepy Jean, reining Hotrod away from her.

On the lookout rock, with the valley dark below them and the stars coming out to one-up the small twinkling lights of the lodge and outbuildings, Mr. Otterbausch waited for the perfect moment, the moment when Sammy was standing with her hands on her hips and saying disgustedly, "I don't see any damn camera," and he swooped in and got her by the braid and kissed her hard on the mouth. She hauled back like she was going to punch him, but she remembered not to punch her boss right when he remembered to let go of her braid—soon enough but a little late. He fell to pieces with apologies and dropped down on his knees to beg her to forget the whole thing, but then he figured as long as he was down there he might as well go whole hog.

"Sammy, I'd like to give you the ranch."

"What?"

"The ranch. I'd like it to be yours as well as mine."

"What for?"

He began to sense he'd made a wrong turn, but he was too drunk and panicked to do anything but press on. He looked up at her dark shape and said, "Well, I'd like to marry you. We could run the ranch together. It'd be yours too. Wouldn't you like that?"

She kicked a rock that went rattling down into the darkening valley. "You think you can bribe me with the ranch? Do I look like a ranch whore to you?"

He sat back onto his butt. "Of course not."

"I don't want it."

"Don't want what?"

"The ranch."

He felt a hopeless burst of hope. "But you do want . . . the rest?"

She waited for a minute before she answered, and he felt so nervous he thought he might faint. But she said, "No."

"You're sure? You're not being stubborn? I didn't mean it like a bribe. I swear, Sammy. I meant that I'd give you anything." Behind them, Sleepy Jean, tied to a tree, squealed at Hotrod, who was tied to another. Mr. Otterbausch tried to stand up but sat back down. He found he was wringing his hands together.

Hotrod whuffed at Sleepy Jean and pulled and pranced at his tree. Sleepy Jean squealed again, lifting her tail. Sammy took a step back from Mr. Otterbausch. "I just don't love you," she said. "I wish I did, but I don't. It's one of those things. I've thought about it. I've tried to get myself to, even, because you're the most decent man I know and you'd treat me good, but I'd feel like a liar."

"I don't mind," said Mr. Otterbausch, raising his voice over Sleepy Jean's.

Sammy whirled around on the mare. "God damn slut horse, stop your yelling!" She stepped close to Hotrod and, as she was pulling his cinch tight, she said, without turning around, "I'm real sorry." She untied the stallion, punched his neck when he made a lunge for Sleepy Jean, climbed on, and rode away. Mr. Otterbausch sat and watched the crescent moon rise. He felt woozy, exhausted, tremulous, like a survivor of a terrible collision. He did not know whether he was more afraid of Sammy leaving the ranch or her staying. Eventually he rode down and finished the whiskey and avoided Sammy pretty well for three months, after which time everything went back to normal and stayed that way. More years went by. He loved her and tried to conceal that he loved her; she pretended that she did not notice he loved her.

Harrison Greene went out to his uncle's ranch once he was very certain his marriage was over. He was a man of great patience, a bird-watcher and a fly-fisherman, and the ink on the divorce papers had to dry for a whole year for him to be certain that he was really divorced, even though by then Marjorie had already been living with Gary-the-Architect for eight months. So he gave up the lease on his sad bachelor apartment, sold most of his possessions, and drove west with his horse Digger in a trailer behind his truck, Illinois unrolling in his side-mirrors. Harrison made his living from larger-than-life paintings of animals and birds. They were perfect down to the last follicle. His life, lived slowly, had eventually bored Marjorie beyond her tolerance, which is why he was surprised that she chose to shack up with Gary of all people, a man who sat in a cantilevered house and made silent, minute movements with his pencil while, across town, Harrison made silent, minute movements with his pencil.

"I think she's really gone," he said to his uncle on the phone.

"Well, yeah, you think? Ha ha ha," Uncle Glen said. Harrison remembered why he had never particularly cared for Uncle Glen. The man was annoying.

"She's moved in with this architect," Harrison continued. "I don't know. Anyway, I was thinking, if you'll have me, it might do me good to come out to your place for a while. I'd pay, of course."

"No need for that. No need at all. Do you still paint?"

"Yeah."

"Maybe you can make a few paintings for the lodge. You still have that horse?"

"I thought I'd bring him along."

"He's a beauty. If you wanted, you could just pay me with that horse. Ha ha ha."

"Ha ha ha," said Harrison.

"All right. Call when you're coming."

The first thing Harrison saw when he drove up the road was a woman riding an ugly Appaloosa. Her braid and the shape of her waist gave her away as a woman, but she rode like a man, back on her hip. When the Appaloosa let go a series of bucks, dolphining up and down along the fence, she whipped him back and forth across the shoulders with the reins and sent him streaking off at a gallop. As she passed, she tipped her hat to Harrison.

"Who's that girl?" he asked his uncle after he had settled Digger in the barn.

"What girl?"

"The one on the Appy out there."

"Most people don't spot her as a girl right away."

"There's the braid."

"Don't go telling Sammy she rides like a girl. Ha ha ha."

"She doesn't, that's the thing."

"You don't remember Sammy?"

"I've never seen her before."

"Sure you have. She's been here fifteen years. Guess you didn't notice her when you had Marjorie with you."

"I don't see why I wouldn't have."

Uncle Glen took him by the arm and turned him away toward the lodge. "You're in here. Next to my room."

Harrison had never seen a girl ride so well. Right away he started tagging along on rides, bringing up the rear in a gaggle of dudes but never losing sight of her hat and her braid beneath it. At first she paid him no notice, but he waited and after a couple weeks he knew she must have at least gotten used to him because when he rode off to investigate a birdsong, she would whistle for him up the trail so he could find his way back. Once she dropped back beside him to say Digger was the best-looking horse she'd ever seen, and when he offered to let her ride him, she said, "Yeah? For serious?"

"Sure. Why not?"

"The Otter hogs all the good ones."

Harrison had a lot to say about Uncle Glen. How he laughed at his own jokes, which weren't even jokes but just things he said. How he had a habit of saying something to your back as you turned to leave a room. How he was so jumpy that Marjorie called him human itching powder. How he longed to rip that preposterous mustache from the man's face. But he said, "I'd think he'd want you to ride them."

She looked alarmed. "Why?"

"Because you're one of the best riders I've ever seen."

She seemed relieved. She shrugged. "The Otter rides good, too.

They're his horses. Marty, sit up there," she shouted at a dude in a bolo tie who was drooping back in the saddle. "I'll tie that stupid-ass bolo of yours to the horn if you don't." The dude looked back over his shoulder, wounded, and she trotted up to the front of the line.

Harrison found with the passing days that Sammy was staking a larger and larger claim on his thoughts. He rode with her as much as he could, and, in the evenings when he went out in the paddocks or the hills with his sketchbook, he found himself only half concentrating because he was listening for her footsteps behind him. She often came out and watched him draw, sitting behind him in the grass. Sometimes he sent her out on Digger, and it was a glorious sight. He made sketch after sketch, and afterwards she always said "That was all right" and rested a hand flat on the horse's neck, leaving a print in his sweat. At night in his bed with Uncle Glen's snores coming through the wall, Harrison filled imaginary canvases with Sammy and Digger done in big, loose brush strokes, more active and alive than his usual Audubon-gets-huge stuff. Having something other than Marjorie to think about was welcome. There was nothing in Sammy to remind him of Marjorie. Marjorie was beautiful. She had delicate wrists and shoulders, and her veins showed through her skin like the roots of baby flowers. Sammy was strong and awkward with weathered skin and a braid too long for a woman her age. Marjorie was busy and jumpy, a jingler of change and a tapper of toes, which made it pretty rich that she called Uncle Glen hyper. She had never sat all the way back in a chair in her life, and she undercooked everything out of sheer impatience. Sammy, on the other hand, might have been reincarnated from a boulder. Marjorie would laugh and laugh and laugh, and her laughter was like birdsong. Sammy's laugh was the sound of air being let out of a tire.

The only problem was Uncle Glen, who, it became clear, was nursing a crush on Sammy. God only knew how long that had been going on. Long enough that his feelings, which Sammy clearly did not return, seemed to have coagulated into some notion of ownership on the old guy's part. He was always popping up wherever they were, making strange non-jokes that only he laughed at, rubbing his paws together and staring at Sammy. When he could, he'd ask Harrison to do him a favor and ride out to check the fence line

while Sammy took dudes in the opposite direction, or he'd send
Harrison into town to buy a bag of bran mash and a bucket when
Sammy was due back in from a ride. After Sammy started riding
Digger, Uncle Glen complained suddenly of an arthritic hip and
turned the choicest horses over to Sammy. He'd watch her ride
from the porch with a glass of something clear sweating on the arm
of his chair.

Sammy must have known that the boss had a thing for her. If she
felt anything for him, it stood to reason that they would have gotten together years ago. Maybe they had. Maybe Sammy broke it off
but Uncle Glen was still carrying a torch. Anything was possible.
Harrison examined Sammy for traces of an attachment to Uncle
Glen — it would be unsporting of him to interfere with a long and
fraught lead-up to love — but he could detect only polite kindness
in her treatment of him. Once, from the window of Digger's stall,
he had watched Sammy as she stood with her arms folded on the
home paddock fence looking at the horses. Uncle Glen came up
beside her and folded his arms on the fence too. Their hats bob-
bled as they talked, and Sammy pointed down the valley. Uncle
Glen looked, but at the side of her face instead of where she was
pointing. Then Glen scooched a few inches closer to Sammy and
then a few more, until their sleeves were touching. After a moment,
Sammy inched down the rail, away from the insistent brush of
Glen's plaid shirt. But Glen closed the gap, and Sammy retreated,
and, like two halves of one caterpillar, they made their way down
the fence, about four feet in the twenty minutes Harrison watched.
Their hats kept bobbling the whole time, and he supposed they
weren't even aware of their awkward tango.

Harrison found his uncle in the ranch office, sitting at his desk
paying bills. "I'd like to take Sammy into town tonight," he announced. "To go dancing."

Uncle Glen ran a finger through the condensation on a glass
that sat on his blotter. "Sammy would rather die than go dancing.
If you knew her, you'd know that."

"There's no harm in asking," Harrison said. "If she'd rather, we
can just sit in a bar."

"Go ahead and ask then. But be careful she doesn't kick you in
the teeth. Ha ha ha."

Harrison pursed his lips and turned away, but his uncle said,

"She's a dead end. Better men than you have tried. No luck for any."

"What men?"

"Just some guys here and there."

"What do you mean 'better'?"

"Nothing, just she doesn't seem to want all that."

"All what?"

"A man. A family. Responsibilities to other people. All I'm saying is she's had other offers, and she's turned them all down."

Harrison brought a sketch of the dog Dirt to Sammy's door. Dirt was ancient and blind now, running low on teeth, and Harrison drew him like that, floppy-lipped and old.

"It looks like him," Sammy said when she saw it. "Ugly bastard." She held the paper carefully, balanced on her fingertips.

"It's your night off, isn't it? Let's go get some drinks."

She glanced up at him, her hand creeping over her shoulder to her braid. "Fine," she said. She shut the door in his face and came out again in five minutes. She looked like she always did, but he smelled something that was neither dust nor horse and might have been perfume. They found two barstools at Jeb's Antlers. She ordered whiskey, and Harrison followed suit. They sat and watched a few couples dancing the two-step to a band that played in jeans and boots on a shadowy stage in the corner.

"I've never been here," she said.

"All these years? There wasn't anyone you'd let take you out?" She snorted.

"Uncle Glen would have been up for it."

"What makes you think that?"

"Look at him. He's your guard dog, sniffing around you, growling at people like me."

She shook her head. "The Otter's got better things to do. He's a good boss."

"Some people say that I'm too slow about things. But old Glen's been biding his time for, what, twenty years?"

"Fifteen," she said. She caught herself and scowled.

"You'd think he'd get it together to try something on you."

"You know what," she said, looking him in the face, "I owe the Otter real big, and he could have tried harder to make me pay him back, but he didn't, and now I owe him some more."

"Are you off men in general or just the ones around here? You'd be doing me a favor to say."

Her hand went up to her braid. "I guess just the ones round here."

"Why did you say you owe the Otter?"

"He helped me out when I was young and didn't have any place to go."

"Why didn't you have anywhere to go?"

"You know. Sad story." She examined her whiskey. "What about you? You got a sad story?"

She had never asked him anything personal before. He knew it was unfair, but he felt intruded upon. "I guess," he said. "Not the saddest in the world. My wife left me for an architect. That's why I came out here. She said I was too deliberate. No, she said I was boring."

"Sounds like a bitch," Sammy said.

"The situation or my wife?"

"Both." She lifted her glass at the bartender.

"Not that things were perfect," Harrison said. His drink was only half gone, but the bartender, without asking, topped it off. "She moved in with the architect, Gary. God knows she can't stand to be alone. She acts like only unlovable people are alone." He thought for a moment about what he had said and then nodded in agreement with himself. "Yeah," he said. "That's right."

Sammy watched the people on the dance floor. He wondered if she was listening, but she said, "Seems to me some people are alone because it's easiest. That don't seem so different from finding an architect because that's easiest." She sipped. The whiskey was cheap and went down like a buzz saw, but Harrison wouldn't have guessed it to look at her. She didn't grimace at all.

"What's your sad story?" he asked. He had been playing with a matchbook, but he dropped it and touched her wrist lightly with his fingers, only for a second. He felt the way he did sitting on a barely broken horse—one wrong move and she would bolt.

"There was this architect," she said, staring him down. "Broke my heart. Lives in Chicago. Name of Gary."

It took him a second to realize she was joking. He felt off balance, something he did not relish. "Very funny," he said.

She smiled into her glass, pleased with herself. He pushed his uncertainty away and tried again. "Your turn," he said. "Sad story. Lay it on me."

She hunched a little and pulled her braid over her shoulder so she could hold its end. "Not too much to tell. A mean dad, mean brothers, mean boyfriend who I ran off with, and then he left me in Canada. My daddy would've killed me if I'd come home. The Otter gave me a job. That's it."

"That's not it. There's more."

"That's it as far as you're concerned right now. No offense."

"Oh, none taken," he said. He emptied his glass and clunked it on the bar. "Well, I think there's only one thing to do, and that is to dance." He stood up and held out his hand.

"I don't dance."

"Sure you do." He took her hand.

"I don't know how," she said, yanking it back.

"Sammy, come and dance." He dragged her off her barstool, and when they were on the dance floor he put one arm around her waist and held her against him so tightly that only the tips of her boots grazed the floor.

"I wish I had a skirt," she whispered.

They drove back in silence, weaving a slow, drunken serpentine over the empty road. In her cabin he had their clothes off while old Dirt was still thumping his tail and rolling his milky eyes around. She said, "It's been so long I might as well be a virgin." She did not cry out but she clutched his hair so tightly that he did.

In the lodge, staring at his barren bedroom ceiling, Mr. Otterbausch listened to the emptiness of his nephew's room. He had heard the truck drive up and their footsteps on the gravel. Now there was nothing but the coyotes yipping in the hills. Mr. Otterbausch, alone in his bed, joined in the silent chorus of the unloved.

Sammy was sorry the Otter was angry, but there was not much to be done about it. He was working her like a dog, sending her out with the dudes, sending her out again as soon as she got back. She knew the method: when the stallions got bad she'd gallop them down to jelly-legs to get their minds off the mares. But it was no good. She'd never be too tired to go to bed with Harrison Greene.

352   MAGGIE SHIPSTEAD

"That was all right," she said to him every time, resting her hand
on his stomach. This business of being happy was something so
long forgotten that she'd forgotten she'd forgotten. She was happy
enough on a horse, but that was over as soon as her boots hit the
ground. She hadn't been happy with a man since before Davey
started being a bastard, which was a while before he drove off while
she was in a truck stop bathroom outside Edmonton. Truth be
told, in the six months or so before Harrison had shown up, she'd
started to think that maybe she should get it over with and marry
the Otter. The Otter had been nice to her for half her life. She
owed him, and she didn't want to leave the ranch. When she was
younger, she'd still thought she'd leave eventually. She'd thought
she wouldn't mind being alone forever. She'd thought lots of
things. Then the years piled up and she got set in her ways, and the
Otter was one of her ways. Sometimes, usually on their dusk rides,
she wondered, for the millionth time, if she could prod her affection for him into something more. But Harrison came along and
reminded her that people couldn't help who they loved.

   Sammy had never had to share her cabin with anyone, but Harrison was so slow and still and quiet she didn't mind him. It was like
having a new piece of furniture that painted pictures. He taught
her how to fly-fish when they could get away from the Otter and
take Harrison's truck down to the river. "One-two," he said, standing behind her and moving her arm back and forth so the fly
stitched the river to the sky. He cooked for her and planted a vege-
table garden behind her cabin. It was only when she asked him
questions that he seemed to freeze up and get irritated. Then he'd
either go off somewhere or he'd kiss her and squeeze her to change
the subject. So she stopped asking him things.

   The summer passed, and in November, after the last of the dudes
had gone and the first snow had come and then the second and
the third, Harrison took Sammy by the hand and told her he had
to go away to visit some people.

   "Like who?"

   "Like my mother for one. And Marjorie for another. We have
some things to settle. Small things. I have to take care of some business too. My agent's been riding me." He grabbed her braid and
tickled her nose with its tip.

   She brushed his hand away. "Are you coming back?"

   "I plan to, yeah." But he was freezing up. His eyes were darting.

"You plan to?"

"That's what I said."

"Don't do me any favors."

"I'm being honest. I plan to come back."

"You mean that?" Stop pushing, she told herself. Let it be.

"I do, but nothing's ever for certain."

"Only that I'll be sitting here in the snow with the Otter, waiting. Feeling like an ass."

"What happened to stoic Sammy?" He pulled her to him and kissed her cheek, then held her at arm's length, by her shoulders. "You stay here where you belong. Take good care of Digger."

She pushed him away. "Here's your stoic Sammy. Have a good fucking trip, Harrison." She tipped her hat and walked off.

He left that day. For a while he called every day, but she wasn't any good on the phone. She wanted to ask him when he was coming back, but she wouldn't. He called less and less. She had never minded winter much, but then she had never been cooped up with an angry Otter before. Most of the other wranglers were off on winter jobs in Arizona or Texas. Just slow-minded Big Georgie was left in the bunkhouse, probably settling in for a long talk with his balls. What made things worse was that, back before Harrison left, Sammy and the Otter had gone out after a wound-up steer, and Sammy hadn't been paying close attention and let the steer go careening at the Otter. Sleepy Jean took a funny step getting out of the way and tweaked a foreleg. Walking back to the lodge (they had left the steer to its fate but of course it decided to turn docile and followed with its nose in Sleepy Jean's tail) the Otter said, "You're getting sloppy, and we both know why, and I'm embarrassed for you."

Sammy was riding, and the Otter was walking next to Sleepy Jean. The dents in the top of his hat looked like an angry face. "That horse is too old for cutting work and you know it," she said.

"I hired you because I thought you'd be tough like a man, not get all moony-eyed the second someone pays you some attention."

"I had some attention before. Someone tried to give me a whole ranch once."

That shut him up, and until Harrison left he mostly glowered at her from afar, leaning like a Halloween decoration against the porch posts and blowing clouds of vapor into the cold air. Usually in winter the Otter was a nuisance but not a menace. He'd show up at her door with Chinese checkers or some other game with lots of small pieces that inevitably ended up in the floorboards when the Otter nervously overturned the whole thing. This year, though, once they were alone, he started picking fights with her, bounding at her through the snow like a pissed-off ferret, wanting to give her shit about the water troughs or some feed he said she'd forgotten to order. His window stayed lit into the early morning, probably because he was up drinking, and she never saw him on a horse.

"You smell like roadkill raccoon," she told him in the tack room.

"Ha!" he said, opening his mouth and eyes wide and grabbing for her. She pushed him off, walked away.

He spent most of his time in Sleepy Jean's stall, wrapped up in an Indian blanket, reading a book. The horse didn't look good. She was an old girl to begin with, but her bum leg had made her crooked everywhere. Swaying around her stall, she looked like she was thinking, "Oh, lordy, my back. Oh, my aching knee." Her skin was as thin and fragile over her bones as rolled-out pie dough. Sammy brought her an apple, and the horse was working on it with her yellow teeth when the Otter's voice came from a dark corner of the stall. "Heard from your boyfriend?"

He knew she hadn't. The phone was in the lodge. "We don't do well on the phone," she said.

"Now that's dedication."

"More like a challenge," Sammy said, holding her palm through the bars of the stall window for Jean to lick.

"A challenge?" The Otter leaned into the light.

"Harrison thinks everyone is as patient as he is."

"Bet you really miss him, ha ha ha. Bet you wish you weren't here with me."

Sammy flared up, tired of the sight of his sallow drunk's face and said, "Yeah, and what about it?"

He smiled at her, showing teeth. The rest of him was going to hell, but his mustache was still as sharp and shiny as a sea urchin. "Patience is a virtue," he said.

Indeed Harrison's leaving seemed to have been the starting pistol for a relay race of misfortune and bad feelings. There was the ugliness with the Otter, and then the wolves got hungry and came down and got a steer right out of the home paddock, and then Sammy hurt Big Georgie's feelings by laughing when he said he

wanted to learn to ride so he could ride Digger someday, and poor
old Dirt kicked the bucket in the second week of December, paws-
up right next to his dinner bowl. Sammy cried because the ground
was too hard for her to get a shovel in, and she had to put him in
the deep freeze. Harrison's drawing of Dirt was too much for her,
and she took it down from above the fireplace. Everything was so
grim that when the knock came at her door on the first sunny day
they'd had in a while, she opened it thinking that the devil himself
might be on the other side. It was the Otter.

"There's a big snow coming," he said.

"Yeah?" She waited for him to say something about how the snow
would probably delay Harrison, ha ha ha.

"It might last a week." He ran a hand over his face, pushing all
the broken pieces around. "Jeannie's not doing well. Four more
months of winter, at least four. She won't get better in the cold. I
thought about trailering her over to Doc Luddy's, but the roads
are bad, and she wouldn't like standing in the trailer that long."
He blinked his red eyes at her. "She's old anyway."

"She's a good old girl," Sammy said cautiously. The Otter was
talking to her like he had in the days before Harrison. Back when
he loved her, was how she thought of it, though she knew he must
still love her or else he wouldn't be so miserable. The winter was
harsh; his horse was dying, and his love was scummed over with
booze and jealousy.

"So," the Otter said, mustache quivering, "I need you to take her
up to the Pearly Gates before the big snow. I think she can walk it
now. I'd hate to wait and then have to have her hauled away. She
should be up there."

Sammy nodded. "Dirt died. I put him in the deep freeze."

He looked past her into the cabin as though for Dirt, and then
he said, "Poor old guy."

The walk to the Pearly Gates was slow. Sammy picked the best
route she could, but still Jean ended up skating on ice and bogged
up to her shoulder in snow a few times. The horse walked on a slow
three beat, bobbing her head. "Well, Jeannie," Sammy said. "Thank
you for all your good work at the ranch and for taking care of the
Otter and all. He's always liked you best, even though he had
better-looking horses. Not that you're ugly, you're just kind of
rough, you know? But you're a good cutter, and you were damn

fast. I don't know what the Otter would have done without you. He's going to feel pretty lonely now, especially because of me. I wish you could stick around to keep him company."

Sammy never liked shooting horses. When it was over and Jeannie's knees had given out, first the back and then the front, and she had fallen down in the snow like someone who was just so tired, Sammy sat with her back against Jeannie's, looking up at the circle of skulls crowned with little snowdrifts. The sky through the trees was a hard winter blue, and she could feel the warmth draining out of the horse. She thought about the Otter down in the lodge, and she asked someone, maybe the skulls, to send Harrison back soon.

She found the Otter in the game room with his glass and his bottle, sitting beneath a huge portrait of Sleepy Jean that Harrison had finished before he left. Jean looked old and tired in the painting. A cue leaned against the billiard table and the balls were out on the green felt. Sammy switched on a lamp.

"Leave it."

"Okay." She came closer and stood leaning against the table.

"Don't say how she was a good old girl and how everything has to die because I damn well know."

Sammy said nothing.

"And don't go stapling her skull to some tree or turning her rib into a scepter or whatever it is that you do. Fucking nonsense. I don't know why you had to make that place all mystical or whatever it is. You can leave Jeannie be. You've done enough."

"I haven't made it anything. It's where I go shoot horses when you tell me to, and if you want to give the shooting job to someone else, or if you want it, you go right ahead. I thought I'd check on you, but I see you're fine. Good night."

"He's not coming back," he said as she turned away. "Lover boy's gone back to his wife but is too big a coward to tell you."

Sammy reached across the table and rolled the billiard balls around, clacking them into each other. "He wouldn't have left Digger."

"But he'd leave you? You're admitting that? He'd leave you but not the horse."

"Aw, shut up. There's no way in hell he'd leave Digger. Fuck all else."

"Sammy, Sammy. He left the horse for you. As payment. Just like he left those for me, for services rendered, ha ha ha." He pointed at a stack of three canvases turned to the wall. She crossed the room slowly, aware of her boots compressing the carpet and the sound of the Otter's breathing, his ratter eyes following her. The first painting was of Digger, the second was of her riding Digger, and the third was of her alone, asleep. "To be clear," the Otter said, "he left them for me, not for you."

She reached down and touched her own closed eyes. She could feel the texture of the canvas through the paint. "I'm sorry," she said.

"For what?" He was leaning forward, gripping his glass.

"That I love him and not you." She let go of the painting and walked out of the room.

The big snow came the next day. Shut in her cabin, she wondered what the Otter's next move would be. It was ten days before the sky snowed itself out and the roads were passable enough for her to drive into town. She told herself she was getting away. She liked the sound of that, getting away, like she was going to Hawaii or Mexico and not just drinking beer at Jeb's Antlers and watching people dance the two-step. She ate potato chips in a motel room by herself; she went to the movies; she bought a new coat. By the time she drove back to the ranch, she was in a forgiving mood. Poor old Otter had gotten his heart broken and never had it set right. One of her brothers had had an elbow that healed wrong and looked like he had a lump of cauliflower under the skin. The Otter's ticker must look like a lava rock by now. She would invite him to play Chinese checkers. But first thing when she got back, she went out to the barn to check on Digger and found his stall empty.

Big Georgie scratched his head and leaned on the fork he'd been mucking with. "Well, yeah, he's not there cause Otter put him on the truck."

"What truck?"

"The auction truck."

"No," Sammy said. "Digger. The big, good-looking horse that's usually in this stall."

"Yeah, I know." Georgie nodded and kept on nodding. "The big horse. Arn came and had the truck all loaded up with the kibble horses and then the Otter threw the big horse on there at the last minute. Did he get sick or something? Cause he looked good to me. He's going to think he's at the wrong party."

The Otter would not open the door of his bedroom no matter how hard Sammy pounded and kicked on it.

"I swear you better be swinging from a beam in there! Do you think nobody else ever lost anything? Do you?"

There was only silence from the other side. Every time she thought she heard a rustle or the tinkle of ice, she charged the door with the worst her fists and words could do, but it was solid oak and would not budge.

"Well," Georgie said when she went back out to the barn and grabbed him by the wooly lapels of his sheepskin jacket, "I reckon they said the auction was tomorrow, and that was yesterday. So," he said, frowning, "I guess it's today."

As Sammy drove, burning up the road to Bozeman, she did two things. First, she prayed, or really begged, for some luck. Just some god damn luck this one time. Second, she reached over and flipped open the glove compartment, feeling for the thick white envelope that she had been checking and rechecking the whole way. She wedged the envelope lengthwise between her thighs and, darting her eyes back and forth between the road and the bills, counted yet again. $6,000. All she had. It had to be enough. She needed it to be enough. Who would pay $6,000 for a few sacks of dog food besides her? Please, she thought, squeezing the envelope like a rosary, please give me some luck here.

The auction was in a low brown clump of livestock sheds. Sammy had to stop twice at gas stations to ask where to go, and at the second one the driver of a big stock truck said to follow him. In the paddocks she saw a brown patchwork of swaybacked horses with shaggy, shit-crusted coats. In the auction hall, every horse they brought out made her pulse race, but it was two hours before they brought out Digger. The crowd murmured. Tall, handsome Digger didn't belong with the broken-down nags that the packers' men were buying for chump change with lazy waves of their numbers. He didn't belong in this parade of the dead. He lifted his head and showed the whites of his eyes and the insides of his nostrils to the crowd. Veins stood out on his head and neck, ran down his legs like tributaries of a mighty river.

"Well, I don't know, folks," said the auctioneer. "Not the usual horse, let's not start at the usual number. I'm asking five hundred."

Sammy lifted her number up and held it there in her trembling hand while the bids went up and up. She held hers like a torch.

"Six thousand one hundred," said the auctioneer. Sammy's arm wavered. He pointed at her. "I have six thousand one hundred." He pointed past her. "Do I hear two from you sir?" Someone over Sammy's shoulder must have nodded, because the auctioneer said, "I have two and I'm looking for three, do I have three?" Her arm stayed up until $6,700, buttressed by whatever had held Sleepy Jean on her feet for a few seconds after the spinning piece of lead lodged in her brain. Then that trembling force let go, and her number fell to her knee. "Sold! For six thousand seven hundred and fifty, and, gents, I think that's both a record high and a bargain. Good for you, sir."

Sammy sat. The men led Digger off the block and brought on another nag. "I'll start the bidding at fifty dollars," said the auctioneer. For the first time, she hoped that Harrison would never return. Then she was seized by the wild thought that he must have been the one who bought Digger. He must have found out and come back. She stood up. No one was standing except her and the man who won. She could not see his face. He was a hat and a pair of hands in the shadows, the number 31 held down at his side. He stepped into the dusty light, and she saw across a sea of hats that it was the Otter. He looked at her with his face twisted around his mustache in an expression of deepest remorse. His sad otter eyes glittered at her, and she felt an answering cry of pity as rough as anything she'd ever felt at the Pearly Gates. Poor Otter with his lava rock heart. Poor Otter who failed at revenge and bought back his heart, rock or not, at the last minute. Even if she'd had a million dollars in her envelope, the Otter would have found a way to outbid her because only the Otter wanted that horse more than she did. She looked at him while the next sad sack horse got pulled out to the block, and he looked at her, and they wondered what was to be done.

WELLS TOWER

Raw Water

FROM *McSweeney's*

"JUST LET ME OUT of here, man," said Cora Booth. "I'm sick. I'm dying."

"Of what?" asked Rodney, her husband, blinking at the wheel, scoliotic with exhaustion. He'd been sitting there for four days, steering the pickup down out of Boston, a trailer shimmying on the ball hitch, a mattress held to the roof of the camper shell with tie-downs that razzed like an attack of giant farting bees.

"Ford poisoning," Cora said. "Truckanosis, stage four. I want out. I'll walk from here."

Rodney told his wife that a hundred and twenty miles lay between them and the home they'd rented in the desert, sight unseen.

"Perfect," she said. "I'll see you in four days. You'll appreciate the benefits. I'll have a tan and my ass will be a huge wad of muscle. You can climb up on it and ride like a little monkey."

"I'm so tired. I'm sad and confused," said Rodney. "I'm in a thing where I see the road, I just don't comprehend it. I don't understand what it means."

Cora rolled down the window to photograph a balustrade of planted organ cactuses strobing past in rows.

"Need a favor, chum?" she said, toying with his zipper.

"What I need is to focus here," Rodney said. "The white lines keep swapping around."

"How about let's scoot up one of those little fire trails," Cora said. "You won't get dirty, I promise. We'll put the tailgate down and do some stunts on it."

The suggestion compounded Rodney's fatigue. It had been a half decade since he and Cora had made any kind of habitual love, and Rodney was fine with that. Even during his teenage hormone boom, he'd been a fairly unvenereal person. As he saw it, their marriage hit its best years once the erotic gunpowder burned off and it cooled to a more tough and precious alloy of long friendship and love from the deep heart. But Cora, who was forty-three, had lately emerged from menopause with large itches in her. Now she was hassling him for a session more days than not. After so many tranquil, sexless years, Rodney felt there was something unseemly, a mild whang of incest, in mounting his best friend. Plus she had turned rough and impersonal in her throes, like a cat on its post. She didn't look at him while they were striving. She went off somewhere by herself. Her eyes were always closed, her body arched, her jaw thrusting up from the curtains of her graying hair, mouth parted. Watching her, Rodney didn't feel at all like a proper husband in a love rite with his wife, more a bootleg hospice man bungling a euthanasia that did not spare much pain.

"Later. Got to dog traffic. I want to get the big stuff moved in while there's still light," said Rodney to Cora, though night was obviously far away, and they were making good time into the hills.

The truck crested the ridge into warm light and the big view occurred. "Brakes, right now," said Cora.

The westward face of the mountain sloped down to the vast brownness of the Anasazi Trough, a crater of rusty land in whose center lay sixty square miles of the world's newest inland ocean, the Anasazi Sea.

Rodney swung the truck onto the shoulder. Cora sprang to the trailer and fetched her big camera, eight by ten, an antique device whose leather bellows she massaged after each use with neat's-foot oil. She set up the tripod on the roadside promontory. Sounds of muffled cooing pleasure issued from her photographer's shroud.

Truly, it was a view to make a visual person moan. The sea's geometry was striking — a perfect rectangle, two miles wide and thirty miles long. But its water was a stupefying sight: livid red, a giant, tranquil plain the color of cranberry pulp.

The Anasazi was America's first foray into the new global fashion for do-it-yourself oceans — huge ponds of seawater, piped or chan-

neled into desert depressions as an antidote to sea-level rise. The
Libyans pioneered the practice with the great systematic flood of
the Qattara Depression in the Cairo desert. The water made one
species of fox extinct and thousands of humans rich. Evaporation
from the artificial sea rained down on new olive plantations. Villages emerged. Fisherfolk raised families hauling tilefish and mack-
erel out of a former bowl of hot dirt. American investors were inspired. They organized the condemnation of the Anasazi Trough a
hundred miles northwest of Phoenix and ran a huge pipe to the
Gulf of Mexico. Six million gallons of seawater flowed in every day,
to be boiled and filtered at the grandest desalination facility in the
Western Hemisphere.

A land fever caught hold. The minor city of Port Miracle bur-
geoned somewhat on the sea's eastern shore. On the west coast sat
Triton Estates, a gated sanctuary for golfers and owners of small
planes. But before the yacht club had sold its last mooring, the
young sea began to misbehave. The evaporation clouds were supposed to float eastward to the highlands and wring fresh rain from
themselves. Instead, the clouds caught a thermal south, dumping their bounty on the far side of the Mexican border, nourish-
ing a corn and strawberry bonanza in the dry land outside Juárez.
With no cloud cover over the Anasazi, the sun went to work and
started cooking the sea into a concentrated brine. Meanwhile, even
as acreage spiraled toward Tahoe prices, the grid spread: toilets,
lawns, and putting greens quietly embezzling the budget of desali-
nated water that should have been pumped back into the sea to
keep salt levels at a healthy poise. By the sea's tenth birthday, it was
fifteen times as saline as the Pacific, dense enough to float small
stones. The desalination plant's reverse-osmosis filters, designed to
last five years, started blowing out after six months on the job. The
land boom on the Anasazi fell apart when water got so expensive
that it was cheaper to flush the commode with half-and-half.

The grocery store papers spread it around that the great pond
wouldn't just take your money; it would kill you dead. Local news
shows ran testimonies of citizens who said they'd seen the lake eat
cows and elks and illegal Mexicans, shrieking as they boiled away.
Science said the lake was not a man-eater, but the proof was in that
gory water, so the stories stayed on prime time for a good number
of years.

The real story of the redness was very dull. It was just a lot of ancient, red, one-celled creatures that thrived in high salt. The water authority tested and retested the water and declared the microbes no enemy to man. They were, however, hard on curb appeal. When the sea was only twelve years old, the coastal population had dwindled to ninety-three, a net loss of five thousand souls no longer keen on dwelling in a case of pinkeye inflamed to geologic scale.

The story delighted Cora Booth as meat for her art. She'd long been at work on a group of paintings and photographs about science's unintended consequences: victims of robot nanoworms designed to eat cancer cells but which got hungry for other parts, lab mice in DNA-grafting experiments who'd developed a crude sign language using the hands of human infants growing from their backs. Once the tenants had fled and the situation on the sea had tilted into flagrant disaster, Cora banged out some grant proposals, withdrew some savings, and leased a home in Triton Estates, a place forsaken by God and movie stars.

Salvage vandals had long ago stolen the gates off the entrance to the Booths' new neighborhood, but a pair of sandstone obelisks topped with unlit gas lamps still stood there, and they still spelled class. Their new home stood on a coastal boulevard named Naiad Lane, a thin track of blond scree. They drove slow past a couple dozen homes, most of them squatly sprawling bunkerish jobs of off-white stucco, all of them abandoned, windows broken or filmed with dust; others half built, showing lath, gray bones of sun-beaten framing, pennants of torn Tyvek corrugating in the wind. Rodney pulled the truck into the driveway at number thirty-three, a six-bedroom cube with a fancy Spanish pediment on the front. It looked like a crate with a tiara. But just over the road lay the sea. Unruffled by the wind, its water lay still and thick as house paint, and it cast an inviting pink glow on the Booths' new home.

"I like it," said Cora, stepping from the truck. "Our personal Alamo."

"What's that smell?" said Rodney when they had stepped inside. The house was light and airy, but the air bore a light scent of wharf breath.

"It's the bricks," said Cora. "They made them from the thluk they take out of the water at the desal plant. Very clever stuff."

"It smells like, you know, groins."

"Learn to love it," Cora said.

When they had finished the tour, the sun was dying. On the far coast, the meager lights of Port Miracle were winking on. They'd only just started unloading the trailer when Cora's telephone bleated in her pocket. On the other end was Arn Nevis, the sole property agent in Triton Estates and occupant of one of the four still-inhabited homes in the neighborhood. Cora opened the phone. "Hi, terrific, okay, sure, hello?" she said, then looked at the receiver.

"Who was that?" asked Rodney, sitting on the front stair.

"Nevis, Arn Nevis, the rental turkey," said Cora. "He just sort of barfed up a dinner invitation — *Muhhouse, seven thirty* — and hung up on me. Said it's close, we don't need to take our truck. Now, how does he know we have a truck? You see somebody seeing us out here, Rod?"

They peered around and saw nothing. Close to land, a fish or something buckled in the red water, other than themselves the afternoon's sole sign of life.

But they drove the Ranger after all, because Rodney had bad ankles. He'd shattered them both in childhood, jumping from a crabapple tree, and even a quarter-mile's stroll would cause him nauseas of pain. So the Booths rode slowly in the truck through a Pompeii of vanished home equity. The ride took fifteen minutes because Cora kept experiencing ecstasies at the photogenic ruin of Triton Estates, getting six angles on a warped basketball rim over a yawning garage, a hot tub brimming and splitting with gallons of dust.

Past the grid of small lots they rolled down a brief grade to number three Naiad. The Nevis estate lay behind high white walls, light spilling upward in a column, a bright little citadel unto itself.

Rodney parked the truck alongside an aged yellow Mercedes. At a locked steel gate, the only breach in the tall wall, he rang the doorbell and they loitered many minutes while the day's heat fled the air. Finally a wide white girl appeared at the gate. She paused a moment before opening it, appraising them through the bars, studying the dusk beyond, as though expecting unseen persons to spring out of the gloom. Then she turned a latch and swung the door wide. She was sixteen or so, with a face like a left-handed sketch — small teeth, one eye bigger than the other and a half-inch lower on her cheek. Her outfit was a yellow towel, dark across the chest and waist where a damp bathing suit had soaked through. She said her name was Katherine.

"Sorry I'm all sopped," she said. "They made me quit swimming and be butler. Anyway, they're out back. You were late so they started stuffing themselves." Katherine set off for the house, her hard summer heels rasping on the slate path.

The Nevis house was a three-wing structure, a staple shape in bird's-eye view. In the interstice between the staple's legs lay a small rectangular inlet of the sea, paved and studded with underwater lights; it was serving as the family's personal pool. At the lip of the swimming area, a trio sat at a patio set having a meal of mussels. At one end of the table slouched Arn Nevis, an old, vast man with a head of white curls, grown long to mask their sparseness, and a great bay window of stomach overhanging his belt. Despite his age and obesity, he wasn't unattractive; his features bedded in a handsome arrangement of knobs and ridges, nearly cartoonish in their prominence. Arn was in the middle of a contretemps with a thin young man beside him. The old man had his forearms braced on the tabletop, his shoulders hiked forward, as though ready to pounce on his smaller companion. On the far side of the table sat a middle-aged woman, her blouse hoisted discreetly to let an infant at her breast. She stroked and murmured to it, seemingly unaware of the stridency between the men.

"I didn't come here to get hot-boxed, Arn," the smaller man was saying, staring at his plate.

"Hut — hoorsh," stuttered Nevis.

"Excuse me?" the other man said.

Nevis took a long pull on his drink, swallowed, took a breath. "I said, I'm not hot-boxing anybody," said Nevis, enunciating carefully. "It's just you suffer from a disease, Kurt. That disease is caution, bad as cancer."

The woman raised her gaze and, seeing the Booths, smiled widely. She introduced herself as Phyllis Nevis. She was a pretty woman, though her slack jowls and creased dewlap put her close to sixty. If she noticed her visitors' amazement at seeing a woman of

her age putting an infant to suck, she didn't show it. She smiled
and let a blithe music of welcome flow from her mouth: Boy, the
Nevises sure were glad to have some new neighbors here in Triton.
They'd met Katherine, of course, and there was Arn. The baby having at her was little Nathan, and the other fellow was Kurt Hackberry, a business friend but a real friend, too. Would they like a
vodka lemonade? She invited the Booths to knock themselves out
on some mussels, tonged from the shallows just off the dock, though
Cora noticed there was about half a portion left. "So sorry we've
already tucked in," Phyllis said. "But we always eat at seven thirty,
rain or shine."

Katherine Nevis did not sit with the diners but went to the sea's
paved edge. She dropped her towel and slipped into the glowing
water without a splash.

"So you drove down from Boston?" Hackberry asked, plainly
keen to quit the conversation with his host.

"We did," said Rodney. "Five days, actually not so bad once you
get past—"

"Yeah, yeah, Boston—" Nevis interrupted with regal vehemence.
"And now they're here, sight unseen, whole thing over the phone,
not all this fiddlefucking around." Nevis coughed into his fist, then
reached for a plastic jug of vodka and filled his glass nearly to
the rim, a good half-pint of liquor. He drank a third of it at one
pull, then turned to Cora, his head bobbing woozily on his dark
neck. "Kurt is a Chicken Little. Listens to ninnies who think the
Bureau of Land Management is going to choke us off and starve
the pond."

"Why don't they?" Cora asked.

"Because we've got their nursh—their nuh—their nads in a
noose is why," said Nevis. "Because every inch of shoreline they expose means alkali dust blowing down on the goddamned bocce
pitches and Little League fields and citrus groves down in the Yuma
Valley. They're all looking up the wrong end of a shotgun, and us
right here? We're perched atop a seat favored by the famous bird,
if you follow me."

Nevis drained his glass and filled it again. He looked at Cora and
sucked his teeth. "Hot damn, you're a pretty woman, Cora. Son of
a bitch, it's like somebody opened a window out here. If I'd known
you were so goddamned lovely, I'd have jewed them down on the
rent. But then, if I'd known you were hitched up with this joker I'd

have charged you double, probably." He jerked a thumb and aimed a grin of long gray teeth at Rodney. Rodney looked away and pulled at a skin tag on the rim of his ear. "Don't you think, Phyllis?" said Nevis. "Great bones."

"Thank you," Cora said. "I plan to have them bronzed."

"Humor," Nevis said flatly, gazing at Cora with sinking red eyes. "It's that actress you resemble. Murf. Murvek. Urta. Fuck am I talking about? You know, Phyllis, from the goddamn dogsled picture."

"Drink a few more of those," said Cora. "I'll find you a cockroach who looks like Brigitte Bardot."

"Actually, I hate alcohol, but I get these migraines. They mess with my speech, but liquor helps some," Nevis said. Here, he sat forward in his chair, peering unabashedly at Cora's chest. "Good Christ, you got a figure, lady. All natural, am I right?"

Rodney took a breath to say a hard word to Nevis, but while he was trying to formulate the proper phrase Phyllis spoke to her husband in a gentle voice.

"Arny, I'm not sure Cora appreciates—"

"An appreciation of beauty, even if it is sexual beauty, is a great gift," said Nevis. "Anyone who thinks beauty is not sexual should picture tits on a man."

"I'm sure you're right, sweetie, but even so—"

Nevis flashed a brilliant crescent of teeth at his wife and bent to the table to kiss her hand. "Right here, the most wonderful woman on earth. The kindest and most beautiful and I married her." Nevis raised his glass to his lips. His gullet pumped three times while he drank.

"His headaches are horrible," said Phyllis.

"They are. Pills don't work but vodka does. Fortunately, it doesn't affect me. I've never been drunk in my life. Anyway, you two are lucky you showed up at this particular juncture," Nevis announced through a belch. "Got a petition for a water-rights deal on Birch Creek. Hundred thousand gallons a day. Fresh water. Pond'll be blue again this time next year."

This news alarmed Cora, whose immediate thought was that her work would lose its significance if the story of the Anasazi Sea ended happily. "I like the color," Cora said. "It's exciting."

Nevis refilled his glass. "You're an intelligent woman, Cora, and you don't believe the rumors and the paranoia peddlers on the goddamned news," he said. "Me, I'd hate to lose it, except you can't sell a fucking house with the lake how it is. Of course, nobody talks about the health benefits of that water. My daughter?" He jerked his thumb at Katherine, still splashing in the pool, and lowered his voice. "Before we moved in here, you wouldn't have believed her complexion. Like a lasagna, I'm serious. Look at her now! Kill for that skin. Looks like a marble statue. Hasn't had a zit in years, me or my wife neither, not one blackhead, nothing. Great for the bones, too. I've got old-timers who swim here three times a week, swear it's curing their arthritis. Of course, nobody puts that on the news. Anyway, what I'm saying is, buy now, because once this Birch Creek thing goes through, this place is going to be a destination. Gonna put the back nine on the golf course. Shopping district, too, as soon as Kurt and a few other moneymen stop sitting on their wallets like a bunch of broody hens."

Nevis clouted Hackberry on the upper arm with more force than was jolly. Hackberry looked lightly terrified and went into a fit of vague motions with his head, shaking and nodding, saying "Now, Kurt, now, Kurt" with the look of a panicked child wishing for the ground to open up beneath him.

When he had lapped the fluid from the final mussel shell, Arn Nevis was showing signs of being drunk, if he was to be taken at his word, for the first time in his life. He rose from the table and stood swaying. "Clothes off, people," he said, fumbling with his belt.

Phyllis smiled and kept her eyes on her guests. "We have tea, and we have coffee and homemade peanut brittle, too."

"Phyllis, shut your mouth," said Nevis. "Swim time. Cora, get up. Have a dip."

"I don't swim," said Cora.

"You can't?" said Nevis.

"No," said Cora, which was true.

"Dead man could swim in the water. Nathan can. Give me the baby, Phyllis." He lurched for his wife's breast, and with a sudden move, Phyllis clutched the baby to her and swiveled brusquely away from her husband's hand. "Touch him and I'll kill you," Phyllis hissed. Nathan awoke and began to mewl. Nevis shrugged and lumbered toward the water, shedding his shirt, then his pants, mercifully retaining the pair of yellowed briefs he wore. He dove messily but began swimming surprisingly brisk and powerful laps, his whalelike huffing loud and crisp in the silence of the night. But after three full circuits to the far end of the inlet and back, the din of his breathing stopped. Katherine Nevis, who'd been sulking under the pergola with a video game, began to shriek. The guests leaped up. Arn Nevis had sunk seven feet or so below the surface, suspended from a deeper fall by the hypersaline water. In the red depths' wavering lambency, Nevis seemed to be moving, though in fact he was perfectly still.

Rodney kicked off his shoes and jumped in. With much effort, he hauled the large man to the concrete steps ascending to the patio and, helped by Cora and Hackberry, heaved him into the cool air. Water poured from Rodney's pockets. He put his palms to the broad saucer of Nevis's sternum and rammed hard. The drowned man sputtered.

"Wake up. Wake *up*," said Rodney. Nevis did not answer. Rodney slapped Nevis on the cheek, and Nevis opened his eyes to a grouchy squint.

"What day is it?" asked Rodney. By way of an answer, Nevis expelled lung water down his chin.

"Who's that?" Rodney pointed to Phyllis. "Tell me her name."

Nevis regarded his wife. "Big dummy," he said.

"What the hell does that mean?" Rodney said. "Who's that?" He pointed at Nevis's infant son.

Nevis pondered the question. "Little dummy," he said, and began to laugh, which everybody took to mean that he had returned, unharmed, to life.

Kurt Hackberry and Katherine led Arn inside while Phyllis poured forth weeping apologies and panting gratitude to the Booths. "No harm done. Thank God he's all right. I'm glad I was here to lend a hand," Rodney said, and was surprised to realize that he meant it. Despite the evening's calamities, his heart was warm and filled with an electric vigor of life. The electricity stayed with him all the way back to number thirty-three Naiad Lane, where, in the echoing kitchen, Rodney made zestful love to his wife for the first time in seven weeks.

Rodney woke before the sun was up. The maritime fetor of the house's salt walls and recollections of Arn Nevis's near death merged into a general unease that would not let him sleep. Cora stirred beside him. She peered out the window, yawned, and said that she wanted to photograph the breaking of the day. "I'll come with you," Rodney said, and felt childish to realize that he didn't want to be left in the house alone.

Cora was after large landscapes of the dawn hitting Triton Estates and the western valley, so the proper place to set up was on the east coast, in Port Miracle, with the sun behind the lens. After breakfast they loaded the Ford with Cora's equipment and made the ten-minute drive. They parked at the remnant of Port Miracle's public beach and removed their shoes. Most of the trucked-in sand had blown away, revealing a hard marsh of upthrust minerals, crystalline and translucent, like stepping on warm ice. Rodney lay on the blanket they had brought while Cora took some exposures of the dawn effects. The morning sky involved bands of iridescence, the lavender-into-blue-gray spectrum of a bull pigeon's throat. Cora made plates of the light's progress, falling in a thickening portion on the dark house-key profile of the western hills, then staining the white homes scattered along the shore. She yelled a little at the moment of dawn's sudden ignition when red hit red and the sea lit up, flooding the whole valley with so much immediate light you could almost hear the *whong!* of a ball field's vapor bulbs going on.

"Rodney, how about you go swimming for me?"

"I don't have a suit."

"Who cares? It's a ghost town."

"I don't want to get all sticky."

"Shit, Rodney, come on. Help me out."

Rodney stripped grudgingly and walked into the water. Even in the new hours of the day, the water was hot and alarmingly solid, like paddling through Crisco. It seared his pores and mucous parts, but his body had a thrilling buoyancy in the thick water. A single kick of the legs sent him gliding like a hockey puck. And despite its lukewarmth and viscosity, the water was wonderfully vivifying. His pulse surged. Rodney stroked and kicked until he heard his wife yelling for him to swim back into camera range. He turned around, gamboled for her camera some, and stepped into the morning, stripped clean by the water, with a feeling of having been peeled to new young flesh. Rodney did not bother to dress. He carried the blanket to the shade of a disused picnic awning. Cora lay there with him, and then they drowsed until the sun was well up in the sky.

Once the drab glare of the day set in, the Booths breakfasted together on granola bars and instant coffee from the plastic crate of food they'd packed for the ride from Massachusetts.

Cora wished to tour Port Miracle on foot. Rodney, with his bad ankles, said he would be happy to spend the morning in his sandy spot, taking in the late-summer sun with a Jack London paperback. So Cora went off with her camera, first to the RV lot, nearly full, the rows of large white vehicles like raw loaves of bread. She walked through a rear neighborhood of kit cottages, built of glass and grooved plywood and tin. She photographed shirtless children, Indian brown, kicking a ball in a dirt lot, and a leathery soul on a sunblasted Adirondack chair putting hot sauce into his beer. She went to the boat launch where five pink women, all of manatee girth, were boarding a pontoon craft. Cora asked to take their picture but they giggled and shied behind their hands and Cora moved on.

At the far end of town stood the desalination facility, a cube of steel and concrete intubated with ducts and billowing steam jacks. Cora humped it for the plant, her tripod clacking on her shoulder. After calling into the intercom at the plant's steel door, Cora was greeted by a gray-haired, bearded man wearing something like a cellophane version of a fisherman's hard-weather kit. Plastic pants, shirt, hat, plus gloves and boot gaiters and a thick dust mask hanging around his neck. His beard looked like a cloudburst, though he'd carefully imprisoned it in a hairnet so as to tuck it coherently within his waterproof coat.

"Whoa," said Cora, taken aback. Recovering herself, she explained that she was new to the neighborhood and was hoping to find a manager or somebody who might give her a tour of the plant.

"I'm it!" the sheathed fellow told her, a tuneful courtliness in his voice. "Willard Kamp. And it would be my great pleasure to show you around."

Cora lingered on the threshold, taking in Kamp's protective gear. "Is it safe, though, if I'm just dressed like this?"

"That's what the experts would tell you," said Kamp, and laughed, leading Cora to a bank of screens showing the brine's progress through a filter-maze. Then he ushered her up a flight of stairs to a platform overlooking the concrete lagoons where the seawater poured in. He showed her the flocculating chambers where they added ferric chloride and sulfuric acid and chlorine and the traveling rakes that brought the big solids to the surface in a rumpled brown sludge. He showed her how the water traveled through sand filters, and then through diatomaceous earth capsules to further strain contaminants, before they hit the big reverse-osmosis trains that filtered the last of the impurities.

"Coming into here," Kamp said, slapping the side of a massive fiberglass storage tank, "is raw water. Nothing in here but pure H's and O's."

"Just the good stuff, huh?" Cora said.

"Well, not for our purposes," Kamp said. "It's no good for us in its pure form. We have to gentle it down with additives, acid salts, gypsum. Raw, it's very chemically aggressive. It's so hungry for minerals to bind with, it'll eat a copper pipe in a couple of weeks."

This idea appealed to Cora. "What happens if you drink it? Will it kill you? Burn your skin?"

Kamp laughed, a wheezing drone. "Not at all. It's an enemy to metal pipes and soap lather, but it's amiable to humankind."

"So what's with all the hazmat gear?" asked Cora, gesturing at Kamp's clothes. Kamp laughed again. "I'm overfastidious, the preoccupation of a nervous mind."

"Nervous about what?"

His wiry brow furrowed and his lips pursed in half-comic consternation. "Well, it's a funny lake, isn't it, Cora? I am very interested in the archaebacteria, the little red gentlemen out there."

"But it's the same stuff in fall foliage and flamingos," Cora said, brandishing some knowledge she'd picked up from a magazine. "Harmless."

Kamp reached into his raincoat to scratch at something in his beard. "Probably so. Though they're also very old. Two billion years. They were swimming around before there was oxygen in the atmosphere, if you can picture that. You've heard, I guess, the notion that that stuff in our pond is pretty distinguished crud, possibly the source of all life on earth."

"I hadn't."

"Well, they say there's something to it," said Kamp. "Now, it's quite likely that I haven't got the sense God gave a monkey wrench, but it seems to me that a tadpole devious enough to put a couple of

million species on the planet is one I'd rather keep on the outside
of my person."

Of Port Miracle's eighty dwellers, nearly all were maroon ancients.
They were unwealthy people, mainly, not far from death, so they
found the dead city a congenial place to live the life of a lizard,
moving slow and taking sun. But they were not community center
folk. Often there was public screaming on the boulevard, sometimes fights with brittle fists when someone got too close to someone else's wife or yard. Just the year before, in a further blow to the
Anasazi's image in the press, a retired playwright, age eighty-one,
levered open the door of a Winnebago parked on his lot and tor-
tured a pair of tourists with some rough nylon rope and a soup-
heating coil.

According to the rules of the Nevis household, young Katherine
was not permitted past the sandstone obelisks at the neighborhood's mouth. But the morning after the dinner party her father
was still abed with a pulsing brain, and would likely be that way all
day. Knowing this, Katherine slipped through the gate after breakfast, wheeled her little 97cc minibike out of earshot, and set a
course to meet two pals of hers, Claude Hull and Denny Peebles,
on the forbidden coast.

She found them by the public pier, and they greeted her with
less commotion than she'd have liked. They were busy squabbling
over some binoculars through which they were leering at the fat
women out at sea on the pontoon barge.

"Let me look," Claude begged Denny, who had snatched the
Bausch & Lombs, an unfair thing. The Bausch & Lombs belonged
to Claude's father, who owned Port Miracle's little credit union
and liked to look at birds.

Denny sucked his lips and watched the women, herded beneath
the boat's canopy shade, their bikinis almost wholly swallowed by
their hides. They took turns getting in the water via a scuba ladder
that caused the boat to lurch comically when one of them put her
bulk on it. The swimming lady would contort her face in agonies at
the stinging water while her colleagues leaned over the gunwale,
shouting encouragement, bellies asway. After a minute or two, the
others would help the woman aboard and serve her something in
a tall chilled glass and scrub at her with implements not legible

through the Bausch & Lombs. The women were acting on a rumor that the sea's bacteria devoured extra flesh. It had the look of a cult.

"Big white witches," whispered Denny.

"Come on, let me hold 'em, let me look," said Claude, a lean, tweaky child whose widespread eyes and bulging forehead made it a mercy that he, like the other children who lived out here, attended ninth grade over the computer. Denny, the grocer's child, had shaggy black hair, a dark tan, and very long, very solid arms for a boy of fourteen. "Fuck off," said Denny, throwing an elbow. "Get Katherine to show you hers. You'll like 'em if you like it when a girl's titty looks like a carrot."

"I'm not showing Claude," said Katherine.

In the sand beside Denny lay a can of oven cleaner and a bespattered paper bag. Katherine reached for it.

"Mother may I?" Denny said.

"Bite my fur," said Katherine. She sprayed a quantity of the oven cleaner into the bag, then put it to her mouth and inhaled.

"Let me get some of that, Kathy," Claude said.

"Talk to Denny," said Katherine. "It's not my can."

"Next time I'm gonna hook up my camera to this thing, get these puddings on film," said Denny, who was lying on his stomach in the sand, the binoculars propped to his face. "Somebody scratch my back for me. Itches like a motherfucker."

"Sucks for you," said Katherine, whose skull now felt luminous and red and full of perfect blood.

"You scratch it for me, Claude," said Denny. "Backstroke, hot damn. Look at those pies. Turn this way, honey. Are you pretty in your face?"

Just last week, for no reason at all, Denny Peebles had wedged Claude Hull's large head between his knees and dragged him up and down Dock Street while old men laughed. Claude loved and feared Denny, so he reached out a hand and scratched at Denny's spine.

"Lower," Denny said, and Claude slid his hand down to the spot between Denny's sacral dimples, which were lightly downed with faint hair. "Little lower. Get in the crack, man. That's where the itch is at."

Claude laughed nervously. "You want me to scratch your *ass* for you?"

"It itches, I told you. Go ahead. It's clean."

"No way I'm doing that, man. You scratch it."

"I can't reach it. I'm using my hands right now," said Denny. "I'm trying to see these fatties."

Katherine sprayed another acrid cloud into the bag and sucked it in. Dust clung in an oval around her mouth, giving the effect of a chimpanzee's muzzle.

"Just do it, Claude," Katherine said. "He likes it. He said it's clean. You don't believe him?"

Denny took the glasses from his face to look at the smaller boy. "Yeah, you don't believe me, Claude? What, I'm a liar, Claude?"

"No, no, I do." And so Claude reached into Denny's pants and scratched, and this intimate grooming felt very good to Denny in a hardly sexual way, so to better concentrate on the sensation, he rested the binoculars and held his hand out for the can of oven cleaner and the paper bag.

After an hour on the beach, Rodney put a flat stone in his paperback, retrieved his pants, and got up to stretch his legs. He had the thought that strolling through the still water might cushion his ankles somewhat, so he waded in and set off up the cove. Forbidding as the water looked, it teemed with life. Carp fingerlings nibbled his shins. Twice, a crab scuttled over his bare toes. He strolled on until he reached the pier, a chocolate-colored structure built of creosoted wood. Rodney spied a clump of shells clinging to the pilings. These were major oysters, the size of cactus pads. He tried to yank one free, but it would not surrender to his hand. It was such a tempting prize that he waded all the way back to the truck and got the tire iron from under the seat. Knee-deep in the water, he worked open a shell. The flesh inside was pale gray and large as a goose egg. That much oyster meat would cost you thirty dollars in a Boston restaurant. The flesh showed no signs of dubious pinkness. He sniffed it — no bad aromas. He spilled it onto his tongue, chewing three times to get it down. The meat was clean and briny. He ate two more and felt renewed. Wading back to shore, a few smaller mollusks in hand, he peered under the wharf and spotted Katherine Nevis on the beach with her friends. The desolation of the town had cast a shadow on the morning, and it cheered Rodney to see those children out there enjoying the day. It would be unneighborly, Rodney thought, not to say hello.

When Rodney got within fifty yards, Denny and Claude looked up, panicked to see a shirtless fellow coming at them with a tire iron, an ugly limp in his gait. They took off in a kind of skulking lope and left Katherine on the beach. Obviously Rodney had caught them in the middle of some teenage mischief, and he chuckled to see the boys scamper. Katherine cupped a hand over the beige matter on her face and looked at her toes as Rodney approached. He wondered about the grime, but instead asked after her dad. "I dunno," she said. "I'm sure he's doing awesome."

Rodney nudged the oven cleaner can with his foot. "Cleaning the beach?" he asked. Katherine said nothing. "Whatever happened to just raiding your parents' booze?"

"He has to drive all the way to Honerville to get it," she said. "He keeps it locked up, even from my mom."

Rodney put the tire iron in his belt and dropped his oysters. He took out his handkerchief and reached for her, thinking to swab her face. She shrank away from him. "Don't fucking touch me," she said. "Don't, I swear."

"Easy, easy, nobody's doing anything," Rodney said, though he could feel the color in his cheeks. "It's just you look like you need a shave."

Cautiously, a little shamefully, she took the handkerchief and daubed at her lips while he watched. The girl was conscious of being looked at, and she swabbed herself with small ladylike motions, making no headway on the filth.

"Here," said Rodney, very gently, taking the hanky from her damp hand. He sucked awhile at the bitter cloth, then he knelt and cradled the girl's jaw in his palm, rubbing at her mouth and chin. "Look out, you're gonna take off all my skin," she said, making a cranky child's grimace, though she didn't pull away. He heard her grunting lightly in her throat at the pleasure of being tended to. A smell was coming off her, a fragrance as warm and wholesome as rising bread. As he scrubbed the girl's dirty face, he put his nose close to her, breathing deeply and as quietly as he could. He had mostly purged the gum from Katherine's upper lip when she jerked away from him and hearkened anxiously to the sound of a slowing car. Arn Nevis's eggnog Mercedes pulled into the gravel lot. He got out and strode very quickly down the shingle.

"Hi, hi!" Nevis cried. His hair was in disarray, and his hands trembled in a Parkinsonian fashion. In the hard noonday light, he looked antique and unwell. Rodney saw, too, that Nevis had a fresh pink scar running diagonally across his forehead, stitch pocks dotting its length. Rodney marveled a little that just the night before, he'd felt some trepidation in the big man's presence. "Kath—Kuh, Kutch." Nevis stopped, marshaled his breathing, and spoke. "Kuh, come here, sweetie. Been looking for you. Mom's mad. Come now, huk—honey. See if I can't talk your mom out of striping your behind."

In his shame, Arn did not look at Rodney, which at once amused and angered the younger man. "Feeling okay, there, Arn?"

"Oh, shuh-sure," Nevis said, staring at a point on Rodney's abdomen. "Thank God it's Friday."

"It's Thursday," Rodney said.

"Oysters," the old man said, looking at Rodney's haul where he'd dropped it on the ground. "Oh, they're nice."

Rodney crouched and held them out to Nevis in cupped hands. Nevis looked at the oysters and then at Rodney. His was the manner of a craven dog, wanting that food but fearing that he might get a smack if he went for it. "Go on," said Rodney.

With a quick move, Nevis grabbed a handful. His other hand seized Katherine's arm. "All righty, and we'll see you soon," said Nevis over his shoulder, striding to his car.

The days found an agreeable tempo in Cora and Rodney's new home. Each morning they rose with the sun. Each morning, Rodney swam far into the sea's broads, then returned to the house, where he would join Cora for a shower, then downstairs to cook and eat a breakfast of tremendous size. When the dishes were cleared, Cora would set off to gather pictures. Rodney would spend two hours on the computer to satisfy the advertising firm in Boston for which he still worked part-time, and then he'd do as he pleased. His was a life any sane person would envy, yet Rodney was not at ease. He felt bloated with a new energy. He had never been an ambitious person, but lately he had begun to feel that he was capable of resounding deeds. He had dreams in which he conquered famous wildernesses, and he would wake up with a lust for travel. Yet he was irritable on days when he had to leave the valley for provisions not sold in Port Miracle's pitiable grocery store. One day he told Cora that he might quit his job and start a company, though he grew angry when Cora forced him to admit that he had no idea what the company might produce. For the first time in his life, he resented Cora, begrudged the years he'd spent at her heel, and how he'd raised no fuss when she'd changed her mind after five years of marriage and said she didn't want children after all. His mind roved to other women, to the Nevis girl, a young thing with a working womb, someone who'd shut up when he talked.

When Cora left him the truck, he often went fishing off the wharf at Port Miracle, always coming home with several meals' worth of seafood iced down in his creel. He would wait until he got home to clean the catch so that Cora could photograph the haul intact.

"Ever seen one of these?" Cora asked him one night. She was sitting at the kitchen table with her laptop, whose screen showed a broad fish ablur with motion on the beach. "This thing was kind of creeping around in the mud down by that shed where the oldsters hang out."

"Huh," Rodney said, kissing Cora's neck and slipping a hand into her shirt. "Snakehead, probably. Or a mudskipper."

"It's not. It's flat, like a flounder," she said. "Quit a second. I wish I could have kept it, but this kid came along and bashed it and took off. Look."

She scrolled to a picture of Claude Hull braining the crawling fish with an aluminum bat.

"Mm," said Rodney, raising his wife's shirt and with the other hand going for her fly.

"Could you quit it?"

"Why?"

"For one thing, I'm trying to deal with my fucking work. For another, I'm kind of worn out. You've gotten me a little raw, going at me all the time."

Sulking, he broke off his advances and picked up his phone from the counter. "Tell you what," he said. "I'll call the neighbors. Get them over here to eat this stuff. We owe them a feed."

He stepped outdoors and called the Nevises, hoping to hear Katherine's hoarse little crow timbre on the other end. No one answered, so Rodney phoned two more times. He had watched the road carefully that morning and knew the family was home.

In fact, Katherine and her mother were out on a motorboat cruise while Arn Nevis paced his den, watching the telephone ring. He did not want to answer it. His trouble with words was worsening. Unless he loosened his tongue with considerable amounts of alcohol, the organ was lazy and intractable. In his mind, he could still formulate a phrase with perfect clarity, but his mouth no longer seemed interested in doing his mind's work and would utter a slurring of approximate sounds. When Nevis finally answered the telephone and heard Rodney's invitation, he paused to silently rehearse the words *I'm sorry, but Phyllis is feeling a bit under the weather.* But Nevis's tongue, the addled translator, wouldn't take the order. "Ilish feen urtha" and then a groan was what Rodney heard before the line went dead.

Until recently, the headaches Arn Nevis suffered had been slow pursuers. A stroll through the neighborhood would clear the bad blood from his temples and he'd have nearly a full day of peace. But lately, if he sat still for five minutes, the glow would commence behind his brow. He would almost drool thinking about a good thick auger to put a hole between his eyes and let the steam out of his head. After five minutes of that, if he didn't have a bottle around to kill it, white pain would bleach the vision from his eyes.

The pain was heating up again when he hung up on Rodney Booth, so he went out through the gate and strolled up to the dry tract slated to become nine new putting greens once the water lease on Birch Creek went through. He set about measuring and spray-painting orange hazard lines in the dirt where a ditcher would cut irrigation channels. Nevis owned most of this land himself, and he was tallying his potential profits when motion in the shadow of a Yerba Santa bush caught his eye. Scorpions, gathered in a ring, a tiny pocket mouse quaking at the center of them. The scenario was distasteful. He raised his boot heel and made to crush the things, but they nimbly skirted the fat shadow of his foot. The circle parted and the mouse shot out of sight.

He glanced at his watch. Four thirty. In half an hour, he had an appointment to show number eight Amphitrite Trail to a prospective buyer. The flawless sky and the light breeze were hopeful portents. Arn felt confident that on this day, he would make a good sale. To celebrate the prospect, Arn took the quart of peppermint schnapps from his knapsack, but then it occurred to him to save it, to drink it very quickly just before the client's arrival for maximum benefit to his difficult tongue.

Eight Amphitrite was a handsome structure, a three-thousand-square-foot Craftsman bungalow, the only one like it in the neighborhood. The plot was ideally situated, up on high ground at the end of the road with no houses behind it. Sitting there on the front steps, Nevis felt a particular comfort in the place, an enlargement of the safe feeling he experienced in restaurants when he found a spot with his back to the wall and a good view of the door. Nevis checked his watch. Ten of five. He opened the bottle and tipped it back. He stretched his tongue, whispering a silent catechism: "Radiant-heat floors, four-acre lot, build to suit."

Arn had just finished the last of the schnapps when a Swedish station wagon pulled into the drive. A young man got out, tall, with soft features, combed sandy hair, and a cornflower-blue shirt rolled to the elbows. He watched Arn Nevis pick himself up off the stairs and come toward him with his hand out. "Mr. Nevis?" the young man had to ask, for Arn did not much resemble the photograph on his website. His white shirt was badly wrinkled and yellowed with perspiration stains, and his hair looked like a patch of trodden weeds. His left eye was badly bloodshot and freely weeping.

"Urt! Guh," Arn Nevis said, then paused in his tracks, opening and closing his mouth as though priming a dry pump. The client watched him, aghast, as though Nevis was some unhinged derelict impersonating the man he'd come to meet. "Guh—good day!" Nevis said at last, and having expelled that first plug of language, the rest flowed out of him easily. "Mister Mills? It's an absolute delight, and I'm so glad you could pay us a visit on this fabulous day."

"Daniel, please," the young man said, still looking guarded. But the anxiety slowly drained from Mills's features as Nevis rolled into a brisk and competent disquisition on 8 Amphitrite's virtues. "That nice overlay on the foundation? That's not plastic, friend. It's hand-mortared fieldstone harvested out of this very land. Clapboards are engineered, and so's the roofing shake, so eat your heart out, termites, and fifteen years to go on the warranty on each."

Nevis was ushering Mills over the threshold when his pitch halted in midstream. Nevis gaped at the empty living room, his mouth open, his eyes stretched with wonder. "My gosh," he said.

"What?" asked Daniel Mills.

"My gosh, Ted, this is that same house, isn't it?" Nevis said, laughing. "From Columbus. When you and Rina were still married."

Mills looked at Arn a moment. "It's Daniel. I—I don't know any Rina."

Nevis's eyes moved in their sockets. He began to laugh. "Jesus Christ, what the hell am I saying?" he said. "My apologies. I've had this fever."

"Sure," said Mills, taking a step back.

"So over yonder is a galley kitchen," said Nevis, leading the way. "Poured concrete counters, and a built-in—"

"Excuse me, you've got something here," murmured Mills, indicating Nevis's upper lip. Nevis raised a finger to his face and felt the warm rush of blood pouring from his nose, dripping from his chin, landing in nickel-size droplets on the parquet floor.

By his sixth week in Triton Estates, an exuberant insomnia assailed Rodney Booth. While his wife snored beside him, Rodney lay awake. His body quivered with unspent energy. His blood felt hot and incandescent. With each stroke of his potent heart, he saw the red traceries of his arteries filling with gleeful sap, bearing tidings of joy and vigor to his cells. His muscles quaked. His loins tittered, abloat with happy news. His stomach, too, disturbed his rest. Even after a dinner of crass size, Rodney would lie in bed, his gut groaning as though he hadn't eaten in days. He would rise and go downstairs, but he could not find foods to gratify his hunger. Whether cold noodles, or a plate of costly meats and cheeses, all the foods in his house had a dull, exhausted flavor, and he would eat in joyless frustration, as though forced to suffer conversation with a hideous bore.

Exercise was the only route to sleep for Rodney. His ankles plagued him less these days, and after dinner he would rove for hours in the warm autumn dark. Some nights he strolled the shore, soothed to hear the distant splashes of leaping night fish. Sometimes he went into the hills where the houses stopped. The land rose and fell before him, merging in the far distance with the darkness of the sky, unbroken by lights of civilization. A feeling of giddy affluence would overtake Rodney as he scrambled along. All that space, and nobody's but his! It was like the dream where you find a silver dollar on the sidewalk, then another, then another, until you look up to see a world strewn with free riches.

On these strolls, his thoughts often turned to Katherine Nevis, that fine, wretched girl imprisoned at the end of Naiad Lane behind the high white wall. He recalled the smell of her, her comely gruntings that day on the shore, the tender heft of her underjaw in his palm. One evening the memory of her became so intolerable that it stopped him in his tracks, and he paused between the dunes in an intimate little hollow where dust of surprising fineness gathered in plush drifts.

Rodney stooped to caress the soft soil, warm in his hand. "Listen, you and me are in a predicament here, Katherine," he explained to the dust. "Oh, you don't, huh? Fine. You stay right there. I'll get it myself."

With that, he unbuckled his pants and fell to zealously raping the dirt. The sensation was not pleasurable, and the fierceness of the act did not sit right with Rodney's notion of himself, but in the end he felt satisfied that he had completed a job of grim though necessary work.

Floured with earth, he made his way to the water and swam vigorously for twenty minutes. Then he crawled into bed beside his wife and slept until the sun rose, minding not at all the pricking of the soft sheets against his salty skin.

The following night Rodney ranged along the shore and back up into the hills, yet his step was sulky and his heart was low. As with the pantry foods he did not care to eat, that evening the great open land had become infected with a kindred dreariness. Squatting on a boulder, Rodney gazed at the column of clean light spilling from the enclosure of the Nevis home. A breathless yearning caught hold. The desert's wealth of joy and deliverance seemed to have slipped down the rills and drainages, slid past the dark houses, leached south along the hard pink berm, and concentrated in the glare above the one place in the Anasazi Basin where Rodney was not free to roam. He stood and walked.

Rodney told himself he would not enter the Nevis property. The notion was to loiter at the gate, have a glimpse of the courtyard, sport a little with the pull of the place, the fun of holding two magnets at slight bay. And perhaps Rodney would have kept his promise to himself had he not spotted, bolted to the top of a length of conduit bracketed to the wall, a fan of iron claws, put there to discourage shimmiers. The device offended Rodney as an emblem of arrogance and vanity. Who was Arn Nevis to make his home a thorny fort? The spikes were pitiful. A determined crone could have gotten past them. Rodney jumped and grasped in either hand the two outermost claws. With a strength and ease that surprised him, he vaulted himself over the hazard and onto the lip of the wall.

He dropped onto the flagstones and the agony in his ankles caused his lungs to briefly freeze with pain. Rodney held his breath, waiting to hear a barking dog or an alarm, but heard nothing. Beyond the batteries of floodlights, only a single window glowed in the far corner of the house. Rodney waited. Nothing stirred.

Crouched in the courtyard, a new oil seemed to rise in Rodney's joints. His body felt incapable of noisy or graceless moves. He removed the screen from an open window and found himself in the Nevises' living room. He paused at a grand piano and rested his fingers in a chord on the sheeny keys. The temptation to sound the notes was strong, so electrified was Rodney that the house was under his authority. The fragrance in the room was distasteful and exciting—an aroma of milk and cologne—and it provoked in him an unaccountable hunger. He padded to the Nevises' kitchen. In the cold light of the open refrigerator, Rodney unwrapped and ate a wedge of Gruyère cheese. Then he had a piece of unsweetened baking chocolate, which he washed down with a can of Arn's beer. Still, his stomach growled. Under a shroud of crumpled tinfoil, he found a mostly intact ham, and he gnawed the sugary crust and then went at it with his jaws and teeth, taking bites the size of tennis balls, glutting his throat and clearing the clog with a second, then a third can of his neighbor's beer.

When he had at last had all he wanted, Rodney's breathing became labored. He was dewed in hot sweat. His bladder, too, was full, but his feeling of satiety there in the kitchen was so delicate and golden that he did not feel like shifting an inch to find a toilet. So he lowered his zipper and relished the sound of fluid hitting terra-cotta tiles, which mingled with the keen scent of his own urine in a most ideal way.

He had only just shut the refrigerator door when a white motion in the window caught his eye. Who was it but Katherine Nevis, the darling prisoner of the house? She plodded across the rear courtyard, on flat, large girl's feet, heading for the little inlet. She shed

her robe, and Rodney was unhappy to see that even at that private hour of the evening, she still bothered to wear a bathing suit.
She dove, and the water accepted her with the merest ripple. For
many minutes, Rodney watched her sporting and glorying in the
pool, diving and breaching, white, dolphinlike exposures of her
skin bright against the dark red tide. When he could put it off no
longer, Rodney stepped through the sliding door and went to her.

"Howdy!" he called, very jolly. She whirled in the water, only her
head exposed. Rodney walked to the edge of the pool. "Hi there!"
he said. She said nothing, but sank a little, gathering the water to
her with sweeping arms, taking it into her mouth, pushing it gently
over her chin, breathing it, nearly. She said nothing. Rodney put
his fists on his hips and grinned at the surveillant moon. "Hell of a
spotlight. Good to swim by, huh?"

Her eyes were dark but not fearful. "How'd you get in here?" the
girl said wetly.

"Oh, I had some business with your dad," he said.

"My dad," she repeated, her face a suspicious little fist.

"Maybe I'll get in there with you," Rodney said, raising his shirt.

"Do what you like," the girl said. "I'm going inside."

He put a hand out. She took it and pulled herself into the night
air. He picked up her robe. Draping it on her, he caught her sour-
dough aroma, unmasked by the sulfur smell of the sea. His heart
was going, his temples on the bulge.

"Stay," he said. "Come on, the moon's making a serious effort
here. It's a real once-in-a-month kind of moon."

She smiled, then stopped. She reached into the pocket of her
robe and retrieved a cigarette. "Okay. By the way, if I yelled even a
little bit, my mom would come out here. She's got serious radar.
She listens to everything and never sleeps. Seriously, how'd you get
through the gate?"

Rodney stretched his smile past his dogteeth. A red gas was coming into his eyes. "She's one great lady, your mom." He put a hand
on the girl's hip. She pushed against it only slightly, then sat with
her cigarette on a tin-and-rubber chaise longue to light it. He sat
beside her and took the cigarette, holding it downwind so as to
smell her more purely. He made some mouth sounds in her ear.
She closed her eyes. "Gets dull out here, I bet," he said.

"Medium," she said. She took back the ocher short of her roll-your-own. He put his hand on her knee, nearly nauseated with an urge. The girl frowned at his fingers. "Be cool, hardcore," she said.

"Why don't you . . . how about let's . . . how about . . ."

"Use your words," she said.

He put his hand on the back of her head and tried to pull her to his grasping lips. She broke the clasp. "What makes you think I want to kiss your mouth?"

"Come on," he groaned, nearly weeping. "God*damn,* you're beautiful."

"Shit," the girl said.

"You are a beautiful woman," said Rodney.

"My legs are giant," she said. "I've got a crappy face."

"Come here," he said. He lipped some brine from her jaw.

"Don't," she said, panting some. "You don't love me yet."

Rodney murmured that he did love Katherine Nevis very much. He kissed her, and she didn't let him. He kissed her again and she did. Then he was on her and for a time the patio was silent save the sound of their breath and the crying of the chaise's rubber slats.

He'd gotten her bikini bottoms down around her knees when the girl went stiff. "Quit," she whispered harshly. He pretended not to hear her. "Shit, goddammit, stop!" She gave him a hard shove, and then Rodney saw the problem. Arn Nevis was over by the house, hunched and peering from the blue darkness of the eave. Nevis was perfectly still, his chin raised slightly, mouth parted in expectancy. His look changed when he realized he'd been spotted. From what Rodney could tell, it wasn't outrage on the old man's features, just mild sadness that things had stopped before they'd gotten good.

Three mornings later, Rodney Booth looked out his bedroom window to see a speeding ambulance dragging a curtain of dust all the way up Naiad Lane to the Nevis home. He watched some personnel in white tote a gurney through the gate. Then Rodney went downstairs and poured himself some cereal and turned the television on.

Later that afternoon, as Rodney was leaving for the wharf with his fishing pole and creel, Cora called to him. She'd just gotten off the phone with Phyllis Nevis, who'd shared the sad news that her husband was in the hospital, comatose with a ruptured aneurysm, not expected to recover. Rodney agreed that this was terrible. Then he shouldered his pole and set out for the wharf.

The day after the ambulance bore Arn Nevis away, Rodney began to suffer vague qualmings of the conscience relating to the Nevis family. He had trouble pinpointing the source of the unease. It was not sympathy for Nevis himself. There was nothing lamentable about an old man heading toward death in his sleep. And his only regret about his tender grapplings with the sick man's daughter was that they hadn't concluded properly. Really, the closest Rodney could come to what was bothering him was some discomfort over his behavior with Phyllis Nevis's ham. He pictured mealtime in her house, the near widow serving her grieving children the fridge's only bounty, a joint of meat, already hard used by unknown teeth. The vision made him tetchy and irritated with himself. He felt the guilt gather in his temples and coalesce into a bothersome headache.

That afternoon, Rodney harvested and shucked a pint or so of oysters. He packed in ice three pounds of fresh-caught croaker fillets. He showered, shaved, daubed his throat and the line of hair on his stomach with lemon verbena eau de cologne. In the fridge he found a reasonably good bottle of Pouilly-Fuissé, and he set off up Naiad Lane.

Phyllis Nevis came to the gate and welcomed him in. "I brought you something," Rodney said. "It isn't much."

She looked into the bag with real interest. "Thank you," she said. "That's very, very kind."

"And the wine is cold," said Rodney. "Bet you could use a glass."

"I could," said Phyllis quietly.

Together they walked inside. Rodney put the fish in the refrigerator. He opened the bottle and poured two large glasses. Phyllis went upstairs and then returned with her baby, Nathan. She sat on the sofa, waiting for Rodney, giving the infant his lunch.

Rodney gave the woman a glass and sat close beside her.

"Thank you," said Phyllis, tears brightening her eyes. "One week, tops. That's what they said."

"I'm so, so sorry," Rodney said. He put his arm around her, and while she wept, she allowed herself to be drawn into the flushed hollow of Rodney's neck. The infant at her breast began to squeal, and the sound inflamed the pain in Rodney's temples, and he had an impulse to tear the baby from her and carry it out of the room. Instead, he swallowed his wine at a gulp. He poured himself a second glass and knocked it back, which seemed to dull the pain a little. Then he settled against the cushion and pressed Phyllis's tearful face into his neck. While she quaked on him, Rodney stroked the tender skin behind her ears and stared off through the picture window. Far above the eastern hills, a council of clouds shed a gray fringe of moisture. The promise of rain was a glad sight in the mournful scene, though in fact this was rain of a frail kind, turning to vapor a mile above the brown land, never to be of use to women and men on earth.

Contributors' Notes

*Other Distinguished Stories
of 2009*

Editorial Addresses

Contributors' Notes

STEVE ALMOND is the author of the story collections *My Life in Heavy Metal* and *The Evil B. B. Chow,* and, most recently, the nonfiction book *Rock and Roll Will Save Your Life.* His next book is a collection of stories, *God Bless America,* that will include "Donkey Greedy, Donkey Gets Punched." He has also self-published two books. *This Won't Take But a Minute, Honey,* is composed of thirty very brief stories and thirty very brief essays on the psychology and practice of writing. *Letters from People Who Hate Me* is exactly that. Both are available at readings.

▪ I'll start with two potentially humiliating disclosures. First, I conceived this story five years ago while lying on my psychoanalyst's couch. Second, my father is a psychoanalyst and a pretty serious poker player. (He does not wear silly hats.) I hope this dispels any expectation that the story is "not autobiographical." The best writing always is, no matter how elaborate the disguise. It's generated by, and commemorates, our deepest preoccupations. For me, this story is about acknowledging who you really are. As wounded and angry as Sharpe might be, he knows himself. Oss has to find out—at great expense. This happens to be a decent executive summary of psychoanalysis itself. A few other notes: I let the story simmer for a long time before sitting down to write it. This wasn't a conscious decision but a function of my life, which is now filled with small children. So sometimes maybe those things we see as distractions are actually serving the needs of the artistic unconscious. This is also one of the few stories I've ever written that might be classified as a thriller. My notions of plot are essentially primitive (push your hero into danger, slow down when it gets bad enough). I don't have the chops to fool the reader too often, and generally consider it dirty pool anyway. But in this case, I wanted to make sure the final showdown contained an element of astonishment as well as inevitability. I'm sure the particulars reflect my own sick fantasies as a former analytic patient. I was also interested in poker as a national obsession—all these men and women who turn to the game out of some desperate need for vitalization. This is what Dostoevsky was writing about in "The Gambler" and what the Judge is setting out in his famous soliloquy from *Blood Meridian* ("All games aspire to a condition of war"). Is it really just a coincidence that poker's popularity skyrocketed during the Bush years? We're drawn to the table not by money but by the thrill of a public confrontation, the chance to experience our own aggression. We're all donkeys waiting to get punched.

MARLIN BARTON is from the Black Belt region of Alabama. He has published two collections of short stories, *The Dry Well* and *Dancing by the River,* and a novel, *A Broken Thing,* all with Frederic C. Beil, Publisher. A second novel, *The Cross Garden,* is forthcoming from Beil. His stories have been published in such journals and anthologies as *The Southern Review, New Letters, Shenandoah, Prize Stories: The O. Henry Awards,* and *Stories from the Blue Moon Café.* He teaches in, and helps direct, the Writing Our Stories project, a program for juvenile offenders just outside Montgomery, Alabama.

▪ In the rural community where I grew up in west Alabama, I heard many stories about a deaf-mute woman who had lived in a house much like the one described in the story. In fact, my cousin Jimbo later lived in that house and I spent many hours there as a boy. Several years ago I came across Library of Congress photographs online that were taken in Alabama by WPA photographers during the Great Depression, including several of my cousin's home. I also found a photo of what may have once been a slave cabin behind a large plantation-style house. There was one indoor photo, and when I zoomed in on a wall calendar to see what year the photo was taken, I realized it was a promotional calendar advertising my grandfather's general store. I felt as if I'd just seen my grandfather's name in a Walker Evans photo. This cabin became the model for the one in the story.

I began to wonder about those traveling photographers—how they lived, where they stayed when they traveled—and then imagined one of them meeting a deaf-mute woman and having more understanding of her than she could have realized. Before I began writing, I'd thought that Mr. Clark would come across as very threatening and sinister, but he didn't emerge that way, which made me go a bit deeper into his character, I think—a good thing. The dialogue was a challenge at first. How do you write dialogue for a character who doesn't speak? But I trusted the reader would understand it was all signing and wouldn't have to be constantly reminded. I hope a sense of silence pervades the story, because that silence is where Janey really lives.

CHARLES BAXTER is the author of five novels and four short story collections. He has also written two books of literary criticism, *Burning Down the House* and *The Art of Subtext: Beyond Plot.* His *New and Selected Stories* will be published by Pantheon in 2011. He was given the Award of Merit for the Short Story by the American Academy of Arts and Letters in 2007. He has taught at Wayne State University and the University of Michigan, and he now teaches at the University of Minnesota and in the Warren Wilson MFA Program. He lives in Minneapolis.

▪ I have always liked stories with dubious narrators given to rationalizations, and "The Cousins" has one such narrator, someone who should give what used to be called "moral support" but doesn't do so until it is too late. The story is built from several bits and pieces: two anecdotes, one told to me years ago by a friend, the other told to me more recently; a dream that I remembered to write down; my memories of New York City in the 1970s; a stanza from one of my own poems; and a monologue I heard in a taxi in Seattle driven by an Ethiopian-American cab driver.

JENNIFER EGAN is the author of *The Invisible Circus,* which was released as a feature film by Fine Line in 2001; *Emerald City and Other Stories; Look at Me,* which was nominated for the National Book Award in 2001; and the best-selling novel *The Keep.* Her new book, *A Visit from the Goon Squad,* was published in June. Also a journalist, she writes frequently in the *New York Times Magazine.*

▪ When I first came to New York, around 1988, I wrote a story called "Safari." It was told from the point of view of a teenage girl whose family is on safari in Africa—something I'd done with my own family in 1980, when I was seventeen. I don't remember much about that early "Safari," except that it was meandering and unfinished, and included a blank-faced actor whom the narrator speculates "assumed expressions only when paid to." Some years later I stumbled on an old draft and was struck by that phrase about the actor, irked that I hadn't found some use for it since.

Then, in 2008, twenty years after the original "Safari," I wrote a story in which a man in his forties, Lou, tells his seventeen-year-old girlfriend about a trip he took to Africa. Although Lou was a minor character in the book I was writing, I couldn't resist pursuing him onto his safari. The actor reappeared (blank-voiced this time rather than blank-faced). Lou's daughter, Charlie, was a stowaway from another failed story, about a girl rescued by her charismatic father from a raw egg–eating cult. I already knew that Lou's son would die as a young man, but it was while writing "Safari" that I realized Rolph's death was a suicide. The piece became a way of exploring, obliquely, some of the deep reasons for that tragedy.

But the real engine of the new "Safari" was Lou's girlfriend, Mindy; only when she began viewing the proceedings through the lens of her structural schema did I have a sense of movement and compression in the story —a hope that this time I'd be able to finish it.

DANIELLE EVANS's work has appeared in magazines including *The Paris Review, A Public Space, Callaloo,* and *Phoebe,* and anthologies including *The Best American Short Stories* and *New Stories from the South.* Her short story collection, *Before You Suffocate Your Own Fool Self,* is forthcoming from Riverhead Books, and she is currently at work on a novel titled *The Empire Has No Clothes.* She received an MFA in fiction from the Iowa Writers' Workshop, was a fellow at the Wisconsin Institute for Creative Writing, and is now teaching fiction at American University in Washington, D.C.

▪ This story started as an image I had of a man in uniform carrying a little girl on his shoulders. I knew that he was not her father and not quite her stepfather, and I was interested in the dynamics of that relationship, perhaps because I was just barely old enough to be on the other side of the equation—to wonder how one was supposed to negotiate boundaries with children of people you might date, instead of being a child second-guessing the intentions of your parents' suitors. I'm not sure why Georgie showed up in uniform, but it probably had something to do with all of the news footage I was watching that year for my thesis on media coverage of Iraq.

For a year or so, the story was just those two figures in my head. I wrote the first few pages of the story in graduate school, and was immediately pleased and charmed by Lanae, but while I knew the emotional arc of the piece, I was stuck on the mechanics of plot. I kept trying to nudge Georgie and Kenny into a melodramatically violent confrontation, and the story kept refusing to go there. Eventually I realized that Esther, instead of being incidental to the conflict between Georgie and Kenny, needed to be the center of the story. I had to let the story I had envisioned as terse, bleak, and violent go to the mall and play with makeup. It became less violent, but the bleakness remained, owing partly to my growing realization that the emptiness of the things Esther was being offered as aspirational was not unrelated to the emptiness Georgie felt upon his return. The idea of lying to win a frivolous contest came from a news story I read, though the nature of Georgie's lie came from his particular circumstances.

For years the working draft of the story was called "Every Single Last M@#ther^&*r on This Planet Is Going to Hell Someday," and though that is still what I call the story in my head, the title seemed probably unpublishable and definitely ungenerous in a story where, as it turned out, I liked all of the characters very much.

JOSHUA FERRIS is the author of *Then We Came to the End,* a National Book Award finalist and winner of the PEN/Hemingway Award. His second novel, *The Unnamed,* was published in 2010.

▪ I find it hard to believe in Naples, Florida, as I find it hard to believe in Las Vegas. There's no centralized spectacle; just the strip mall in its full ascendancy. We're talking miles and miles, unfurling in a Hanna-Barbera loop, of single-story retailers, including my favorite, Not Just Futons and Barstools. Panther-crossing signs dot the highways, those stripped and well-paved corridors flanked by redoubts of an old Florida wild that endures continuously only in the Everglades. This is not the south Florida of Zora Neale Hurston or Peter Matthiessen. The story of the rape of the land is an old one, as are those told of retired Q-tips, early-bird specials, and the parade of ambulances pulling out of the planned communities.

I suppose I started writing "The Valetudinarian" because I liked the word *valetudinarian,* defined by the *OED* as "a person in poor or indifferent health, esp. a person who is constantly or unduly concerned with his or her own health." I was reacquainted with it in an elegy for John Updike (whose final Rabbit book is a fine Florida novel). I put *valetudinarian* together with the name Arty, a name I liked to hear my father-in-law say (he's friends with an Arty, who as far as I know shares nothing in common with the one in the story). That was the start of the character. Next I considered Arty's phone. It would be an old black rotary, sitting mutely and calmly day after day in Arty's lonely condo, until his birthday arrived. The refrain "Happy birthday to me" came next. That's how I write a story, bit by bit, with sustained and single-minded focus that's relinquished only after a final draft—in this case, thirteen weeks of work.

LAUREN GROFF is the author of a novel, *The Monsters of Templeton,* and a collection of stories, *Delicate Edible Birds and Other Stories.* She has an MFA from the University of Wisconsin–Madison, and her work has appeared in journals including *The Atlantic, Ploughshares, One Story,* and *Glimmer Train,* and anthologies including *The Best American Short Stories, 2007; The Best New American Voices, 2008;* and *Pushcart Prize: Best of the Small Presses,* volume 32. Her second novel, *Arcadia,* is slated for publication in 2011. She lives in Gainesville, Florida, with her husband and little boy.

▪ "Delicate Edible Birds" is the title story in a collection sparked by the lives of real women. It always surprises me how the heat and pressure of years of writing temper my characters and turn them into people quite different from those who first capture my interest: in the process, they stop being the subjects of the stories and begin to act more like muses. This story is no exception. It all came about when I read *The Collected Letters of Martha Gellhorn,* edited by Caroline Moorehead, and fell in love with the brave, witty, gorgeous, angry, and deeply vulnerable Gellhorn. She was a war reporter, a fiction writer, and, less important (to me), the third wife of Ernest Hemingway. Her voice stuck in my head for years until I reread my old dog-eared copy of Maupassant from college and remembered the story "Boule de Suif," from which I shamelessly stole the journalists' situation. I owe the ortolan to François Mitterand, who had eaten the bird at his last meal: the image of the president of France on his deathbed, hiding from God behind a napkin so that he could gulp down a wee bird, seemed at first hilarious. The more I considered it, though, the more it broke my heart.

WAYNE HARRISON lives Springfield, Oregon, with his beautiful wife and two young daughters. His stories have appeared in *The Atlantic, Narrative, McSweeney's, Ploughshares, The Sun, New Letters,* and other magazines, and he is at work on a novel. His short story "Charity" was a BASS distinguished story of 2009. He teaches writing at Oregon State University and with the UCLA Extension Writers' Program.

• This story is close to my heart because, among other things, it reminds me of the person I used to be. For five years after high school, I turned wrenches as a general repair mechanic in Waterbury, Connecticut. This was in the early nineties, when you didn't need a computer science degree to perform a tune-up. We were genuine grease monkeys with aching backs and manifold burns and hamburgered knuckles. I miss that life. I don't remember it involving politics or posturing or concern about tenure. BASS wasn't a collection of good stories back then; it was a fish you caught over beers at the lake. For all our boasting about cars and the twelve-second quarter-miles we'd run, we were humble enough not to try and make art out of the world. Sometimes what I wouldn't give to go back for an afternoon: a Winston in one hand, a cup of hundred-mile coffee in the other, my mind on the low compression of a number six cylinder and nothing else.

JAMES LASDUN was born in London and now lives in upstate New York. He has published several books including *The Horned Man,* a novel, and *Landscape with Chainsaw,* a collection of poems. His story "The Siege" was adapted by Bernardo Bertolucci for his film *Besieged.* He co-wrote the screenplay for the film *Sunday* (based on another of his stories), which won Best Feature and Best Screenplay awards at Sundance. His story "An Anxious Man" won the inaugural UK National Short Story Award in 2006. It is included in his latest collection, *It's Beginning to Hurt* (FSG 2009).

• This was an unusual story for me, in that it was based on a real event —the accidental death of a neighbor. Finding a tone and point of view that would do justice to the tragic nature of what happened while also allowing me to extend things in the direction I wanted to take them was extremely hard, and I had dozens of false starts before I got anything that seemed to work even remotely. I suppose I could have written it as reportage, but somehow the event, with its odd mixture of human drama and deus ex machina chance (or mischance), seemed to call for the imaginative freedom of fiction. My own feelings of affection and shock and loss were very bound up in my desire to write about it, and I wanted to write something that would give form to those feelings. A certain amount of transformation seemed necessary.

REBECCA MAKKAI's first novel, *The Borrower,* will be published by Viking in the summer of 2011. This is her third consecutive appearance in *The Best American Short Stories,* and her work appears regularly in journals such as *New England Review, Shenandoah,* and *The Threepenny Review.* She lives north of Chicago with her husband and children.

• In a workshop many years ago, the writer David Huddle asked us one week to attempt "souped-up prose," and then gleefully refused to explain what that was. My response was a linguistically mangled story in which a literature professor levitates in the middle of a lecture on magical realism. It was short (since I wasn't quite sure what to do after my main character flew out the window), strange, and—mercifully—remains unpublished. Several years later, the idea came to me that it could be salvaged only as part of a series of stories in which professors are victimized by the literature they teach. (I should add here that I have nothing against professors; any literary aggression is most likely the manifestation of my fears of how I'd have turned out had I followed through with my plan to earn a living teaching Comp. 101.) I haven't yet found the nerve to write the rest of the series—a professor of cavalier poetry stuck through with a saber? a modernist who falls to literal pieces?—but the story of Alex shooting down the albatross was the one that begged to be told.

BRENDAN MATHEWS was raised in Albany, New York, and grew up disappointed that the city no longer resembled a William Kennedy novel. He spent a decade in Chicago working in nuclear weapons journalism, architectural salvage, and a variety of ill-fated dot-com ventures, and later received his MFA from the University of Virginia. His stories have appeared in *The Virginia Quarterly Review, Epoch, TriQuarterly, Cincinnati Review, Manchester Review,* and other journals. He teaches at Bard College at Simon's Rock and lives in western Massachusetts with his wife and their four children. He is working on a novel about assassins, big band music, and the ghost of William Butler Yeats.

▪ I wrote the first draft of what would later become "My Last Attempt to Explain to You What Happened with the Lion Tamer" at the end of my first year in graduate school. I was thirty-five years old, and just a year earlier my wife and I had quit our jobs in Chicago, sold our house, and moved with our one-year-old daughter to Charlottesville so that I could make a serious go at writing. I will leave it to the reader to determine why this seemed like a good time to write a story about a man who steps into a cage full of lions with little more than a chair, a whip, and an irrationally large portion of self-confidence to protect himself.

Whatever the reason, my notebooks from that period were full of lion tamers, often in atypical lion tamer situations: a lion tamer takes his parents on a cruise, a lion tamer goes to a wedding, a lion tamer tries speed-dating. But the story didn't come together until I wrote a line — "He wasn't even a good lion tamer, not until she showed up" — that pushed the lion tamer out of the spotlight and conjured up both a narrator and a "she" to be the third point in the triangle. For a long time, I tinkered with the easy stuff: I brushed up the circus lingo, switched to a longer title, and cut two gorgeous, entirely unnecessary pages about the lion tamer's ex-girlfriend. The story should have been easy to give up — *A story about the circus? Narrated by a lovesick clown?* — but the more time I spent with these characters, the more I started to see that the action wasn't in the center ring but in the shadows, out on the midway, and in the lonely nights after the crowds went home. At some crucial moment, I nudged the point of view and made the story a direct address from the clown to the aerialist. It forced me to rethink almost every word I'd written, but it also added a darkness, a weight, and an intimacy that the story had always lacked.

It took five years to go from the first draft to *The Cincinnati Review.* Through that time, this was the story I would pull out of the drawer when other stories were done, or weren't working, or needed time to cool before the next round of revisions. It was a refuge, a reward, even a guilty pleasure. Eventually I started to realize that the crazy little story about the circus wasn't just a distraction. I had written the closest I had come to a love story.

JILL MCCORKLE is the author of five novels and four story collections, most recently *Going Away Shoes,* which includes the story "PS." She lives in Hillsborough, North Carolina, and teaches in the MFA program at N.C. State University.

▪ I was recently asked by someone what I would want to be were I not a writer. My immediate answer was "therapist," suggesting that we do similar things: meet people, hear all about their life stories, and then try to make sense out of all the pieces. I then joked that the good part about being the writer of these people and their stories is that you got to see them all the way to the other side or at least far enough to glimpse resolution. I said it would drive me nuts to have invested lots of time and energy in a person and all the events of that life, only to have him or her pull up roots and move on without a trace—another town, another therapist, who would know? And that led me to write "PS"—a letter written by a woman to her marriage counselor to fill him in on all that has happened since he last saw her. As often happens, I began with lots of ideas that made me laugh but by the end had really gotten to know the woman buried under all those sessions. And yes, I was very happy to see her make it all the way to the other side.

KEVIN MOFFETT is the author of the story collection *Permanent Visitors*. His short fiction has appeared in *McSweeney's, New Stories from the South, Tin House, Harvard Review,* two previous editions of *The Best American Short Stories,* and elsewhere. He has received the Pushcart Prize, the Nelson Algren Award, a National Magazine Award nomination, and a grant from the National Endowment for the Arts. He teaches in the MFA program at Cal State, San Bernardino.

▪ When I first started writing, I was a big fan of rules, commandments, anything that sounded as if it could be proclaimed from a mount. Never write about dreams. Never dramatize phone conversations. I made note of the rules, underlined the important ones, double-underlined the really important ones. I've long abandoned most of them, except one: never write about writing.

In his Nobel speech Orhan Pamuk said that a writer "must have the artistry to tell his own stories as if they were other people's stories, and to tell other people's stories as if they were his own." My challenge wasn't in finding a way to write about writing—this was made easier by the premise of a father publishing in the same literary magazines as his son—it was to write something personal that wasn't abjectly biographical. I tried to skirt this by using a narrator who is, in many ways, an agglomeration of my worst qualities. Prideful, a little clueless, resolutely unheroic, a devotee of the band Yes. This allowed me to disconnect from whatever did happen to me when I was a writing student, and to be faithful to what should happen to the narrator. I had a lot of fun writing this story. Many thanks to Jordan Bass and Eli Horowitz for making it better and for publishing it.

TÉA OBREHT was born in 1985 in the former Yugoslavia and spent her childhood in Cyprus and Egypt before eventually immigrating to the

United States in 1997. After graduating from the University of Southern California, Téa received her MFA in fiction from the Creative Writing Program at Cornell University. Her short stories have appeared in *The Atlantic,* among other places. Her first novel, *The Tiger's Wife,* was excerpted in *The New Yorker,* and is forthcoming in spring 2011.

▪ For the better part of my college years, my family lived abroad in a small riverside German town called Heidelberg. Visiting them was a sensational pleasure: there were Christmas festivals and summer boat races, and long, rainy daytrips to nearby mountain castles, and with all these influences it wasn't long before I was planning an elaborate and gloomy novel, preferably set in a bygone east German wintertime. I was, unfortunately, forever returning to Los Angeles too soon, and the mood for my gloomy novel—chocolates and Christmas knickknacks aside—could not hold up under the southern California sun. In August 2006 I was raring to move to Ithaca, New York, to begin graduate studies at Cornell, and I had a vivid and optimistic vision of myself cocooned in my partly subterranean apartment on the edge of town, shuffling into the kitchen to prepare hot cocoa, while my gloomy novel, helped along by inspiring, snowbound strolls through the woods, gelled at last into something substantial, something entrenched in reality.

Considering the conduciveness of my new environment—an inflexible schedule regulated by felled power lines, snow-jammed doors, and daily treks around the front of the building to dig out my apartment window, not to mention new responsibilities like outwitting the snowplow and finding sustenance—I was surprised to find that, somewhere between November 20 (first appreciable snowfall) and April 16 (final snowfall totaling around fourteen inches), I had given up on my gloomy German novel and written "The Laugh" instead.

For me, writing has turned out to be an exercise in deprivation: I write most comfortably in the absence of the things or people I am writing about. Having grown up under the sun of Cyprus and Egypt, and having followed, in my college years, a more or less sunlit trajectory, I hadn't realized to what extent warmth launches the senses, how reliant my writing is on climate, or how much the absence of sunlight, sharpened by the ever-growing pile of *National Geographic*s at my Ithaca bedside, would make me long for even the smell and sound of the sub-Saharan Africa I had never seen.

LORI OSTLUND'S first collection of stories, *The Bigness of the World,* which includes "All Boy," received the 2008 Flannery O'Connor Award for Short Fiction and was chosen as a 2009 Notable Book by The Story Prize. The stories appeared in *New England Review, The Georgia Review, Prairie Schooner,* and *The Kenyon Review,* among other journals; a story from the collection received the Lawrence Foundation Award. In 2009 Ostlund was the recipient of a Rona Jaffe Foundation Writers' Award. She grew up in a hardware store in a town of 411 people in Minnesota and currently lives in San Francisco. She has been appointed the Kenan Visiting Writer at the University of North Carolina–Chapel Hill for 2010–11, during which time she hopes to finish her first novel.

▪ My stories generally take shape slowly, but I wrote most of "All Boy" over a two-week period in March 2008. I was exhausted at the time, having taken part in a botched strike at the ESL school in San Francisco where I worked. I resigned after a week, realizing that the only good thing about the job was the students, and drove to Albuquerque, where I had lived for many years, to housesit for a friend. My first morning there, I took a long walk with another friend, who told me, in passing, about an acquaintance of his, a mother deep in denial about her son, her denial most eloquently and heartbreakingly manifested though her insistence on telling stories about her son that ended with the refrain, "I guess he's just all boy." I've always had a soft spot for boys like Harold, boys who prefer words and stories to motion, boys who get called "sissy" and "fag."

My writing often unfolds like a connect-the-dots exercise. Anecdotes and images pop into my head, and my job is to figure out how they all tie together. The toenails, for example, came from something that I observed in the bathroom of the famous Frontier Restaurant in Albuquerque in 1988: a woman in a business suit helping a homeless woman cut her toenails. A former colleague told me that her childhood babysitter locked her in the closet and that her father did not fire the babysitter until he later learned that the babysitter had used his toothbrush. The toothbrush had appeared in another story of mine, and so I came up with the socks, wanting to preserve this notion of an unbearable intimacy. I soon discovered that Harold liked being in the closet, a place that ultimately became symbolic as I began to better understand both him and his father. Endings are always hardest for me; I know when an ending is wrong (though I often spend time trying to convince myself otherwise), but that doesn't make the right ending easier to find. After many months, I realized the obvious: that "All Boy" needed to end back in the closet.

I'm especially pleased that this story appeared in *New England Review*. Not only is it one of my favorite journals, but also Carolyn Kuebler and Stephen Donadio are great to work with and were the first to publish a story from my then in-progress collection back in 2006, a publication that sustained me through several frustratingly dry years.

RON RASH is the author of three collections of poems, four novels, and four collections of stories. His collection *Chemistry and Other Stories* and his novel *Serena* were PEN/Faulkner Award Finalists. He teaches at Western Carolina University.

▪ In 2004 I read a short local newspaper article about a small plane that had crashed in the North Carolina mountains. The plane had not been found for six years, and then only by accident. A bear hunter had stumbled upon it. I clipped out the article and placed it in a pencil and spare change container on my bureau. Years passed and the clipping yellowed, but I'd see it often, tuck it back into the container after taking out coins or a pencil. I knew a story was in that article. I just didn't know whose story it was. When I finally realized the story centered on a child discovering the plane, the rest came quickly.

KAREN RUSSELL is the author of a collection of stories, *St. Lucy's Home for Girls Raised by Wolves.* She has taught creative writing and literature at Columbia University and Williams College and is currently a Cullman Fellow at the New York Public Library. Her first novel, *Swamplandia!,* is forthcoming from Knopf in spring 2011.

▪ In graduate school I read an incredible essay by André Aciman, "Arbitrage." Aciman borrows a financial term to discuss what he calls "mneumonic arbitrage," our habit of trading away the present moment for a perch in an imaginary future, "firming up the present by experiencing it as a memory."

This was back in 2006; this story had a long gestation! For weeks after reading Aciman's essay, I remember wandering around acutely aware of my own "arbitrage," this boil of mental activity whereby I was always converting the present into a future memory. Nal, the protagonist of my story, does this too. He uses each minute of his life as thread and weaves a grand picture of "the Future." Then, when his mother gets fired and that future unspools, it's extraordinarily painful for him; he feels cheated, even if what he's lost never existed anywhere outside of his own mind. In this story I wanted to channel Nal's outrage and confusion—his panicked teenager's sense that the "right" future has been stolen from him.

I'm not sure where the seagulls came from. In retrospect, it seems a little bonkers to have ever thought, "Of course, what this story needs more of are time-traveling seagulls!" Maybe for me, the horror of the gulls has something to do with the fizzy sensation that many unseen forces must be altering our lives in the future. And the unsettling fact that things are going to happen to us and to our loved ones without any regard for our beliefs about what's "meant to be."

One of the funnier challenges for me with this story was writing about that American sport we call "basketball." Cheston Knapp, my editor at *Tin House,* had to gently explain some basic physics of the game. He pointed out, for example, that Nal might not be able to dribble the ball so well on a court covered with "iridescent rocks," or whatever Virginia Woolf-y line I originally had in there. We joked that I should write a Victorian sports story, with sunset purple prose: "Nal embraces the ball. Oh, how can he bear to part with it! And yet he must. He must heave his ball toward that aureole in the sky, the 'hoop.'"

I am extremely grateful to my fantastic agent Denise Shannon and to the genius editors Carin Besser and Cheston Knapp, who helped this story so much.

JIM SHEPARD is the author of six novels, including most recently *Project X*, and three story collections, including most recently *Like You'd Understand, Anyway*, which was a finalist for the National Book Award and won The Story Prize. He teaches at Williams College.

▪ "The Netherlands Lives with Water" began, as I assume nearly all of the stories in that issue of *McSweeney's* did, with an e-mail from the issue's editor, Jordan Bass, inviting me among others to become part of a special issue involving stories focused on single cities around the world twenty-five years into the future. And probably like nearly all of the writers who said yes, I read along in the e-mail vaguely intrigued but also thinking, *Now, why would I want to do something like this?* until I got to the kicker: *McSweeney's* would also *send* me to whatever city I chose.

Well, now: *that* was different. Sure, I could do a story about *some* city, couldn't I? What cities *were* there in Tahiti, anyway?

I really did rack my brains for a justification to send myself to the South Pacific, but came up with nothing. Sea level rise due to global warming is one of my many preoccupations, and that was certainly going to be a problem for the Pacific Islands, but I had trouble envisioning how a story would work, mostly because the future victims in those cases were in such a passive position, sitting by helplessly while they waited for the inundation.

Thinking about sea level rise led me directly to the Dutch, of course, who I knew were proud of how energetically and proactively they were already approaching the problem. I'd recently finished Elizabeth Kolbert's cheerfully saturnine and harrowing *Field Notes from a Catastrophe*, with its memorable chapter on what the Dutch were facing and how they were facing it. *That* collision—between the Dutch and the oncoming, implacable disaster of climate change — *did* get my imagination going, mostly because I was simultaneously moved by and skeptical about the optimism the Dutch expressed concerning their long-term chances of keeping their nation afloat. I was also struck by how much they'd already accomplished —staggering engineering feats—as well as the extent to which those feats already were beginning to appear inadequate. In other words, I felt myself to be in the presence of intensely powerful and nearly equal conflicting values and/or feelings: always a good sign, in terms of the production of literary fiction, as far as I'm concerned.

It took only a week's worth of research to narrow my choice of city down to Rotterdam, which, alas, by all accounts was dumpier than either Amsterdam or The Hague, but was also both more economically crucial to the country and in much more immediate danger.

And then more help presented itself. An old friend, Kerry Sulkowicz, called to offer some business and government contacts he knew in the water sector in Holland. I was happy to have them but assumed, given the responsibilities of the men whose names he'd passed along, that I'd be lucky to talk to any of them.

But this was the Netherlands. Not only did those contacts contact me; two of them rearranged their schedules so that we could meet, and one —Djeevan Schiferli, who worked with IBM's new water division—facilitated all sorts of other contacts that he thought might be helpful, and then spent the day with me, schlepping me to sites I needed to see. I kept reminding everyone, somewhat meekly, that I was only writing a short story for a magazine called *McSweeney's,* and not a cover article for the *New York Times Magazine,* but they all seemed unfazed. I was a writer who shared their interests and was in need of help. So they helped. It was one of those moments when I've been acutely aware that I wasn't in the United States.

So: "The Netherlands Lives with Water," even more than my other stories, owes its existence to other people who inspired it and then facilitated its construction. If you don't like the story, well, that's my fault. If you do, thank Jordan Bass, Elizabeth Kolbert, Kerry Sulkowicz, Arnoud Molenaar, Jaap Kwadijk, Jos van Alphen, Pavel Kabat, and especially Djeevan Schiferli.

MAGGIE SHIPSTEAD grew up in Orange County, California. She graduated from Harvard in 2005 and earned an MFA at the Iowa Writers' Workshop. Currently she is a Stegner Fellow at Stanford.

▪ In the summer before my second year of grad school, I was driving from California to Iowa and stopped to spend a couple nights with my aunt and uncle who live in Boulder. I've made a lot of very long drives with my dog, and those days of sitting and doing nothing but watching the country go by have occasionally germinated a story. "The Cowboy Tango" started pretty much out of the blue—I got out of bed in Boulder to write the first page, then turned out the light and went to sleep. I wanted to write about a tiny world within a vast landscape, where the characters have an abundance of physical space and yet are bound by emotional claustrophobia.

WELLS TOWER is the author of *Everything Ravaged, Everything Burned,* a collection of short fiction. Tower's fiction and journalism have appeared in *The New Yorker, Harper's, McSweeney's, The Paris Review, GQ,* the *New York Times,* the *Washington Post Magazine,* and elsewhere. Tower is the recipient of the Plimpton Prize from *The Paris Review* and two Pushcart Prizes, and was named Best Young Writer of 2009 by the *Village Voice.*

▪ I wrote "Raw Water" for an issue of *McSweeney's* whose theme was stories set in the year 2024. The story's inspirational germ was a news item about a bunch of scientists kicking around the idea of flooding desert valleys with ocean water as an antidote to sea level rise. So I wrote a story about a manmade sea gone wrong, and the folks unfortunate enough to live on its shores. But the story was still lacking in the sci-fi urgency department, said Eli Horowitz, editor at *McSweeney's.* And I said, "How about if the bacteria in the lake are, like, supercharging everybody's Darwinistic faculties. You know, making them act like monkeys?" Perfecto, Eli said, and I went from there.

Other Distinguished Stories
of 2009

CAMPBELL, BONNIE JO
Home to Die. *Boulevard,* vol. 24,
issues 2 & 3.

CATES, DAVID ALLAN
Rubber Boy. *Glimmer Train,* issue
70.

CHACE, REBECCA
Looking for Robinson Crusoe.
Fiction, issue 55.

COOK, K. L.
Bonnie and Clyde in the Backyard.
Glimmer Train, issue 73.

COOKE, CAROLYN
The Snake. *Idaho Review,* vol. 10.

CROSS, EUGENE
Rosaleen, If You Know What I Mean.
American Short Fiction, vol. 12, issue
46.

DAHLIE, MICHAEL
The Children of Stromsund. *Tin
House,* vol. 11, no. 1.

DOBOZY, TAMAS
All the Black Hearted Villains. *Agni,*
no. 70.

DOERR, ANTHONY
The River Nemunas. *Tin House,* vol.
10, no. 4.

ERVIN, ANDREW
The Light of Two Million Stars.
Conjunctions, no. 53.

FENNELLY, BETH ANN, AND TOM
FRANKLIN
What His Hands Had Been Waiting
For. *The Normal School,* vol. 2,
issue 2.

FERRIS, JOSHUA
A Night Out. *Tin House,* no. 40.

FLYNN, LOUISE JARVIS
Irish Twins. *New England Review,* vol.
30, no. 3.

FRANZEN, JONATHAN
Good Neighbors. *The New Yorker,*
June 8 and 15, 2009.

FRIED, SETH
Frost Mountain Massacre. *One Story,*
issue 124.

FUREY, RACHEL
Birth Act. *Sycamore Review,* vol. 21,
issue 2.

GAIGE, AMITY
Belinda. *Yale Review,* vol. 93, no. 3.

GANESHANANTHAN, V. V.
Hippocrates. *Granta,* issue 109.

GAUTREAUX, TIM
Idols. *The New Yorker,* June 22, 2009.

GAVALER, CHRIS
G.O.D. *Hudson Review,* vol. 62, no. 1.

GENI, ABBY
Captivity. *Glimmer Train,* issue 73.

GOOLSBY, JESSE
Derrin of the North. *Harpur Palate,*
vol. 9, issue 1.

HAGY, ALYSON
Lost Boys. *Idaho Review,* vol. 10.

HAIGH, JENNIFER
Desiderata. *One Story,* issue 125.

HAMMOND, ALLIS
Tuesday's Child. *Black Warrior Review,*
vol. 36, no. 1.

HARVEY, GILES
The Indifferent Beak. *Agni,* no. 70.

HEULER, KAREN
Joey, the Upstairs Boy. *Alaska
Quarterly Review,* vol. 26, nos. 2 & 3.

HOMES, A. M.
Brother on Sunday. *The New Yorker,*
March 2, 2009.

HORACK, SKIP
Borderlands. *Narrative Magazine.*

HORROCKS, CAITLIN
At the Zoo. *Paris Review,* issue 188.

HUDDLE, DAVID
Volunteer. *Georgia Review,* vol. 63,
no. 1.

JOHNSON, NORA
The Road to Hofuf. *Confrontation,* no.
104.

PEARLMAN, EDITH
Tale. *Cincinnati Review,* vol. 6, no. 1.
PEDERSEN, ASHLEIGH
Small and Heavy World. *Iowa Review,*
vol. 39, no. 2.
PERABO, SUSAN
Shelter. *Iowa Review,* vol. 39, no. 1.
POWERS, RICHARD
Enquire Within upon Everything.
Paris Review, no. 190.
PROSE, FRANCINE
A Simple Question. *Conjunctions,* no.
53.

QUADE, KIRSTIN VALDEZ
The Five Wounds. *The New Yorker,*
July 27, 2009.
QUINLAN, EMILY
The Green Belt. *Santa Monica Review,*
vol. 21, no. 1.

REENTS, STEPHANIE
Creatures of the Kingdom. *Epoch,* vol.
58, no. 3.
REISMAN, NANCY
Ear to the Door. *Glimmer Train,* issue
73.
RIVECCA, SUZANNE
None of the Above. *American Short
Fiction,* vol. 12, issue 46.
ROW, JESS
Lives of the Saints. *Ploughshares,* vol.
35, no. 1.

SAUNDERS, GEORGE
Al Roosten. *The New Yorker,*
February 2, 2009.
SAUNDERS, GEORGE
Victory Lap. *The New Yorker,*
October 5, 2009.
SCHLOSS, ARIA BETH
Toward a Theory of Blindness.
Glimmer Train, issue 70.
SHIPSTEAD, MAGGIE
The Water Snake. *Mississippi Review,*
vol. 85, no. 4.

SILBER, JOAN
Fools. *Northwest Review,* vol. 47, no. 2.
SNOWBARGER, JEFF
Bitter Fruit. *Tin House,* issue 42.
SORRENTINO, CHRISTOPHER
The Pride of Life. *Open City,* no. 28.
SPENCER, ELIZABETH
Return Trip. *Five Points,* vol. 13,
no. 1.

THOMPSON, JEAN
Soldiers of Spiritos. *Northwest Review,*
vol. 47, no. 2.
TÓIBIN, COLM
The Color of Shadows. *The New
Yorker,* April 13, 2009.
TROYAN, SASHA
Hidden Works. *Ploughshares,* vol. 35,
no. 1.

WATSON, BRAD
Vacuum. *The New Yorker,* April 6,
2009.
WOODRING, SUSAN
The Smallest of These. *Ruminate,*
issue 11.

YATES, STEVE
A Report of Performance Art in the
Provinces. *TriQuarterly,* 132.

Editorial Addresses of American and Canadian Magazines Publishing Short Stories

African American Review
http://mc.manuscriptcentral.com/aar
$40, Nathan Grant

Agni Magazine
Boston University Writing Program
Boston University
236 Bay State Road
Boston, MA 02115
$20, Sven Birkerts

Alaska Quarterly Review
University of Alaska, Anchorage
3211 Providence Drive
Anchorage, AK 99508
$18, Ronald Spatz

Alimentum
P.O. Box 776
New York, NY 10163
$18, Paulette Licitra

Alligator Juniper
http://www.prescott.edu/alligator
_juniper/
$15, Melanie Bishop

American Letters and Commentary
Department of English
University of Texas at San Antonio

One UTSA Boulevard
San Antonio, TX 78249
$10, David Ray Vance, Catherine Kasper

American Short Fiction
P.O. Box 301209
Austin, TX 78703
$30, Stacey Swann

Amoskeag
Southern New Hampshire University
2500 N. River Road
Manchester, NH 03106
$5, Allison Cummings

Antioch Review
Antioch University
P.O. Box 148
Yellow Springs, OH 45387
$40, Robert S. Fogerty

Apalachee Review
P.O. Box 10469
Tallahassee, FL 32302
$15, Michael Trammell

Apple Valley Review
Queen's Postal Outlet
Box 12

Kingston, Ontario K7L 3R9
Leah Browning

Arkansas Review
Department of English and
Philosophy
P.O. Box 1890
Arkansas State University
State University, AR 72467
$20, Janelle Collins

Arts & Letters
Campus Box 89
Georgia College and State University
Milledgeville, GA 31061
$15, Martin Lammon

Ascent
English Department
Concordia College
901 Eighth Street
Moorhead, MN 56562
$12, W. Scott Olsen

The Atlantic
600 NH Avenue NW
Washington, DC 20037
$39.95, C. Michael Curtis

Bamboo Ridge
P.O. Box 61781
Honolulu, HI 96839
Eric Chock, Darrell H. Y. Lum

Barrelhouse
barrelhousemagazine.com
$9, The Editors

Bayou
Department of English
University of New Orleans
2000 Lakeshore Drive
New Orleans, LA 70148
$15, Joanna Leake

Bellevue Literary Review
Department of Medicine
New York University School of
Medicine
550 First Avenue
New York, NY 10016
$15, Danielle Ofri

Bellingham Review
MS-9053
Western Washington University
Bellingham, WA 98225
$20, Brenda Miller

Bellowing Ark
P.O. Box 55564
Shoreline, WA 98155
$20, Robert Ward

Blackbird
Department of English
Virginia Commonwealth University
P.O. Box 843082
Richmond, VA 23284–3082
Gregory Donovan, Mary Flinn

Black Warrior Review
P.O. Box 862936
Tuscaloosa, AL 35486–0027
$16, Christopher Hellwig

Blue Earth Review
Centennial Student Union
Minnesota State University, Mankato
Mankato, MN 56001
$8, Ande Davis

Bomb
New Art Publications
80 Hanson Place
Brooklyn, NY 11217
$25, Betsy Sussler

Boston Review
35 Medford Street, Suite 302
Somerville, MA 02143
$25, Joshua Cohen, Deborah Chasman

Boulevard
PMB 325
6614 Clayton Road
Richmond Heights, MO 63117
$20, Valerie Dixon

Brain, Child: The Magazine for
Thinking Mothers
P.O. Box 714
Lexington, VA 24450–0714
*$19.95, Jennifer Niesslein, Stephanie
Wilkinson*

Briar Cliff Review
3303 Rebecca Street
P.O. Box 2100
Sioux City, IA 51104–2100
$10, Tricia Currans-Sheehan

Callaloo
MS 4212
Texas A&M University
College Station, TX 77843–4212
$48, Charles H. Rowell

Calyx
P.O. Box B
Corvallis, OR 97339
$23, The Collective

Canteen
70 Washington Street, Suite 12H
Brooklyn, NY 11201
$35, Stephen Pierson

Carpe Articulum
8630 SW Scholls Ferry Road, Suite 177
Beaverton, OR 97008
$59.95, Rand Eastwood

Chattahoochee Review
Georgia Perimeter College
2101 Womack Road
Dunwoody, GA 30338–4497
$20, Marc Fitten

Chautauqua
Department of Creative Writing
University of North Carolina,
Wilmington
601 S. College Road
Wilmington, NC 28403
$14.95, Jill and Philip Gerard

Chicago Quarterly Review
517 Sherman Ave
Evanston, IL 60202
$17, S. Afzal Haider

Chicago Review
5801 South Kenwood
University of Chicago

Chicago, IL 60637
$25, V. Joshua Adams

Cimarron Review
205 Morrill Hall
Oklahoma State University
Stillwater, OK 74078–4069
$24, E. P. Walkiewicz

Cincinnati Review
Department of English
McMicken Hall, Room 369
P.O. Box 210069
Cincinnati, OH 45221
$15, Brock Clarke

Colorado Review
Department of English
Colorado State University
Fort Collins, CO 80523
$24, Stephanie G'Schwind

Columbia
Columbia University Alumni Center
622 W. 113th Street
MC4521
New York, NY 10025
$50, Michael B. Sharleson

Commentary
165 East 56th Street
New York, NY 10022
$45, Neal Kozody

Confrontation
English Department
C. W. Post College of Long Island
University
Greenvale, NY 11548
$10, Martin Tucker

Conjunctions
21 East 10th Street, Suite 3E
New York, NY 10003
$18, Bradford Morrow

Crab Orchard Review
Department of English
Southern Illinois University at
Carbondale
Carbondale, IL 62901
$20, Carolyn Alessio

Crazyhorse
Department of English
College of Charleston
66 George Street
Charleston, SC 29424
$16, Anthony Varallo

Crucible
Barton Collge
P.O. Box 5000
Wilson, NC 27893
$16, Terrence L. Grimes

Cutbank
Department of English
University of Montana
Missoula, MT 59812
$12, Lauren Hamlin

Daedalus
136 Irving Street, Suite 100
Cambridge, MA 02138
$41, James Miller

Denver Quarterly
University of Denver
Denver, CO 80208
$20, Bin Ramke

Descant
P.O. Box 314
Station P
Toronto, Ontario M5S 2S8
$28, Karen Mulhallen

Dogwood
Department of English
Fairfield University
1073 N. Benson Road
Fairfield, CT 06824
Pete Duval

Ecotone
Department of Creative Writing
University of North Carolina,
Wilmington
601 South College Road
Wilmington, NC 28403
$16.95, David Gessner

Epiphany
www.epiphanyzine.com
$18, Willard Cook

Epoch
251 Goldwin Smith Hall
Cornell University
Ithaca, NY 14853–3201
$11, Michael Koch

Esquire
300 West 57th St., 21st Floor,
New York, NY 10019
$17.94, Fiction Editor

Event
Douglas College
P.O. Box 2503
New Westminster
British Columbia V3L 5B2
$24.95, Rick Maddocks

Fantasy and Science Fiction
P.O. Box 3447
Hoboken, NJ 07030
$39, Gordon Van Gelder

The Farallon Review
1017 L Street
No. 348
Sacramento, CA 95814
$7, The Editors

Fiction
Department of English
The City College of New York
Convent Ave. at 138th Street
New York, NY 10031
$38, Mark Jay Mirsky

Fiction Fix
www.fictionfix.net
April E. Bacon

Fiction International
Department of English and
Comparative Literature
5500 Campanile Drive
San Diego State University
San Diego, CA 92182
$18, Harold Jaffe

The Fiddlehead
Campus House
11 Garland Court
UNB PO Box 4400
Fredericton
New Brunswick E3B 5A3
$55, Mark Anthony Jarman

Fifth Wednesday
www.fifthwednesdayjournal.org
$20, Vern Miller

Five Points
Georgia State University
P.O. Box 3999
Atlanta, GA 30302
$21, David Bottoms and Megan Sexton

The Florida Review
Department of English
P.O. Box 161400
University of Central Florida
Orlando, FL 32816
$15, Susan E. Fallows

Flyway
206 Ross Hall
Department of English
Iowa State University
Ames, IA 50011
$24, David DeFina

Fourteen Hills
Department of Creative Writing
San Francisco State University
1600 Halloway Ave.
San Francisco, CA 94132–1722
$17, Charles Rech

Gargoyle
3819 North 13th Street
Arlington, VA 22201
$30, Lucinda Ebersole, Richard Peabody

Georgetown Review
400 E. College Street
Box 227
Georgetown, KY 40324
$9, Steven Carter

Georgia Review
Gilbert Hall

University of Georgia
Athens, GA 30602
$30, Stephen Corey

Gettysburg Review
Gettysburg College
300 N. Washington Street
Gettysburg, PA 17325
$28, Peter Stitt

Glimmer Train
1211 NW Glisan Street, Suite 207
Portland, OR 97209
$36, Susan Burmeister-Brown, Linda Swanson-Davies

Grain
Box 67
Saskatoon, Saskatchewan 57K 3K9
$30, Terry Jordan

Granta
841 Broadway, 4th Floor
New York, NY 10019–3780
$39.95, John Freeman

Grasslands Review
Creative Writing Program
Department of English
Indiana State University
Terre Haute, IN 47809
$8, Brendan Corcoran

Green Mountains Review
Box A58
Johnson State College
Johnson, VT 05656
$15, Leslie Daniels

Greensboro Review
3302 Hall for Humanities
and Research Administration
University of North Carolina
Greensboro, NC 27402
$10, Jim Clark

Gulf Coast
Department of English
University of Houston
Houston, TX 77204–3012
$16, Nick Flynn

Hanging Loose
231 Wyckoff Street
Brooklyn, NY 11217
$22, Group

Harper's Magazine
666 Broadway
New York, NY 10012
$21, Ben Metcalf

Harpur Palate
Department of English
Binghamton University
P.O. Box 6000
Binghamton, NY 13902
$16, Barrett Bowlin

Harvard Review
Lamont Library
Harvard University
Cambridge, MA 02138
$16, Christina Thompson

Hawaii Review
Department of English
University of Hawaii at Manoa
1733 Donagho Road
Honolulu, HI 96822
$20, Che S. Ng

Hayden's Ferry Review
Box 875002
Arizona State University
Tempe, AZ 85287
$14, Cameron Fielder

High Desert Journal
P.O. Box 7647
Bend, OR 97708
$16, Elizabeth Quinn

Hotel Amerika
Columbia College
English Department
600 S. Michigan Avenue
Chicago, IL 60657
$18, David Lazar

Hudson Review
684 Park Avenue
New York, NY 10065
$62, Paula Deitz

Hunger Mountain
www.hungermountain.org
$12, Anne de Marcken

Idaho Review
Boise State University
1910 University Drive
Boise, ID 83725
$10, Mitch Wieland

Image
Center for Religious Humanism
3307 Third Avenue West
Seattle, WA 98119
$39.95, Gregory Wolfe

Indiana Review
Ballantine Hall 465
1020 East Kirkwood Avenue
Bloomington, IN 47405–7103
$17, Jenny Burge

Inkwell
Manhattanville College
2900 Purchase Street
Purchase, NY 10577
$10, Peter Acker

Iowa Review
Department of English
University of Iowa
308 EPB
Iowa City, IA 52242
$25, David Hamilton

Iron Horse Literary Review
Department of English
Texas Tech University
Box 43091
Lubbock, TX 79409–3091
$15, Leslie Jill Patterson

Isotope
Utah State University
3200 Old Main Hill
Logan, UT 84322
$15, The Editors

Italian Americana
University of Rhode Island
Providence Campus
80 Washington Street

Providence, RI 02903
$20, Carol Bonomo Albright

Jabberwock Review
Department of English
Drawer E
Mississippi State University
Mississippi State, MS 39762
$15, Michael P. Kardos

Jewish Currents
45 East 33rd Street
New York, NY 10016–5335
$30, Editorial Board

The Journal
Ohio State University
Department of English
164 W. 17th Ave.
Columbus, OH 43210
$14, Kathy Fagon

Juked
110 Westridge Drive
Tallahassee, FL 32304
$10, J. W. Wang

Kenyon Review
www.kenyonreview.org
$30, The Editors

Lady Churchill's Rosebud Wristlet
Small Beer Press
150 Pleasant Street
Easthampton, MA 01027
$20, Kelly Link

Lake Effect
Penn State Erie
4951 College Drive
Erie, PA 16563–1501
$6, George Looney

Lalitamba
110 W. 86th Street, Suite 5D
New York, NY 10024
Florence Homolka

The Literary Review
Fairleigh Dickinson University
285 Madison Avenue

Madison, NJ 07940
$18, Minna Proctor

Louisville Review
Spalding University
851 South Fourth Street
Louisville, KY 40203
$14, Sena Jeter Naslund

Madison Review
University of Wisconsin
Department of English
H. C. White Hall
600 North Park Street
Madison, WI 53706
$25, Miles Johnson

Make
www.makemag.com
Tom Mundt

Mānoa
English Department
University of Hawaii
Honolulu, HI 96822
$22, Frank Stewart

Massachusetts Review
South College
University of Massachusetts
Amherst, MA 01003
$27, David Lenson, Ellen Dore Watson

McSweeney's
826 Valencia Street
San Francisco, CA 94110
$55, Dave Eggers

Meridian
Department of English
P.O. Box 400145
University of Virginia
Charlottesville, VA 22904–4145
$12, Julia Hansen

Michigan Quarterly Review
0576 Rackham Building
915 East Washington Street
University of Michigan
Ann Arbor, MI 48109
$25, Laurence Goldstein

Mid-American Review
Department of English
Bowling Green State University
Bowling Green, OH 43403
$12, Michael Czyzniejewski

Minnesota Review
Department of English
Carnegie Mellon University
Pittsburgh, PA 15213
$30, Jeffrey Williams

Minnetonka Review
P.O. Box 386
Spring Park, MN 55384
$17, Troy Ehlers

Mississippi Review
University of Southern Mississippi
118 College Drive #5144
Hattiesburg, MS 39406–5144
$15, Frederick Barthelme

Missouri Review
357 McReynolds Hall
University of Missouri
Columbia, MO 65211
$24, Speer Morgan

Montana Quarterly
2820 W. College Street
Bozeman, MT 59771
Megan Ault Regnerus

n + 1
68 Jay Street, #405
Brooklyn, NY 11201
$23, Keith Gessen, Mark Greif

Narrative Magazine
narrativemagazine.com
The Editors

Natural Bridge
Department of English
University of Missouri, St. Louis
St. Louis, MO 63121
$15, Mark Troy

New England Review
Middlebury College

Middlebury, VT 05753
$30, Stephen Donadio

New Letters
University of Missouri
5100 Rockhill Road
Kansas City, MO 64110
$22, Robert Stewart

New Millennium Writings
www.newmillenniumwritings.com
$12, Don Williams

New Ohio Review
English Department
360 Ellis Hall
Ohio University
Athens, OH 45701
$20, John Bullock

New Orphic Review
706 Mill Street
Nelson, British Columbia V1L 4S5
$30, Ernest Hekkanen

New Quarterly
Saint Jerome's University
290 Westmount Road
N. Waterloo, Ontario N2L 3G3
$36, Kim Jernigan

New Renaissance
26 Heath Road, #11
Arlington, MA 02474
$38, Louise T. Reynolds

The New Yorker
4 Times Square
New York, NY 10036
$46, Deborah Treisman

Nimrod International Journal
Arts and Humanities Council of Tulsa
600 South College Avenue
Tulsa, OK 74104
$17.50, Francine Ringold

Ninth Letter
Department of English
University of Illinois
608 South Wright Street

Urbana, IL 61801
$21.95, Jodee Rubins

Noon
1324 Lexington Avenue
PMB 298
New York, NY 10128
$12, Diane Williams

The Normal School
5245 North Backer Ave.
M/S PB 98
California State University
Fresno, CA 93470
$5, Sophie Beck

North American Review
University of Northern Iowa
1222 West 27th Street
Cedar Falls, IA 50614
$22, Grant Tracey

North Carolina Literary Review
Department of English
2134 Bate Building
East Carolina University
Greenville, NC 27858-4353
$25, Margaret Bauer

North Dakota Quarterly
University of North Dakota
Merrifield Hall, Room 110
276 Centennial Drive Stop 27209
Grand Forks, ND 58202
$25, Robert Lewis

Northwest Review
5243 University of Oregon
Eugene, OR 97403
$20, Ehud Havazelet

Notre Dame Review
840 Flanner Hall
Department of English
University of Notre Dame
Notre Dame, IN 46556
$15, John Matthias, William O'Rourke

Noun vs. Verb
Burning River
169 S. Main Street, #4

Rittman, OH 44270
Chris Bowen

One Story
232 Third Street, #A111
Brooklyn, NY 11215
$21, Maribeth Batcha, Hannah Tinti

On Spec
P.O. Box 4727
Edmonton, AB T6E 5G6
$24, Diane L. Walton

Open City
270 Lafayette Street, Suite 1412
New York, NY 10012
$30, Thomas Beller, Joanna Yas

Orion
187 Main Street
Great Barrington, MA 01230
$35, The Editors

Our Stories
www.ourstories.com
Alexis E. Santi

Oxford American
201 Donaghey Avenue, Main 107
Conway, AR 72035
$24.95, Marc Smirnoff

Pak N Treger
National Yiddish Book Center
Harry and Jeanette Weinberg Bldg.
1021 West Street
Amherst, MA 01002
$36, Aaron Lansky

Pank
Department of the Humanities
Michigan Tech
14000 Townsend Drive
Houghton, MI 49931
$15, The Editors

Paris Review
62 White Street
New York, NY 10013
$34, Philip Gourevitch

PEN America
PEN America Center

588 Broadway, Suite 303
New York, NY 10012
$10, M. Mark

The Pinch
Department of English
University of Memphis
Memphis, TN 38152
$25, Kristen Iverson

Playboy
730 Fifth Ave.
New York, NY 10019
Amy Grace Lloyd

Pleiades
Department of English and
Philosophy
University of Central Missouri
Warrensburg, MO 64093
$16, Kevin Prufer

Ploughshares
Emerson College
120 Boylston Street
Boston, MA 02116
$30, Ladette Randolph

Potomac Review
Montgomery College
51 Mannakee Street
Rockville, MD 20850
$20, Julie Wakeman-Linn

Prairie Fire
423–100 Arthur Street
Winnipeg, Manitoba R3B 1H3
$30, Andris Taskans

Prairie Schooner
201 Andrews Hall
University of Nebraska
Lincoln, NE 68588–0334
$28, Hilda Raz

Prism International
Department of Creative Writing
University of British Columbia
Buchanan E-462
Vancouver, British Columbia V6T 121
$28, Rachel Knudsen

A Public Space
323 Dean Street
Brooklyn, NY 11217
Brigid Hughes

Puerto del Sol
MSC 3E
New Mexico State University
P.O. Box 30001
Las Cruces, NM 88003
$10, Evan Lavender-Smith

Redivider
Emerson College
120 Boylston Street
Boston, MA 02116
$10, Matt Salesses

Red Rock Review
English Department, J2A
Community College of Southern
Nevada
3200 East Cheyenne Avenue
North Las Vegas, NV 89030
$9.50, Richard Logsdon

River Oak Review
Elmhurst College
190 Prospect Avenue
Box 2633
Elmhurst, IL 60126
$12, Ron Wiginton

River Styx
3547 Olive Street, Suite 107
St. Louis, MO 63103–1014
$20, Richard Newman

The Rome Review
www.theromereview.com
Tarek Al-Hariri

Room Magazine
P.O. Box 46160
Station D
Vancouver, British Columbia V6J 5G5
$25, Clélie Rich

Rosebud
N3310 Asje Road
Cambridge, WI 53523
$20, Roderick Clark

Ruminate
140 N. Roosevelt Ave.
Ft. Collins, CO 80521
$28, Brianna Van Dyke

Salamander
Suffolk University
English Department
41 Temple Street
Boston, MA 02114
$23, Jennifer Barber

Salmagundi
Skidmore College
Saratoga Springs, NY 12866
$20, Robert Boyers

Santa Monica Review
1900 Pico Boulevard
Santa Monica, CA 90405
$12, Andrew Tonkovich

Sewanee Review
735 University Ave
Sewanee, TN 37383
$48, George Core

Shenandoah
Mattingly House
2 Lee Avenue
Washington and Lee University
Lexington, VA 24450–2116
$25, R. T. Smith, Lynn Leech

Slow Trains
P.O. Box 100145
Denver, CO 8025
Susannah Indigo

Sonora Review
Department of English
University of Arizona
Tucson, AZ 85721
$16, Astrid Duffy

South Dakota Review
University of South Dakota
414 E. Clark Street
Vermilion, SD 57069
$30, Brian Bedard

Southern Humanities Review
9088 Haley Center
Auburn University
Auburn, AL 36849
$15, Dan R. Latimer

Southern Indiana Review
College of Liberal Arts
University of Southern Indiana
8600 University Blvd.
Evansville, IN 47712
$20, Ron Mitchell

Southern Review
Old President's House
Louisiana State University
Baton Rouge, LA 70803
$40, Jeanne M. Leiby

Southwest Review
Southern Methodist University
P.O. Box 750374
Dallas, TX 75275
$24, Willard Spiegelman

Subtropics
Department of English
University of Florida
P.O. Box 112075
Gainesville, FL 32611–2075
$26, David Leavitt

The Sun
107 North Roberson Street
Chapel Hill, NC 27516
$36, Sy Safransky

Sycamore Review
Department of English
500 Oval Drive
Purdue University
West Lafayette, IN 47907
$14, Mehdi Okasi

Think
P.O. Box 454
Downingtown, PA 19335
$20, Christine Yorick

Third Coast
Department of English
Western Michigan University

Kalamazoo, MI 49008
$16, Daniel Toronto

Threepenny Review
2163 Vine Street
Berkeley, CA 94709
$25, Wendy Lesser

Timber Creek Review
8969 UNCG Station
Greensboro, NC 27413
$17, John Freiermuth

Tin House
P.O. Box 10500
Portland, OR 97296–0500
$29.90, Rob Spillman

TriQuarterly
629 Noyes Street
Evanston, IL 60208
$24, Susan Firestone Hahn

Upstreet
P.O. Box 105
Richmond, MA 01254
$10, Vivian Dorsel

Vermont Literary Review
Department of English
Castleton State College
Castleton, VT 05735
Flo Keyes

Virginia Quarterly Review
One West Range
P.O. Box 400223
Charlottesville, VA 22903
$32, Ted Genoways

War, Literature, and the Arts
Department of English and Fine Arts
2354 Fairchild Drive, Suite 6D45
USAF Academy, CO 80840–6242
$10, Donald Anderson

Water-Stone Review
Graduate School of Liberal Studies
Hamline University, MS-A1730
1536 Hewitt Ave.
Saint Paul, MN 55104
$23, The Editors

Weber Studies
Weber State University
1405 University Circle
Ogden, UT 84408–1214
$20, Michael Wutz

West Branch
Bucknell Hall
Bucknell University
Lewisburg, PA 17837
$10, Paula Closson Buck

Western Humanities Review
University of Utah
255 South Central Campus Drive
Room 3500
Salt Lake City, UT 84112
$16, Barry Weller

Willow Springs
Eastern Washington University
501 N. Riverpoint Blvd.
Spokane, WA 99201
$18, Samuel Ligon

Witness
Black Mountain Institute
University of Nevada
Las Vegas, NV 89154
$10, The Editors

Yale Review
P.O. Box 208243
New Haven, CT 06520–8243
$33, J. D. McClatchy

Zoetrope
The Sentinel Building
916 Kearney Street
San Francisco, CA 94133
$24, Michael Ray

Zone 3
APSU
Box 4565
Clarksville, TN 37044
$10, Amy Wright